NIGHTMARE VISION

Ahead on the pavement a mother was seeing her young daughter off to Sunday School. Zipping up her coat and kissing her on the lips.

'Steve, get off me. Let go!'

'Nick. For Chrissakes stand still and listen.'

'Let go.'

'Listen.' Steve spoke slowly; he was willing the words into my brain. 'Listen to me. It wasn't Slatter who killed John. Slatter was nowhere near your house. In fact, Slatter is probably already dead.'

'Dead? How the hell can Slatter be dead?'

'Something's happened. Something . . . just so weird. Insane. People have gone crazy. All of them. They've just gone ape-shit crazy. Don't take my word for it. Look.' Steve nodded at the woman kissing her child.

I looked. This time I saw properly.

The mother wasn't kissing her child. *She was eating her face . . .*

'All of Simon Clark's stories resonate and confront, while the dialogue and descriptions run true. Clark is worth seeking out'

Fear

Also by Simon Clark in New English Library paperback

Nailed by the Heart

About the author

Born in 1958, Simon Clark lives in Doncaster, South Yorkshire. His short stories have appeared in several magazines and anthologies, including *Darklands 2, Dark Voices 5* and *The Year's Best Horror Stories* (four times). He has published a collection of short stories, *Blood and Grit*, and his work has been broadcast on BBC Radio 4. His first novel, *Nailed by the Heart*, was published in 1995 in hardcover by Hodder and Stoughton and in paperback by New English Library. *Blood Crazy* is his second novel. More horror novels by Simon Clark are scheduled for publication by Hodder and NEL.

For Doreen and Peter Clark, my parents.

Get this message into your head.
You, too, have a monster to kill.
– And this book just might save your life.

THE FIRST PART

THE DAY THE WORLD WENT MAD THIS HAPPENED:

Chapter One

THE START OF THE END OF EVERYTHING

'What happened?'

Baz stared at the blood.

Fresh and red and wet, it drenched the paving slabs in a slick that looked big enough to paddle your canoe through.

I elbowed him in the ribs.

'I said, what happened, Baz?'

He looked up at me, his eyes egg-size with shock.

'I've just watched them shovel the poor bastard off the pavement ... Christ. What a mess. That cop there puked all over his car ... They've seen nothing like it, Nick. They can't handle it.'

Baz talked like he was firing a machine gun at nightmare monsters. If you ask me, he had a psychological need to tell me what happened.

'They say – they say he'd just walked out of Rothwell's, crossed the street when – slam! slam! Poor bastard never knew what hit him. He was dead before the ambulance got here.'

All around us Saturday morning shoppers stared at the blood. That mess of red had got them by the short and curlies.

On the balls of their feet, cops ran, directing traffic, cordoning off the street with candy-striped tape or repeating that famous lie that no one ever believes: 'Move along. There's nothing to see.'

They sweated in the Spring sunshine. On their faces weren't the usual expressions of our seen-it-all policemen.

'An axe, Nick ... A bastard axe ... Can you believe that? Laid into him with it right there outside the shop.'

'Who was it?'

'Jimmy ... Jimmy somebody. You'll have seen him round town plenty. About seventeen. Went to the art college, had a pony tail. Always swanned round with a green guitar under his arm ... Smashed that up, too. Like they wanted to kill both of them ... him and his guitar.'

'You saw it happen?'

'No. I got here just as they scraped him off the street. I saw the people who'd seen it happen, though. They were flaked out across those seats over there like they'd been neck-shot. Just flat out from shock. I tell you, Nick, it was like a fucking war or something. Blood on the street. People shaking and throwing up. You know, like you see on the news or ... or ...'

The charge that fired the words like silver bullets from his lips suddenly exhausted itself. His red face turned white and he said no more.

From a hardware store came two old ladies carrying buckets of water. They poured them onto the blood which was setting to jelly in the warm sun. It took four more buckets before the blood slid off the paving slabs and into the drains where it was swallowed with a greedy sucking sound. There were solid chunks of red in there. Like cuts of raw meat.

Eventually only wet pavement reeking of disinfectant was left. Now there really was nothing left to see. But Baz still stared at the wet slabs.

I said, 'Someone must have really hated the kid to do that to him.'

'They did. Jesus Christ they did. They unzipped him like a holdall.'

'Do they know who murdered him?'

'Yeah.' Baz looked up. 'It was his mother.'

The day the world went mad I was on my way to McDonald's' with two things on my mind.

One. The *Big Mac* I was going to stuff down my throat.

Two. How was I going to hurt that bastard, Tug Slatter?

Normality oozed through the town as thick as toothpaste through its tube. People shopping; little kids in buggies; big kids hunting down the record and game stores, their pocket money red-hot in their hands. Total, utter, complete small town normality.

That was until I saw the blood on the street.

They tell you this at school.

Every so often in history, there will come this colossal event that splits time in two. You know, like the birth of Jesus Christ. Everything before – BC. Everything after – AD.

On my way to McDonald's it happened again. After two thousand years the old Age, Anno Domini, had died a death.

Naturally, like everyone else at the time I didn't know it. Any more than a passer-by seeing that baby squawking in a manger somewhere in suburban Bethlehem would have known that the world was going to change PDQ.

At that moment, as I left Baz watching five slightly moist paving slabs, life – on the surface – was returning to normal. New shoppers flowed into town, kids in buggies got stuck into ice creams, lovers walked hand in hand. And they saw paving slabs wet with nothing more than water.

So, I showed the wet stretch of street my back and I headed toward the building with the golden arches that formed the magic *M*.

Now I was hungry. All I wanted was that *Big Mac*, fries and a monster coke rattling with ice.

Of course, I was ignorant as shit. I didn't know the truth. That before long I'd look back and call this:

DAY 1
YEAR 1.

Chapter Two

WHO THE HELL'S NICK ATEN?

Before we get any further into this, something about me.

I'm seventeen. The name's Nick Aten (yeah, yeah, it rhymes with Satan).

Mother Nature sprang me on middle-class parents. Father: an investment advisor. Mother: an accountant.

Things changed a bit when I was born one Sunday morning, 3 March. My mother had already given up work when she fell pregnant so the Atens had to shave back on some of life's luxuries. Not that they didn't want a baby. They'd been trying for years. There had been three miscarriages before me. And one son who had lived two weeks before the doctors gave up the fight and let him die. My parents called him Nicholas and cremated him.

In my mother's drawer there's a bundle of cards, the deepest condolences kind with angels and babies sleeping 'safe in the arms of the Lord.'

They are for a dead boy called Nick Aten. People sometimes ask if it feels weird to see your name on these cards. There it is in black and white. Documents to say you're dead. A bit like seeing a video of your own funeral.

I laugh it off.

As a snotty-nosed two-year-old, I would spend my days stalking around the garden carrying a stick. With this stick I'd whack the ground, bushes and Mum's prized bedding plants.

When they asked, 'Why are you hitting the bushes, Nicholas?'

I'd reply, 'Nick killing monsters.'

When I was three a rat somehow sneaked into the dining room. There I was, sat on the rug, happy as Larry, playing with my bricks. My new baby brother snug in his layback chair.

Ten minutes later when mum came into the room, she screamed and sprayed a mugful of coffee across the wallpaper.

Because there I stood, a statuette of Aphrodite in my hand, watching the rat. It lay twitching its legs, with its rat brains looking like pink cottage cheese stuck to the head of the statuette.

Unusually tidily for me, I'd picked out its titchy rat eyes and dropped them into my Dad's tankard he'd won in some tennis tournament a million summers before.

That passion for killing monsters is probably my most valuable asset.

Since it happened – that BIG DAY ONE – I've had plenty of time to wonder if that passion – that obsession – to kill monsters was somehow imprinted onto my mind in the womb. That it was my destiny.

Before I sat down with a pile of paper to write this, I looked at manuals to see how you're supposed to write a book. They say it's important to make you understand what I'm like. What makes me tick. So you will understand why I did the things I did.

Here goes.

I've no real life-time friends. But I had a life-time enemy. Tug Slatter. We fought one another on our first day at school. The first time he tried to kill me – I mean actually terminate my existence on planet Earth as opposed to merely ruining my face – was when we were fourteen. I'd aerosolled TUG SLATTER'S QUEER on the wall of the local scout hut. Slatter broke three fingers of my left hand with a fence post.

Broken fingers don't sound life-threatening, but I was using them to protect my skull at the time.

I left school at sixteen. No qualifications. I've had three jobs: glass collector in a night club. Trainee plastics extruder. And, last of all, driving a pick-up for a general dealer.

So. If you'd seen me walking down the street on that Saturday morning what would you have seen?

A seventeen-year-old, dark hair, jeans, trainers, leather jacket. Your first impression would be, 'He's a cocky bastard.' (And I was).

You're thinking now I'm nothing more than a small-town bad boy. Maybe. Maybe not.

Mum and Dad watched me grow into what I am with a bemused expression. They knew they could do nothing to change me. My dad's response was, 'Nick'll either end up a millionaire – or in jail.'

Sometimes my antics would wear down mum's stamina, then she'd grumble, 'Do you know the sacrifices your father and I have had to make for you?' You know the rhythm of it. You'll have heard it all before.

But I was never in serious trouble. I didn't torture cute animals. And probably the only person who knew the way I ticked was my uncle, Jack Aten.

He was a lot like me. Left school with no qualifications and no desire to join the rest of the pen-pushing Atens. Ambition sizzled inside him. He wanted to be a rock guitarist. For fifteen years he toured with one of those bands who although they play honest to goodness rock music never make it as far as a recording contract.

When I was eleven Jack Aten came back. Starved bony thin, he made you think he'd been somehow scorched.

I guess now he'd married himself to heroin. So it was a case of return home, get off it – or die.

Jack used to spend a lot of time at our house. Sometimes we'd play crazy golf (for some reason he loved crazy golf – then he liked crazy things and crazy people). When we went out on these jaunts he'd always carry a can of beer from which he'd take little sips. He'd make one can last two hours. I thought it was great. I was with this rock rebel.

Now I know he was drip-feeding alcohol into his blood. It knocked just enough of the sharp edges off reality to make life bearable.

Now and again he'd ask in a joke upper-crust accent, 'I say, Nick-Nick. Am I alive?'

'You're alive, Jack.'

'Thanks, old man. Sometimes I forget.'

Nights he'd play his guitar in his room, so softly you could hardly hear it. Whenever I heard the music my skin would prickle cold. The music reminded me of a documentary I'd seen about whale songs. I'd hear the tones of the electric guitar floating down through the floors and I'd remember the part about the whale with five harpoons through its back and how the whale sang as it died. The dying whale song – Jack Aten's gentle guitar sounds. In my head the two things were one and the same.

When I was fourteen life killed Jack Aten. He was thirty-eight. Cancer of the bollocks.

They say some cancers are a kind of suicide, grown by men and women who can't change their shape to fit into the narrow slot that society inflicts on them.

For twelve months I didn't open doors like you and the Reverend Green. I kicked them open. Ask me a question, I'd snarl you an answer. I was a balloon full of rage stretched tight to rupturing point. All I wanted to do was run to a mountain top. Then roar at the sky to bury me.

I was the little kid who wanted to kill monsters. As the years passed the monsters disappeared.

I grew up to enjoy a night out with the lads, a few beers. Happiness was a *Big Mac*. Ecstasy two *Big Macs*.

Now all that's changed.

The monsters have returned.

And I've got the biggest monster of all to kill.

It's not a monster you'd recognise immediately. It doesn't look like the ones you see in kids' books, with leather wings, claws and teeth like steak knives. But it's a monster all the same. And if I don't kill it it will eat my bones as sure as you shit tomorrow.

In a way, this book is an instruction manual on how to kill that monster. Because remember this.

You, too, have your own monster to kill.

That's why I'm locking myself away in here for a month. I'm just going to sit down and write the bloody thing as it comes, all right? No frills, no poncey literature. But nor am I going to cut corners, or cut the bad things. This is what happened to me. Also it'll help clear my mind for what I've got to do next.

No one's likely to find me here. It's February. It snows like someone's torn a hole in the sky. The house is miles from anywhere. On three sides of it there's thick forest. In front there's a dirty great river that's more than a mile wide.

Sometimes, to clear my head after hours of word crunching, I go down to the shore to skim stones. There are still a lot of things floating in the water. They look like rotting logs, hundreds of them, day and night, going with the flow of the river down to the sea. I'll throw pebbles or snowballs at them. In the same kind of way any other seventeen-year-old would.

The only time it looks bad is when the undertow rolls them over. One end of the rotting log lifts smoothly out of the water. Then you know what it really is. You see the holes where the eyes were.

I shrug it off. Throw more pebbles. Then kick my way back through the snow, turn up the gas fire, get the pen back in my hand and I attack the paper again. I have to get what's in my head down onto paper.

Throughout my life, I've never wondered about the big – and I mean the REALLY BIG – mysteries. And yet over the last eight months I got answers. Answers to those questions that scholars and people just like you have been asking for three thousand years.

I didn't go looking for them. They dropped into my hands like stones from the sky.

It's important you know.

What you do with it is up to you.

Chapter Three

ALL CALM BEFORE THE STORM

'You know where he'll be. We could take him now.'

'Revenge, they say, is a dish best served cold.'

'Yeah, and in the meantime that shit Slatter thinks he's got away with it.' Steve Price kicked a can rattling away down the road. 'He's laughing at us, Nick.'

'Cold, I said. Not stale. We'll pay him back. But we don't rush it. We work out a plan.'

After the burger blow-out in McDonald's we'd walked back from town to my house.

Steve Price, blond hair, round-faced, with a passion for football and Oriental girls, was my best friend. We'd knocked around together for the last five years. Now he was itching to take a crack at Slatter.

As we'd sat there behind the plate glass in McDonald's, chewing burgers, we'd seen Tug Slatter parading his ugly, tattooed face through town.

'You know where he'll be going, Nick?'

I knew. Slatter was patrolling his territory. Dressed in his uniform of denim shirt, jeans, brown leather belt and pit boots. Cigarette in the corner of his down-turned mouth, shaved head swinging from side to side like a bad-tempered pit-bull looking for someone to bite.

He'd slouch through town from the market to the High Street, trying to catch some kid's eye. When he did it'd be the old routine.

Slatter: 'Oi. What you want?'

Puzzled kid: 'Pardon?'

'Don't come that with me. You know what you did.'

'No. What?'

Slatter, aggressive: 'You were looking at me.'

'I wasn't.'

Slatter moves closer. Eye contact cobra sharp. 'You did. And I didn't like the way you were doing it.'

'I didn't. I—'

'Damned well did. You were looking at me.' Slatter bunches hands. 'You think you're better than me, eh? Want to make something of it?'

Kid knows what's coming now. Frightened, he sees those tattooed fists coming up with their biting snakes and hand-picked letters across the fingers spelling out HATE and KILL.

He doesn't have to try hard to imagine himself lying on the ground spitting out broken teeth while this ugly ape kicks the living shit out of him.

Slatter: 'You don't just walk through town, you know, just staring people out.'

The kid guesses the safest way out. He goes for it. Show this tattooed gorilla he's undisputed boss.

'I'm sorry ... Look ... I really am. I didn't mean to.'

'Don't look at me like that again. All right?'

'I'm sorry. I didn't mean to.' (The kids stops short of calling Slatter SIR – just.) I was only walking down ... I ... I mean I—'

'All right. But don't do it again. I don't like it.'

Respect – induced through terror – is meat and drink to Tug Slatter.

Kicking stones, we turned into my home street.

'Tomorrow night,' I told Steve. 'We want to pick the right time.'

'What we going to do to him?'

'After what he did – something that really hurts the bastard.'

'But what? He's armour-plated.'

I grinned. 'Give me time.'

Lawn Avenue reeked of normality. A road of Victorian town houses lined with lime trees that look terrific in the Spring. Kids riding bikes, and the sound of someone playing a piano floating through an open window.

I'd lived in Lawn Avenue all my life. It seemed nothing special to me, but Steve thought it posh. 'You know, I've never ever seen dog crap on the pavement round here,' he'd say.

'That's because all our dogs have their backsides sewn up at birth. You know, you can lay in bed at night and hear them in their kennels just bursting like balloons.'

As we walked up the driveway Steve asked, 'Still clean?'

'It better be.'

I checked my pick-up. It wasn't one of Ford's most freshly minted vehicles but it was mine, it was paid for. I'd resprayed it myself a flame red then stencilled in white above the radiator grille its name – THE DOG'S BOLLOCKS.

That would have made Jack Aten laugh. Sometimes I'm sure I do half-crazy things to amuse his ghost.

'Clean as a whistle.' I patted the wing.

'Anyway, you don't think he'd be stupid enough to do the same again.'

'I don't see why not, Steve. He's got as much imagination as that worm there. Once he's learnt a good trick he'll repeat it ad nauseam.'

'Ad what?'

'Until we're sick of it, Steve, until we're sick of it.'

'It looks alright now.' Steve ran his fingers across the paint work. 'No scratches.'

'You should have seen it yesterday. Tyres flat – and he'd smeared shit all over it. Paint work, glass, lights.'

'Bastard.'

'It had set like concrete. And I'll tell you another thing.'

Steve raised his eyebrows.

'It wasn't dog shit.'

'You mean. . . .'

'I mean it was pure Slatter. I couldn't shift that stink out of my head all day.'

'What now?'

'Now we go inside and decide how we are going to hit back.'

'Hi, Steve. How's your dad keeping?'

My dad pulled himself to a sitting position on the sofa and brushed cake crumbs off his sweatshirt.

'Fine, thanks,' said Steve. 'He's taking a load of stone down south this weekend.'

'So I thought I'd baby-sit for him,' I said. 'And make sure Stevie doesn't get frightened all alone in that big, dark house.'

The three of us laughed easily.

Steve's mum and dad had divorced years ago. The weekends his dad worked away a few of the gang would stop over at his house and make a party of it. Lately a gang of girls had been promising to stay too. Suddenly weekends were starting to get not just exciting but electrifying.

I told my dad about the murder. He was as horrified as I expected him to be. He kept shaking his head in disbelief. That kind of thing just didn't happen in a small town like Doncaster.

He looked at his watch. 'I take it you two lads have come to interrupt my honest relaxation.' He reached down beside the sofa and came back with a can of beer. He smiled, exposing the gap in his top front teeth through which he could make the loudest whistle I've ever heard. 'It's not one of those video nasties again?'

'Not this week. I taped a concert last night. We thought we'd watch it this afternoon . . . that is, if you're not watching anything, eh . . .'

'This old horse opera?' My dad took a deep swallow of beer. 'It's only the one I saw the night I proposed to your mother. But you watch what you want. It's as bad as I remembered the first time around. You know nostalgia ain't what it used to be.'

He stood up. Cake crumbs showered onto the carpet.

'You're living dangerously,' I said. 'Mother will go absolutely, totally insane when she sees the mess.'

My dad pulled a face. 'I'm safe. I'll blame it on you two.'

He crossed the deep carpet that mum hoovered with religious zeal every day and left the empty beer can on the window sill.

'Hey, Nick-Nick.' My fifteen-year-old brother called from the doorway, swinging a carrier bag in his hand. 'Got any spare cash?'

'Not if you're going to waste it on anything stupid like dictionaries and exercise books.'

'Nah. Robbo's selling me a couple of his CDs.'

'Thank God for that. It's time you started mis-spending your youth.'

'Don't listen to your brother,' dad said. 'He'll either end up a millionaire or—'

'IN JAIL.' We chorused the old Aten catch phrase.

'There's some spare cash in my tin. Not the one shaped like a coffin. The one with the naked lady – so cover your eyes when you get it.'

John saluted. 'Thanks, Nick-Nick. You're a hero.'

The image of my brother standing there in the doorway, eyes flashing happily, big freckled face grinning, is nailed permanently to my mind. It was the last time I saw him alive.

He ran upstairs, his feet thumping heavily. I heard my bedroom door open, then footsteps crossing to the bedside table. A pause.

He was counting the money. He'd take not a penny more than he needed. I heard the feet pass back out onto the landing toward his room.

Then nothing more.

'You shouldn't give your hard-earned away like that, Nick.' Dad shook his head, smiling, flashing that gap in his teeth again. 'He gets money of his own.'

'I know, but he fritters it away on history books and junk like that.'

My dad picked up a hammer from the sideboard and pointed it at me playfully. 'I'll find out how much John's paying for them and I'll give you the money back Monday. Now watch that concert, I've got a job that needs doing upstairs.'

Casually swinging the hammer, he walked out of the room. I trawled through the drawer in the video cabinet for the tape. As always I'd not bothered writing on the memo label so there would be a five-minute interval of swearing and false starts before I found what I was looking for.

As I pulled out the tapes mum came in with a plateful of sliced cake and tea – all part of the Saturday afternoon ritual. In her track suit, her dark hair short and neat, she looked ten years younger than she was. Within minutes she would get Steve laughing and chatting shyly.

'I keep telling Nick he should get a decent office job like yours, Steve,' she said, smiling brightly.

'Oh, I think he enjoys what he does, Mrs Aten.'

'Judy.'

'Sorry . . . Judy. He couldn't stand being tied to a desk.'

'I hope the police never look in the back of that truck he drives. There are enough rumours about Mr Karowski to sink a battleship.'

Upstairs my dad had begun his DIY. Thump. Thump. Thump. It sounded like he was tapping nails into solid brick.

My mother chatted happily over the thumping, handing out more cake to Steve who could never bring himself to say no.

'Found it,' I said as pink lasers cut slices out of the TV screen.

'Oh, I'll leave you to it. Anyway, I've got a boatload of ironing to do. If you want anything I'll be in the kitchen.'

She left, singing lightly to herself.

As I stood up I noticed my dad's empty can. Lucky she hadn't seen that otherwise dad would have been in for an ear-bruising. Crushing the can, I dropped it into the bin.

Upstairs the hammering stopped.

Suddenly something struck me as strange. Never, ever, in my seventeen years on this planet had I seen dad drink beer of an afternoon.

'Looks as if it's going to be a good concert, Nick.'

It was. I sat down to watch it and forgot the beer can completely.

Chapter Four

LIFE IS A BASTARD

Steve kicked us out early.

Well, you have to agree, 8.30 is excruciatingly early for a Sunday morning. His dad was due home by mid-day so he needed to restore the house so it didn't look like a truckful of drunks had crashed through the front door. Which was more or less what had happened.

The girls we hoped would show, didn't. We ended up getting drunker while playfully shoving one another over the furniture.

The three of us hopped over Steve's back garden wall to cut across the fields, leaving Steve to do what he could with the house while repeating for the thirteenth time that morning:

'My dad's going to kill me when he gets home.'

With the morning sun already hot on our necks, we plodded across empty meadows. My mouth tasted as if a toad had died of the blister in there, then been buried beneath my tongue.

The others went their separate ways as we reached the edge of town, leaving me to plough the last mile through the long grass alone. What thoughts I could keep together mainly centred on how I could do the most damage to Tug Slatter.

I saw no one. I heard nothing. It was only a Sunday morning in Spring with nine-tenths of the population enjoying a lie-in.

I climbed the fence into our back garden, scaring the birds up into a blurry cloud. Then, cutting down the passageway into the front garden, I checked my pick-up. Still clean. Slatter hadn't chosen to do an encore just yet.

I noticed my dad's car was missing from the drive. Nothing unusual about that. Some Sundays he'd drive into town to pick up the newspapers. My mother would probably still be in bed. My brother certainly would. Saturday nights he'd watch old horror films in his bedroom into the early hours – then sleep until lunchtime.

'HI HONIES, I'M HOME!' It was my customary greeting in a voice guaranteed to sandpaper anyone's nerves.

The usual 'Shut up! I'm trying to sleep!' never came. They were sleeping with the lid on that morning. I headed for the kitchen.

'Pigs!'

I shouted it again as I pushed a pile of hacked bread to one side of the table and clicked the top back on the butter tub.

If that was my dad who'd left the mess he was playing a dangerous game. Mum would go berserk. Not that he'd normally do something like this.

Come to think of it, he'd NEVER do anything like this. After eating his cornflakes he'd wash his dish then stick it back in the cupboard. The only other culprit could be—

'John! You are dead! You'd better clean this lot up before mum sees it.'

No reply. Jesus ... Maybe beneath that home-work-loving line-toeing fifteen-year-old there was a rebel after all.

Five minutes later I dropped my empty bowl in the sink and, still crunching a massive mouthful of cornflakes, I went upstairs.

Upstairs the house was tidy and quiet.

I changed into my slob-around jeans. Then I decided to roust John and mention the fact that if he wanted to live until lunchtime he would have to clean up the mess in the kitchen.

I pushed open the door.

And I saw something that stopped my breath.

My brother's bedroom had ceased to exist.

Oh, the four walls and window were still there. But the stuff that made it my brother's bedroom wasn't.

The bed had gone. The wardrobes, furniture and all the posters of Greek temples and Egyptian statues had gone with it. Instead, in the middle of the floor, nearly touching the ceiling light, was a pyramid.

I stood there and actually laughed out loud.

What I saw was impossible. I laughed again. But this time it was forced. I began to feel cold. Like someone was slowly dipping me into a mountain lake.

Someone had been in here, taken the furniture and then smashed all my brother's possessions. Because that pyramid was built out of books, computer games, childhood toys, holiday souvenirs, comics ... Everything that John had ever been given, collected, saved for, bought. Every fucking thing.

Jesus Christ.

That bastard ... Slatter.

As I stood there I could see things in my mind's eye. Slatter looking through the bedroom window, bluebird tattoos at either side of his eyes, a grin hacking open his ape face. Then climbing in to smash the place to smithereens.

Tug Slatter had done this. I believed that. But what on earth had he done with the bed and furniture? Where was my brother? He'd have been asleep in here.

I saw it. But a big chunk of me did not believe it.

I didn't move. I just looked. My chest aching, my breathing sounding strange in my ears.

The bastard had been thorough. Far, far more thorough than when he'd done the job on my pick-up with the fruit of his own backside.

Books hadn't just been ripped in two. Every page had been torn to pieces the size of postage stamps. John's computer – he'd loved the thing, he actually polished it – had been reduced to bits the size of my thumbnail.

Shaking my head, mind-kicked, I began picking through the pyramid. Examining a fraction of computer game or a shred of one of John's precious history books. There was his video of the first man on the moon. As I touched it, it fell from the pyramid to expose more of John's treasures. His pirate chest money box, more computer games. A torn mask. A model car. A ...

My fingers stopped above the mask.

John never owned a mask.

But here was a life-size mask. It had partly open eyes. Life-like hair. A nose . . .

I pushed my hand into the pyramid to pull at the mask. It wouldn't come. It had been fixed to something solid.

As I pulled somebody shoved the room. It spun so fast around me I could hardly see the walls and window flashing by. Only the mask stayed in focus.

Made from grey rubbery stuff, it was torn from mouth to ear, opening up a cheek like a parcel, exposing a row of teeth messed with red. The eyes reflected the light shining into the room, making it look as if they were alive. Or had been once.

I remember looking at the thing and seeing a mask.

But I hear myself shouting:

'John! John! John!'

Then I was in the street. My throat burning like I'd drunk bleach. I was still shouting. This time for help.

It was like a dream – you shout but no one hears.

Lawn Avenue was empty. The trees shifted slightly in the morning breeze – and I stood there and screamed to a world with stone ears that my brother lay dead in his bedroom. His face nearly torn in two.

Chapter Five

I'M GOING TO KILL SLATTER

'Where we going, Steve?'

We were walking along Thorne Road. Christ Church, shining as white as a bone in the sun, hurt my eyes. Overhead, rooks circled like black snowflakes. The traffic lights at the junction flicked through red, amber, green. There were no cars on the streets.

'Steve. Where we going?' My throat burned as the words came out.

Steve walked by my side. I'd not seen that expression on his face before. It reminded me of a kid at school whose dad had been broken in half in a factory accident. No expression. The face looked like it had been chiselled from concrete. Only the eyes leaked pain.

'Steve . . .'

He stared straight ahead. I didn't know if he was ignoring me or whether my butchered throat couldn't produce a voice.

Why was I walking with Steve? Toward town, sure. But what for? Doncaster's a ghost town Sunday mornings.

Steve, why did he look like that? Maybe his father had fallen asleep at the wheel and . . . shit . . . why didn't my brain work? It was as if I'd lost a lump of the stuff – the lump with the memories . . .

Christ, I must have been in one hell of a fight. Who'd hit me so hard that I felt like one of the living dead? It'd have to be someone like Slatter.

SLATTER!

Memory exploded inside my head.

Back over the garden fence that morning. Hacked-up bread in the kitchen; John's bedroom; the pyramid.

I yanked at Steve's arm, spinning him to face me. 'Steve. Slatter's killed John. I – I got back this morning. I went into his bedroom. It's all – all ... I found John. He'd ripped his face. He's dead, Steve, he's dead.'

Steve looked at me. His stone face not altering. When he spoke it was very low. 'Nick. Don't you remember? You ran back to my house. You told me about John.'

Steve began walking but I grabbed him by the arm. 'I'm getting Slatter for this. I'm going to tear his skin off. I'm going to do what he did to John.'

Steve shook his head.

'Steve, you don't have to help. I'll do it myself. I'm going to kill Slatter. John will ...' The words jammed up inside of me. I screamed and kicked a wall. 'I'll get the bastard. I don't care if I do time ... Slatter ... SLATTER!'

I was losing it again. I came to with Steve holding me by the shoulders. He looked me in the face for a full ten seconds before he said something that nearly knocked me flat.

'Nick. It wasn't Slatter.'

'Of course it was Slatter. Slatter wants to destroy me. My pick-up. Then John ... I'm—'

'Nick, listen. It wasn't Slatter. Keep still. No, I'm not letting go. Just listen. Slatter didn't kill John.'

'Of course it's Slatter.'

'No.'

'If it wasn't Slatter who the hell was it?'

'I think it was ...' He broke off, shaking his head furiously. 'I don't know, I don't know.'

I pushed him away and walked in the direction where Slatter lived. My pace savage.

Steve followed, having to jog to keep up. We cut off Thorne Road into rows of terraced housing that fill the budget end of town.

'Nick ... Wait. Give me five minutes to explain.'

'No way. Slatter's dead. That's the end of it.'

Ahead on the pavement a mother was seeing her young daughter off to Sunday school. Zipping up her coat and kissing her on the lips.

'Steve, get off me. Let go!'

He'd hooked his hand around my jacket collar. The only way to shift him was to batter him in the face. And I was ready to do it. Then shove by mummy kissing her little girl. The only thing that existed for me right then was the aching need to baptise my hands in Slatter's blood.

'Nick. For Chrissakes stand still and listen.'

'Let go.'

'Listen.' Steve spoke slowly; he was willing the words into my brain. 'Listen to me. It wasn't Slatter who killed John. Slatter was nowhere near your house. In fact, Slatter is probably already dead.'

Now that did stop me. I just stared, blood pumping through my ears.

'Dead? How the hell can Slatter be dead?'

'Nick. Something's happened. Something ... something just so weird. Insane. I don't know – I can't say what.'

'Have you cracked or what?' I twisted out of Steve's grip and stood there, staring at him.

'Nick. People have gone crazy. All of them. They've just gone fucking, ape-shit crazy.'

'I can't handle this now. Just piss off, will you.'

'Don't take my word for it. Look.' Steve nodded at the woman kissing her child.

I looked. This time I saw properly.

The mother wasn't kissing her child. She was eating her face.

Chapter Six

THE SOUND OF KILLING

'The noise started after you left this morning, Nick. I went outside. The noise was the sound of people killing one another.'

As we walked along the deserted road Steve told me what had happened to him.

'They weren't fighting. There were two sets of people. One set were doing the killing. The other set were being killed.'

'Why are they attacking us? Did you see who they were?'

He nodded, his eyes fixed in front of him.

I said, 'Cops ... Why aren't there any cops when you need them?'

'I live next door to a cop. A sergeant from the town station.'

'He couldn't do anything?'

'Oh, he could do plenty.' Steve nodded. 'He was murdering his own children.'

'Wasn't anyone trying to stop it?'

Steve shrugged.

'What did you do?'

'Me?' Steve shot me a look. 'I ran. That's right, Nick. I'm a damn coward. I was running when I saw you coming up the street to my house. You were out of it, old son. I thought you were one of them.'

'Jesus ... I've got to find my parents. I've got to tell them.'

'No, Nick. That's not a good idea.'

'Why, for Chrissakes? They've got to know about John. I don't know where they are. I don't know if they've been attacked. Or – or—'

'Nick. I don't think they've been harmed. And don't worry about finding them. If what I think is right, they'll be looking for you.'

'What do you mean?'

'Nick. Right now the world seems to have gone mad. But there's a pattern to it.'

'What pattern?' I was still in shock. I couldn't get my head around this. 'What are you talking about?'

'Remember what happened yesterday. Down there in the market place.'

'That kid was murdered.'

'By?'

'By his mother.'

My brain fought to process this data. I couldn't. It was all mad. Images streamed senselessly through my head. John lying in the pyramid. The little girl near Christ Church. Her mother eating her face. The deserted roads. The town centre. So silent you could hear the rooks calling overhead.

At that point we didn't know where we were walking. Maybe we were instinctively hunting for signs of normality. This was the town we'd both known for seventeen years. We knew every shop, road and alleyway. And today it looked normal. There was no litter on the streets. Cars were parked in an orderly way by the kerbside. Only there were no people.

We passed a café with its Xpelair humming. A beautifully normal sound. It even carried a shot of warm oil and onion smells from the night before.

'What's happening, Steve? Why are people acting like this?'

Without looking at me he shrugged.

'Steve, you said you thought parents were killing their children.'

'Mainly.'

'When I said I wanted to look for my parents . . . You said not to bother . . . That they were probably looking for me. What do you mean?'

'What do I mean, Nick? I mean I saw mothers and fathers, ordinary people I've known all my life, killing their children. They were tearing them apart. That's what I saw. Why are they doing it? Jesus Christ, I don't know why.'

Suspicion detonated like Semtex inside my head. 'You think my parents killed John?'

'I think . . . Shit. Will you take a look at that?'

I looked in the direction he was staring.

There were people in the High Street. At that moment they were doing nothing.

Nothing apart from watching us. With nearly a hundred yards separating us I wasn't scared. Physically they weren't intimidating. They could have been a group of thirty or so churchgoers, gathering on the pavement for an impromptu meeting. There were no children with them.

Your elders will tell you spending your time in nightclubs teaches you nothing. Not true. It teaches you this. You learn body language. And when you're seventeen knowing how to read body language keeps you in one piece. You instinctively recognise when someone walks toward you whether they're going to ignore you, say hello, or take a belt at you.

When that group of Doncaster men and women turned to look at us, a ripple of movements ran through them. As easy as you read these words you could read their hostility – and intent.

I said, 'They're going to have a go at us.'

Steve nodded. 'At least they'll never catch us from here. Come on.'

We turned.

Where they had come from I don't know. They must have leaked from the back alleyways. Blocking the pavement ten yards away were a dozen men and women aged anything from their twenties to one old guy of eighty-plus with a deaf aid and walking stick. Normally you wouldn't have looked twice at this bunch.

But their eyes belted out a different message.

They burned with hatred. The muscle beneath their faces was so tight skin creases radiated from their mouths and eyes. Whatever changes had taken place inside their heads changed the shape of their faces. These were facial expressions no one on this planet had seen before.

'Nick. Run . . . Run!'

The men and women didn't move. But you sensed the muscle tension building in their bodies. Their shoulders began to slowly rise.

I felt a punch in my side.

'Wake up, Nick. Run!'

I ran, cutting between two closely parked cars and belted across the road.

Steve wasn't behind me. I stopped at the far side and looked back.

He hadn't been fast enough. I saw him fighting to twist free. That blond head strained from side to side as fists punched down on him; arms wrapped around his shoulders and chest.

I ran back until I was only separated from the mob holding Steve by a parked car.

'Steve!'

He twisted his head to look at me. Blood poured like tears from his eyes.

'Run, Nick! Run!'

Agony cracked from this throat. They were killing him.

I climbed onto the roof of the car and beat the metal with my fists, like I was trying to scare away a pack of wild dogs.

What in God's name could I do?

How he managed to keep on his feet I don't know. Women wrapped their arms around his neck as if they wanted to kiss him. But they were biting his face. Holes appeared in his cheeks.

'Nick . . . Oh, Jesus . . . Nick! Niiiarrrr . . .'

I was screaming, 'Leave him, leave him, leave him . . .'

They took no notice.

A heavy shape bounced across the car inches from me. A fat man threw himself onto the clump of bodies. Steve went down.

They were all over him. A mound of kicking, biting, punching men and women.

Steve's destruction was all that mattered. They even ignored me, although their bodies slamming into the car nearly rocked me off as they fought for their share of the obliteration.

That's what it was. Like a jilted bride tearing up the photograph of her ex. They were shredding my best friend to the tiniest pieces they could.

I jumped from the car and ran.

I stopped when I could go no further. I'd reached the top of the multi-storey car park after running up the ramps that linked the concrete decks.

Within twenty minutes my heart had slowed to near normal. I looked out over Doncaster. In the sunlight it looked pretty much like it always did. St George's Church looking like a Gothic wedding cake beside the art college. Railway tracks gleamed like snail trails. No trains ran. North Bridge spanned tracks, canal and river completely deserted.

From here I could see the streets, shops, shopping mall. The silent pattern of changing traffic lights. Red, amber, green.

The place was normal. It wasn't mad. No one was mad.

That's it. It was me who was mad. Me, Nick Aten.

Or maybe Slatter – it had to be that twat Slatter – had spiked my beer last night with acid. I was hallucinating.

For Chrissakes, Aten. Snap out of it. Get the stuff out of your system. Eat. Drink. Piss it from your body.

The thoughts scrambled across the grooves of my brain. Nothing clear connected. I just hung onto the idea I'd been drugged. Taking a deep breath I walked down the ramps back into town.

It was people-free.

I walked the streets. Not knowing where I was going, just hoping the effects of whatever had been dropped in my drink would wear off. Once I saw kids sleeping in a doorway. Only I knew deep down they weren't sleeping because of the way they lay, arms and legs stretched out.

As I neared McDonald's I slowed down. There was movement behind the counter. I passed the expanse of plate glass, trying not to appear too interested in what was happening.

Normality was happening. Two teenage girls in uniform stacked burgers in the hot trays. One reached over to lift out a basket of fries and shake them onto the drain tray. I could smell heaven.

I walked through the door.

Inside it smelt even better. Mobiles advertising kids' specials with a Ronald McDonald toy hung from the ceiling, turning slowly.

'Can I take your order, sir?' The girl's bright smile was a shot of pure antidote. The world was nice and normal again.

'*Big Mac*, please.' I pulled out the money.

'Would you like fries with that, sir?'

'Please.'

'Would you like a drink with your meal, sir?'

'A large coke ... Thanks.'

Then I didn't look at her clean smile, I looked into her eyes.

It was the worst mistake I could have made. Behind the smiling face were the eyes of a frightened little girl. In that one second of eye contact we communicated more deeply than if we'd sat round a table and talked for an hour.

It was all true. The nightmare was reality. There was blood on the tarmac. Teenagers lay dead in their beds, chewed to pieces by mum and dad in the night. She'd seen it, too.

She snapped off to punch the till presets. I handed her the money but kept my eyes down on the tray.

'Thank you – enjoy your meal.'

The other girl watched me hard from behind the burger racks. She was waiting for me to say, 'What the hell are we doing? There's genocide out there. Why are we pretending nothing's happened?'

The only person you can really lie well to is you.

McDonald's was deserted apart from its two teenage staff. It seemed normal, civilized. I wanted it to stay that way. I took the tray upstairs to eat in what could have been a film set of heaven with its marble columns, flowers, vines and sense of tranquillity.

After I'd finished I automatically dumped my rubbish in the bins and went to the toilet. The men's door opened only a few inches. Something soft blocked it. I pushed hard and looked down. I saw a Reebok on the end of a leg.

I quit the door as if it had suddenly erupted in boils. For a moment I stood there, wanting a piss but not knowing what to do.

At last I put my head round the corner of the ladies' door. It was pinkly empty. Feeling stupidly self-conscious I went as quickly as I could and left, still zipping my jeans.

The two girls watched me come downstairs, their eyes huge with fear. I've never seen a drowning man clinging to a life belt, but I'm sure if I did he wouldn't hang on more tightly than one of those girl's was hanging onto that McDonald coke dispenser.

I got through the door feeling their eyes on my back. What could I do? What could I say? I was in shock. My brain was black lead inside my skull. I should have tried to help them – they were just frightened kids.

I didn't.

I hit the street not knowing where I was going but walking quickly. If I walked purposefully then maybe a purpose would come. Some idea of where to go.

The police?

No. When was the last time you saw a teenage cop?

I saw the car, the roof dimpled where I'd jumped onto it. There was a purpose after all in the direction I was walking. I had to check on Steve. He might be alive.

I edged slowly round the car. First I saw the mess in the gutter that looked like black-red treacle. Lying flat on the paving slabs was my friend. I didn't know if he lay face up or face down. They'd been thorough.

As I stepped forward a black shape rushed at my face, whipping my cheek with something soft, then it was gone. I looked up to see a rook flapping up to the roof tops, a piece of food hanging from its beak.

I walked away.

Before me the traffic lights ran through their sequence. Red, amber, green. Neon signs flashed in the stores. Six TVs in an electrical store played an old U2 video. Then the sense of dislocation squeezed back again. Perhaps it would have been easier to walk through a post-nuclear holocaust town with burned-out buildings and rusting car wrecks. But here was madness and murder in a town with clean pavements and traffic lights signalling to empty highways. My friend lay broken on the street while a TV in the Post Office window chuntered in green letters:

GOOD MORNING DONCASTER.

THE WEATHER TODAY – SUNSHINE: 21C.

EVENTS SUNDAY, APRIL 16.

REGENT'S SQUARE SPRING FETE. 1PM.

FOR CARE OF THE ELDERLY WITH DIGNITY, THE—

As I stood there the screen died.

And at that moment I knew the town itself had begun to die. The traffic lights went out; screens in the electrical stores blanked; VDU timetables at the bus stop faded to black.

Electricity is like blood flowing through your veins. You don't notice it till it stops.

Now there was something cold and inert about the town. The buildings, even in sunshine, seemed suddenly dark. It was quieter. All the air conditioning units and Xpelair fans that provide the subliminal hum had died too.

For the first time I realised that loneliness wasn't just people not being there. Loneliness has form, it's got a presence so huge you feel it pressing against you. You have to do something or it begins to smother you.

I couldn't just keep circling the town like a calf circling around its dead mother. She was dead. I had to break away.

In the end, I didn't have to make the decision.

A hundred yards ahead of me, gathering in a swarm, were men and women. They were moving in from side streets. Some were the ones that had attacked Steve. They had his lifeblood drying to cracks on their hands and faces.

I cut down a side street that lead in the direction of the station. It took me by McDonald's. Smoke now filled the restaurant. I never did find out what had happened to the girls who'd served me twenty minutes ago.

People seemed to seep from the brickwork. They headed in the direction of Clock Corner, the traditional centre of town, as if there was going to be some announcement and the call had gone out to meet there. I saw no one under the age of twenty.

From the distance came the cry of someone in pain. After a second it cut to nothing.

Sweating-scared now, I ran down a narrow service alley. But walking towards me were five men of about forty. I forked off to the left along a narrow back street flanked by high brick walls.

This's getting shitty, this's getting shitty . . .

I looked back. The men were following me.

Shit.

Ahead, blocking my way, was a hulking great orange truck, the driver's door open against the wall.

Heart juddering, breath turning ragged, I ran faster. I'd have to duck under the high door of the van and run until I bust. Or I'd be like Steve. The bastards would dance on my heart and lungs then leave me to be picked by rooks.

I slammed through the gap between the truck and the wall then ducked under the door, but stayed crouching there, the door above my head. Twenty yards ahead three men walked slowly along the alley toward me.

No, it wasn't a deliberate trap. But it had become one.

Behind me, the other men had nearly reached the tailgate of the truck. I scrambled into the cab.

At that moment I felt God still loved me. The keys swung from the ignition.

The engine fired as I slammed the door and punched the lock shut. Outside two faces appeared to stare in at me. They were impassive; no expression – just like those of the mob before they attacked Steve and me.

Hands shaking, I struggled to knock off the handbrake while revving the motor until clouds of blue rolled down the alley. The guys in front had nearly reached the truck; the faces at the window pressed closer; the muscle beneath those faces tightened into an expression of sheer, fucking, alien fury.

'Come on, you stupid bastard!' I yelled at myself. My hands and feet were like mashed potato. Nothing worked; the engine roared like a bleeding elephant; gears screamed, shredding splinters of steel. Beside me the door handle turned. They wanted in. They wanted to tear my skin. They—

BANG! Gear connected to axle.

The truck moved. I stamped on the pedal. The engine roared and the brick walls blurred orange. I was, thank Jesus and all his sweet, sweet angels, really shifting.

I looked away from the side window. I didn't want to see what happened to the faces.

I thundered that truck along the alley like a shell through its barrel, a paint-stripping hand's breadth to spare at each side.

The truck powered out from the side of McDonald's, the building now blazing. I swung right.

It was a one way street. I was going the wrong way. But I couldn't care less.

I wouldn't stop this big orange truck until the town was miles away. What'd I do then? God only knew . . .

Chapter Seven

STAY TUNED TO THIS STATION. AN IMPORTANT ANNOUNCEMENT FOLLOWS THIS MESSAGE

Cutting myself from Doncaster felt like cutting an umbilical cord that had connected me with that town for seventeen years.

It hurt. But I had to do it or it would kill me.

The truck was slow, as noisy as a tank, but its sheer bulk felt reassuring.

I cut off onto minor roads that took me into the flat countryside that surrounds Doncaster in a vast pancake of fields.

There was no traffic. I saw no one. No one moving, that is. I powered the truck through small villages, sometimes seeing a shape at the side of the road. Often they looked like big dolls or just a mound of children's clothes. I knew what they were.

In the front garden of a vicarage with roses climbing round the front door were the remains of a bonfire. Charred shapes with arms stretching up as stiff as branches lay in the ash.

A country hotel. From the window three young men hung head first down the walls like carnival decorations. In a dislocated way I wondered how it had been done. I guessed they had been dangled out of the windows while someone had nailed their feet to the window ledges. Beneath each corpse blood streaked down the wall.

Memories of the drive come back to me now. Bright and hard but somehow broken and disconnected. Miles of road cutting through fields and woodland. The nailed boys. Blue sky. Torched bodies, crisp as burnt toast. Lots of birds. A sports car burning in the middle of the road like a gigantic firework, pumping out sparks and smoke. The truck crushing through bushes at the road side as I swerved to avoid it.

I drove aimlessly for a couple of hours, circling the same few miles of countryside. Every so often I'd pass the hotel with the nailed boys. At one point I even found myself heading back into Doncaster.

I passed a school playing field where perhaps three hundred adults tore pieces from figures that looked like scarecrows. I turned the truck, flattening a road sign, then headed back into the countryside.

Ten minutes later I parked the truck in a field beneath some trees.

The truck contained about ten thousand bottles of spring water. HAMPOLE PRIORY SPRING sang the labels. At least I wasn't going to die of thirst. In the cab I found the driver's plastic lunchbox.

I remember feeling unreasonably bitter that whatever had happened to the truck's driver hadn't happened sooner. The sandwiches were gone leaving two apples and a large pork pie. The pie had a half moon shape missing from it where the trucker had taken a huge, slobbering bite.

The burst of anger over something as trivial as the pork pie actually settled me down mentally. Here was something I could concentrate my irritation on. Ten thousand bottles of frigging water and a part-masticated pie. Shit to the dead kids decorating the landscape, here was something I could handle. I could even see the guy's teethmark slicing through the pink meat. I strode round the truck, kicking the wheels and swearing.

Then I sat on the grass, wrapped my arms round my knees and shook for ten minutes.

After that I didn't feel so crazy any more. I picked off the bits of crust and meat that had made contact with the trucker's lips and tongue, ate the pie, then drank water – lots of it. Fear dehydrates you.

I didn't know why I didn't think of it earlier but I tried the truck's radio. Usually you get the crack and pop of dozens of stations as you spin the dial. All I got from FM was a hiss. On AM I picked up three stations. One played uninterrupted classical music. Another played old disco songs back to back with no DJ. Eventually the music stopped to be replaced by a sound like an electric razor.

Station three was more promising. I tuned in to hear a single word '. . . message.' Then came orchestral versions of popular hymns. For five minutes I sat in the truck, swinging one leg out the door, listening to *Hills Of The North Rejoice* before it suddenly faded. Then came the voice.

'You must stay tuned to this station. An important announcement follows this message.'

All Things Bright And Beautiful followed. I waited, actually gripping the steering wheel until my hands ached. This was it. I'd find out what was happening. And what I should do next. Again came the rapid music fade-out.

'You must stay tuned to this station. An important announcement follows this message.'

I waited. More music. Then came the same message. I punched the steering wheel, swore and waited some more.

For an hour I sat listening to the shit-awful music and the automated voice repeating the same few words. In the end I switched it off and went for a piss against a tree.

The sun was touching the horizon when I realised I'd have to find somewhere to sleep. It was tempting to sleep in the cab. But a three-ton chunk of iron the colour of day-glo tangerines in the middle of the countryside shines like a moon in a midnight sky. I didn't want to wake with faces pressed to the windows.

Carrying two bottles of Hampole Priory Well water and the trucker's apples, I headed through the trees to where the land fell away into a valley. I knew the place well enough. We used to cycle there as kids. Spanning the valley is a huge viaduct carrying a motorway. No traffic moved on it. Beyond the viaduct at the far end of the valley is a small village with a church tower poking up through the trees.

It all came back to me as I walked down the paths winding through the trees. We'd come up here with air pistols and spend hours hunting through the woods, not hitting a damn thing but enjoying every minute of it.

Beneath a rock outcrop were a couple of small sandy caves. They were always dry and that's where we'd make camp for an hour or two. And they were private. You could only reach them by climbing a near-vertical bank of grass.

I crawled into one of the caves.

Now. There was nothing more to do but lie down and shut my eyes.

Chapter Eight

INSIDE ME I FEEL ALONE AND UNREAL

At something past midnight I woke. Suddenly alert, my ears ringing with the quiet. I crawled over the cave floor to the entrance and looked out.

The night was cool, peaceful. No stars or moon. Below, the cloudy black shapes of forest trees.

As I looked out a sudden blast of light shot from one side of the valley to the other. It came from the direction of the village, its reflected glare silhouetting the viaduct carrying the motorway high across the valley.

From what I could see it came from the church on the hillside.

At that moment, squatting at the cave entrance I could believe that the interior of the church was filled from pew to roof beam with a solid block of eye-blistering light. Then someone had thrown open the doors of the church.

Unleashed, the light leapt out across the valley in a beam so hard and straight it looked like a second bridge, solid enough to drive a truck across.

One, two, three ... I found myself counting. At five the light snapped off; darkness returned so heavily it was suffocating.

I crawled back into the corner of my cave. What was the light? Who had made it? Why?

I didn't know. The only truth I did know was that the world tonight was different from the one I woke up in that morning.

How did I feel right then?

There's a song by Syd Barrett. It's called *Late Night*. It describes how it feels to slide into mental illness. There's a line in the song that goes: *Inside me I feel alone and unreal*. If you've ever heard it you'll know it's the saddest song in the world.

Curled up in the cave corner that lyric went round and around my head. *Inside me I feel alone and unreal*.

Christ ... Poor Nick fucking Aten. If only I'd been a university professor of philosophy or some high-powered shit like that you'd hold in your hands the words that explained logically and clearly what was happening. You would have a description as clear as glass of civilization lying belly-up and busted.

But I couldn't. Inside me I felt alone and unreal. The song haunted my head like a ghost. I was alone. I was scared. I didn't know if this time tomorrow I would still be alive.

Later, I heard a voice singing. It was my mother's. I'd heard her singing thousands of times when I woke up on a morning as she made breakfast.

Then I'd hear her calling in her bright, it's-a-beautiful-morning voice. 'Nick. Time to get up ... If you're not down here in five minutes you'll get nothing to eat.' The night was heavy, my mind rambled on alone in the dark. The words from my mother seemed to be, 'If you're not down here in five minutes I'll come up there and eat you.'

Mum's ghost voice would not stop.

'Nick. Breakfast's ready. Nick, your brother's dead. Nick, you're next ... you're next.'

The cave walls tightened around me closer. Inside me I feel alone and unreal.

Chapter Nine

FOOD AND DRINK AND HOPE

DAY 3. YEAR 1. I woke from a deep sleep just after six. I sat at the cave's entrance eating the trucker's last apple and drinking a bottle of spring water. Sleep is the best cure for a psychological battering. I felt sane and in control.

As I crunched the apple down to the core I brewed up my own theory about what had happened. The military are always developing new weapons. The trend was to develop ones that killed or disabled people but left property and land intact. Hence nerve gas, biological weapons and those neutron bombs that are supposed to wipe out armies but leave buildings fit to move your Aunt Flo into the very next day.

I ate the apple nodding wisely as the theory ran through my head.

Our military or a foreign power had developed a weapon that affected the mind only. Whether a gas or some electro-magnetic neural disrupter I didn't know. But they had a mind-busting weapon. That weapon had been used against Doncaster. Probably during that Saturday night I spent at Steve's.

Clearly it only affected adults. And that effect drove them to kill their children. Whether that was the intention Christ knows but that is what happened. Or at least that was what my theory told me.

Your mind finds a mystery uncomfortable. Like that bit of grit inside an oyster's gut. You have to wrap that mystery in a pearl of an answer – it doesn't really matter if it's right or completely crackers. An answer makes you feel better and that's all that counts.

I quit the cave and headed up through the valley. As I walked three objectives fell quickly into place.

1. I wanted to eat.

2. I wanted a new set of wheels. The truck was about as discreet as a three-inch zit on the end of your nose.

3. I wanted out of this area.

I guessed the neural disrupter had only affected a few square miles. I imagined driving back to the normal world where the army waited at roadblocks to whisk survivors back to normality. There'd probably even be CNN waiting with cameras to get the survivors' stories.

These thoughts were a comfort to me. They gave me hope.

I knew where I was going. Further up the valley there were a few big houses. Some quite isolated.

The first one I reached looked like a baked skeleton with black walls and still-smoking timbers. A burnt-out Rolls Royce stood on the drive.

The next was a converted farmhouse complete with a swimming pool in the barn.

First I knocked on the door then ran back to hide in the bushes. No one came.

I cut down the side of the house, feet crunching overloud on the raked gravel. The stable doors were open. No horses but three cars parked side by side. Two sportscars and a hulking Shogun 4x4. Perfect.

The bugger was locked.

On the patio at the back I found a child's go-cart. It had been thoroughly cut to pieces with a saw. Hanging from a child's climbing frame, swinging in the breeze, were two black bin liners. They could have been full of hedge clippings, but I doubted it.

For a minute I was ready to quit this house.

Get your fucking head together, Aten. You need that Shogun.

I hunted through the rockery, hoisted out a chunk of limestone the size of a football and lobbed it at the patio window. It bounced off the toughened glass.

Shit . . . It takes some skill to be a vandal.

Next, I heaved the rock at the kitchen window. It disappeared in a crash loud enough to wake the dead. I froze, expecting someone to charge from the house and cut me in two. Nothing.

I climbed through the window. This was breaking and entering but I didn't feel a shred of guilt. The civilized bit of Nick Aten was already withering.

After checking that the place was deserted (the kids' bedroom turned me sick) I went down and sat on the sofa for ten minutes. A couple of Scotches from the bar helped.

On a table stood a photograph of a family. Beautiful people, mum would have said with a wink, slightly catty, slightly envious. The father had slick executive looks, the mother was glamorous and well-jewelled.

Between them sat two little girls with plaits. They now resided in the plastic sacks hanging from the swing.

I put the happy family portrait face down and went to find food.

There was plenty of it. There was no power but the refrigerator felt cool. The gas cooker still worked so I made a breakfast big enough to bust the intestine of Homer Simpson. Eggs, ham, steak, mushrooms, coffee, more Scotch.

Now I felt fuelled and in gear.

The keys to the Shogun hung from a hook in the kitchen.

It was hit and miss but I loaded supplies into the back of the car. Food, Scotch, cans of beer, soft drinks, a spade, a tool kit, a long-handled axe, a wicked-looking diver's knife. From the wardrobe I took a leather jacket. It was new and smelt so richly of leather you could taste it. I slipped it on.

I'd got the car, I'd got the supplies: now I'd find where the sane world started.

Chapter Ten

YOU'VE NEVER SEEN A RIVER LIKE THIS ONE

Finding where the sane world started wasn't going to be as easy as I thought.

The motorway wasn't blocked, exactly. It was full.

I stopped the car in the middle of the bridge that crossed the motorway, got out, leaving the engine running and the door open, then looked down.

Beneath me the six-lane highway stretched out in a long S curve, flanked at each side by corn fields. A sign set on the embankment said simply: THE SOUTH.

I had planned to hit the motorway then hammer the Shogun south. In an hour or less I imagined myself reaching the normal world with the army at the checkpoint telling me where to go next. I probably wouldn't even need the food I'd dumped in the back of the car.

But I wouldn't be using this motorway. From one end to the other, as far as I could see, was a river. A vast, sluggish river, squeezed between grass bankings. A river of human beings.

Like a river they all flowed in the same direction, from north to south, at the same slow pace. Thousands of people – you could not see an inch of road tar.

A burnt-out truck a hundred yards to the south forced them to part like a river flowing round a rock, then they merged again, to flow on in their single-minded migration.

There was something mind-numbing about this flow of people. I imagined myself climbing over the fence to jump down the thirty feet to land on them.

Like you saw singers at rock concerts hurling themselves onto an audience so tightly packed they could roll over them like you roll across a bed. I could do that. I could go with them. There was something at the end of the motorway that they wanted. And, oh shit, they wanted it so badly they were prepared to walk for hours down this road with no food, no drink, no rest. They were like those on a pilgrimage to see the coming of the Lord.

Not one looked up at me. Their ten thousand eyes burned south.

I unglued my hands from the railing and stepped back – shaking.

I walked round the Shogun breathing so deeply it hurt my lungs. When I felt balanced again I looked down at the river of people. I looked harder this time, making myself see individuals, not a mess of heads.

I was searching for a child. Or at least someone who looked under twenty.

Thousands marched silently beneath me. I never did see a single child. However, I did notice blood marks on some of the walkers' faces. They had killed their children too.

I got back into the car and stamped the pedal so hard that the big tyres spun on the Shogun, powering me away from the river of lunatics.

My plan remained the same. If I headed back to Doncaster I knew I could join another road south.

As Doncaster's suburbs began to slip by I slowed down. There were wrecked cars, burnt-out buses. A school was burning so brightly it looked as if a crack had opened in the Earth and a chunk of hell was bursting through.

At a crossroads I looked right. A group of middle-aged men and women walked in my direction. Some carried ten-foot poles topped with objects that although I couldn't identify made me suddenly cold in the warm car.

I had intended driving straight on but looking to my left I saw an orange VW Beetle, parked at a clumsy angle. Two girls, one about eighteen, the other elevenish, were changing a flat.

They were doing a good job. The car was jacked high and the younger girl was wheeling the spare toward the other girl.

They were dead meat.

The group of adults had seen me for sure, and possibly the girls. They walked purposefully in my direction.

Pulling the car a sharp left, I stopped alongside the VW.

The eighteen-year-old, long blonde hair, wearing jeans and a sweatshirt, ignored me and hoisted the spare onto the hub.

The younger girl, wearing riding jodhpurs, her blonde hair tied into a pony tail, just stared at me as if I'd dropped from a golden-winged spaceship.

In the rear view mirror I saw the group with the poles had nearly reached the crossroads.

I leaned through the window. 'I reckon you've got about ninety seconds to leave that and get in.'

The older girl still ignored me and began tightening the wheel nuts.

'Eighty seconds.' I lightly revved the engine. 'Forget it. Get in the car.'

The younger girl looked at the older one. 'Sarah!'

Sarah threw down the wrench. She wasn't frightened, she was angry. 'All right, all right . . .' She shot me a hard look trying to read what I was like. Would I drive round the corner, then take a Stanley knife to their throats?

'Get in.' I opened the back door from the inside, still keeping one hand on the steering wheel and glancing in the rear view. The pole carriers were a hundred yards behind and closing quickly.

The oldest girl, Sarah, opened the VW door. 'Vicki, out. We're going with this . . . gentleman.'

Another girl, about tennish, wearing pink-rimmed glasses and with the same colour hair in a pony tail, jumped out of the car, ran to the back door of the Shogun – then she stopped.

'Wait a minute.'

She ran back to the VW.

The girl behind me shouted in such a high-pitched voice it pierced my skull. 'Vicki! Hurry up! There's people coming! They'll catch us!'

'Vicki!' Sarah ran to the car looking as if she'd drag the brat back by the hair. Vicki bounced into the back seat of the VW, pulled out a fluffy rabbit toy, then ran back to the Shogun. She slid in beside the other girl. Sarah joined her, slamming the door shut so hard I felt the air compress against the back of my neck.

When I looked back at the mob this time they were close enough for me to see their expressions. Some of them had broken into a run.

The two youngest girls lay down in the back seat, hands over their ears, eyes screwed shut. Sarah looked back, composed, even curious.

I wasted no time in hitting the gas – we took off like a rocket, leaving the orange VW to its fate.

THANKS . . . I waited for her to say the word. She didn't.

'My name's Nick Aten.' For a second I thought she was going to stay mute.

Then she held up her hands so I could see them in the rear view. They were black with filth. 'Have you got any tissues?'

The car's owner had thoughtfully provided a drum of wet wipes and I handed them back.

Sarah wiped her hands, then her face. There was a bruise turning blue on her left cheek. From the look on her face she had reached a decision. She'd decided to trust me.

'I'm Sarah Hayes. These are my sisters, Vicki and Anne.'

'Where were you going?'

'Doncaster. We had to drive over a lot of broken glass on the way in. I think we picked up the puncture there.'

'Have you got relatives in Doncaster?'

'No.'

One of the girls piped up. 'We're going to the police station. We're in trouble.'

'Vicki.' Sarah glared at her to shut her mouth.

'Why can't we tell him, Sarah?' The little girl sounded as if she'd start crying. 'He's the first nice man we've seen. He might help us.'

'We don't know him. He might . . . he might be on his way to work or something.'

I nearly laughed. Big sister was still trying to pretend the world was sane.

I told them, 'I'm in trouble too.'

The two youngest girls leaned forward, eyes round. 'What you done?'

'Nothing really. But I think it's the same trouble as you. Look, there's no point in going into Doncaster. It's full of . . . It's not safe at the moment.'

Vicki hugged the rabbit. 'We've got to go to the police. We've got to tell them what happened.'

'What did happen?'

'It doesn't matter.' This was big sister, Sarah.

A seventeen-year-old male can't look at a girl without ticking off the usual list.

Attractive? Nice breasts? Fit figure? Etc, etc . . . If you're male and over fourteen you know what I mean. To that list I'd add *Was she intelligent*? The answer was a thumping *Yes*: Sarah had got looks and she was nobody's fool.

'Where are you taking us, Nick Aten?'

'Have you eaten today?'

'No.'

The younger girls chorused. 'We're starving.'

'Then I'll drive somewhere quiet and we'll have a picnic. I've got stacks of food in the back.'

I drove away from town. Occasionally I glanced back at Sarah. Her eyes had a metal edge to them – also they told me they had seen a slice of hell this last forty-eight hours.

I thought she'd say nothing for while. Shock can lock memories away in a steel box and bury it deep in the mind. But as I looked at her in the mirror her eyes locked onto mine and she told me what had happened to her.

Chapter Eleven

THIS IS WHAT HAPPENED TO SARAH HAYES

Sarah lived with her family on a farm. On Sunday morning, Day 2, she had got up, dressed, then gone out into the farmyard where her parents stood leaning with their backs to a wall.

'Morning,' she had said, smiling. 'Are Vicki and Anne out riding?'

That's when her father punched her in the face.

'Kill her, James. Kill her,' shouted her mother. 'Kill her before she hurts anyone else!'

Shock numbed the initial pain of her father's punch, but it knocked her back onto the dirt. Mother reached out for daughter, a knife in her hand, her eyes blazing hatred.

Dazed, Sarah acted on instinct. She ran back to the house, clawed her way upstairs and locked herself in the bathroom. It was a solid door but the bolt wasn't: designed for modesty not survival.

As she backed away from the door someone knocked on it. Her father. 'Come on out, Sarah, love. We've got to talk to you. It's important.'

If her father had tried he could have kicked in the door inside thirty seconds. But for some reason he talked. He told Sarah over and over how he and her mother loved her. And the plans they had for her. If only she'd unlock the door.

Sarah, too shocked to think, sat on the floor.

'Come on, Sarah, love. Your mother's making you a cup of tea. Open the door.'

She couldn't *think* what to do, so she did what her guts *told* her to do.

She ran the water. 'I'm just going to wash, then I'll come out.'

Leaving the water running, she climbed out of the window onto the flat roof of the conservatory. From there, she swung herself off the roof, hanging by her hands from the guttering, before dropping into the flower bed.

Legs threatening to give way, she managed to jog round the house. As she ran she heard the sound of her VW Beetle.

Her sisters had seen what had happened to her, got the car started and were desperately trying to drive the thing. Eleven-year-old Anne in the driving seat, revving the engine until it rattled, tried to get it in gear but didn't know she had to depress the clutch pedal. Metal struck metal, the old German car shrieked.

Sarah pushed both sisters into the front passenger seat then reversed the car across the yard as her father belted from the house. One look at his face told her *RUN*.

As she drove down the drive he charged the car, punching through the passenger window with his fist.

Sarah thrashed the motor and the car left him behind. Immediately he stopped running and just stared after them.

Five minutes later Sarah parked the car – then she threw up in a hedgebottom.

After that, the sequence of events was similar to mine. Driving round, shocked. Listening to the same message on the radio. Seeing the aftermath where parents had torn apart their children.

By late afternoon both sisters were complaining of hunger. Sarah found a deserted village store. They could have taken what they wanted but the Hayes sisters had been brought up nicely with a private education. Looting wasn't on the curriculum so Sarah left the few coins she found in the car to pay for the loaf of bread and chocolate they took.

Sunday night they slept in the car in a wood. The next morning she decided to drive to Doncaster police station.

If I hadn't found them as they tried to change the tyre I think the three sisters – or some part of them – would have joined the other objects that topped the ten-foot poles carried by the mob.

Chapter Twelve

WHY ARE THEY TRYING TO KILL US?

'What's happened? Why are they trying to kill us?'

Shrugging, I opened another beer. Sarah sat on the wooden bench that looked over the fields and tried to work out what had happened. It was a mystery she wanted to solve so much it hurt her more than the bruised cheekbone.

'I went to bed Saturday night. I'd watched TV with my parents. They were perfectly normal. Dad even brought home a Chinese meal. Then when I woke up Sunday morning they tried to kill me.'

'Had your father ever brought home a Chinese meal before?'

'No. He always said he never fancied eating—' She shot me a look with those clear blue eyes.

'What do you mean, Nick? What's eating Chinese food got to do with . . .'

'Not much, probably. Only the last time I saw my dad he was drinking beer in the afternoon. Nothing odd about that except I'd never seen him ever drink beer before during the day.'

'You mean they were starting to change even then?'

'Probably. But the changes were so slight you didn't notice them at the time.'

'But what caused it?' Sarah beat her knee to the rhythm of the words. 'What caused most of the population to turn into homicidal maniacs?'

'Not *most* of the population. *All* the *adult* population.' I told her about the river of lunatics I'd seen on the motorway. 'As far as I can tell everyone over twenty has been driven stark, barking mad. I haven't seen any kids affected.'

'But how?'

I nearly told her my neural disrupter theory. In the cold light of day it sounded too half-assed. I shrugged again.

She started pacing in front of the bench. 'Is it something in the water supply? In the air? Like a nerve gas? Is it a virus? Why should it send people not just mad, but ... but it seems to implant in parents a – a craving to kill their own children ... I mean they're not fighting each other, they're banding together, they're flocking like birds ... they want ... they seem to need to ... oh God ... God ...'

Sarah suddenly sat down rubbing her forehead, like she was trying to massage the mystery from her brain.

And she obviously had brains. She was trying to work out logically what had happened. I'm short on brains. I opened another beer. Why should I try and work out what happened? There'd be plenty of scientists and psychologists and all that shit working on what had hit Doncaster for years to come.

I walked round the hilltop. Castle Rising is a straight-sided little hill that pokes out of the flat countryside like a monster zit. I'd not chosen it for its picturesque setting but its views of the surrounding fields. If the crazy people should come we'd see them a mile off.

Sarah's sisters sat on a blanket, eating sandwiches. I avoided them. They never stopped asking questions.

'Will mummy and daddy be all right now? When can we go home? Who'll look after Pookah and Chestnut?' (Their ponies.) 'If that car isn't yours whose is it then? Won't we get into trouble if we don't go to school?'

I completed the circuit of the hilltop and sat beside Sarah. A faint fatherly instinct suggested I put my arm around her and tell her everything would be okay. But at seventeen you don't do that kind of thing.

'Sarah. I planned on driving south. I reckon we should be out of the affected area after a few miles . . . You and your sisters can come along if you like.'

'Thanks . . . And thanks for picking us up back in town. You took a risk.'

'Don't worry about it.' I drained the can. 'We'll have another half-hour here then we'll be off.'

I picked a patch of soft grass on the sloping hillside and lay down. Sunshine warmed my face and the beer and sandwiches made me feel that the world was going to be all right after all. My eyes closed.

The birds sang, the two youngest girls were laughing. At this distance it sounded musical.

I let myself imagine I was drifting on a cloud, a mile high above the countryside; it was as soft as cottonwool. I relaxed into it; I relaxed and I relaxed and I floated out of this world.

'Nick! Here, quick!'

I ran down the hillside so fast that when I tried to stop I skied the rest of the way, my trainers buzzing over the grass.

'What is it? What's wrong?'

Then I stopped and gawped stupidly at the two people in front of me.

'Mum . . . Dad.' I had to laugh out loud then or cry hysterically. 'How did you find me? Are you all right? Did – did you see what's happened in Doncaster? They – they . . . It's all—'

'Nick . . . It's all right, Nick. We know what happened.'

My dad, smiling, showing the gap in his top teeth, walked up and put his arm around me. The hug was tight and loving. Mum hung back, pushing back her hair. Her smile was pure mother love.

'Nick, I bet you'd given us up for dead,' she said. 'Whatever happens we'll never leave you again.' She kissed me on the cheek. If she could she would have picked me up like a toddler and hugged me.

'Come on, let's go home. The car's parked on the road.'

'John's waiting to see you. He's been dying to show you those new games he bought.'

A cold lump squeezed through my guts to my legs. A bastard dream.

I shook my head. 'Yeah. John's dying to see me. And where's Uncle Jack? Playing crazy golf?'

My mother laughed like a teenage girl. 'No. We left him practising his guitar in the kitchen.'

I still wanted to go with them. I really did. I wanted them to strap me in the back of dad's car and ride home like I was seven years old. But something deeper said:

NO. RUN LIKE HELL, NICK ATEN. SHOVE YOUR PARENTS AWAY AND RUN, RUN, RUN. THEY'RE GOING TO QUEER YOU UP, BOY.

'Here you are, Nicholas.'

'You know he's going to either end up a millionaire one day or end up in jail.'

Run, Nick, run!

Too late.

Mum and dad pushed me down and held me flat on the ground, my arms outstretched. I was seven years old, not strong enough to stop what they were going to do to me.

'Now, Nicholas, don't be silly. I'm not going to hurt you.' It was the voice my mum used when she used to cut my toe nails. 'You want to look like John, don't you? Lie still. Anyone would think we were trying to kill you.'

Mum held a knife in front of my face.

'If it bothers you,' dad said, 'think about your favourite programme. *The Munsters*, isn't it? Lie still, Nicholas, don't wriggle like that. It'll be over in a minute.'

No!

Stop!

I stared down at my bared chest as mum eased the blade into the skin. Dad began to whistle *Ten Green Bottles* through the gap in his teeth.

A red smile opened in my chest.

Not breathing, I watched her calmly cut through the chest wall. Like a plump red fruit my heart pumped there, its white roots, the arteries, disappearing into bloody meat.

Mum grasped a handful of arteries and began cutting through them as I'd seen her cut rind from bacon, snapping the tougher bits with her fingers.

Each broken artery was agony. I screamed.

'Don't be silly, Nicholas,' she said. 'Another minute and I'll be done. Then you can join your brother. Now hold still while I cut your big one.'

Muthaaaaaaaaa ...

I was sitting on the grass, grunting. When my eyes focused I saw Sarah looking down at me, her eyes wide.

'Are you all right, Nick? I thought you were having a heart attack or something.'

I breathed deeply and rubbed my sweaty palms against the grass.

'Can I get you anything, Nick? A drink?'

I shook my head. The pain felt real. My parents seemed real. I looked down the hillside to make sure they weren't really there.

'Come on,' I said, standing. 'Let's get back to the car.'

'Nick.' She touched my arm. It was the first time she touched me. 'Nick, are you sure you're okay?'

I made my face smile. Inside I felt shit. 'Yeah. Thanks. Just a stupid dream.' I ran my hand across my chest feeling for the hole and feeling stupidly relieved that there was nothing there.

'Was it bad?'

'It was nothing. Forget it. Come on, I want to get back to civilization before it gets dark.'

Chapter Thirteen

THE FIFTY MILLION DOLLAR RUG

'Are you sure it's safe this way?'

'No.'

Sarah looked out at the passing houses. Some were burning. 'You might have been better using the by-pass.'

'It still takes us too close to the town centre.' I turned onto a road that linked the industrial areas with another motorway. That one, I hoped, empty. If it was we could be out of the madlands within the hour. In the back seat Anne and Vicki were half asleep.

'Watch it,' Sarah said. 'They're in the bushes.'

'I see them.'

Alongside the road ran a six-foot mound planted with shrubs that screened the factories from the road. It was sprinkled with men and women sitting on the ridge. None looked under twenty-five.

'What do you think they're waiting for?'

'The second coming . . . People like them to join them.' I shot her a grim smile. 'Or people like us.'

I dropped the speed to twenty-five. Ahead debris littered the road. A truck had ploughed off the road, gouged out a chunk of banking, then dropped on its side.

'Jesus, just look at that,' whispered Sarah. 'Look at all that money.'

The security truck had cracked open like an egg. Bank notes ran across the road like a fifty million dollar rug. I drove through them sending up a spray of fifties like a speedboat cutting through the ocean.

I could have stopped and picked it up. For a minute or two I would have been a millionaire – before the crazy bastards on the bund tore me in two.

'Nick!'

I hit the brake. 'What?'

'There's a boy back there.'

Vicki shouted, 'He's running after us!'

Anne screamed. 'Quick. Drive away, Nick. He'll catch us.'

'He's not one of them. He's too young.'

The boy was about fifteen. God knows where he came from, but he came leaping down the slope onto the road about a hundred yards behind us. Even from this distance you could tell he was terrified.

He ran toward us, his eyes locked on the car. His arms wind-milled, the sports jacket flapped open.

I slipped the car into reverse. I'd meet him half way.

'Get ready to open the back door, Vicki. No, not yet. Wait until he's – shit.'

I nearly reversed into her. An old woman had limped down the banking to stand between me and the running youth. He ran faster, arms going wildly. And I saw why. Running down the banking after him was a mob of adults.

They wanted his blood.

I began to psych myself up. The old woman wouldn't let me reverse past her. I'd have to reverse over her. It made sense. Her eyes told me she was mad. Mad, bad and dangerous.

Into reverse. Pedal down. Bang. Easy.

Come on, Aten. Come on you soft prick.

Shit . . . I couldn't do it.

I stared back at the woman, and I knew I couldn't run the mad old bitch down.

'Watch it, Nick. They're coming for us.'

More crazies were running across a factory yard. A six-foot chain link fence separated them from us. Slowly they began to climb it. Soon they would be dropping down onto the road right next to us.

Behind us the youth had closed the gap to perhaps forty yards.

I rolled the car forward.

'What are you doing, Nick? Don't leave him behind.'

'I'm not. But we can't let ourselves get caught. Those lunatics will tip the car over. He'll make it, he's well ahead of the pack.'

The kid had got a good start – he was fast. I took the car up to five miles an hour.

As he ran his wallet flew from his jacket pocket. For a moment I thought he'd be mad enough to stop and pick it up. But he just glanced back at it bouncing in the gutter, then he looked back at the car, like a sprinter looking at the finishing tape. He didn't shout or yell – he sank everything into running.

From the mound a fat man ran in a slow, lolloping stride. Gravity helped the man, pushing his pace faster than he'd ever make on the flat.

The man snatched at the youth.

'Oh, God,' Sarah's voice punched my ear. 'They've got him, they've got him.'

I twisted back to watch the chase.

The fat man had hold of the youth by the jacket. As I watched the youth held his arms straight back. Smoothly he slipped out of the jacket leaving the fat man holding it in his hands.

'He's going to make it, he's going to make it. Come on! Come on!' I shouted till my ears hurt.

From the passenger side came a loud crack.

I turned to see an old guy beating the window with a walking stick. He struck again and a star crack appeared.

In the back the girls screamed. They screamed again as he grabbed the handle and swung open the door.

I pumped the car forward to twenty leaving him spinning across the road to fall flat on his face.

'Shut the door, Vicki, and lock it.' Sarah's face was white. 'You too, Anne.' Sarah opened her door as we rumbled along. 'He'll have to get in here with me.'

I slowed the car to five miles an hour.

The kid was tiring now. His red face screwed in pain.

Behind him the mob were gaining. He should have made it though, he really should.

For no reason on a clear stretch of road he tripped. He went down flat onto his chest, arms stretched out. I stopped the car.

It all happened too fast.

The mob were on him like a tidal wave. One second he was there, down on the ground, looking up at us, panting. Then he disappeared under a crowd that kicked, punched, ripped.

I accelerated away. Ten seconds later we could see nothing.

Sarah slammed shut her door and turned on me. 'Stop! I said stop!'

I shook my head.

'Stop! Help him!'

'I can't. It's too late.'

'Nick . . . Stop.'

'I said – it's too late! HE IS DEAD! OKAY?'

We drove on without speaking. In the back the girls were crying.

Chapter Fourteen

SLATTER

We weren't going to make it.

Doubt started to flow as we drove away from the boy being torn to shit on the road. Now I couldn't stop it.

Too many things could go wrong. Too quickly we could end up like the poor bastard back there. Punctures ... Engine failure ... Roads blocked by barricades ... Or maybe a few hundred crazies would simply pull the car apart around us.

What the hell do I do then?

There's a chance I could outrun them. What about the two girls in the back? Would I risk chucking away my own life to save them? Maybe it was best to get rid of them as quickly as possible?

What you going to do, Nick? Leave them at the side of the road? Why not make it quick for them – use the knife.

No. I could find a house for them. Leave them with plenty of food, then get help.

I ran through the possibilities as I drove in the direction of the motorway which would take us south.

I was still chewing over a plan when I saw someone I knew walking up the centre of the road toward me.

I slowed the car to ten miles an hour.

There he was. Mr Nightmare himself. Another dream perhaps. No ... there he was – alive and ugly.

'Tug Slatter.'

'Who?'

Sarah leaned forward to look at the man as we slowly rumbled toward him.

Slatter looked like he always did. Light blue denims, pit boots, shaved head swinging from side to side, cigarette in his mouth that he smoked not for pleasure but as a means of making a statement. That statement was: 'I fucking well hate you.'

He never even looked at us as we approached.

It was only as we slowly passed that he snapped his eyes away from the road to look at me. The eye contact was short, hard and cold. The blue bird tattoos at either side of his eyes only seemed to concentrate the force of his glare.

I felt his contempt for me come in a wave as he broke eye contact.

Psycho.

I accelerated away. In ten minutes Slatter would be dead. The road would take him directly to where the loonies squatted on the bund. Slatter – dead. Those words I liked.

'Aren't you going to warn him?' Sarah couldn't believe I'd just driven by him.

'When he sees them he'll turn back.'

From the corner of my eye I could see her shaking her head. First I was a coward, leaving the boy to his fate. Now I was callous not warning someone I obviously knew. She was starting to hate me.

'Why don't you take the man with us?' That was Vicki, her eyes all serious behind her glasses.

'He'll be fine. Now sit back and get some rest. We'll be on the motorway in a minute. There's some chocolates on the back shelf.'

'But why won't you let that man come with us? Those people might hurt him.'

'He wasn't going in our direction. The chocolates are in the blue box.'

'Is that his name? Tug?'

'Yes.'

'Why do they call him Tug? Tug's not a proper name.'

'Jesus wept. How the hell do I know? He's not my brother or anything.'

Sarah stabbed a look at me. 'She's only curious. There's no need to be so touchy.'

'I'm not being touchy.'

'Why didn't we pick him up, then? There's room for him, for God's sake.'

'We don't have an unlimited supply of fuel, Sarah. Extra weight means we use it faster ... We run out ... We're stuck.'

'Rubbish.'

'Look, Sarah ... I don't know how far we'll have to drive to get out of the affected area. If there is something in the atmosphere that sent people insane will it start to affect us if we hang around too long?'

'Nick Aten. You are a coward.'

That did it. The scream of the tyres stabbed my ear drums.

Sarah looked at me with those calm blue eyes. 'Where are we going?'

'You'll see. And don't say to me ... don't you ever damn well say to me I didn't warn you.'

It took seconds to catch up with Tug Slatter. He heard the car but he didn't look round.

I drove so that the passenger window would be alongside Slatter. I spat the words. 'Sarah. Tell him to get in. No, not up front. In the back behind you. Anne, move closer to your sister.'

Sarah opened the door and asked Slatter to get in. He looked at her for a second then sat in the back. He could have been accepting a lift from his grandma for all the notice he took.

I roared back down toward the motorway, shooting glances at Slatter in the rear view. He smoked the cigarette, flicking ash onto the seat. He never acknowledged me.

For a good five minutes we drove like that. A silence so dead you could lay it out in a coffin and bury it.

In the back seat the two girls stared in awe at Slatter's tattoos.

When the cigarette smoke made them cough Sarah opened the window an inch.

Slatter grunted. 'Shut it.'

Sarah glanced at me. I stared ahead like a dummy. She shut the window with a loud sigh.

We drove on. I could feel the tension building like gas in a beer bottle.

Two miles to the motorway. I put my foot down. The sooner we got where we were going the better. My neck began to ache.

Sarah opened the vents on the dash.

I waited for Slatter to open his ugly mouth.

The car tyres drummed the cats' eyes, the speedo rested on fifty, the gauge showed the tank three-quarters full. If the car had been fitted with an occupant stress gauge its needle would have been kissing the red.

I glanced into the rearview. Slatter was staring at me. When they lock onto you, those eyes punch you in the gut.

The silence was going to break one way or another, so I decided to be the one to do it. Maybe after all this shit Slatter would be forced to see the world in a new light. Not a planet full of men waiting to be kicked or women waiting to be screwed.

Without looking back I said, 'I'm heading south. We're getting out of the affected area.'

No reply. Not even a sign he'd heard me. Press on, Nick. I introduced the girls. I told him what had happened to me. Slatter said nothing. I finished off repeating that I reckoned it best to drive south. 'We should be out of it in a couple of hours.'

'You're wasting your time.' Slatter's voice was flat.

'Why?'

'Let me drive.'

'Why on Earth should I?'

'Because you drive like a girl.'

'My car. I'm driving. Tug, you said I'm wasting my time driving south. Why's that? What do you know?'

'Because it's like this everywhere. Stupid twat.'

Sarah and her sisters watched the conversation like spectators at a tennis match, eyes flicking from one man to the other.

'Slatter, how the hell do you know?'

'I just do, that's all.'

'So, where were you going? You'd have got yourself killed if I hadn't picked you up.'

He shrugged, not interested.

I stopped myself shouting. 'I'm still driving south – it's worth a try.'

'Your time, your petrol, you damn well waste it.'

'It's better than going back to Doncaster. Have you seen the place, Tug? Dead people in the streets. It's full of lunatics waiting to kill you. It's a mess.'

'Nothing's changed much then, has it? It's always been a bastard dump.'

'Jesus Christ, Tug, isn't there anything that worries you?'

'Yeah.'

'What?'

'You calling me Tug. I don't like to hear my name come out of the mouth of a faggot.'

'Shit ... I don't believe you, Slatter. The world's gone insane; civilization's just hit the fan – and all you want to do is pick a fight.'

'Fight? I don't need to fight you. You're a streak of piss.'

I clenched my jaw so tight it ached.

'Aten. I want to drive.'

'No way, Slatter. NO WAY.'

'Take me back to Doncaster.'

'This is my car. We go where I say.'

'Where's that, then? You don't know, do you? You haven't got that tart of a mother to tell you what to do.'

'I know where I'm going ... I'm going south.'

'Suit yourself.'

We were hitting sixty when he opened the door and started to get out.

Anne's and Vicki's screams fused with the sound of the tyres as I crunched the brake. Slatter was out of the car before we even stopped. Lighting another cigarette he walked back the way we'd come, head swinging from side to side.

My hatred for the bastard ran deeper than I'd felt anything before. Under my breath I hissed, 'Don't mention it, Slatter. I don't need thanks for saving your frigging skin. Any time ... pal.'

As I drove away I wound down the window to shift the cigarette smoke, and the smell of Slatter.

'He's not a real person, is he?' asked Anne. 'I think he's got to be a monster.'

'You're right.' I laughed with the sheer relief of getting shut of him. 'He's a monster all right.'

Vicki said, 'He frightened me.'

'Me too.' Sarah looked at me. Her eyes softened – it was the nearest thing to an apology. 'Who is Tug Slatter, Nick?'

'A nobody. Forget him. Now where's those chocolates? I'm starving.'

Slatter was going back into the jaws of death in Doncaster. He'd be cold by suppertime.

But I knew right then as I drove down the slip road onto the deserted motorway that if I'd dropped Slatter off at the gates of hell he'd walk right through it.

And walk out the other side, smoking a cigarette, and looking as if he'd made the place his own.

Chapter Fifteen

A KIND OF NORMALITY

We'd been living in the cottage three days. My turn to cook. Sarah in a skirt and striped T-shirt sat on the sofa flicking through a holiday brochure.

'Supper's ready. The wine's on the shelf.'

'Fancy a beer?' asked Sarah.

'Why not?'

'Spaghetti bolognaise. A man of many talents. Where did you find the meat?'

'It's tinned. I stuck in a jar of bolognaise sauce and my own special ingredient.'

'Which is?'

'Half a mugful of red wine. The tip from the Nick Aten guide to smart cuisine is whatever you cook, add booze. It transforms it.'

'I had you down for a good-for-nothing slob.' Sarah smiled as I handed her the plate. 'You've got hidden depths.'

'Well hidden. Now eat up before it gets cold.'

'You sound like my mother...'

That killed the conversation for a while.

Over the last three days we'd been able to begin to relax. Now we were getting to know one another as people. Not merely shell-shocked survivors who happened to share a car.

She downed her wine in one then refilled her glass. 'Nick. How long do you think we should stay here?'

'Give it a few more days. We've got food, shelter, we're miles from anywhere. No point in rushing it after what happened on Monday.'

'It's not your fault, you know. You did what you could.'

After leaving Slatter to his fate we'd hit the motorway and barrelled south. For twenty miles there were no hold-ups, just the occasional abandoned car. In the distance we saw towns and cities. Some were burning.

After hours of driving my arms and shoulders hurt like hell; the tension clamped my jaws together so tightly my teeth ached. As the motorway approached another burning city we saw the road ahead was completely blocked with a wall of smashed trucks and cars. It didn't look like a deliberate barricade. If anything it looked as if people had driven suicidally into the wreckage. There was no way past and the sun hung low in the sky.

We were scared. We didn't know the area. We didn't know if we'd turn a corner to find a thousand crazies blocking the road.

I U-turned and took the first motorway exit. Then I headed into the countryside.

We found the cottage in a forest. Unlocked and deserted, it seemed like paradise. Of course, there was no electricity but water still ran from the taps, and it had one of those old kitchen ranges where you can cook over an open fire.

For the last three days it had rained. We did nothing much but eat and sleep. Vicki and Anne went through a cycle of arguing, crying for mummy, long silences, then back to arguing again. I drove to the nearby village – deserted apart from dead boys and girls – and returned with a car load of supplies, clothes, toys and games. After that they seemed happier with something to occupy them.

Now they were upstairs asleep and I was eating spaghetti with their big sister and trying to work out what the hell we should do next.

'Do you think that ape Slatter was right?' Sarah sipped her wine. 'That all the world's like this now?'

'No. Even if there had been a nuclear strike there'd be large areas still unaffected. If we drive far enough we'll find towns that are completely normal.'

'God . . . It's a mess though, isn't it? It's like something out of the Bible. Thousands must have died. Cities destroyed. If the madness is permanent the government are going to have to keep them somewhere. Whole counties are going to have to be turned into mental institutions.'

'Thank God it's not our problem . . . Cold?'

'A bit . . . Yes.'

She was shaking but it probably had damn-all to do with the temperature. I pushed more logs onto the fire. Soon the flames blazed white up the chimney, filling the room with a pulsating light so bright we didn't need candles.

After we'd eaten we sat together on the sofa just watching the flames dance like it was the latest TV poll-topper.

I couldn't help thinking about my parents. Because I hadn't seen them crazy like the rest I couldn't believe that they weren't normal. I knew that if they walked through that door right now they would be like they had always been. Level-headed adults who put their children's interests first.

Sarah hugged the cushion to her chest. 'Perhaps it was in the water. A drug or toxin.'

'But who'd do a thing like that?'

'Terrorists.'

'But why aren't we affected? It only seems to have sent people over the age of twenty insane.'

'Adults have different levels of hormone in their bodies to children and adolescents. Perhaps the hormones reacted with the drug. Or the gas.'

Outside, rain rattled the windows from out of the darkness. Sarah closed the curtains. She said when it grew dark she didn't like to see the tree trunks that surrounded the cottage. They looked like ghost sentinels. Waiting for something to happen.

When she returned she sat next to me on the sofa. Sometimes when she got close like that I felt a buzz of excitement. A dozen times these last three days I had wanted, just out of the blue, to reach over and hold her hand or stroke her blonde hair.

The beer didn't help my resistance. I wanted to touch her.

Nothing wildly sexual but what I wouldn't give to just sit there on the sofa with my arm round her, watching the flames alive in the grate.

Sarah pushed her hair back over her shoulder. On the wall behind her, her shadow image, distorted and gigantic from the log fire, mimicked the motion. She was beautiful – if she'd read from the Yellow Pages I'd have drunk in every word.

'You said you saw people heading south on a motorway.'

'There were thousands of them. It was a people river. You can't imagine what it was like unless you saw it with your own eyes.'

'So adults haven't simply gone mad. I mean they're not just running round, screaming. There's a pattern.'

'There's a pattern all right. Parents kill their children. Adults who have no children kill anyone under the age of twenty.'

'But it's almost as if they're following new instincts. They're killing. Yes, we've seen that. But they are also flocking like birds. As soon as there's a big enough group something tells them to march south. Nick, they're migrating.'

'Migrating?'

'Yes. Like birds. But where?'

I shrugged. 'One day we'll know. Anyway, the effects of this madness might be temporary. Tomorrow all these people might wake up in a field a hundred miles from home wondering just how the hell they got there.'

'God, I hope you're right.'

'Wine?'

'Please.' She paused, then: 'Are you sure you're comfortable sleeping on this sofa?'

There was more to that question than met the eye. I'd slept three nights on the sofa. Upstairs there were two bedrooms with a double bed in each. The two younger sisters in one and Sarah in a double bed by herself.

I told her I was fine and we talked small talk. What we said with our mouths didn't really matter. We were communicating with our eyes and the way we moved our heads and hands, and the way she stroked back that long hair that shone in the firelight.

'How's the face?' I asked looking at the dark bruise on her cheekbone.

'It doesn't hurt. But it's still swollen. You can feel it.'

Sarah had invited me to touch her. She pushed back a strand of hair and leaned sideways across the sofa toward me. When her eyes looked directly into mine I felt electricity buzz through my blood stream.

Gently I stroked my finger tip across her cheek. It didn't stop there. I couldn't stop myself. I carried on gliding my fingertips across her skin, down to her throat, then in one movement to the back of her neck beneath her hair.

She slid across the sofa cushions toward me, her hips lifting against her skirt.

The kiss. Soft. Shot with sweetness, warm. And she kissed me as much as I kissed her.

I breathed her in, her smell of soap and skin and hair. I tasted her.

We held each other tightly, kissing. I let my hands stroke down her arching back to where her T-shirt was tucked into her skirt. She was ready for it all, her breathing hot in my ear. I wanted to see her naked by firelight.

Then I broke the clinch. Trembling and breathing fast I stood up. She looked up, her blue eyes bright.

Suddenly I felt awkward. 'I'll get more wood for the fire.'

Sarah sat smiling at me. 'I'm warm enough. Anyway, I'm going to bed now. I feel more than a little bit drunk.'

'Me too.'

I knew we'd sleep in our usual places tonight. Sarah upstairs, me on the sofa. Call it courtship convention but something told me not to rush things to fast. Tonight I felt hot and giddy and Sarah seemed the loveliest thing in the world.

I wouldn't make love to her tonight.

But tomorrow night, I told myself as she kissed me on the cheek before going upstairs, tomorrow night we would.

Chapter Sixteen

BAD DREAMS NEVER GO AWAY

I dreamt this:

I opened the door of the cottage. Standing there were Mum and Dad. They looked pleased to see me.

'Hello, Nick,' dad said.

'Are you looking after yourself?' Mum seemed concerned. 'Are you getting enough to eat?'

Dad's smile broadened showing the gap in his top front teeth. 'We know you've been hearing rumours that we intend to kill you.'

My mother looked at me hard. 'We don't want to kill you, Nick. But we have to.'

'The sooner you come home, Nick, the sooner we can get it over with. Your mother wants to wear your heart on her sleeve. So don't be a silly boy, Nicholas. Tell him, Judy, tell him we want him home. It's your favourite for tea, then straight upstairs for the killing, easy as one-two-three ...'

'Did you kill John?'

Dad smiled, exposing his gap teeth. 'Ask him yourself.'

I looked down. Between them, as if my parents held the hands of a two-year-old was John. His head was as I remember it, the size of a teenager's, but his body had shrunk to the size of a toddler's. His eyes were open but dull, his mouth had become a bruised hole and the rip in his face had dried black.

Then the screaming started.

I woke on the sofa. The screaming continued.

Vicki and Anne. I rolled off the sofa and ran upstairs, pulling up my jeans as I went. Sarah, dressed in pants and T-shirt, was already through the bedroom door.

The two girls were hiding under the bedclothes screaming so loudly it felt like needles being driven into my ears.

Sarah tried to pull back the blankets. 'Vicki ... Anne. What's wrong? Anne, shut up and let go of the blanket. Now. What's the matter?'

Anne's eyes were round as she sat there, holding the blanket up to her chin. 'We saw a man.'

'Looking in through the window,' wailed Vicki. 'He frightened us.'

The curtains were partly open.

My nerves were stripped. 'How could he look through the window? It's ten feet from the ground.'

'Big man,' whispered Vicki.

'Don't be ridiculous. Men don't grow to that—'

'Nick,' Sarah said quietly. 'I'll take care of it.'

I shrugged and fastened the belt on my jeans.

Sarah sat on the bed. 'Don't you think you could have imagined it?'

'No.'

'Which one of you saw the man?'

'We both did. He was a big man, looking straight in the window at us. His eyes were really staring. He didn't like us.'

I looked out the window. 'No sign of giants.'

'Nick, don't tease them.'

'Sarah, Anne, Vicki. Look for yourself. There's no one there. This window is a good ten feet from the ground. There's no ladder against the wall.'

'But we *did* see someone, Sarah.'

Vicki looked as if she was going to cry. 'You believe us, don't you, Sarah?'

Hysterical schoolgirls weren't the way I wanted to start the day. Irritated, I snapped, 'What did he look like then?'

There was a pause while Vicki thought about it. Then she pointed at me and said, 'The man looked like him.'

That derailed me. Sarah shot me a pointed look that obviously asked: Nick Aten? A peeping tom?

'It wasn't me. Jesus. What would I want to look in your damn bedroom for?'

Sarah turned to ice. 'Was it you, Nick?'

'Was it hell. How could I ... More to the point WHY in God's name should I want to look in at these two whining brats?'

'You tell us, Nick. We don't know you. On the surface you've been nice but you're showing us you're a bastard now. For all we know you might have been in trouble with the police for this and God knows what else in the past. Okay, we don't know you ... but we've seen people you know.'

'Who?'

'That ape we picked up. Tug somebody or other.'

'Tug Slatter? If you think—'

'I do think, Nick Aten. If you know animals like that then what the hell are you like, Mr Aten? What are YOU like?'

Suddenly I felt like the condemned man. And for some stupid reason I felt guilty. Whatever it was that drove men and women crazy, was it beginning to affect me too? Had I somehow scrambled up the drainpipe to leer insanely through the window? I began to sweat.

The three girls stared at me. In their eyes I was a dangerous loony. First I was peeping. What next? Downstairs in the kitchen there were plenty of sharp knives. Just a moment, girls, I want you to say hello to Mr Knife and Mrs Pain.

Then Sarah said, 'Vicki, how do you know it was him? You weren't wearing your glasses.'

'I never said it was him, stupid. I said it looked LIKE him.'

Sarah sighed explosively. 'You mean it *wasn't* Nick looking through the window?'

'No. It just looked like him.'

'Either it was or it wasn't. Was he dressed?'

'I think so, but I didn't see what he was wearing.'

Sarah shot me an apologetic look then asked her other sister, 'Anne. You saw him. What did he look like? The colour of his hair?'

'Oh, it was like Pookah.'

'Pookah's her pony,' Sarah explained. 'It's a piebald.'

'What's that mean?

'It's a mixture of black hair and grey.'

I said nothing. I tipped my head forward and pointed at my black hair.

'Oh, I noticed something else,' Anne said. 'He had a big gap in his teeth just here.' She pointed at her front upper teeth.

'A gap in his teeth . . . I'll check outside,' I said.

Sarah grabbed my arm. 'Nick. What's wrong?'

'Nothing's wrong.'

'You look awful. You're as white as a sheet.'

I nearly told her then that Anne had just described my father.

Outside the rain had stopped; a rising breeze shook the trees that surrounded the cottage in their thousands. It made the sound of the sea.

I walked round the cottage while breathing in the cold air. Nothing had changed. Shogun still parked by the cottage; the doors of outbuildings still closed; their contents untouched. I didn't see any strange footprints, but as the area consisted mainly of turf I didn't expect to find any.

Sarah joined me. 'Anything?'

'Nothing.'

'Are you sure you're all right? When Anne described the man you looked as if you'd been kicked.'

'Listen, I'm fine. Okay?'

Her blue eyes watched me, hurt. I was playing the rough bastard.

'I'm sorry, Sarah. It's stupid really. I don't believe for one minute there was anyone looking in your sisters' bedroom window . . .'

'But?'

'But the description she gave could have been my father.'

'That's impossible. He couldn't have followed you all—'

'I know it's impossible. It shook me, that's all. Sarah, you were attacked by your parents. I can't shake off this feeling mine are following me. You see, they killed my brother.'

It was the first time I had openly admitted mum and dad had killed John. I knew it now. They had. But the words still hurt.

'Nick. I'm sorry. Come inside, I'll make you a coffee . . . Nick . . . Nick. Where are you going? For God's sake be careful.'

At the back of the cottage was an outbuilding. The slate roof sloped steeply. But it was climbable. I hauled myself up. At the ridge tiles I stood up, feet planted firmly on each side of the roof.

When I straightened I was six feet from the cottage – and I looked straight into Anne and Vicki's bedroom window. They were making their bed when they saw me.

The screams were piercing.

'Shit . . . Vicki! Anne! It's me, Nick! Quiet. I said BE QUIET!'

It did the trick. I slid down to the ground where Sarah waited.

She nodded. 'Someone could have looked in.'

'It's possible.'

'Where you going?'

'I'm going for a look round. There's an axe in the shed. I'll take that. You lock yourself in the cottage. I'll be back in half an hour.'

'Twenty minutes. If you're not back by then, I'm putting Anne and Vicki in the car and driving out of here.'

I took the axe and began a walk that took a rough spiralling route away from the cottage.

There was bugger all apart from trees. The wind blew them, shaking off heavy lumps of water that exploded on my head.

I saw rabbits, birds, trees, plenty of trees, miles of bloody trees but nothing human. I made it back to the cottage in twenty minutes.

The Hayes sisters sat in the car.

'You waited for me then, Sarah?'

'We were going to give you another five minutes. Anything?'

'Nothing. Come on back inside. We'll get something to eat.'

I'd gone out, I knew, to search the woods for dad. There was no one there. Vicki and Anne had imagined it.

After that we didn't do much of anything. The rain stayed off so I checked over the Shogun and topped up the tank from a can. Sarah came out to watch me at one point, her arms folded over her breasts, long hair blowing back in the breeze.

'I'm sorry about this morning, Nick. Vicki and Anne are still upset about what happened.'

'Don't worry about it. It's a wonder we're not all swinging through the trees screaming our heads off. This is the biggest piece of shit to hit the fan since Noah's flood.'

She kissed me on the cheek then returned to the cottage. Blushing, I checked our food stocks. They were adequate but I'd have to hunt out more supplies in a few days. As I counted canned beans questions ran through my head. Should we stop or should we go? The cottage seemed safe for now. But more than once I thought of the Goldilocks-and-the-three-bears scenario. Should we try and find where the sane world started once more?

And I remembered last night when Sarah and I kissed. What would happen tonight?

There were no answers, only questions. I started counting bags of sugar.

Evening came. Vicki and Anne went off to bed. Sarah cut bread in the kitchen.

'Nick, would you get me the cheese?'

It was an innocent enough request but it was a set-up. To get the cheese from the cupboard I had to get past her, between the table and worktop. As I moved sideways through the gap between Sarah, her back to me, and the table, she arched her back and pushed gently back. I had to brush by her, my groin sliding across her bottom.

It doesn't seem much in cold print. But it was probably the most erotic experience I'd had with my clothes on.

She said nothing, but gave me a shy smile as she licked the butter from her finger. My heart changed gear and I felt a giddy flush. 'I'll get some wood for the fire.'

What's that Rod Stewart song? *Tonight's The Night.*

The night, cool and clear. A full moon lit the trees making the leaves twinkle silver. Beneath the leaves the tree trunks marched off into the dark in pale columns. Back at the cottage the candlelight showed downstairs windows as yellow oblongs. Upstairs they were black. Anne and Vicki were asleep.

Despite everything – my brother, Steve, cities on fire, madmen – all I could think about at that moment was Sarah. Her blonde hair flowing down to her bottom. Her bare arms and the little gold chain round one wrist. The thought of seeing her naked by firelight was pure, mind-blowing, body-vibrating excitement.

I wanted to run back right then but I walked to the edge of the wood, sucking in the cold air. I wanted to return poised and in control. Not looking like Homer Simpson slobbering over a bucketful of chocolate.

Moonlight splotched on the grass between trees. No breeze to ruffle the leaves. Absolute stillness.

Sarah was waiting for me. I imagined her smile as I walked into the cottage. Her arms coming up around my neck.

It was only as I began to walk back to the cottage that something registered in my head.

There were too many trees.

I looked back into the forest. The tree trunks were closer together than earlier in the day. No. Get a grip, Aten. Again that feeling cracked through my head. I was losing my grip. I was going mad too.

'S easy to do. 'S easy, Nick. Just imagine the trees are creeping up to cluster round the house. They reach out their branches like grannie's knotty arms to hug you tight.

No, Nick. I bit my lip hard enough to bring reality juddering back. The reason why the trees are flocking toward the cottage is because they aren't trees at all. They are . . .

People.

My eyes tuned to the gloom and I saw them.

What I'd taken as hundreds more tree trunks were men and women. They were standing scattered through the forest as far as I could see. And they were looking at me.

I began walking backward. An object clunked against my foot.

I looked down.

Casually lying on his side, the upper part of his body supported by one elbow, like he was enjoying a sunny afternoon in his garden, was a man. About fifty with a stubbled beard, he looked up at me. No expression on his face but his eyes shone like balls of blue neon in the moonlight. He did not move. He only watched. And I felt terror come at me like a knife and cut me through.

I froze. The madman's eyes held me there. I waited for the avalanche of people to fall on me and kill me there in the wood.

Without moving my head, I scanned the hundreds of men and women standing there like mannequins. They must have crept up to us like a tide creeps up a beach.

They were waiting for something to trigger them to attack. Perhaps a movement from me, or just some animal instinct inside them.

Slowly, slowly, I began moving back to the house. I walked backwards. My guts told me to keep facing them. Only pray you don't fall over anything.

By the time I reached the cottage door my mouth had dry-welded shut. Sweat soaked me. And, Christ, I just wanted to run and scream.

I looked back at the people. Not one of them had moved, but I sensed a change in them. They had seen their prey. Soon they would hunt.

'I thought you'd got lost.'

Sarah sat on the rug in front of the log fire. She'd brushed her hair so it fell down over her shoulders, arms and chest like a golden cloak.

I stared at her. She must have thought I'd been struck stupid.

As I closed the door and slid the bolt I whispered, 'Sarah. Get Vicki and Anne. We're going.'

Sarah's face flashed shock. 'They're here, aren't they?'

'They are all around the fucking cottage ... Now move, Sarah. Please.'

She shifted, fast and silent. In five minutes Vicki and Anne stood yawning in the kitchen. Sarah said to her sisters, 'Listen. We're going out to the car. No one talk, make a noise, or let go of my hand.'

She looked at me which I guessed meant, *Okay, let's do it*.

I snuffed the candles, picked up the axe, then slid back the bolt. I went first; Sarah, gripping her sisters' hands, followed. We had to get into the car as quickly and as silently as we could. Then blast out of there like a bullet from a gun.

The people still stood weirdly in the wood. Like statues. I could see more lay under the trees in that strange, casual way. On their sides, lifting themselves up on one elbow. Vicki hung back staring back at the hundreds of eyes gleaming from out of the darkness.

Sarah gently pulled her to the car.

At that point I guessed the nearest was about forty yards from us. If they charged now, we'd be ripped to pieces.

As I stood between the girls and the nearest lunatics, axe at the ready, Sarah pushed her sisters into the back seat.

I saw Vicki reach across to the back door and give it a hefty pull to shut it. A door slam would have sounded like a gunshot in this silent forest.

The best I could do was to simply jam my arm between the door and the bodywork.

The door hit my forearm with a soft thump. Quiet, but the pain shot up my neck like a bullet.

Sarah, eyes big with concern, came round the car to help but I waved her to get in the passenger seat. She did, closing the door without a sound. As soon as I clicked the rear door gently shut Anne locked it.

Then I was in the driver's seat, door locked, turning the ignition and whispering, 'Come on, sweetheart, first time . . . first time.'

It did. The engine purred – the sweetest sound I've ever heard.

At first I didn't switch on the lights. I waited until the speedo was nudging twenty before I hit the switch. As the beams blew away the dark the car lurched and bumped over something in the road. The girls let out gasping cries, but the back wheels bounced straight over it and we were away.

We could have run over a branch. But I knew it wasn't. It was something soft . . . fleshy, lying on the road. I drove the car away into the night.

Chapter Seventeen

DO YOU WANT TO LIVE OR DO YOU WANT TO DIE?

We drove through the night to get back to Doncaster. Sarah agreed. We felt safer in a place we knew.

On the edge of town just before the North Bridge spans the river, canal and railway lines there's one of these out-of-town retail parks, fronted by a massive car park. It consists of six or seven huge stores that sell furniture, DIY, carpets and electrical goods.

Vicki saw the people first and squealed for us to stop.

We parked a hundred yards from the nearest store. What we saw were a group to-ing and fro-ing, carrying all kinds of stuff – chairs, boxes, bedding, you name it. Sarah leaned over my side so she could see through my window. 'Well . . . What do you think?'

'They look young,' I said. 'So let's take a closer look.'

At first I thought kids were looting the stores. As I drove up I saw they were organised. They were bringing goods from outlying stores to one central store that had the makings of a compound outside the front doors. No sooner had I parked by a row of trucks then a tall, smiling youth was striding toward us. I got out of the car.

'Hi, I'm Dave Middleton. Nice to see you.'

He appeared genuinely pleased to see us and shook everyone's hand in turn, while asking our names. Late teens, well spoken, even though dressed in jeans and a sweatshirt he had a well groomed look.

He said, 'The first question I have to ask is – do you want to live? Or do you want to die?' The smile dropped for a second.

'Well, what do you think?' asked Sarah, puzzled.

'Sorry.' The smile flashed back. 'I have to be brutal and ask it right out. We're trying to get a community together here. Some people have been turning up who are, quite frankly, time wasters. We've no room for passengers. You look worn out, Nick. You too, girls. I'll get coffee organised and you can get to know us.'

Smiling, he led us inside. It was a furniture store so there was no shortage of chairs and sofas to sit on. Within five minutes we had coffee and sandwiches.

'I'll be back in two ticks. We're just making this place secure.'

I didn't know Dave Middleton, but I knew what he'd been like in life before the sanity crash. I could see him from a cash-fat family; no doubt he was a youth leader at the local church. Without trying the mental picture came of him leading a group of clean-cut kids through the mountains singing hymns in *Joy to the World* voices.

A good-looking, clean-living guy who I never saw in my world of red-hot nightclubs. I'd seen them at school, though, and I hated them. Now I saw they had their place on Earth. Level headed, good organisers, Dave Middleton was doing the Phoenix bit and pulling a crowd of kids out of the ashes of a burning civilization.

Half an hour later he took us on a conducted tour, long legs springing him along, like he was showing us around his beloved church.

'I was on a camping weekend with some friends when it happened.' He sounded indestructibly cheerful. 'I know it's only a few days since, but things came together quite quickly . . . This is where the girls sleep. What we're not short of is beds. Boys sleep in the warehouse at the back there. This way, please. Watch your feet, Sarah, Michael's been careless with the packing . . . Michael, don't forget to put the plastic sheets in the sacks. We don't want anyone falling over them. Right, where was I . . . Oh, that's it. Within two days we'd collected fifty-six people, some we literally picked up from the street – from toddlers to the eldest, that's Rebecca Keene, she's eighteen. We put together a convoy of vehicles and set out to find somewhere safe to stay. This seemed the best. It's secure. There are no windows apart from those at the front where the main doors are. We're going to protect that area with a barbed wire compound. You'll notice we've got electricity. The store has emergency generators.'

We followed him upstairs into what would have been the manager's office. Its mirror windows looked out across the hangar-size store, beds and furniture stretching to the distant doors. Children and teenagers buzzed up and down the aisles each with their own task – none slacked.

'Excuse me a moment.' Dave picked up a microphone. His voice rolled across the place like God's own. 'Rebecca Keene. Rebecca Keene and Martin Del-Coffey to the office, please. Oh, and can I have everyone's attention? Will all those handling barbed wire remember they must wear gloves. Thank you.' He swivelled back to smile at us. 'Right, I'll introduce you to the Steering Committee.'

Steering Committee. By that I guessed he meant 'bosses.'

Sarah caught my eye. Just a bit, she raised her eyebrows. If we weren't running for our lives she'd have found this amusing.

Me? Me, I'd have laughed my frigging socks off.

Then Dave Middleton went into detail. He listed the vehicles, food and bottled water reserves, medicines, the group's objectives. He even had something called a mission statement he'd written in blue and red and pinned to the wall. As he talked a bony girl in a blue headscarf joined us, very sober faced. Another holy roller, I decided. This was Rebecca Keene. Then came a sixteen-year-old with wispy blond hair and a high forehead. His untied laces trailed along the floor. This was the steering committee.

'I must confess.' Dave smiled. 'We're self-appointed. Once we're settled we'll hold elections so everyone can decide who will be in charge. Rebecca and I have experience of leading youth groups through our work at St Timothy's. Martin Del-Coffey here is our resident genius. You might have seen features on him in the local newspaper. He has the highest recorded IQ for his age in the area covered by Doncaster's Education Authority.'

Bully for him. I'd have said that a week ago. Not now though. My cockiness had been yanked out. I nodded politely.

Rebecca spoke in a schoolmistress voice. 'It's individuals of Martin's calibre who will restore our society to what it was before.'

'Only better.' Martin did not smile. He was there for brains not for charm.

'Excuse me.' Dave spoke into the PA. 'Alpha team. Alpha team. Lunchbreak. Remember to be out of the canteen by twelve. We've lots of work to get through today.'

On the shop floor I saw a third of the kids stop whatever they were doing and head for a doorway at the back of the store.

The steering committee questioned us and I realised we were being assessed. If we didn't reach a certain mark were we out the door?

At one point a boy of about eleven tapped on the door and gave some kind of report. 'We've done the circuit, Dave.'

'Anything?'

'Mr Creosote in a house on Briar Lane.'

'How many?'

'Just the one, Dave. There's something wrong with his leg. He can't walk right.'

'Well done, Robert. Get some lunch. After that check the river banks as far as Carnel's.'

Sarah raised her eyebrows. 'Mr Creosote?'

Rebecca said, 'It's a generic name for the affected adults. A girl used the name Mr Creosote to describe one of the adults that had become ill. The younger ones carried on using the name. It stuck. Now the mentally ill adults have become Mr and Mrs Creosote.'

'It's a way of sugar coating a very bitter pill, Miss Hayes.' Martin leaned back picking his fingernails. 'It frightens the children to say we're being hounded by a million madmen. Mr Creosote doesn't sound completely sinister, does it now?'

A week ago I'd have wanted to slap the arrogant egghead. I nodded meekly.

'From what we've seen adults are the only ones affected.' Sarah, brisk, still hunted answers. 'They attacked their own children – if they have no children they attack anyone under the age of twenty.'

'Nineteen.' Martin found his fingernails fascinating. 'We've not found anyone nineteen or older who is sane. We've not encountered anyone insane under that age. Whatever attacked their minds was brutally selective.'

Sarah leaned forward bunching her fists on her knees. 'But what caused it?'

'That, Miss Hayes, is what I intend to find out.'

Dave said, 'Martin is excused normal duties. He's been assigned to research. It's his job to track down the cause.'

'From what I can determine so far,' Martin said, 'the condition is similar to the mental illness schizophrenia.'

'I've heard of it,' said Sarah. 'It's curable.'

'Yes, in most cases it can be treated with drugs. But I said *similar* to schizophrenia. Not the same. Many of the symptoms are present. Paranoia and delusions. Mr and Mrs Creosote seem to be actually afraid of their children – perhaps when they see us they don't see their sons and daughters but disgusting, frightening monsters that they feel compelled to destroy before we destroy them. Also you'll have noticed their intellect has been top sliced, rendering them sub-human. They no longer drive cars, live in houses, or use tools.'

Dave added: 'We've seen bizarre patterns in their behaviour. Have you?'

I told them about the mass migration south I'd seen on the motorway.

'We've seen them laying out bottles,' Dave said, 'cans, even jewellery in patterns in car parks and fields. Patterns that although intricate are just . . . just—'

'Just plain potty.' For the first time Martin sounded interested in the conversation. 'It suggests that these patterns have purpose and are very, very important to Mr and Mrs Creosote.' He smiled. 'Consequently it appears that Mr Creosote is attempting to communicate with someone.'

'Who?'

Martin raised his eyes. 'Someone up there.'

We talked more, then Dave leaned forward. 'Sarah. Nick. The question is, would you like to join our community?'

What else could we say?

We said it together. 'Yes. Thank you.'

'If you would just fill in these, please.' Rebecca handed us a sheet of paper. 'It's a short questionnaire. It's important we know something about you and what talents you possess so we can use you most effectively within the community.'

Dave Middleton had re-created a slice of civilization in a furniture store in the middle of madland. I knew then I'd hate having to conform and follow the orders of a smarmy church boy.

But I had answered his question truthfully when we first met.

Yes, I wanted to live. So far, Dave Middleton's way was the only way.

Chapter Eighteen

ORGANIZATION

Rebecca gave me my orders. The following day I found myself using a forklift truck to stack cases of beans in the warehouse. Kids of all ages, degutted by terror, worked like robots. I watched a sixteen-year-old hooligan with home-made tattoos cry his eyes out when Rebecca told him he wasn't working hard enough. Poor bastard had been working his bollocks off.

'Hi, Nick.' Sarah smiled brightly.

'Long time no see. Sleep well?'

'Fine, thanks. Sorry, can't stop. Too busy.' She showed me the clipboard. 'I've been promoted to admin. Bye.'

I watched her go, blonde pony tail swinging sexily.

PING! Miss Keene's voice over the PA: 'Beta team. Beta team. Break time. Recommence work 10.30.'

'Hey, mate,' I called to the red-eyed hooligan. 'Which team have they put you in?'

'Alpha.'

'I'm Gamma. Are those Latin letters or names of atoms or what?'

He was too scared to reply. He worked harder.

As I shifted baked beans by the ton I kept an eye on the to-ing and fro-ing. More survivors joined the community. Most were brought in by the boys who patrolled the area on bikes. One fifteen-year-old girl had to be carried in, her face a bruised lump set with two staring eyes.

Later, two teenagers ran into the compound. One had shit himself.

They were taken for drinks and the regulation questionnaire. The steering committee were building an empire.

PING! 'Gamma team. Break time. Gamma team.'

On the way to the canteen I saw Mr Genius Del-Coffey in his office. He lay back in a chair, feet on the desk, shoe laces hanging down. Piles of books, laptop computers. An Asian girl of about sixteen was reading to him from a book called *Psychology Today*. The door was wide open.

Basically he was wanking off. And he wanted everyone to see.

The canteen was full of kids drinking coke, but hardly anyone spoke. I found myself reading the staff club's fixture lists for football and table tennis. Teams of men and women who were either dead or mad by now.

PING! 'Nick Aten to the delivery bay, please.'

In *Mash* the medics were interrupted in their high jinks by the speakers announcing 'Incoming wounded.' I got incoming self-raising flour.

I got there as Dave Middleton was legging up and down organizing kids to stack bagged potatoes.

'Not in the dump bins, Katrina. Over by the doors – they need to be well ventilated. Hi, Nick. Sorry to have to buzz you down. We need to get the flour off the truck quick. Now, Sarah, can you make a note of—'

Before I got a chance to reach the forklift a boy skidded his mountain bike in through the warehouse doors. He was panting hard.

'Dave . . . It's Mr Creosote. He's back!'

Chapter Nineteen

DOES IT ALWAYS HAVE TO BE THIS WAY?

The name Mr Creosote killed Dave's *Joy to the World* smile. He slapped the clipboard against his leg. But he didn't swear.

'Where?'

'Down by the river footbridge.'

'How many?'

'Nine. They're just hanging around.'

Dave turned to me. 'You see, it's always the same pattern. They flock like birds. A couple arrive. Then one more. Then another three. A couple of hours later there's a hundred. Only when there's a certain number, a – a kind of critical mass, do they move in.'

He seemed to be working it through for his own benefit so I just nodded as he talked.

'Same routine as last time, Dave?' asked the boy.

'Let's not be hasty. They might disperse. We can't keep running every time we see Mr Creosote. John, go back and keep an eye on the bridge. Report back every fifteen minutes. Straight away if they start moving. Nick ... There's a path down to the river bank back there. I need you to go and keep an eye on the road on the far side of the river.'

Dave disappeared to push the gang working on the barbed wire stockade around the store. We were building a fortress.

The situation wasn't dangerous at the moment. But my stomach tensed. When Mr and Mrs Creosote decided to move, they moved fast. I'd have been happier getting Sarah and her sisters into the car and ready to shift if we had to.

Nevertheless, I cut down the path to the river.

The River Don was wide and deep there. It was unlikely they'd swim across. Mr Creosote would walk the extra half mile down stream to the bridge then cross there.

And there they were. Walking out of town, on the other side of the river, were the insane population of Doncaster.

I found myself looking at each face. I was looking for mum and dad.

Among the strangers, I did see some adults I knew. The guy who had the florist's at the end of Lawn Avenue. The fat lady who worked in a town centre café. A bouncer from Trixies. I recognised them but whatever weird mind occupied their heads had altered the expressions on their faces. It pulled the muscles tight round their eyes so they scowled, like a stone in their shoe irritated them.

They passed by, not looking across the river in my direction. I saw a cop with his face burnt down one side – it didn't seem to bother him. He flowed by like the rest, eyes locked on something invisible above the heads in front of him.

A few carried things on poles. I looked away.

In the river a dead boy drifted by, white ribbons streaming out of his stomach to float in the water behind him.

I turned my back on all this shit and rubbed my face.

The mad people of Doncaster were coming to get us too. The Steering Committee's barbed wire would not save us. The lunatics would roll over that like flood water.

'Piss off ... Why don't you just fuck off and leave us alone!' Before I knew what I was doing I was shouting and pitching stones at the mad bastards. A useless and loony thing to do. But I had to do something. I couldn't take all this shit, shrug my shoulders and say 'Oh dear.'

Mr and Mrs Creosote took no notice. They walked on. The stones I threw fell short, splashing into the water.

Ten minutes later a boy on a bike pedalled down like Lucifer himself wanted to chew on his left bollock.

'Get yourself back up here . . . We're moving out.'

Rebecca and Dave were efficient organisers. Within half an hour we
were ready to hit the road.

Sarah, holding Vicki and Anne's hands, followed me across to the
Shogun.

'Is this what it's going to be like, Nick? Squatting somewhere for a
few days, then those things forcing us to move on?'

All along the convoy of trucks, buses and Land-Rovers, engines
were bellowing. Blue smoke swirled around us.

'Nick.' Dave ran up, carrying a clipboard. 'I've got you travelling
with Jo over there in the yellow mini-bus. Sarah's riding in the bus
up front with her sisters.'

'I've got the car. It's got a full tank.'

'It's too small. It's a waste of resources. Girls, hop out of the car
and get on the bus up front. We've got to—'

I held Dave's arm. It felt as thin as a stick. 'Dave. I'm taking my
car. The girls ride with me.'

He was going to – not argue with me – reason with me, but time
was running out. Family Creosote was swarming over the footbridge.

'Okay, okay. We'll talk about it later . . . Jo, stick close this time.
Don't hang too far back.' He went back to talk to the mini-bus
driver as I climbed into the Shogun and crashed the door shut.

Sarah looked at me. 'That told him.'

'Yeah. He's going to have to watch that mouth doesn't run away
with him.'

The convoy slid out of the retail park like a long, lumpy snake.
We travelled slowly, bumper to bumper. Heads stretched out of
windows looking for trouble.

We needn't have looked for it. It came soon enough.

Chapter Twenty

THEY'RE CHASING US

'Faster, Nick. They're chasing us.'

'Hurry up!'

'They're not chasing us, Anne ... Vicki, calm down and stop jumping up like that.'

'They're frightened, Nick,' said Sarah.

'There's nothing to worry about. They're over a mile away. We're driving away from them.'

'Can't you go any faster?'

Through clenched teeth, I explained, 'Vicki, you see this long line of trucks and buses? It's a convoy. That means we can only go as fast as that truck in front.'

The convoy, nose to tail, close as dogs smelling one another's backsides, did a frustrating fifteen miles per hour. Orders from Miss Keene. She didn't want anyone being left behind. We wouldn't have left a tortoise behind at that speed.

There were ten vehicles. Every vehicle but mine carried a number from 1 to 9. Number nine was the yellow mini-bus behind me at the back of the convoy. Number 1 was the bus leading the convoy. That contained the Steering Committee. They hadn't time to fit all the vehicles with CBs otherwise we'd have had directives crackling over the speaker every 6.3 minutes.

Sometimes the convoy would suddenly stop. Twice the truck in front shunted into the Land-Rover in front of it. What else could you expect from teenagers with a few hours' tuition?

Then we'd lumber off again, engines over-revving, gears crashing. We took a roundabout route to avoid the town centre. The houses looked abandoned now. We saw no one.

I asked Sarah, 'What now? Have they got a plan?'

'The plan is to find somewhere safe for the community to settle. Their experience is that they find somewhere for a couple of days then Mr Creosote finds them, then they have to run for it again.'

'Community? They think this is permanent, then?'

'Martin thinks so.'

'Martin Del-Coffey. Huh, praise be to God that he was spared, eh? Hell, what's wrong now?'

'It's Dave,' Vicki squealed. 'He's got out of the bus. He's running away. Mr Creosote's chasing him.'

Sarah sat up. 'He's not being chased. He's found a boy at the side of the road. He's rescuing him.'

'There's Mr Creosote in a field over there.' Anne pointed.

'Anne, that's a scarecrow. Uh . . . We're moving again.'

A pattern established itself. We'd drive along minor roads, then the convoy would bump to a stop. Dave would leg it across the road and come back with more kids. Once we stopped for a fifteen-year-old pushing his dead nephew along in a supermarket trolley. Another mile, then it was two girls on a wall. One soaked head to ankles in blood.

Once Dave ran into a house and returned carrying a half-starved five-year-old girl.

My own feelings sparked between irritation and admiration. Dave Middleton, the clean-living, church-going guy – the kind I detested. Yet he had the guts to go into houses where he could have walked into a roomful of lunatics. There was no doubting his dedication to saving everyone he could get his hands on.

We drove on. Sometimes stopping as a kid climbed on the bus up front, plucked from certain death by Saint Dave of Doncaster.

The suburbs fell away and we headed into open countryside.

Sarah stretched her neck up to see into a field. 'There's one of the messages they mentioned.'

'What messages?'

'Those that Mr Creosote are making.'

In the field hundreds of bottles had been laid in lines across the turf. We were high enough to see it formed a cross. As we drove by the bottles flashed like a heliograph in the sunlight.

'Who do you think they are trying to contact?' asked Vicki, her eyes big behind her glasses.

'Sit down while I'm driving.'

'They can't be trying to contact us, that's for sure,' said Anne. 'They are trying to kill us.'

Vicki said: 'A girl told us that because we've been so sinful God has punished us by making our parents loony, and now they are sending these messages to God asking him to end the world.'

I wanted to say one word: Bollocks.

Sarah said gently, 'Those are just rumours . . . silly rumours.'

'It's true. The girl said that whenever Mr Creosote speaks it's not his voice that comes out but God's.'

More bollocks. Mr and Mrs Creosote were just plain swinging through the trees gibbering like a crazy baboon. Nothing more than that.

Sarah's problems were more practical. 'The real worry is if someone falls sick. We've no medical skills. Even something like appendicitis'd be a killer now.'

'Don't worry,' I said. 'The great Mr Del-Coffey will cut you open with one hand while holding a textbook in the other. No doubt composing an ode to the fall of civilization while he's at it.'

'Martin's important to us now, Nick, and don't you forget it. Last night he said the teachers are as good as dead, we have to teach ourselves now or the human race will become extinct.'

'Last night? You and Del-Coffey?'

'Yes, with Rebecca and Dave – we were discussing what we must do to establish a viable community.'

'Sounds cozy.'

She gave me a cutting look, then sat curling her hair round her fingers.

I stared at the tail lights of the truck in front trying to guess what she was thinking and knowing the painful truth. Civilization can die tomorrow but jealousy's here to stay.

* * *

We drove for another hour, looping round Doncaster. No one spoke. We stopped a couple more times. But I didn't bother to see who got on Dave's bus.

'We're going to a farm!' Vicki's voice pierced my ear. 'Dave's taking us to a farm.'

The convoy pulled into a farm yard. A burnt-out tractor stood in front of the barn. Dave told us to stay put while he checked the buildings. Five minutes later we got the thumbs up.

Dave loped up. 'Nick, en route we found some older teenagers. You know all there is to know about trucks so would you mind giving them some tuition? We need more vehicles and drivers.'

We walked up to number 1 bus as the door opened and the latest batch came out blinking into the sunlight.

'I'll introduce you to them, Nick. This is—'

As the first one stepped off the bus I knew there was a God. And that God had made up his ubiquitous mind to torment me for every sin I had ever committed.

'Tug Slatter.'

Slatter leered through his tattoos. 'Hello, sweetheart.'

Chapter Twenty-One

THEY'RE COMING TO GET ME

I woke in the back seat of the car to see the note under the wiper.

Pencilled on the front of a piece of paper folded in half: *NICHOLAS ATEN*. I read the note and felt like I'd been kicked in the back.

> *Nick.*
> *Come home. Urgent news for you.*
> *Love – mum & dad.*

'Slatter. Slatter! Wake up, you bastard.'

'Piss off, Aten.'

'Look at this. I said look at it.'

He came out of the sleeping bag like a sullen bear. I shook the note in his face. 'I've a good mind to shove this down your throat. With my boot.'

'If you don't take that thing away from my face I'm going to break your bastard neck.'

He looked up. The eyes, flanked by tattooed blue birds, bore into me as aggressively as ever.

'Aten. I don't know what the fuck you are talking about.'

'This. You stuck it under the wiper of the Shogun.'

'What would I want to do that for?'

'To get at me, that's what for. Did you think I'd be stupid enough to think my parents would find me here and leave me a note?'

'I didn't do it.'

'Course you damn well did.'

'Is it my handwriting?'

I knew Slatter's moron style well enough. 'No ... But that doesn't—'

'Is it your mummy's handwriting?'

'Of course it isn't.'

The pause was a mistake. He read doubt in my face and lay back, laughing, his hands behind his head.

'It's not your handwriting, Slatter, but I know you got someone to do it.'

Slatter didn't reply. He stared up at the truck's ceiling. It was his usual habit of suddenly switching off as if the world and people in it had disappeared.

'What seems to be the problem here?' The sixteen-year-old was one of Dave's church chums.

In a matter of fact way, Slatter said, 'Fuck off.'

Bible boy fucked off.

'Saw your mother yesterday, Aten.'

Jaw muscles tightening I glared at Slatter.

'She looked in a bad way.' He nodded solemn. 'She'd been shagged by the town donkey.'

It was one of his damn pointless comments designed to provoke you. I shook the note again.

'If you do this again, I'll kill you.'

As I strode away furiously, I heard him say to himself, 'It's a good laugh. But I didn't write the note.'

I really wanted to kill the psychotic bastard. But I had a big problem. I believed he was telling the truth.

We stood in line for breakfast which was cooked outside on camping stoves.

I carried the note in my pocket; the words I carried in my head. *Come home. Urgent news for you. Love – mum & dad*

One of Slatter's sick tricks. Years of punishment had pumped a little cunning into his brain. He still had a pathological need to fight people, but he'd learnt to provoke them so they hit first. Then he could stand there in front of the probation officer/cop/judge and say, 'He hit me first.'

Worse than feeling the victim of Slatter's sadism was doubt. Was the note genuine? The notes I'd seen at home. A piece of paper folded against the kettle: *Nicholas*. Then the message: *Nick. Gone shopping. Meat pie for you. Love – mum*. Or something like that. Of course the handwriting was different but there was something about the rhythm of the message that was the same.

'Eggs and beans?'

I nodded and took my plate back to the car. I could be home and back in an hour. It wouldn't be that dangerous. Pull up to the house in Lawn Avenue, stay in the car, sound the horn – see what happens then.

Dave walked up like he'd got springs in his plimsolls. He asked me to check on one of the Land-Rovers after I'd eaten. Rebecca Keene and two church buddies were going to drive across country to a remote hotel. 'It's near where St Timothy's have their summer camp. If the hotel's deserted we'll move there. We'll have good accommodation, kitchens, fresh water supplies. That'll come from the stream. There's trout this big in there. We'll be able to build a thriving community.' Dave enthused while I thought about driving back home. I could feel the shape of the folded paper in my back pocket, maybe—

'Nick . . . Nick, can you do that for me?'

'Uh, what do you want me to do?'

'You're our mechanical expert. Can you check number 2 Land-Rover's engine and tyres?'

Rebecca and her companions were away by nine. Normally they could have been there and back in five hours, but Rebecca wouldn't risk driving faster than twenty-five. On the roads farm animals roamed wild. You hit a cow at fifty, you wreck the car.

I asked around if anyone'd seen Slatter putting the note under the wiper. No one had. Slatter had taken himself up into the hayloft in the barn. There he sat, dangling his pit boots above everyone's heads while drinking from a bottle of vodka. A sixteen-year-old girl had got the hots for him and danced behind him talking non-stop. She'd have to watch it. Once an old girlfriend of his had said something hadn't liked and he'd rammed his hand inside her mouth and tried to pull out her tongue.

When Slatter started spitting vodka on the people below they moved outside. If this went on I wondered if Dave would try kicking Slatter out of the community.

Sarah was helping younger girls boil water on the camping stove out in the yard, her long blonde hair tied back.

'What do you make of this?' I handed her the note.

She read it then looked at me, her blue eyes trying to gauge my feelings. 'What do *you* make of it, Nick? Practical joke?'

'Yeah.'

'A sick one. Was it Slatter?'

'It's not his handwriting, but he probably put someone up to it.'

'What did you intend doing with this?' She held up the note.

'I'd like to nail it to something solid – Slatter's forehead, for instance.'

'Forget it, Nick.' Her voice was gentle and touched some part inside of me. She twisted the note into a spill and lit it from the stove. As the flame neared her fingers she dropped it on the ground. Then she kissed me on the cheek while squeezing my forearm between her two hands.

'It's not worth fighting over, Nick. If you'd take my advice keep well away from Slatter. He's digging himself into a hole anyway. Yesterday he headbutted Simon because he saw him reading a Bible. A couple more incidents like that and the Steering Committee are going to order him out.'

'Excuse me.' Dave's voice sang out across the yard. 'Boys, girls, ladies, gentlemen ... Can I have everyone's attention, please?'

We shuffled round to the middle of the yard so we could see him standing there in the back of a pickup, smiling, his arms out in a communal embrace.

Slatter was nowhere in sight.

'You probably know by now that Rebecca, Luke and Clifford are on their way to the Esk Hotel in Eskdale. I don't know if you know the area but it lies in a beautiful valley with forests, meadows, and a stream fed by mountain springs. Rebecca's going to find out if it's safe for us to move up there. If it is we should be in our new home by tomorrow. The hotel is a converted country mansion with nearly fifty bedrooms, so we can all live under one roof together. There's a huge dining room with a minstrel's gallery. I know you'll all like it there. However.' He held up a finger, his face serious. 'It will be no picnic. The disaster that has befallen us is enormous. We face great danger. Not just from the mentally ill adults but from natural threats to our survival – hunger and disease. Yes, there might be places that haven't been affected by the madness. Yes, we might be rescued. But we can't rely on that. We must be prepared to survive alone. As if we are the only people alive on Earth.'

Ripple of applause.

'We have enough food for months to come. But it won't last forever. We on the Steering Committee believe we must become self-sufficient as quickly as possible, growing crops, keeping live-stock, making tools, even our own clothes.'

The speech went on – basically it was the belt-tightening, shoulder-to-the-grindstone kind of speech. Tough times ahead but God willing etc.

I found my attention being pulled to Sarah. She listened atten-tively, nodding now and again. Just looking at her was the most pleasurable thing I'd done that day. I looked at her smooth face. I wanted to touch it. I looked at those wonderfully shaped lips. I wanted to kiss them.

Mentally I had begun to map the rest of her body when something hard came out of the sky and hit me.

Chapter Twenty-Two

ATTACK

The first I knew was one hell of a thump in my back which knocked me flat.

A bare foot, toes crusted with dirt, stamped down three inches from my face. Twisting my body across the earth, I saw the man snatch at Sarah. He lifted her up in his arms like she was a child then started to cut through the crowd like a snow plough.

It seemed I knelt there forever, watching the man carry Sarah away.

He must have been sixty, his bald head burnt red with exertion, but he moved like an athlete.

'Nick!' Sarah struggled, her hair torn free to flare out around her head.

The man had nearly reached the edge of the yard before I'd kicked off after them, jumping over fallen kids.

He was going like a loco: his eyes stared like glass balls through Sarah's cascading hair. I ran hard and dived at his pounding legs, wrapping my arms around them. The momentum carried him and Sarah forward, but he went down. Sarah bounced onto the track ahead of him.

He reached out grasping at her but she rolled away. His hands hooked into the dirt to pull himself toward her, dragging me along still gripping his legs.

Then more bodies fell on us. Christ, I thought, there's more of the bastards. We're dead.

Then I recognised Dave straddling the man's chest. More kids grabbed his arms and legs as he twisted and strained like a baboon on crack.

Dave panted orders, 'Get his legs, Peter. No, sit on them . . . sit on them!'

I shouted for Curt to grab the man's head as it whipped from side to side to butt Dave's arms.

'Rope! Get a rope!'

The old man's dentures slid out in pieces. He coughed blood.

'Shit . . . It's on me. His blood!'

'Shut up, Curt – just hang on.'

Laurel and Hardy could have done it quicker but at last we'd got our first Mr Creosote in captivity, tied with orange nylon cord.

Grunting like an excited pig he strained against the cords. They cut through his arms like wire. His glass-ball eyes stared at the sky.

'Sarah. You okay?' I put my arm round her shoulder. She was shaking and trying to get her breathing under control.

'My arm's a bit sore but I'll be all right.'

I hugged her. 'I'll get you a coffee.'

'No, no. Just leave me to get my breath back. I'll be all right.' Face white, she limped to sit in the Shogun.

Curt wiped the man's sputum and blood from his arms with a rag. He looked as if he was going to start crying again.

'What on Earth are you going to do with that?' asked Dave as Slatter walked up with an iron bar the length of his arm.

Slatter nodded at the tied man. 'Crack him with it.'

'You'll do nothing of the sort.'

'What ya gonna do with him, then? Keep him as a pet?'

Dave looked at Slatter in horror. He'd realised we'd adopted a tattooed monster. 'No, Mr Slatter. We're not going to kill him. There's a lock-up store in the barn. Come on, we'll carry him in there . . . Watch his mouth, he might bite.'

Slatter shrugged and walked away.

The man did not struggle as we carried him to the barn and put him in the store.

Dave snapped shut the padlock. 'If we can talk to him we might begin learning something.'

Sarah was back. 'Hadn't someone better cut the rope – he's going to cut himself to pieces it's so tight.'

'Don't worry,' I said, looking in at him through the narrow gap in the door. 'He's getting out of it in any case.'

Dave sighed. 'That's one problem solved, anyway. We'll work out how to get food and drink in there later. Now, we might as well get started. Simon, ask Martin Del-Coffey to come across. Curt, take a good look round to make sure there's no more Mr Creosotes about. Peter . . .'

I left them to it and took Sarah to one side. She looked in control.

'Thanks, Nick. You saved my life. Again.'

I smiled. 'Don't mention it. You'd have done the same.'

'Only quicker.' She smiled back and gave me a gentle punch on the chin. 'Well, thanks to you we've our very own Mr Creosote. But something tells me he's not going to sit down and tell us why everyone over the age of eighteen went mad, or who they are signalling to with their bottle patterns.'

'It'll give Del-Coffey something to do.'

I watched him stroll nonchalantly into the barn, laces trailing.

'Hello. Hello in there.' Del-Coffey tried to sound the authoritative scientist. 'Can you understand what I am saying? Hello. Can . . . you . . . understand . . .'

They'd have had more luck trying to contact the poor bastard with a ouija board.

'Come on.' Sarah pulled me by the hand. 'Leave them to it.'

'Where're we going?'

'Somewhere quiet, Nick.' She smiled. 'I just want to sit on your knee for a while.'

That's what we did. The sun had broken the clouds and we sat on a grassy slope away from the farm. Sarah on my knee, her arm around my neck. We talked about the past. Those intimate things people talk about sometimes. A kind of exchange of secrets that binds you closer.

Sarah told me, 'After I'd finished school I was going to take a year out. A friend and I ... No, it's okay, Nick, it's a she ... We were going to India. I'd found out about a charity that works with children in Calcutta. I would have spent six months there. But to tell the truth, if I'd found it was work I wanted to do I'd have made it permanent.'

'Your parents were happy about that?'

'They never knew. They wanted me to go to university. Officially, my ambition was to study law, but I decided sitting round in courts waiting to prosecute people for not returning their library books wasn't for me. What about you, Nick?'

'Sometimes you get people who are born without a tongue or eyes. I was born without ambition. My plans were to earn a bit of money, drink more beer and have a good time.'

We talked on. I enjoyed the sun warm on my back, the pressure of her body against mine and the way the breeze sometimes lifted her hair against my face in a light, tickling sensation that, for me, felt out of this world.

'Nick. Do you think Slatter would have killed that man?'

'Yeah, I think he'd have had a go. It's sinking into Slatter's thick skull that law and order have disappeared with civilization. He knows he can do whatever he wants now.'

Her arms tightened around my neck. 'Keep out of his way, Nick.'

'I intend to. What happens when we get to this hotel, then? Will the Steering Committee hold elections for leadership?'

We talked for another half hour before walking back to find Vicki shouting at Tug Slatter. I ran back to the yard, my stomach screwing tight.

'Give me them back.'

'No.'

'Why not?'

'That tart, Aten, needs them. Then when he looks into the mirror he can see just how big a faggot he actually is.'

'Give them back ... You'll break them.'

'Give them back,' pleaded Anne. 'Vicki can't see without them and she hasn't got a spare pair.'

Slatter stood there, face as ugly as sin, Vicki's glasses dangled over her head. She jumped for them. Each time she did he flicked them higher. Tears wet her face.

I said, 'Give them back, Slatter.'

'These are yours, Aten. Got nice pink rims. Go with your faggot face.'

'Look . . .' I made eye contact and held it. 'Give them back. All right?'

'You gonna make me or what?'

I looked into that tattooed face and hated every millimetre of it. There should have been horns coming out of that shaved head.

'Give them back, Slatter.'

'All right, Aten. Take them from me.'

He wasn't laughing, or even enjoying himself as most bullies would. As salmon are driven up rivers to spawn, something inside Slatter drove him to be a bastard.

Others in the yard moved back to give us space. They knew what was brewing.

I judged my chances. I needed to put him down in one. Kick to the balls? Punch to the jaw? As soon as he was down I'd have to keep kicking until he couldn't get up again.

If he got the better of me I'd be lucky to get out of this without broken bones at least.

'Nick,' hissed Sarah. 'It's not worth it. We'll get more glasses. Leave it . . . Vicki, come here.'

Vicki tried to jump for the glasses. Slatter spread his hand across her face and pushed her cruelly back.

'Slatter.'

'Come . . . and . . . take . . . them . . . from . . . me . . . Aten.'

'Tug, look what I found.'

It was the girl who'd pinned herself to him. She was too pissed to know what was happening and blundered in holding a bottle of vodka. Her lips were scarlet with lipstick and she'd daubed on black eye shadow. Her blouse was unbuttoned far enough to expose her bra. Slatter read her body language as easy as a road sign.

With an animal snarl, he chucked the glasses into the air then strode back to the barn. 'Come on then, you stupid bitch.'

Giggling, the girl followed.

Slatter had thrown the glasses hard enough upward for Sarah to catch them safely as they dropped down.

I'd begun to sweat.

'Close one,' she said.

'Too close for comfort . . . You know, Sarah, one way or another, Slatter'll have to go.'

Chapter Twenty-Three

ANOTHER MESSAGE, ANOTHER DEATH

7 a.m. The day began with two things.

One. Another note appeared beneath the wiper of the Shogun. *Come home. Urgent news for you. Love – mum & dad.* I screwed it into a ball and kicked it over the wall. It was a sick joke. I decided not to let it get under my skin.

Two. Rebecca Keene returned. She climbed out of the car with her two companions as we bunched round to hear the news. She told us in her schoolmistress voice that they had had an uneventful journey. The hotel was deserted – ideal for our purposes. She wore a new bandage on her left hand but didn't mention it.

During our open air breakfast the story went round that Rebecca had been bitten by a dog.

'Poor bloody animal.' Curt, the tattooed hooligan, stuffed his mouth with bacon. 'Bet it dies of food poisoning.'

'Nick, sorry to interrupt.' Dave came up. 'After breakfast would you check the vehicles?'

'When we setting off?'

'That's to be decided. But we need to know the vehicles will get us there in one go.'

'I can't guarantee they won't break down.' I guessed somehow the vehicles had become my responsibility. 'Dave, I know you were in a hurry getting the convoy together but we haven't got any spares for them. Truck number 2's radiator hose is cracked and the yellow mini-bus's mileage would have taken you round planet Earth four times . . . In other words the engine's shit.'

The smile didn't blip. 'Do what you can, Nick. I know you'll do a good job.'

'But I can't work miracles. No spares. Not enough tools. For a start we should ditch the mini-bus and find a replacement.'

'Nick, we'll see if we can pick up another on the way. I don't want people leaving the camp today. We might have to leave at short notice.'

Curt's eyes went big. 'What? Have we got Mr Creosote on our tails again?'

'No, Curt. The patrols haven't seen anything yet.'

8 a.m. I got stuck into vehicle number one, checking fluid levels and hoses. I wasn't a mechanic but I probably knew more than anyone else there – that made me the expert.

Sarah brought me coffee. I was glad to see her.

'Thanks for getting Vicki's glasses back from Slatter yesterday.'

'Don't thank me. We were lucky that time.'

'Vicki's very sensitive about her glasses. When she was younger mum was always having to tell her off about them. Vicki was constantly forgetting where she'd put them. When she was six she even dropped them down a drain. Dad went hairless. Now if Vicki misplaces them she has fits until we find them again.'

'Does she need to wear them all the time? Once Slatter finds someone's weak spot he plays on it.'

'She's blind without them.'

I took a drink of the coffee. 'They say that Rebecca got bitten by a dog. Is she all right?'

'A dog? No. She cut her little finger climbing a fence. There's nothing like kids for starting rumours.'

'That's something that the Steering Committee will have to watch. Stupid rumours could be dangerous if they panic the kids. They're still saying that Mr Creosote is talking to God and all this is divine punishment.'

'I'll mention it to them.'

'So you've been promoted to the Steering Committee?'

Grinning, Sarah blushed. 'Drink your coffee, Mr Aten. We want all these vehicles in tip-top condition by noon.'

'See that water in the tub over there, Miss Hayes? After I've done the trucks, I'll turn that into wine.'

She laughed and I felt desire bite me you know where. If we'd not joined this convoy maybe we'd be shacked up cosily together somewhere. Now I slept in the Shogun; Sarah in the farmhouse.

As we talked two sisters, I called them the Singing Sisters, came up. They were about ten and twelve, went everywhere together, blonde curly hair shining like halos, and everywhere they went they sang in harmony.

The eldest Singing Sister spoke to Sarah. 'Excuse me, Miss Hayes. Dave needs to see you.'

'Duty calls, Nick.'

'Sarah, try and convince Dave to find a replacement for the yellow mini-bus ... sorry, vehicle number 9. The engine's shot to buggery.'

'I'll ask.' Smiling, she squeezed my arm, then ran lightly across the yard.

I returned to work, annoyed that Saint Dave of Doncaster could command Sarah's presence whenever he wanted.

'Shit.' The wrench slipped and I grazed my knuckle. 'Shit, shit and double shit.'

11 a.m. Martin Del-Coffey lounged back in an armchair in the barn, one leg crossed over his knee, his laces dangling. A laptop computer rested on his stomach. He still played the role of bored intellectual. The Asian girl, Kitty, stood outside the door of the lock-up looking through the gap at our Mr Creosote. She made notes on a clipboard.

'Has he been chatting to God this morning?' It was my break and I'd taken my coffee into the barn.

Del-Coffey waved a limp hand. 'Not even a murmur to one of the lesser angels. Take a look.'

Kitty stood back to let me look through the gap.

Mr Creosote stood in the cell sideways on to me. His mud-caked clothes made him look like the town tramp, his bald head gleaming faintly in what light trickled through the ventilation grill in the ceiling. He stared at something on the wall. I shifted my position to see what it was. There was nothing there – just an expanse of blank concrete. But he stared at it, eyes as bright as light bulbs, like it was a dazzling technicolour vision sent by God Almighty himself.

'Does he always stand like this?' I asked.

'Mostly. He's said nothing. He's eaten nothing.'

'What do you think of these rumours that Mr and Mrs Creosote have a hotline to God?'

'I think, Mr Aten.' Del-Coffey pressed a key on the computer and read what scrolled up the screen as he held a conversation with me. 'I think a student of human behaviour would find it fascinating. God has driven our parents mad. And, mad, they have been supernaturally programmed to destroy their young. Us. God has done this because we have sinned most horribly. And now, Mr Creosote is communicating with God, either with the bottle patterns, or verbally – or both. He is asking God to finish the Divine work and end the world.'

'You believe that?'

'Do I buggery . . . It demonstrates though, does it not? That if you gather together a lot of frightened human beings, who haven't the slightest clue what's happening, they invent answers. The more outlandish the answers the more they believe them. It's a wonder they haven't seen snow on Mr Creosote's boots.'

'Snow on their boots? What do you mean?'

'Mr Aten, haven't you heard the Snow On Their Boots legend? No? In the First World War, Britain reached a point where it looked as if it would lose to Germany. Russia was our ally. The rumour spread like wildfire that a million Russian troops had landed in Britain to help defend King and Country. Trouble was, the population was as frightened of Russians as it was of the Germans. Panic. Pandemonium. The Russians are coming! People hid anything of value up trees, in holes in the garden . . . And do you know how the rumour started?'

'No.'

'Everyone believed Russia was a very cold place . . . and someone saw – said they saw – soldiers with snow on their boots. Ergo, they were Russian soldiers. *Comprende?* People were too stupid to realise that even the coldest Russian snow would melt during a three-day sea voyage from Russia to Liverpool. No Russians, Mr Aten. Nor does Mr Creosote talk to God.' Pleased with himself, Del-Coffey tapped the computer keys. 'Also in the First World War, during the battle of Mons, the British forces were being defeated when the ghostly archers of Agincourt appeared and slew the Hun. The genesis of that rumour was a fictional story, *The Bowmen*, by Arthur Machen who was—'

'What's planned for him in there, then?' Del-Coffey's lecturing was beginning to grate. 'Are we taking him with us?'

'No. If you put your nose to the door you'll realise he's lost some of his civilised niceties.'

'Pardon?'

'Your nostrils will tell you that Mr Creosote is suffering from a case of crowded trouser syndrome.'

'In English, what's that?'

'He's shit himself, Mr Aten, he's shit himself.'

'If Slatter had his way, he'd kill him.'

'Ah, Mr Slatter. I caught him this morning tormenting poor Mr Creosote. He just kept repeating, "Do you like it in there? Do you like it in there? Fucken basturd. Do you like it in there?"'

I grinned. 'Maybe we should put Slatter in there with Mr Creosote and let them sort one another out.'

'Nice idea. I'll be glad to give Mr Creosote the push, though. We're not learning anything from him, but Dave thinks we should persist. That if we discover what sent adult humanity schizo then maybe we can cure them. Or prevent the same happening to us.'

'We're okay so far.'

'We are. But we've found no one over the age of eighteen who is sane.'

'So?'

'So what happens, Mr Aten, on your nineteenth birthday?'

'*All things bright and beautiful, all creatures great and small . . .*'

The Singing Sisters appeared. 'Mr Del-Coffey, would you come to the farmhouse, please. Dave needs to see you urgently. Rebecca is very poorly.'

12 noon. Standing in line for lunch, Curt grumbled, 'Damned

meatballs again. Damned instant mash. Why can't we have something different for a change? In there...' He pointed his spoon at the farmhouse. 'They'll be living like lords.'

Not true. I knew Dave Middleton would eat what we ate. He was one of those people so honest it's sickening.

But two days ago Curt would have stood in line, eyes still red from sobbing into his vest, and been pathetically grateful for whatever was slopped into his bowl. Now he was grumbling. Earlier I'd seen a fourteen-year-old girl refusing to wash a zillion breakfast plates. If it demonstrated anything it was that the human spirit was returning from wherever sheer naked, run-for-your-life terror had sealed it. Kids were starting to say, 'No.'

1.30 p.m. With oil black up to my elbows I was slaving on the mini-bus engine. Oil leaking through the cracked rings had bunged up the plug to prevent one of the cylinders firing.

The Singing Sisters turned up holding out a sheet of paper. 'It's got Nicholas Aten written on it.' The youngest smiled, her chubby face dimpling.

'So you guessed it was for me, right?'

'Yes.'

'Just give me a minute to wipe my hands ... Thanks ... Wait a second – who gave you this?'

'No one. We found it stuck in the gate at the end of the driveway.'

They marched away singing. My hand was shaking by the time I unfolded the note.

Nick,

Come home. John waiting to see you. Uncle Jack too.

Love – mum & dad.

Nightmares of my parents haunting me flickered back into my head so brightly I had to sit down against the mini-bus. When I found out who was playing this sick joke I'd break their damn necks. Slatter was the—

Slatter should have been the prime suspect. He could have got someone to write the note. He knew I had a brother called John. I'd lay a bet, though, he didn't know I had an Uncle Jack.

Sweat oozed from my face. I looked round the yard at people

from four to eighteen carrying boxes of food, and I suspected each and every one. Why was someone playing this shitty trick on me?

'Another one?'

I looked up, shielding my eyes against the sun. 'Hello, Sarah. Yeah, another one.'

'Same message?'

I nearly told her but – 'Yeah. No doubt someone's laughing fit to burst their bag. One day I'll catch them at it. Then I'll kick them so high they come back down covered in frost.'

She knelt down by my side and squeezed my leg. 'I'm sorry, Nick. There are some cruel people about.'

'Don't we know it. The world's full of them these days.' I tore up the note. 'What's new, Miss Hayes? Are we moving out yet?'

'No. Rebecca's not well. Dave wants to wait until she's better.'

'What's wrong with her?'

'We don't know. Martin and Kitty are going through the medical books, but the symptoms could fit a dozen complaints.' She looked at me, troubled. 'I don't like the look of her, Nick. I think it's serious.'

6 p.m. I'd spent the afternoon working on the mini-bus. I'd managed to get it running on all cylinders and kicking out clouds of blue smoke, but I was far from happy with the thing.

We had no word on Rebecca but in the afternoon the bedroom curtains were snatched shut. Every so often Kitty would run white-faced to the trucks to look through the supplies.

By 6.30 people were stopping doing their chores and began gathering outside the farmhouse door.

I went to clean up in the stream that ran at the back of the farmhouse. I noticed Slatter slouching through the trees at the other side. The girl with the eye makeup followed him as best she could in her high heels across the grass.

'I'm sorry, Tug. ... I'm sorry...' She kept repeating as they disappeared amongst the trees. I saw a red mark on her cheek.

7 p.m. The barn was deserted. People hung round the farmhouse door waiting for news.

I looked in on Mr Creosote. He stood in the same position,

staring at the wall. He saw something marvellous there. God knows what.

As I watched, his knees bent a little, then straightened. Gently, he began to bob up and down, like a guitarist in a rock group getting into the rhythm. The light-bulb eyes still stared, fixed at the point on the wall. His lips moved slightly now as if he was whispering.

Whispering to God, Mr Creosote?

I coughed. No reaction. 'Hello . . . Can you hear me?'

He couldn't, or maybe he ignored me. He carried on with his silent whispering and gentle knee jigs.

I looked at him and thought about my own parents. Could they be like this? Their own shit hot in their pants? Gazing at visions? No. I could not believe that. Somewhere they were hiding. As sane as me.

Suddenly, Mr Creosote froze in mid-jig, cocked his head to one side and held it there. The eyes blazed. He'd heard something. What was it? The call of his own kind?

I shivered as I left the barn.

7.20 p.m. Dave opened the farmhouse door and stood on the top step. He looked round the assembly and said, 'Rebecca Keene died five minutes ago . . . Nick. Can you help me for a moment?'

Did I hell want to go into the farmhouse, but I followed.

At the top of the stairs Simon was wringing his hands. 'How can we be sure? We can't be certain . . . No one knows enough to . . . We're just kids, for Chrissakes . . . We've no medical training . . . How do we know Rebecca is dead?'

In the last few days I'd seen enough death to believe I'd been toughened against it.

It was still a shock. One look at her lying hunched on one side, her face looking as if it was moulded from lard, her mouth pulled into a crimson O, told you life had gone from that eighteen-year-old body.

In Dave Middleton's band of survivors Rebecca Keene was the first to die.

Chapter Twenty-Four

A DIFFERENT KIND OF PAIN

'Do you want to go first?'

'No. I'm scared. It's dark down there?'

'I'll be with you, Susan.'

'I'm still scared.'

'We'll go down together, then. Hold my hand . . . There – that's better, isn't it? Now, hold it tight.'

The voices of the little girls, the Singing Sisters, although nearly whispers, were enough to wake me. I came to groggily, still tasting the whisky on my lips.

I rubbed my face and sat up in my sleeping bag. That night I was in the barn. Dave thought it best if we took turns sleeping near Mr Creosote's lock-up. In case he started behaving differently, started talking, or simply tried to break out.

I looked round for the voices. The Singing Sisters should be asleep in the farmhouse. I listened.

'Now. I'll count to three.'

'Are you sure it'll be all right?'

'Yes, Susan. It will be all right. Hold onto my hand. Tighter.'

'I'm frightened.'

'Remember what I told you. This is magic. We will see mummy and daddy.'

'Will mummy and daddy be nice again?'

'Yes, of course they will. Now, hold onto my hand tightly. One, two, three . . . jump.'

A terrible, terrible feeling of dread cut through me. My head snapped up.

From out of the darkness two girls glided down, halos of blonde hair around their heads.

I held up my hands in this futile, this fucking stupid futile attempt to catch them both.

They stopped five feet above my hands with a sound like a gunshot that still echoes in my head. Then they swung like little blonde dolls on the end of their ropes.

At that moment, my heart felt as if it had cracked like an egg.

Stiff, I walked out through the doors of the barn into the farmyard, the mud cold beneath my bare feet.

I did not know whether I wanted to shout, or just run and run and let the night swallow me whole. I wrapped my arms around myself and shivered.

When I was five, dad would wrap me in a blanket and carry me out to show me the night sky. He'd point out the stars. Those same stars that burned harder and brighter now the streetlights had died.

Far away in the distance, someone began to whistle. A slow, haunting sound. It was faint, but the night air carried the notes well enough for me to recognise the tune.

Ten green bottles hanging on a wall,
If one green bottle should accidentally fall . . .

Chapter Twenty-Five

REMEMBER THIS: DON'T PLAY THE HERO

The yard buzzed as we loaded the camping gear into the trucks; engines cranked into life. Del-Coffey moved the fastest I'd ever seen him move. He loped along the line of vehicles telling the drivers to get ready – we were pulling out in five minutes.

I stood with Dave Middleton by the lead bus as Del-Coffey, panting, climbed on board.

'Get the lazy bastards to hurry up.' Del-Coffey's face was as red as a strawberry. 'Creosote's not going to take forever to get here. If they cut across the fields they can block us leaving the yard.'

'We've plenty of time,' said Dave. 'Also, I think you've forgotten something.'

'I've forgotten nothing. Let's get out of this pig-sty.'

'We still haven't decided what we're going to do with the old guy in the lock-up.'

Del-Coffey laughed but I could tell he was just plain scared. 'You *are* joking? Dave, there are two hundred of the murdering bastards watching us from that hill and you want to fart around with the one locked up in the barn. Jesus H. Christ . . . Leave him, for Godsakes. His pals'll be here any minute. Let them liberate him. Now . . . Come on!'

'Martin,' Dave spoke calmly. 'We don't know if they'll release him. If they don't he'll starve in there.'

'That, old boy, is your problem. We're leaving, even if I have to drive this bloody bus myself.'

'The Creosotes are more than two miles away. All we have to do is work out some way to safely unlock the door then we'll be on our way to the hotel.'

'It's too dangerous. The moment you unlock that door he'll burst out of there and break your neck.'

'Okay, Martin. Just give me a minute to think . . . Right. You take the convoy out onto the road. Follow the route Rebecca prepared before . . . Well, just follow that. I'll catch you up.'

Del-Coffey looked at him in disbelief. 'You're going to risk your life to let out some mad bastard who'll kill you given half a chance? Your funeral, mate.'

Del-Coffey scrambled into the bus and started it up.

Dave turned to me. 'Nick, will you lend me the Shogun? Once I've let the old man out I'll catch up with the convoy and you can have it back.'

'You're taking a hell of a risk. If anything happens to you all these kids are up shit creek.'

'Don't worry. I'll think of a way to get our chap free without risking my own neck.'

'Let me stay and help, then.'

This surprised him. He looked up at me, touched. 'Thanks, Nick, I appreciate it. Look, it's best if we have another pair of hands. I'll see if Curt will volunteer to stay with us.'

'Are you sure? He looks tough but it doesn't take much to frighten him.'

'He'll be okay.'

Dave headed off down the convoy looking for Curt. I went back to the Shogun and got Sarah and her sisters to join Del-Coffey in the bus up front. Then I backed the Shogun across to the barn.

The plan had been to stay here for a couple more days until the shock of Rebecca's death and the two suicides had subsided. But like all plans they had a tendency, at the drop of a hat, to be shot to buggery.

Dave Middleton had buried the three girls with his own hands in a nearby cemetery. Driving back to the farm he'd spotted Family Creosote massing on a hillside two miles from the farm. There was no alternative but to up and go. The mob could be beating up the drive to the farm within thirty minutes.

From the barn doorway I watched the convoy lumbering out onto the road. I felt cold. I was sure Del-Coffey wouldn't wait for us. Without Rebecca Keene as backseat driver Del-Coffey put his foot down, leaving the rest of the convoy to follow as best it could.

'What you going to do with him?'

'Slatter?'

'No, it's your fairy bloody godmother, who'd you think?'

Slatter oozed out of the shadows at the back of the barn like a bad memory. 'So, what's happening to him in there?'

'That's what Dave and me are going to work out. Why haven't you left with the convoy?'

'You know what? You should kill him. Pour diesel in on him through the vent in the roof, then drop a match in.'

'No. We're going to work out a way to get the door open without him killing one of us. Why aren't you on the bus, Slatter?'

He looked at me with those cruel eyes. It was an effort for him, but he was thinking. 'Aten. What did your parents do to you?'

'Nothing. I was out when it happened.'

'Then they'll be looking for you. When they catch you they'll cut you to fuck.'

'They'll not find me.'

'They will, Aten. They'll follow you till the day you die.'

'Yeah, and what do you know?'

Slatter fixed his eyes on me, then pointed at the lock-up. 'Because that mad fucker in there is my father.'

With that, Slatter spat on the floor and walked out into the yard.

Anyone else I'd have said I was sorry. Not Slatter: I just watched the back of his tattooed neck as he stared into space, smoking a cigarette.

I looked through the gap into the lock-up.

Christ Almighty. I jumped back a yard, my heart beating like a power hammer.

When I got over the shock, I looked in again. Cautiously this time. I hadn't expected to see that.

Mr Creosote, Slatter senior, stood at the other side of the door. The light-bulb eyes stared back into mine. He just stood and stared, his lips twitching in a way that told me something excited him. He seemed to sense something was going to happen soon.

'Nick,' Dave strode into the barn followed sulkily by Curt. 'Nick, Creosote's on the move. I reckon we've got fifteen minutes to release the gentleman in there and get away from here. Is Tug helping?'

'I don't think he will. Did you know it's his father in there?'

'Good Lord, no. Does he want us to try and take him with us?'

'No, he doesn't want to do that. In fact, what he really wants to do is torch his old man.'

'Heaven help him. Well . . . We haven't time to worry about that now. Let's just get the door open, then we can go.'

Curt stood in the doorway looking in the direction of family Creosote. 'They're really shifting, Dave. They've made it as far as the crossroads.'

'Don't worry, Curt,' said Dave. 'That still gives us another ten minutes. Listen, this is what we do. Unlock the padlock – quietly – tie string to the steel pin that fits through the latch, there. Then run the string over that beam to the car. We climb in the car, I pull the string, that lifts out the pin – hey presto. Mr Creosote's a free man. Now, who's got the padlock key?'

We looked at one another.

'Bloody Nora!' Curt turned white. 'I forgot to ask Del-Coffey for it. He's taken it with him.'

I wanted to hit the idiot. My patience with him had already been wearing thin. That morning I had heard him laughing with some other kids as Dave made wooden crosses for the grave of the Singing Sisters and Rebecca.

Through his loose lips Curt had chuckled. 'I suppose now you could call them the Swinging Sisters.'

'Curt, there's a bunch of keys in the farmhouse. Fetch those. There might be a spare for the padlock.'

Curt sweated. 'We haven't got time. Them crazy bastards are cutting across the fields. They'll be here in five minutes.'

'Five minutes is enough, Curt. We are still civilized – we do not leave people locked up in a cell to starve. Bring the keys.'

Swearing, Curt ran to the house. I noticed Tug had climbed into the back of the car and sat watching us, his face expressionless.

The mob were half a mile from us. They were climbing over a fence in a dark wave. Dave had been generous giving them five minutes to reach us. I gave them three.

It only took a minute to tie the string to the padlock and trail it over the beam and through the open front passenger window of the car. I would drive, Dave would pull the padlock free from the safety of the car.

Curt came running back, panting through his loose wet lips. 'They've made it as far as the bridge, Dave. It won't be long now. I think we—'

'Get in the car, please, Curt.' Dave's patience was out. 'In the back seat next to Tug. Nick and I will handle it now. Try the keys, Nick, please.'

There must have been twenty keys on the iron ring and my fingers were like frozen sausages. I pushed the first key into the padlock. Jesus, first time lucky ... Shit. The key part turned but wouldn't shift the lock mechanism. Try again, Nick.

My blood thudded in my ears. I kept shooting glances over my shoulder at the driveway. Any minute now it would be swarming with lunatics hungry for our skin.

'Don't worry, Nick. I'll keep a look out.'

By key six I was ready to quit. Suddenly it seemed a pointless exercise to let the madman out – he'd only kill us if he got the chance anyway. But we were playing the game Saint Dave of Doncaster's way. From the cell I heard a loud snort, almost the kind of noise horses make when they get excited.

My hands shook now as I forced the next key into the slot. This is stupid, Nick. You're going to get yourself killed ... Get in the car, and drive, drive, drive, Nick. You're going to get yourself peeled like a banana and—

'Got it, thank God!'

'Thank God indeed.' Dave still sounded cool. I was sweating like a pig on its way to the bacon factory.

'Now, Nick. Just release the lock. Leave the pin through the latch. Is the string still tied to it?'

'Yep.'

'Let's go.'

We ran back to the car. I revved her up as Dave climbed into the passenger seat and took up the string's slack.

'Come on, come on!' Curt's eyes bulged. 'The bastards are coming up the road!'

Slatter, sitting in the back, smoked a cigarette, and for all the notice he took of what was happening he could have been simply on his way to tea at Auntie Flo's.

Dave gently pulled the string. I saw the padlock jiggle. He pulled harder.

In the back Curt yelled, 'Get a frigging move on! They've nearly reached the gates!'

I snapped back. 'Curt. Shut it . . . Or you can get out and walk.' That shut him up. He sat in the back staring at me, his loose lips shaking.

'No. The wretched thing's stuck.' Dave gave the string a tug. 'The padlock moved but I can't slip it up out of the catch.'

I made a decision. A totally damn stupid decision – but I went for it. 'Dave. Get behind the wheel.' I climbed out of the car.

'What you doing?'

'I'll just pull the thing out and run for it. Be ready to drive as soon as I'm back in the car.'

I don't know if Dave said a prayer for me but I saw his lips moving before I ran back into the barn.

Two yards from the lock-up door I saw the padlock had all but come out of the latch. I was standing with my hand out ready to lift the thing off when I heard the crash.

The door exploded open, kicked from the other side.

I froze still, arm stretched out. In the doorway the man stood, his light-bulb eyes burning into mine. If he'd moved then I wouldn't have stood a chance.

I snapped round and ran. The Shogun's passenger door yawned wide open and I just dived for it, bouncing head first into Dave's shoulder. He pumped the pedal and we were buzzing round the yard in a skidding turn.

I slammed my door shut as the madman bounded out of the barn.

I expected him to chase us, braying on the glass. Instead he sprinted across the yard and jumped onto the burned-out tractor to stand, one foot on the seat, one foot on the charred tyre rim. He froze there, glaring at us, like some schizoid baboon, as we skidded the car round the yard and down the driveway to the road.

We pulled out as the first Creosotes rounded the corner fifty yards away. Within seconds the car left them behind.

I slumped in the passenger seat like a wet piece of rag.

'We should be back with the convoy in a few minutes,' said Dave, smiling. 'You did a good job, Nick. That took a lot of courage.'

I said nothing, but I made up my mind there and then. Whatever happens, Nick Aten. Never, ever, play the hero again.

Chapter Twenty-Six

SURPRISING HOW QUICK THE ROT SETS IN

'Nick. Look at that.' Sarah leaned forward in her seat to get a better view. 'We expected buildings and the fabric of civilization to decay, but I didn't think the rot would set in so soon.'

I looked in the direction she looked. There was a lake where no lake existed the week before.

'We've had some heavy rain,' I said, slowing as the brake lights of the truck in front flashed red. 'I didn't think we'd had that much.'

'Doncaster's fairly low lying so there are lots of pumping stations dotted about to get rid of the water that accumulates in the drains.'

'So, no electricity, no pumps pumping.'

'That's about the size of it. A lot of the land around Doncaster is reverting to swamp.'

'Look at the church,' cried Anne from the back seat.

Vicki jumped up to look. 'It's like a boat, all surrounded by water.'

'It looks as if we're going to get a taste of it now,' I said slowing the Shogun. 'Lift up your feet so they don't get wet.'

I was joking but it was close. Ahead the road was flooded up to the axles. We ploughed through it more than a hundred yards before reaching the dry road at the other side. Just then I'd seen a glimpse of the shape of things to come. It might take years but leaf falls, floods, soil erosion, plant growth would eventually make the roads vanish from the face of the Earth.

We joined the Selby Road and headed north. We saw no one. In the back the girls fell asleep. In low voices Sarah and I talked.

'It's going to be dark before we reach Eskdale,' I said.

'We won't try and do it in one day. Dave plans to camp for the night once we're away from the major towns.'

'Sarah, do they know what killed Rebecca?'

She shrugged. 'Martin's sure it wasn't contagious. The two that went with her are fine. The guess is that it was some kind of blood poisoning from the cut on her finger.'

'Talk about babes in the damn wood. We don't know anything, do we? Probably your average GP would have diagnosed what was wrong with Rebecca and saved her bloody life with an injection. I mean, are we going to blunder round dying of 'flu and measles and rickets?'

'We're going to have to learn, Nick.'

'Maybe what we will learn is that we don't have a hope in hell . . . I keep thinking what those two girls did in the barn. Had they the right idea? Quit while you're still healthy. In five years time are we going to be covered in lice and boils and be digging in the shit for worms to eat?'

Her voice was small. 'I don't know, Nick. We can only try.'

Reaching Eskdale should have been a pleasant drive through the countryside. Now it had become a dangerous journey through a new world I called the Madlands.

We were just kids who didn't know shit. The place was lousy with madmen who, given half a chance, would strip the skin from our faces. We'd no weapons, and even if we had we wouldn't know how to fire the damn things.

The world was just plain mad, bad and dangerous. And I was scared. My eyes darted from left to right just looking for monsters to jump out and gobble us whole. Even at rest stops when I closed my eyes all I saw was the mad staring light-bulb eyes of Slatter's father, or the Singing Sisters gliding out of the darkness with golden halos. Then the ear-stabbing crack of the ropes snapping tight.

'Nick . . . Are you all right?'

'Yeah.'

'Do you want me to drive? You look on edge.'

'I'm okay. What's wrong?'

'Nothing. I was just telling you there's another one of the patterns made by the Creosotes in the field across there. It looks like a stick man made out of foil plates.'

I shivered, goose bumps raised like boils on my arms. 'I don't know about you, Sarah, but I'm just about ready to believe in this Creosote-communicating-with-God business.'

'I know the feeling. It's because we're frightened. We start looking for simple answers. Martin Del-Coffey said: Take away civilization from a man and you aren't left with a man without civilization, you are left with a completely different animal.'

'It'll take more than a teeny philosopher to get us out of this crap in one piece.'

'It *will* take more than that, Nick. But we have to remember not to allow fear to take control of us. Martin said we must be aware strange things will happen to us mentally. We've all gone through a harrowing ordeal, we've seen terrible things, people literally torn to pieces. We're frightened. For a while we are going to live in constant danger. It's inevitable that more of us will die. Consequently we will become more irrational, we are likely to become extremely superstitious; probably even paranoid.'

'What's that mean? Paranoid?'

'In a nutshell, we're going to be afraid of our shadow. And we're likely to irrationally blame people, even things, for our misfortunes, like the Nazis blamed the Jews for all their problems and how the—'

'You're beginning to sound like Del-Coffey.'

'But don't you see he's right? He's trying to make us understand what will happen to us. It's like you get 'flu and your doctor tells you what symptoms to expect. Fever, aches, weakness. We're going through nothing short of a nightmare. There'll be a psychological impact on us with its own symptoms – superstition, irrational fears, paranoia. But if we know the symptoms we can deal with them.'

I asked her suddenly. 'Are you on the Steering Committee?'

'Yes. I am.'

'You're Rebecca's replacement?'

'No . . . Dave asked me, that's all.'

We drove in silence for the next twenty minutes. Then without apparent reason the convoy stopped suddenly.

A minute later Dave came springing down the line of vehicles.

'Nick ... We've a problem.'

I followed him back to one of the trucks. One glance at the steam hissing from beneath the cab told me what was wrong.

'The radiator hose has split,' I said. 'I told you it was cracked when I was checking the vehicles back at the farm.'

'Can you do anything with it, Nick?'

'It depends how bad it is. Like I said, we've no spares. What you can do is get me a couple of eggs.'

'Eggs?'

'It's okay, Dave, I don't want to eat them. If the hose isn't completely ruptured I'll crack the eggs into the radiator and they'll seal the leak. With luck that'll get us as far as the hotel.'

He went to get the eggs while I lifted the flap. Steam billowed out around the convoy. The hose wasn't beyond the point of no return yet. While it cooled I grabbed a couple of buckets and went in search of water.

'We're not far from the River Ouse,' Dave told me. 'It's just across that field there. Do you need any help?'

'No, thanks.' The truth was I wanted some time by myself. The suicide of the girls was beginning to bite.

I pushed through the gap in the hedge and crossed the field to the river. It took just seconds to fill the buckets but I grabbed a few minutes to sit on a rock and watch the water go by.

The river was a good fifty yards wide. Birds swooped down low over it to peck midges from the air. Somewhere a fish jumped with a splash. The peace was relaxing and as the minutes passed the world didn't seem so frightening any more. I began to look forward to reaching the hotel. Maybe I would end up sharing a room with Sarah.

As I stared at the water I heard the whistle.

I knew that sound. My head came up sharply, my eyes searched the far banking until I saw them. A man and woman stood there at the edge of the river looking back across at me.

Dad waved. 'Nick! Where on Earth have you been? We've been looking for you for days!'

A bullet couldn't have winded me more.

'Nick,' called mum. 'Are you all right?'

'Yes.' My voice felt as if it didn't belong to me. 'I'm okay. What about you? Are you—'

'Nick, we can't hear you properly. Work your way downstream and cross at the bridge.' They began to walk along the far bank, waving me to follow.

'Hurry up, Nick,' shouted mum. 'We can't wait here.'

'What's happening?' I called. 'Where are you going?'

'We can't talk now. We've got to go.'

'But what on Earth's happened? Dad . . . Dad . . .'

They didn't stop. Mum looked back and shouted. 'Have you heard the news, Nick? It's marvellous, isn't it?'

'What news? Mum . . . Dad . . . Come back, I don't know where you're going. Come back!'

As I followed them through the bushes alongside the bank I nearly ran smack into Curt.

'What's wrong, Nick? Why you running?'

'I'm following them.'

'Who?'

'Those, on the other side.'

'Why? They're Creosotes, they'll kill you.'

'They're not damn Creosotes, they're my parents.'

He looked at me, scared. Just then I looked pretty wild and he must have wondered if I'd gone over the edge into the wonderful world of Creosotedom too.

'Dave . . . Dave sent me to find you, Nick. They need to get going. There are some Creosotes following us back up the road. Another ten minutes and they'll be here.'

'Piss off.'

He stood and stared at me, his lips flapping.

'I said piss off!'

Just then I wanted to feel my fist smack into that Sloppy Joe mouth. I snarled and made a run at him.

He cried out like he'd been kicked and scrambled back up the field to the convoy.

I ran along the river bank looking for mum and dad. They were gone. This time it hadn't been a dream – they were real. It would've been better if they'd jumped up and down screaming they wanted to kill me. They hadn't. They just seemed like my down-to-earth parents who'd heard some exciting news. Like the time they burst into the house to tell us that they'd won the TV in the prize draw.

Were they mad? Were they sane? I did not know.

Dave found me sitting on the bank, flicking pebbles into the water.

'You okay, Nick?'

'Yeah, so-so.'

'I heard that you've seen your parents . . . Are you sure it's them?'

'Positive.'

'You gave Curt a scare, you know? He's blabbing his eyes out.' Dave's smile was kind; he squatted beside me and began flicking stones too. He talked in a matter-of-fact way for a while; he told me how he'd returned home after the camping weekend to find his two brothers dead in bed. There was no self-pity.

I hated myself for hating him.

'Curt said there were some Creosotes down the road.'

Dave smiled. 'Curt's a jittery so-and-so. There's about ten a good two miles away. We've plenty of time. Anyway, I like it here. It's relaxing, sitting by water. Did I ever tell you I once hooked a pike in this river? The thing was the size of a whale. It pulled me in head first. I never did land the thing. It bent the hook out straight as a nail and disappeared.' We laughed and talked some more, then we collected the buckets and walked back to the convoy.

Ten minutes later the convoy was back on the road again.

We drove on through the countryside and I knew before long I would meet my parents again. The question of whether they were sane or not would be answered then . . . if they tried to kill me.

Chapter Twenty-Seven

A MEXICAN STAND-OFF

That afternoon it began to rain hard. The convoy lumbered north-wards along twisting country lanes. At three, we pulled off into a roadside picnic area for a rest-break. Under the iffy shelter of some trees we set up the camping stoves.

I went to check on the truck – the hose now sealed with hardboiled egg was holding – then I looked at the mini-bus. The plug had fouled again. I cleaned the thing the best I could. As I worked I thought about my parents. Something had happened to them. What, I didn't know – but they thought it was something marvel-lous. And I thought about Slatter's mad father, obsessively hunting his own son.

Dave strode busily by. 'When you've finished, Nick, grab yourself a coffee and something to eat. We're moving on in five minutes.'

'Dave. I don't think this mini-bus is going to hold out much longer. The plug's fouling every – Dave . . . Dave!'

He was gone. In his head was his task agenda. The mini-bus came way down the list.

As I walked back through the rain to get my coffee, I saw Sarah confronting Slatter. My heart sank: more shit was about ready to hit the fan.

'What's bothering you, Slatter?' I asked calmly.

'I just thought I'd get these so I could see you better.'

'Slatter. Give Vicki her glasses back.'

'I always thought you looked like shit, Aten. I just thought I'd take a look through these to make sure ... Ah ... Yeah. You look like shit all right.'

Sarah said gently. 'Please, Tug. Give them back to Vicki. She can't see without them.'

Big mistake. Never try and appeal to Slatter's good side. He hasn't got one. And if you admit what he's doing is going to hurt more than he thought – well, that's bleeding Christmas come early for the bastard.

'Piss off, blondie. I need 'em now.' He leered through his tattoos. 'Or are you going to ask lover boy to take 'em off me?'

'Come on, Slatter. The convoy's ready to pull out.'

As soon as the others in the convoy saw what was coming they packed up ultra-quick and locked themselves safely into the vehicles.

We stood like that in the rain. Waiting for someone to do something. I hoped Slatter would get wet and cold enough to simply quit this line of action and get in the back of his truck. He waited, staring me out through the tattooed bluebirds.

Dave's bus sounded its horn then pulled out, the rest of the vehicles following. We were left behind with the Shogun.

'Come on,' said Sarah to Vicki. 'Get in the car.'

Anne was already in the back seat. As Sarah sat in the front passenger seat I whispered, 'When you see me run, get behind the wheel and drive as fast as you can.'

'No, Nick. Whatever you're planning, don't do it.'

'Look, Slatter just wants the excuse for a fight. He'll not rest until he's pulped my face. What we'll do is this. I'm going to grab the glasses and leg it for that field there.' I looked in the direction of a ploughed field that resembled six acres of wet chocolate. 'Slatter'll chase me. You see where the road forks off to the right across the top of the field? Wait for me there. I reckon I can run faster than Slatter. Once I'm in the car we'll rejoin the convoy.'

'You can't leave Slatter. He'll die out here by himself.'

'Will he buggery. He'll survive. Only he won't be plaguing us any longer – that's all that matters.'

'Nick ...'

'Shush, I'll see you later.' I walked back the fifteen paces toward Slatter.

'Last chance, Slatter. Give me the glasses.'

'You know, these glasses are starting to piss me off. I'm going to smash them to shit if you don't take them. Here.' He held them out in his great tattooed paw. As he did so, he circled round until he was between me and the car. He'd guessed I'd planned to grab the glasses and run back to the car and leave him here. As it was he put himself just where I wanted him. Now I was nearer to the field I intended to cut across.

'Would you have really set fire to your father, Slatter?'

'Yeah.'

'Why?'

'Why not?'

'Do you think he's still following you?'

He made an animal grunt that I guess meant yes.

'I saw my parents, you know. They're following me too.'

'Then they'll be fucking ape shit as well. This is the one time in my life I'm going to do you a favour, Aten. My advice is kill them the first chance you get. Or they'll kill you.'

'Why should I wait for them to do it? *You* want to kill me, don't you?'

'Nah . . . I just want to pretty your face up a bit.'

'Why? Why have you spent your life hating me?'

'Because—'

GOTCHA!

I whipped the glasses and ran. He was ready for me to run to the car. The idiot didn't know what hit him when I ran in the other direction, vaulted the fence and ran up the ploughed field, the glasses in my hand.

'You're dead, Aten!'

He ran after me.

It was tough work. The wet soil stuck to my shoes until I was running with a great clump of mud at the end of each leg.

Halfway across the field I was panting, my leg muscles ached, rain and sweat blinded me. I could hear the thump of Slatter's pit boots behind me. Looking to my left, I saw the Shogun speeding up the lane to the top of the field.

Another sixty seconds and Slatter would be all alone. Waiting for daddy to call ... Ha-Ha! I felt a delirious rush of energy. *Slatter's history!*

I heaved on across the slop, mud squelching around my feet, water soaking me through – this was bloody murder – but it would be worth it.

It all turned to shit when I felt the bang on the back of my head. I went face down into the mud.

Slatter reached down and pulled the glasses out of my hand.

'You say that brat with the pigtails can't see without these, Aten?'

'She needs them. Look, just give them back, and we—'

He bent over me so I could see, then he snapped the arms off. 'Bastard glasses.' He threw the spectacle arms back over his shoulder.

'Oh, shit, Slatter. There's no need to do that. Damn...'

Watching my face for the reaction, he calmly snapped the glasses so the lenses were separated. He threw them, too. Then he raised his boot above my face like he was going to step on an ant.

I don't remember any more.

Chapter Twenty-Eight

SEX

First my lips split apart. Next, my eye cracked open. I was dead meat, lying in darkness.

I rocked my head to the left. My neck hurt.

With an effort I cracked open the other eye. I gently fingered each eye in turn. They were puffed and coated in crispy crumbs of something that might have been blood. My face felt stiff and swollen.

I remembered Slatter and the ploughed field. Where I was now God only knew.

As I lay there trying to get my brain firing on all four cylinders light exploded into the room.

'So . . . You're awake at long last.'

I recognised Sarah's voice.

'Yeah . . . But feeling half dead.'

'You're lucky not to be a hundred percent dead . . . If you have any more bright ideas like that, I'll stamp on your head myself.'

'Is that what he did?' My eyes focused enough to let me see Sarah nodding. She sat on the edge of my bed.

'Dave reckons the only thing that saved you was the soil was so soft he stamped your stupid head right into it.'

'Are we at the hotel?'

'No such luck. It took me half an hour to drag you across to the car. Then Dave came back for us. He'd found this motel so we're stopping here the night. We've been here...' She looked at her watch, her blonde hair falling over her face. 'Five hours.'

'Where's Slatter?'

'He took off on foot back the way we came.'

'He'll come back ... Christ, it's the first time I've been in a bed for ... Hell, I can't remember how long since.'

Sarah lit a candle. I saw her concerned eyes looking down at me. 'He made a mess of your face, you know. It's one big bruise.'

Then without warning, completely out of the gob-smacking blue, she leaned over and kissed me on the forehead.

'You're a fool,' she said stroking my hair. 'But I'm a bigger fool. I've got a soft spot for you, Nick Aten. Now ... You stay there and I'll get you some soup. Chicken okay?'

'Fine, nurse.'

'I'll bring some bread, too ... Don't worry, you've still got all your teeth, so you can chew.'

By the time she got back with a tray I was pulling my shirt on.

'Where you going?'

'I need to look at the yellow mini-bus. I want to do a proper job of cleaning the plugs before we set off tomorrow.'

'You'll not get out of that bed, boyo.' She pushed me back. 'It's nearly dark anyway. No ... Stay where you are, Nick, or I'll hide your jeans.'

Stiffly I slid back in, trying to hide the look of pain on my face.

'It needs looking at. The engine's a mess.'

'You can see to it tomorrow. Dave has just told me he plans to stay here at least two nights. A lot of the kids are getting cranky. The shock of what happened to Rebecca and the two sisters is beginning to tell. He's already had to bring back one boy who decided to go it alone on his bike.'

Sarah fed me the soup. I looked up at her face, just getting a different kind of nourishment from watching her blue eyes. We talked for a good hour before she kissed me goodnight and blew out the candle.

I wished she hadn't gone. It would have felt good to hold another human being.

* * *

The next day.

The plug came out as tarred up as before. I used a nail to gouge away the worst of the burnt-on oil. As I worked on the mini-bus's engine beneath a dripping tree Dave loped up.

'Nick, are you sure you feel fit enough to do that?'

'It needs sorting. The cylinder's not firing.'

'How are you feeling?'

'Sore. Has Slatter come back?'

'No. We haven't seen him since it happened.'

'Slatter'll have satisfied his inner craving now he's pulped me. He'll probably be quiet for a day or two.'

'If he doesn't show by eight tomorrow we'll go without him anyway.'

'How long to the hotel now?'

'If we get a clear run, perhaps four or five hours. Once there we can rest and take stock.'

'Do you think we'll make a go of it at the hotel?'

'I don't see why not. If we can cultivate some fields with corn and vegetables, and there's bound to be sheep and—'

'No. I don't just mean food.' I leaned back, wiping my hands on a rag. 'That will probably be the least of our problems. Even if Family Creosote leave us alone we're still going to run into trouble.'

'What do you mean?'

'I mean who's going to be boss? Who's going to tell us what to do – then make sure we do it?'

'For a while the Steering Committee will run things then we'll hold a free election to determine the membership of the next Committee.'

I laughed. It hurt my face – but I laughed so loudly David Middleton, Jesus's little sunbeam, looked startled.

'Look, Dave, a lot of these kids aren't reasonable or sensible human beings. Did you know that? They're not like the nice kids you take on these Church youth weekends. Most are, but a lot are vicious little bastards.'

'We're in a mess, Nick. They'll see the dangers and the need to pull together, behave responsibly and—'

'Will they shit. They're quiet now because a bunch of them are in shock. But they're starting to come out of it. You can see it with your own eyes. I remember Curt from school. He's been in trouble with the police, he gets into fights in clubs – correction, he waits until there's a fight, then he kicks whoever's on the floor. The girl with red hair who's always complaining – she's been busted for selling drugs. Like you, I went to school and kept my eyes open. You know as well as I do some kids are bullies, some steal, some use threats and violence to exploit ones younger or weaker than themselves.'

'So, what are you saying?'

'That you are going to have to wave a big stick, Dave, if you hope to get some of these kids to do what they are told.'

Dave shook his head, sad that I was talking that way. 'I agree some of these people are rough diamonds, but I believe they haven't been given a real chance in life. We will reason with them and give them a sense of responsibility.'

My head ached when I shook it and I went back to work on the mini-bus.

The room felt cold after two days' rain. I sat on the edge of the bed and stared at the framed print of sunflowers on the wall. The TV sat dead in the corner. Even if we had electricity I was sure there'd be nothing but static on the thing now.

They say you don't miss something until you lose it. How bloody true. What I wouldn't give to watch some old film. Maybe something like *It's a Wonderful Life* that I'd seen a million times before. Familiarity's reassuring.

I was ready to snuff the candle when the tap came on the door.

It opened. 'Hi, how you feeling?'

'Fine, Sarah, thanks. I'm just wondering whether to watch the in-house movie or the World Wrestling Summer Slam Spectacular.'

She stepped in, looking cute in a towelling robe. She'd brushed her long hair down over one shoulder, so it covered one breast.

Suddenly awkward, we said nothing for a moment until she held out a can. 'I found some beer in the back of the car.'

'Thanks. Just what the doctor ordered.'

'You're quite privileged, you know. You're the only one with your own room. Even Martin's having to share with Dave. I'm sharing with Anne and Vicki and two other girls. It's cramped.'

'Sit down.' I smiled. 'I'm rattling around in this place like a pea in a packing case.'

We opened our beers and sat again feeling awkward.

'Nick,' she suddenly sounded brisk. 'I've been thinking. Life is going to be difficult, in fact it's going to be a battle to survive. People are going to start acting like animals to get what they want. I can see a time when there will be no pleases or thank-yous. Those tough enough are going to just take what they want – food, clothes ... anything.'

'What are you saying, Sarah?'

'I'm saying, Nick ... God, I wish there was an easier way ... What I am saying is, soon girls may not have the right to say no, so ...' She took a huge breath. 'So, I want you to be the first one.'

We looked at one another: her eyes searched my face, reading what she saw there.

I leaned forward to kiss her gently on the lips, my ears rang, and I felt a light burn inside me.

She smelt clean, a faint perfumed smell with something musky beneath.

Her arms came up around my head and she pulled my face to hers harder now. The pains went from my face and neck and I only felt the whisper of her hair on my bare arms and the pressure of her lips.

I felt her hunger. When I slipped my hand inside her dressing gown, I felt the beat of her heart as much as her breast beneath my fingers.

As we kissed she slipped off the dressing gown and all I knew was the heat of her body. Time meant nothing as we kissed on the bed, but still I found myself holding back until she whispered, 'I'm ready now. Do it ... I want you to do it.'

I was nervous, afraid to hurt her. But apart from a gasp she did not cry out. She only held me tightly until it was over.

An hour later I felt her hands touching me again. This time she made love to me as much as I made love to her.

Chapter Twenty-Nine

THE RETURN OF THE BEAST

The convoy left the hotel by eight. Sarah and her sisters rode in the Shogun with me. Vicki wore the glasses that Sarah had done her best to repair with sticking plaster, but she could only wear them for short periods before they began to irritate her.

Slatter? There was no sign. With any luck he'd have run into Father Slatter and the pair would have cancelled one another out.

Sarah's cheeks still carried a flush from the night before. Every so often we'd make eye contact only to break it with secretive smiles.

I constantly checked the rearview for the yellow mini-bus. If its exhaust was blowing blue smoke I was happy. That meant the faulty cylinder was still firing and burning oil. It wasn't perfect but it meant Jo, the driver, had at least adequate pulling power – the mini-bus was chocker with canned vegetables as well as its five passengers.

Before we set off Dave had tried to persuade me to ditch the Shogun and ride in the mini-bus. He told me he wasn't happy with me driving after all those knocks on the head. I told him otherwise and belted myself into the Shogun. Shaking his head, saddened by my rebel streak, he returned to the big bus up front.

We had been driving for twenty minutes when Sarah breathed in sharply.

'My God . . . Here it comes . . .'

In the rearview I saw a grey Rolls Royce come swerving along the road to overtake the convoy. Driving, larger than life, Mr Nightmare himself.

'Tug Slatter.' Sarah shook her head. 'He's found us, then. Just look at the idiot. He's going to kill himself.'

'Yip Pee,' I said under my breath. 'He'd be doing us a big favour if he did . . . Jesus, what's he playing at?'

Where Slatter had got the Roller from I don't know but he was driving the car so it scraped down the full length of a stone wall, grating paint, chrome trim and mirrors off the car in a spray of debris.

'Why's he doing that?' asked Anne.

'Because he is completely mad,' replied Sarah.

'I know him of old,' I told them. 'He enjoys destroying property. The more someone values it the more he gets a kick from trashing it.'

Vicki shrieked. 'Look, he's trying to run down the dog! Oh . . . He's killed it. The rotten man killed the puppy.'

I looked down the line of crawling vehicles. 'He's gone right over the top of it. He's not hit it.'

The puppy staggered, shaken, into the grass verge. Behind us the mini-bus stopped and Jo ran across to pick it up. She looked it over then hugged it like it was a baby before running back to the mini-bus.

Slatter sped off along the road to disappear into the distance. The convoy crawled on. Rain began to fall again: huge drops like glass balls exploded on the car.

We rolled through a small village, complete with pond and ducks and a rustic church.

'Ooh,' said Vicki, 'look at that big cross in the churchyard. Doesn't Jesus look funny?'

'Heads down, girls,' I said quickly. 'And keep them down. Sarah, don't look. It's not worth it.'

She turned her head the other way to watch the ducks splashing in the pond. 'What is it?'

I whispered, 'When was the last time you saw Jesus wearing a wristwatch?'

Someone had nailed their own son to the cross.

The land changed. Hills swelled out of the fields and the trees looked wilder as we headed away from the flat agricultural lands that run from Doncaster to York. Villages got smaller, signs of civilization fewer.

It seemed as if Family Creosote, as soon as they had finished what business they had with their sons and daughters, had simply walked away from their homes to join the mass migration.

At a bend in the road, a neat section of fence had been chopped out. I looked along the set of tyre tracks across the turf to where a lake began. The top half of the grey Rolls Royce showed above the water.

The convoy slowed and Slatter climbed onto the truck in front.

'One day he'll break his thick neck,' I said, 'or someone will do it for him.'

The rain got heavier, crackling on the metal work around us. It made the hills look bleak.

We reached a motorway that cut the landscape in two and saw them moving from north to south.

It was the same as I'd seen on the motorway near Wentbridge, a river of human beings. Adult-kind were still following the call of something wonderful that we could not see.

Sarah looked at me, her eyes wide. 'You told me about it, but it's fantastic. Look at them all. Look at the expressions on their faces. It's like they've been promised the second coming.'

'It's scary,' said Anne.

Vicki pulled on her taped glasses. 'Will mummy and daddy be down there?'

'No.'

'Why do they look like that? They look like children on Christmas morning.'

I shook my head. 'God knows . . . Come on, Dave, get a move on. It's not safe to hang around here.'

We were crawling along a road that ran parallel to the motorway which ran along a deep cutting below us. The grassed banks were steep but it wouldn't take the Creosotes long to climb up to our road.

I glanced back at the mini-bus. Happily, it still pumped out plenty of blue smoke. In the front passenger seat a girl held the rescued puppy.

As we drove I couldn't stop looking down at the people river. One of them stood on a car roof in the middle of the motorway. He stared south, as if he was pointing the way with his chin.

It was as we rolled past on the road above him that his head moved abruptly, like a hawk spotting fresh prey.

I looked down into those homicidal eyes glaring up at us and I felt a wave of liquid ice roll through me.

'Hurry it up, Dave,' I hissed, 'they've spotted us.'

Ahead the road curved to the left and up to cross over a bridge to the other side of the motorway. The lead bus followed the road round.

Then stopped.

Dave and Jonathan climbed out.

'Idiots!' I punched the steering wheel. 'They can't stop here!'

Down on the motorway the people river had stopped flowing. When they saw us a ripple ran through them.

At the head of the convoy Dave and Jonathan were talking and looking at something on the bridge I could not see.

'Damn. Sarah. Get ready to drive if that lot down there start to climb the banking.'

'Where you going? Nick. Stay here!'

'Don't worry, I'm just going to kick ass. If we stay here much longer we'll be dead.'

Vicki and Anne let out squeals of fear.

Swearing noisily, I ran hard to the head of the convoy.

'What's wrong? We can't stop here.'

'Well, we can't go on.'

'Like bollocks we can't.'

'Look.'

Three burnt-out cars had shunted together on the bridge blocking the way. I kicked a stone. 'Damn it, Dave, they're only poxy cars!'

'Nick, we'll need everyone out to roll them clear.'

'Oh yeah, and in thirty seconds they'll be torn limb from limb. Haven't you noticed what's on the motorway?'

'Nick, fetch Martin Del-Coffey, we'll discuss what's best to—'

'Stuff Del-Coffey.' I snapped. 'We need to shift those wrecks now.'

'Nick, I think—'

'Button it, Dave ... The pair of you, back on the bus and be ready to roll.'

I ran back to the third truck and yanked open the door. Slatter lay on the driver's bunk, staring at the ceiling, smoking a cigarette. I jumped on the step to the cab. And pushed the driver. 'Get across into the passenger seat. Quick. I don't care if you do have to sit on Curt's knee. Do it, if you want to see dinner time ... Slatter.'

'Piss off, Aten. I'm busy.'

'How would you like a wager?'

'You've got nothing I want. Or nothing I can't take from you.'

'Oh, yes, I have. I've got a litre of vodka. And I know you've nothing left.'

He raised his eyebrows in a couldn't-care-less way. I hoped my shot in the dark was right, that he'd pissed all his booze against a tree.

'Are you on, Slatter? Think you've the guts?'

'What we betting on?'

'That you can't use this truck to shift those cars on the bridge in the time it takes me to get back to the car.'

Slatter slid off the bunk into the driving seat and pushed me in the chest. I fell back into the road.

By the time I'd got to my feet he'd shifted gear and was pumping the truck forward like an armour-piercing shell. I heard Curt screaming.

I walked backwards to the Shogun watching as the truck two-wheeled it round the bend, thundered onto the bridge and hit the cars.

A tank couldn't have done it better. The tangled wrecks split as easily as tangerine segments in a blast of glass and metal. The truck lumbered uphill and stopped at the top.

I made the Shogun as the lead bus followed the truck across the bridge.

'Nick. Hurry. They're coming up the banks.'

Sarah pointed. They were swarming up like flood water, hundreds of them.

The convoy was slow moving off. The truck in front wasn't moving at all. 'Come on, come on ... Jesus, has someone nailed their tyres to the road or what ... Thank God for that.'

We were moving. Not as fast as I liked but the idiots were at least rolling in the right direction.

I glanced in the rearview at the yellow mini-bus. Then I looked ahead as we rolled up onto the bridge and—

Bastard.

I twisted my head to look back. There was no blue smoke pumping from the mini-bus exhaust. She'd fouled her cylinder again.

'Keep going, baby,' I hissed. 'Keep going.'

The Shogun was over the bridge. The mini-bus followed. I could see Jo frowning; all wasn't well, but at least she kept the motor pulling them forward. By her side the girl hugged the puppy to her breast.

We rumbled up the hill. I looked down to the motorway. Some of the mob had reached the top of the banking and were following the road over the bridge after us. They were running.

Sarah gripped my arm. 'Hell, look down there.'

Shit. Hundreds more of the mad bastards were swarming up the bank on our side. I shot a glance back at the mini-bus. Still following.

I shifted down a gear as we hauled up the steep hill.

Behind us the mini-bus followed, but slower. As I looked back it jerked, stopped, then began rolling back.

'Jesus Christ, it's stalled!'

You can stand on a shore and scream at a wave to stop. Does it hell. It comes roaring up the beach to bury the sand.

I yelled for them to stop. They didn't. The wave of madmen swept silently over the mini-bus. It was as simple as that.

They buried it with their bodies as they hacked at the mini-bus like it was a living monster that threatened their own lives. A side window splashed into crystals. I sat there, the Shogun crawling uphill, and I watched Jo look back at me, her hands holding the steering wheel. At her side the girl held the puppy close; she put her hand over its frightened eyes.

Then they were all gone.

All I could see were hundreds of men and women covering the mini-bus.

No one spoke. Silence rang like a bell in a vacuum.

I drove on after the convoy as it crawled toward the dark hills. The rain fell heavier. Cold filled the car.

We were a little thread of frightened humanity crawling between a black heaven and wet earth.

We had all seen our own futures back there, stamped to death on the road. We were without hope. All we could do was keep moving and pray to God that the death shadow that followed wouldn't catch us – at least for a little while longer.

THE SECOND PART

HOW OLD WERE YOU WHEN YOU LOST YOUR VIRGINITY?
WHO WAS THE LAST PERSON YOU SLEPT WITH?
PICK FIVE WORDS TO DESCRIBE YOURSELF.
DO YOU BELIEVE IN GOD?
IF YOU COULD HAVE ANY QUESTION ANSWERED, WHAT
WOULD IT BE?
       (EXCERPT FROM A TYPICAL CELEBRITY
              QUESTIONNAIRE)

Chapter Thirty

DO THIS, BECAUSE THERE'S NO TOMORROW

SEX. BOOZE. GUNS. DRUGS. FAST BIKES – FASTER CARS AND LOUD, LOUD, *LOUD* MUSIC.

Christ! Life is fun!

PICTURE THIS.

A long, sizzling hot summer. Eskdale – a valley miles from anywhere, with woods and fields and meadows, and just slipping through it a cool, cool stream.

Bang in the middle of the hillside sits the hotel. It's a hundred years old, and has a garden so big you could graze a herd of buffalo there – and the lot is surrounded by a ten-foot-high brick wall.

LISTEN TO THIS.

The place is alive with three hundred shouting kids. They're in the middle of the biggest party planet Earth has ever seen. They run round the gardens, roll on the lawns and bounce around the patio.

Teenagers stripped of everything but their laughter splash in the outdoor pool, spray from naked bodies hitting the water flashes like diamonds in the sunlight. Couples frigging in the deep end send waves breaking across the tiled paths.

That loud, LOUD music beats from the speakers the size of basketball players' coffins. At the instrumental break the kids stop

what they're doing – and I mean everything they're doing – to yell to
the beat:

NO SCHOOL!
NO RULES!
NO SHIT!
YEE-OWW!!!

And they howl like rutting werewolves.

SMELL THIS!

Curt's cigar, it's the size of a chair leg. A hundred cigarettes
turning the air blue. On the lawn a pig roasts on an open fire.

FEEL THIS!

I'm on the Harley D, powering down the drive to the gatehouse,
the wind zithering my hair, tyres drumming the cobblestones,
tickling you from head to timbuch-too. Sarah sits up tight behind,
burying her face into my neck and laughing until she can laugh no
more. Her blonde hair blowing straight back like a pennant.

The open-top Porsche we're racing skids into the orchard, smacks
into a tree, knocks apples down like rain. Jonathan spills his beer
and rolls out laughing in a stream of apples.

I shout back over the engine, 'Hungry?'

'Starved!'

'Let's go bite some hot pig.' I ride up through the trees by the
statues of Eros and Artemis, up the lawn to the mother of all
barbies. We rip the pig and get stuck into the hot juicy meat.

'Trouser's going to have to stop screwing,' I said as the seventeen-
year-old came staggering out of the bushes, pulling up the gold
trousers that gave him his name. 'The twat can hardly walk.'

Grinning, he held up eight fingers.

'Eight today?' I shook a handful of steaming pig at him. 'Aye, and
the rest.'

We left the Harley Davison for someone else to ride and walked
back to the pool where bottles and cans were set out on tables along
with buckets full of cigars, cigarettes, pills – the full nine yards.

'Oh, baby . . . Oh, bay-beeee . . .' Curt looked as if he was going
to say something vital about the survival of homo sapiens but his
eyes glazed and he collapsed back onto the sun lounger, the cigar
resting on his stomach. When it burnt through his Zippo T-shirt he
yelped and rolled off into the pool.

'Hey, Nick ... me old buddy, Nick Aten.' Big amiable smile plastered on his face, Boxer, a giant with a dandelion clock fuzz of black hair dropped one of his paws onto my head. 'How you doing?'

'I'm doing fine, Boxer.'

'Listen, Nick, mate. What you gone and done with your buddy, Slatter?'

'Slatter! My buddy? You've got to be kidding ... Hey, pass a can, no, not Buds, the Special Brew ... No, thank Jesus and his merry men, I haven't set eyes on Slatter in a fortnight.'

Boxer chuckled, well sozzled. 'He's a bloody weird one, isn't he? It's like trying to hold a conversation with that statue over there ... Good tattoos though. I'd have 'em done like those but they don't show up with skin this colour. Listen, listen, Nick, mate, when we've sobered up after this one ... D' ya want to come with me and Jonathan and what's-iss-name to get some more ammo for the Kalashnikov? Christ, I didn't think I'd be able to say that, I'm well gone ... Kalashnikov. Yeah, do fancy it, if ... if your lady love'll let you go ...' He chuckled and patted my head in his friendly big giant kind of way.

Sarah smiled. 'Only if you look after him this time. I don't call camping out in the nearest bar you come to for three days an effective supply-finding expedition.'

'If it wasn't for Curt dropping his cigar down the back seat of the car and setting it on fire we'd have been back the same day ... Oh, blimey, here comes Jonathan. What's he got this time? Nick! Get down! He's aiming for your head!'

Jonathan had made it back from the Porsche with a load of apples in his T-shirt. He lobbed them like hand grenades at me. They fell short into the pool, one bouncing on the head, Newton-style, of a youth kissing a girl. They never even noticed.

With a wild laugh Jonathan jumped in the pool. He surfaced, shouting, 'You know this is a great way to wash your clothes. Now for spin dry.' He hauled himself out of the pool and went whirling away across the lawn, spinning water drops from his outstretched arms.

Sarah and I sat side by side watching the revel. Overhead the sky turned deep blue as the sun floated down to the hills. Music beat up the air. There was wall to wall talking, laughing, eating, drinking. Two hooligans arm wrestled, naked seventeen-year-old girls ran through the wood, Simon was spitting whisky into the barbecue. It burst into balls of flame that singed his eyebrows. He did it again.

Behind us half a dozen thirteen-year-old boys were tattooing each others' noses and cheekbones with the Red Indian Brave look that was the numero uno at the moment.

The music hit the instrumental link, to the rhythm everyone chanted:

NO SCHOOLS!
NO RULES!
NO SHIT!
YEE-OWOWOW...

Then the music abruptly cut, and there was ear-bruising silence.

Pause, then: 'Jesus Christ . . . Not again . . .'

'That's the tenth time in three days . . .'

'Eleven.'

'Where's Dave?'

'Someone get Dave freaking Middleton. What's he playing at?'

'Curt was saying that he cuts the generator deliberately.'

'Miserable dog.'

Someone went to fetch Dave Middleton; we grumbled, feeling suddenly awkward now the music had gone. 'Noise keeps you clothed. Silence makes you naked,' said a girl.

We beat empty beer cans together like cymbals until Dave Middleton arrived.

So, you'll realize a lot of stuff'd flown under the bridge since Dave Middleton's convoy rumbled through the hotel gates that day in April.

The first few weeks went the way Dave planned. He and the Steering Committee efficiently drew up work programmes that got everyone busy. Scavenging parties went out in trucks; pretty soon the barns we were using for stores were stacked from floor to roof joist with food, shoes, clothes, hardware. Thanks to our discovery of an abandoned BNFL security post on the road between Calder Bridge and Sellafield, we even had a respectable armoury of assorted firearms and *mucho* ammo.

We collected more survivors – the community grew fast, adding more skills so we could look after ourselves better. A seventeen-year-old girl joined who'd been a trainee nurse. Boxer had actually been in the army eight months before civilization bellied up. He gave us firearm training. We found generators and once more we had electricity.

I captained Beta scavenging team and we ranged further and further from Eskdale, bringing back fuel by the tanker load, cylinders of gas for cooking and heating.

We saw the cities were looking weird now.

Plants were beginning to grow in town centre streets. Corpses had become skeletons. We began to have trouble with wild dogs so we'd shoot a few to remind them that humans were still kings of the world.

In one town a river had broken its banks and now flowed down the high street, complete with otters swimming in and out through Woolworth's doorways, and ducks nesting in Burger King.

Animals had been escaping from zoos and circuses. In Nottler we saw a troop of monkeys hanging out at the police station. There were elephants wallowing in the local canal.

The summer got hotter. And that's when things started to change.

People got tired of hard work day after day, they got tired of Steering Committee work rotas, they got tired of Dave Middleton full bloody stop.

Scavengers still went out in their trucks but instead of returning with the flour on Dave's list they came back piled high with cigarettes, sound systems, games machines, motorbikes.

Dave reasoned with them. He prayed for them.

And the kids realised he didn't carry a big stick.

For the last couple of months ninety-nine percent of us had dedicated ourselves to one, shining, golden goal.

FUN.

Thirty or so kids locked themselves into the attic rooms with the games machines and we didn't see them from one day to the next. Occasionally one would wander out. White face, dark eyes, unhealthy looking, but brain fizzing with strategies for the electronic battles they fought. We called them The Spooks.

So: Whatever you want to do – DO IT!

That was the national anthem now. You like bikes. Great, get the biggest, fastest mother you can and torch up and down the roads all day.

Guns? Grab your Uzi and go waste some sheep.

Some just liked to relax fishing. Only the way they did it was to go up to the reservoirs and chuck in sticks of dynamite.

The rest partied.

We looked different now. Clothes got spectacular. Tattooing your face was IN for the under-fifteens.

Martin Del-Coffey didn't like what was happening. He quietly oozed off to shack up with his books, computers ... oh, and Kitty, in a house down in the village.

Slatter more or less kept himself to himself. Sometimes he'd beat people up for a little light entertainment but the only bother I got from him was verbal.

Sarah and I shared a grand room overlooking the driveway.

We hadn't seen a single Creosote since we reached Eskdale. And life was twice as nice as paradise.

Boxer was angry. 'What the hell kept you, Middleton?'

'I've been unblocking the drain again ... You – you just can't keep stuffing anything you like down the toilets and expect it to flush away. When we worked out—'

'The generator's packed in again. What the hell you doing with it?'

'Me?' Dave moved in the jerky, twitchy way he'd developed lately. 'Me? Can I be everywhere at once?' He looked round at us; his eyes like piss-holes in the snow. 'I'm working eighteen-hour days to keep this place functioning. I get no help, I only get abuse. No one does anything any more. You're animals ...'

Laughter.

'I – I planted crops in the spring. You used the fields for your truck races. Everything's ruined.'

'We've got food, you stupid twat,' shouted Curt. 'Why should we work like slaves when we've got everything we need?'

Everyone agreed.

Boxer spat. 'Get the generator back on.'

'I don't know if I can, I ...'

'What's wrong with it?'

'It might be out of fuel, it could be ... I – I don't know ... just wearing out. I—'

'Who's supposed to maintain it?'

Dave had to massage his aching head before pulling out a name. 'Anthony ... Yes, yes ... Anthony.'

Boxer bunched his fists, bad tempered now. 'Where's Anthony?'

Curt said, 'He's one of the damn Spooks. It's that lot with their computers that are draining off all the power.'

'You!' Boxer pointed to a twelve-year-old boy. 'Fetch Anthony. Now!'

The boy ran off to the hotel.

We waited, awkward. These days silence was the thing that was too loud. We needed music to kill it.

The boy returned.

'Boxer ... Anthony says he's too busy to come down, and he wants to know why the power's off again.'

'Shit.' I thought Boxer was about to detonate. 'Go back and get Anthony. Curt, you go with him. Drag him back by his hair if you have to.'

I looked at Sarah. She raised her eyebrows. We'd not seen Boxer as mad as this.

Minutes later, the boy and Curt returned with a dozen sulky Spooks. Even the sunset was too bright for them and they rubbed their sore eyes.

'Which one's Anthony?' snapped Boxer.

'Me,' said a lanky, grey-faced teenager. 'Why are the generators out?'

'That's what we want to know.'

'Why ask me? Middleton sees to it.'

'But you were on the rota. It's your responsibility, Spook.'

Dave watched: his tired eyes registered that something was building. So did the crowd round the swimming pool. No one talked.

Anthony got defensive. 'I've not touched the thing in weeks. So why the hell should I do it?'

The Spooks nodded. They sided with Anthony.

'But you were trained to look after it,' said Dave in a low voice.

'You were supposed to strip it down every three weeks to clean the plugs.'

'Why should I be the one? You're doing damn all, Boxer. You do it.'

I saw it coming. Anthony did not.

Boxer's fist blurred through the twilight. The punch slammed square in the middle of the Spook's face. He went down flat.

For a second I thought he was actually dead. He stared up at the sky, the eyes sightless. Then he blinked and gave a moaning kind of cry. Blood ran down his T-shirt like a waterfall.

The Spooks cringed backwards.

'Stand still, you zombie shits . . . I said stand still.' Boxer's army training came back. The Spooks ignored him and began to move back to the hotel.

In a single movement Boxer slid the heavy leather belt from his jeans and laid into the Spooks, using the belt like a whip.

They came back yelping, their hands and faces covered in red marks. One tried to run for it. Boxer expertly tripped him, then yanked him vertical by the hair. The Spook howled.

When they were in line, Boxer snarled, 'I am sick of this. No discipline. Everyone doing what they damn well like. That goes for everyone. Not just the Spooks. In future everyone listens to Dave Middleton – they do what he says. Or . . .'

Boxer pulled Anthony to his feet and showed us his splattered nose. 'Or . . . there are going to be a hell of a lot more people looking like this.'

Totally unexpected – but suddenly we had order once more.

It lasted fourteen days.

And Dave Middleton, standing there exhausted, and shocked by the unChristian behaviour, had twenty-two days more to live.

Chapter Thirty-One

'IF WE'RE GOING TO SURVIVE, WE NEED TO LEARN MORE'

By the following morning it'd become clear Boxer was king. He said he wasn't, that Dave Middleton was still in charge. But Boxer called the shots now.

After breakfast people were assigned 'duties' and were hard at work again. The party was over.

As I walked down toward the tanker truck I'd been ordered to service, a cigarette butt bounced down onto the ground in front of me.

I looked up, squinting against the sun. Ten feet above my head, sitting astride the stable roof, like the Devil himself, was Tug Slatter. The first thing I noticed were his pit boots.

Usually they were clean. Now they were pasted in so much dried blood it looked as if he'd paddled through a slaughter house.

'What's been happening, Aten?'

In as few words as I could I told him. The last thing I wanted was to stand chatting to the tattooed ape.

Slatter spat, missing me by a yard. 'About time someone took charge. Middleton's shit.'

I didn't disagree. 'What about you, Slatter? You haven't been around for a couple of weeks. Been far?'

'Far enough. My old man caught up with me. He'd been following me ever since we left the farmhouse where that Keene bitch snuffed it.'

'Where is he now?'

'I sorted him out.'

I looked back up at his bloody boots and didn't have to try hard to guess what had happened.

'Aten. You'll have to do the same with yours.'

'My parents? The last time I saw them was on the Selby road before we got here.'

'That's because you go round with your faggot eyes shut.'

Slatter swung himself round, bloody boots leaving rust-coloured smears on the stone wall and disappeared.

I shook my head and carried on walking. It was a typical Slatter wind-up. Mum and dad were miles away. They might even be dead.

I reached the truck, pulled out the tool kit from the cab and set to work. Boxer wanted the truck to bring back more fuel before winter set in.

Ten minutes later Martin Del-Coffey ambled up, laces trailing through the dust.

'You look busy, Mr Aten.'

'That's because I am. We don't see much of you these days. What do you want?'

'You don't beat about the bush, do you, Mr Aten?' He looked at his clean fingernails. 'I heard what happened last night, and that Eskdale has a new lord and master. What's he like?'

'Boxer? He's seventeen. He trained for a few months as a soldier. If you ask me, deep down he felt guilty about partying all summer with the rest of us. What he really craves is order and discipline. I guess in a few weeks we'll all be in uniform and saluting.'

'Well, in a situation like this, you need a leader who wields a big stick. Middleton's democratic, let's-all-co-operate-as-reasonable-human-beings modus-operandi was doomed to failure.'

'Oh, so you saw it all coming, did you, Del-Coffey? Is that why you took off to live in the village?'

'I needed peace to work.'

I snorted and hammered loose the air filter.

Del-Coffey went on, 'He's got the right leadership qualities then?'

'How the hell should I know? I'm a grease monkey. I can't give you a psychological personality profile, can I?'

'Maybe not, but you're streetwise, Nick Aten, you know the kind who rises to the top of the pecking order. The kind of guy who can lead a gang.'

'Boxer's no bully. He's not bright but with a bit of guidance from Middleton he'll get the community in shape again.'

'So he's the kind of person who'll listen to reason?'

'Ah . . . So you *did* have a motive for coming up here.' I blew dirt off the filter. 'You want something from him.'

Del-Coffey smiled. 'See, you're not as ignorant as you pretend, Nick. Very perceptive of you. The truth is I need help with research. Kitty and I are working every hour God sends.'

'You won't get it. Boxer's told us plain and simple – what's done is done. All he wants here is a comfortable routine with everyone sticking to a timetable.'

'I'll reason with him.'

'Your funeral, Del-Coffey. Curt tried to persuade Boxer that getting up before nine was a mug's game. Now Curt's lip looks like it's got a chunk of raw meat stitched to it.'

'Listen, Nick. The Creosotes are changing. They might pose a greater threat now than they did back when this catastrophe started.'

Del-Coffey looked round as if afraid he would be overheard, then he leaned forward. 'Three weeks ago I saw twenty Creosotes gather on the big hill that looks over the hotel. They arrived about an hour before sunset. You lot were in the middle of a party, and so stoned you probably couldn't see much past the end of your noses, never mind half a mile away.' Del-Coffey's hands shook, excited. 'I watched through my telescope. They just stood there and very, very intently watched what was going on in the hotel grounds. At dusk they turned round and walked away over the brow of the hill.'

'They just stood and watched?' I looked up at his face. 'So? That's good news, isn't it? They watch but they no longer attack us.'

'They haven't attacked yet. That doesn't mean they won't try in the future. If we're going to survive, we need to know more.'

'Well, there's only twenty of them. There's three hundred of us – and we've enough guns and ammo to fight a war.'

'But if you could have seen their faces, Nick. You look at them and you know, *you just know*, they are planning something.' He took a deep breath. 'From my findings over the last few months, my conjecture is that adults are undergoing some kind of transformation here.' Del-Coffey tapped his head. 'What we saw in Doncaster, that savage and insane behaviour, was only the first stage in a continuing process. Adults are undergoing a psychological metamorphosis. Although their bodies are the same their minds are being retuned. Like when you buy improved software for your computer, the hardware's the same but its performance is better. Do you follow? Or if you replace the engine in your car with a more powerful one ... Remember Slatter's father? He could hear things none of us could. I watched those adults on the hill. They were half a mile away and yet they could see what was going on at the hotel as if they were looking through binoculars. And listen to this ... I was in the house in the village, and when I called Kitty to the telescope, the Creosotes on the hill actually turned their heads to look down at my house. They had actually heard me. No, Nick, don't pull a face, it's not fantasy. The changes in their heads have radically improved the way they process data coming in through the senses: hearing, seeing, smell ... I'd put their audio ability on a par with a dog's, which is very good indeed.'

'Okay, Martin. So, you're telling me this: a bunch of loonies that look like tramps are turning into supermen.'

'No, not exactly. But the psychological metamorphosis is improving certain aspects of their minds.'

'Well ...' I wiped my hands on a rag. 'You go tell Boxer that and he'll either laugh you to shit or he'll crack your nose.'

'It's true, Nick. We need to send teams out to conduct field research. We need to know where the Creosotes migrated to; we need to know who they were signalling to; what the symbols laid out in fields meant and what—'

'Where are those Creosotes now? If Boxer sees them he might at least hear you out.'

Del-Coffey shrugged. 'God knows. They stayed two days to watch the hotel. Now they've disappeared. I found signs they had stayed in the next valley up near the dam.'

'What you need to do is show Boxer a mob of blood-thirsty

Creosotes ... Words like 'research,' 'hypotheses' and 'psychology' don't exist in his vocabulary.'

Del-Coffey pulled an envelope from his back pocket. 'I've got photographs.'

'How did you get these?'

'On the second evening. I managed to sneak up the next hill with the camera and a telephoto lens.'

The black and white photographs were as clear as I expected them to be, taken as they had been by Eskdale's resident genius. They showed twenty men and women, watching the hotel and its residents at play. They looked like naturalists closely observing our behaviour patterns – as if they would take that knowledge away and use it in some strategy they were creating.

Their clothes were shabby, hair long, scruffy, the men bearded. An old man carried a long pole. Ever eaten a kebab with vegetables and meat on a skewer? There were little heads threaded on the pole.

Del-Coffey pointed to the man with the pole. 'That's my uncle. He helped my mother raise me. And those,' he pointed to the head pole. 'I think those are my cousins.'

Suddenly the bees buzzing through the flowers sounded very loud. I pointed to the photograph of a man and a woman standing on the brow of the hill.

'And those are my parents.'

Chapter Thirty-Two

SEX AND MURDER

The fourteen days were up.

Dave Middleton had seven days left.

'Oh...'

'I didn't hurt you?'

'No ... Nice ... Oh, very, very nice.'

I lay on my back, Sarah above me: the early morning sunshine penetrated the curtains in a blaze of flaming glory.

Naked, she pressed down onto me, sighing, letting her head drop forward so her hair washed across my bare chest.

Boxer's orders. Work six days a week. On the seventh day it's R&R. Rest and Recreation. Sarah and I hungrily obeyed.

She kissed my face and throat and chest, moving hard now, panting. My hands caressed her breasts, tanned golden by day after day of sunshine.

'Don't leave me, don't you ever leave me, don't, ah ... Nick, don't leave me ... promise.'

'I promise ... Ah ... I'd be mad ... to leave ... this ... You are BEAUTIFUL! JESUS...'

Ten minutes later we lay still, limbs and bedding tangled, watching the dust motes ride the sunbeams.

'It's better, isn't it, Nick?'

'It gets better every time.'

'No ...' She giggled. 'I'm not talking about sex now. The community's better now Boxer's in charge.'

'Don't you miss the awesome powers you used to wield on the Steering Committee?'

'No. Power seems attractive when you haven't got it. When you have it, it brings problems, loads and loads of problems.'

'Such as?'

'Jealousy. Some people, Nick Aten, resented being told what to do. Don't pull a face, it's true. And there was responsibility for people's lives and well-being. We lost people on the way here. If we'd been smarter and more experienced they'd still be alive now ...'

'You're thinking of Jo and the others in the mini-bus?'

'In fact, they would still be alive if we'd listened to you, Nick.'

We talked for a while. The situation did seem better; we were even relieved that the summer-long party was over; it had, maybe, been a kind of wake for our past life, family and friends who had been obliterated on that day in April.

Sarah stroked my stomach thoughtfully. 'Dave Middleton's happier now; things aren't being run exactly the way he wants but at least there's some kind of order, the community's working again. And he was right, you know. One day we're going to have to learn to survive properly and that means planting crops, looking after live-stock, even making our own clothes and tools.'

I grunted. Sarah's gentle stroking was more interesting than what she was saying.

'The only person who's still cheesed off,' she said, 'is Martin. Did you hear about when he went to Boxer to ask for people to be assigned for research? What he got were Boxer's boots to polish. Six pairs. Nick, are you listening? Nick ... Ahhh! Not with your tongue – it tickles ...'

Shrieking with laughter, she pulled me over her. We rolled onto the floor laughing.

We were still making love when we heard the gunshots.

Someone was shooting rats, or crows, or tin cans – who cared. Sarah's long legs were wrapped around my back. This was my universe beneath a cotton sheet – a place full of heat, excitement and endless delight.

* * *

The hammering on the door came fifteen minutes later.

'Nick! Sarah!' Dave's voice came through the door like a bullet. 'Get downstairs as quickly as you can! Something terrible's happened.'

'What's wrong? Dave, what is it?' called Sarah as she pulled on her T-shirt. Dave was already gone, hammering on other bedroom doors down the passageway.

As I dragged on my jeans the feeling hit me as bright as the bloody sunshine. 'The shit's just gone and hit the fan again.'

We stood under the apple trees looking down at him.

Dave pointed with a stick. 'Eight, nine . . . ten. Holy Father, the poor boy. There's another one. Eleven bullet wounds.'

Whoever had shot Boxer had done a thorough job. He lay flat on his back looking like he'd been dipped in blood. One bullet had drilled through the back of his head, straight through his brain to partly erupt from his forehead. The bullet looked like a brass stud set in the skin.

'Creosotes?' asked Simon, his face as white as paper.

Dave shook his head. 'Murder.' He covered the body with a blanket. 'One of *us* did this . . . Simon. Bring a couple of the older ones to move the body to the stables. We'll bury him later. Billy . . . Christopher.' Two twelve-year-olds came forward. 'Please go round everyone in the community and ask them . . . No, tell them . . . They must assemble on the driveway in front of the main entrance at eleven o'clock sharp. I'm going to make an announcement. Janet, will you please run down to the village and ask Martin and Kitty to join me in my office. Thank you.'

At ten to eleven we were all waiting. Martin stood at the front, near the steps up to the main entrance where Dave would make his speech. Sarah had already guessed it would be a belt-tightening, shoulder-to-the-grindstone sermon, followed by an announcement that there would be democratic elections for a new Steering Committee and leader.

No one talked. The sun climbed higher. It grew hotter. Sweat began to run down my forehead.

Dave Middleton appeared. He held out his arms in the communal embrace we knew of old, his expression serious.

He opened his mouth – but he never got a chance to speak. Out from the hotel swaggered Curt and Jonathan. Curt pushed Dave firmly forward down the three steps to the driveway.

Dave turned annoyed but he shut his mouth when he saw Curt carried the Kalashnikov and Jonathan a pump-action shotgun.

Curt shouted, 'Listen. We're going to cut through the crap. Someone's topped Boxer. We're going to find out who did it – and believe me they'll wish they were never frigging well born.'

Jonathan smirked while Curt talked.

Curt lifted up the assault rifle so everyone could see it. 'Until this is sorted out, me and Jonathan are taking charge. Get it? From now on – we're your bosses.'

They'd wasted no time in breaking into Boxer's gunroom. Or maybe they just took the key from his body.

'Jonathan's going to read out a list of names. Those people come and stand behind me. The rest can piss off. Ah-ah ... When I give the order, boys and girls.'

Jonathan read out the names. Sarah caught my eye as two dozen delinquents, bullies, morons and good-for-nothing shits who had caused all the trouble in the community lined up behind Jonathan, smug grins twisting their faces.

'And just to remind you we mean business.' Curt pulled back the bolt on the Kalashnikov. 'I'll give you to the count of three to get down on your knees. One, two—' He pulled the trigger blasting a stream of bullets low over our heads.

With the explosions hammering our eardrums we scrambled on all fours across the dirt to hide in the bushes.

Chapter Thirty-Three

TYRANNY

The long, hot summer ended with a bang. The afternoon they buried Boxer the mother of all thunderstorms battered Eskdale. Rain turned fields to mud; rivers ran down the roads.

The following morning, the first day of October, as our new masters slept off the effects of the wake they had held for Boxer, I walked through the orchard under a sky full of cloud mountains. With me were Martin Del-Coffey, Sarah, Kitty and Dave. Our expressions were just plain worried.

'I really thought the community was coming together again.' Dave lightly rubbed the blister on his cheek where Curt had stubbed out his cigar after Boxer's funeral. 'Boxer maintained discipline. Everyone was back at work again.'

I said, 'Boxer could crack heads but he wasn't bright. When you're leader you have to keep looking back over your shoulder to see who's coming up with the knife.'

'So now we have these two gentlemen.' Del-Coffey sniffed. 'You know they're petty tyrants. All they'll do is run this place to gratify their own perverted appetites.'

Dave shook his head; inside he was hurting. 'Jonathan ... I can't believe it of him. He was actually in the choir of St Timothy's. He taught at Bible study classes.'

'This last few months has changed people,' said Sarah. 'By all accounts Curt had been in trouble with the police over the last few years: Nick's told me if there was a fight in a nightclub Curt was often at the back of it.'

'But he always disappeared as soon as the fists began to fly,' I added. 'Now he's developed into a real hard nut.'

Sarah looked at each of us sharply. 'I don't think we're under any illusion who murdered Boxer yesterday?'

Del-Coffey looked round uneasily as if the apple trees had fruited ears.

Sarah drove on. 'Curt and Jonathan did it. They lured Boxer down here, then shot him. They had this takeover planned.'

Kitty said in her soft Asian tones, 'And from what I have seen they are quite shrewd. Immediately they have recruited those who might pose a future threat to them and are buying their loyalty with possessions and power. And from what I have heard on the grapevine Curt is going to create a harem for himself.'

Del-Coffey picked an apple from the tree. 'And these girls are going to have no choice in the matter. You can add rape to the crime of murder.'

I suddenly felt uncomfortable. 'Hey, hold on. Is this a meeting of the Steering Committee or what? You are talking as if we're actually going to do something about all this. You know there's no cops we can go to; we can't stick those guys in jail.'

'That's exactly what we're saying.' Dave's red-rimmed eyes fixed on me. 'Nick, we have to take back ... no, seize, grab onto control of this community and never let go. If we don't, all we can look forward to in the short term is torture and slavery from those thugs ... In the long term we'll die – you can be sure of that. If we're not farming the land within the next twelve months we'll die of starvation.'

'And death might come faster than that.' Del-Coffey bit into the apple. 'Tell them, Kitty.'

'Martin and I have continued to study the affected adults we call Creosote. There are small groups moving round the area. Everyone has seen the photographs Martin has taken. Some of the individuals have been identified as mothers and fathers of members of our community.'

'But they don't pose a threat, do they?' I objected. 'The most they've done is watch their sons and daughters here at the hotel. At the moment that seems as life-threatening as mummy and daddy walking down to school at play-time to watch their kids playing hopscotch.'

'But don't you see, Nick?' Sarah sounded exasperated. 'There is some instinct that drives our parents to find us. And to watch us. We all know what happened six months ago. Martin and Kitty believe it will happen again. Only this time it won't be a frenzied, mindless attack. Nick, our mothers and fathers are studying us . . . Then they will work out a way of finishing what they started.'

'So,' said Dave, 'what we need to do is this: we will—'

'Dave . . . Not that way. Keep away from the hotel.' Del-Coffey cut off towards the bottom of the orchard. His voice dropped to a whisper. 'In a day or two our new bosses are going to get very paranoid. Every time they see more than two people talking together – the way we're doing at present – they're going to suspect we're plotting a *coup d'état*.'

Sarah glanced back at the hotel. 'And that's exactly what we're going to have to do.'

'Look,' I said. 'I think we're being too hasty here. Why not give it a week or two? Curt might settle down once he sees being boss isn't so easy.'

Del-Coffey bit off another lump of apple. 'We can't wait. One. I've seen enough of those two to know they'll be first-rate tyrants. With Curt's sadistic streak that'll make life unpleasant for us all. Two. If Family Creosote walk up to those gates now, there's damn all we can do to stop them killing every single one of us.'

Dave said, 'This is what we do, then: we remove Curt and Jonathan as leaders. Then we appoint a new leader. Boxer, for all his faults, showed us the way. We need someone who's not afraid to discipline wrong-doers fairly but firmly – very, very firmly.'

I asked, 'Who will be leader?'

'We'll cross that bridge when we get to it,' said Dave. But I noticed he and Del-Coffey looked at one another as if sharing a secret.

'Then,' said Del-Coffey, 'we have to turn the hotel into a fortress. We've got the ten-foot walls and the gates. But we need to dig a deep ditch around the outside of the walls, then beyond that security fencing topped with barbed wire. Probably an electrified fence would be pretty useful, too. Around the perimeter we will have watch posts. We will have a team of armed guards, trained to deal with any Creosotes should they attack. Within the compound will be—'

'Wait a minute, wait a minute.' I held up a finger. 'I know I'm thinking a lot more slowly than any of you. But you said we had to remove Curt and Jonathan as leaders. It might seem a minor detail but they're armed to the teeth – so are their bodyguards. We've no guns, so how do you propose to do it?'

They looked at me as if I'd poured cold water on a flawless plan. I was sorry about that. But I remembered Boxer's bullet-punctured body. And I wanted to stay alive.

Chapter Thirty-Four

HAREM

Twenty-four hours later Sarah was still mad at me. She came back into our room, slamming the door. Her eyes flashed, her hair swung about her shoulders as she paced the floor.

I sat up in bed and groaned. 'Look, when are we going to stop this argument? What do you expect from me? I've listened to what you, Del-Coffey and Dave Middleton have said. Okay, kick out Curt and Jonathan, appoint a new leader. I agree, but how the hell do we do that? Those guys are armed and dangerous. Why not give them a few weeks? With experience they might turn out to be good leaders.'

'Not if you heard what I've just heard.'

'And what's that?'

'Do you know what happened this morning? No, you lie there in bed and rot. I'll list them for you. One: Martin Del-Coffey has some drums of fuel in his garage. Those two bastards said that they wanted them. Martin asks why. And do you know what they did, Nick? Broke two of his fingers. He didn't even say no, they couldn't have the fuel. He only asked why.' She paced, punching one hand into the other. 'Two: young children have been beaten for not keeping quiet outside our new leaders' rooms. Three: at this moment, Curt is sitting in the dining room writing a list. It's a list of girls' names. Now, listen to this . . . Curt intends to personally make all the girls on the list pregnant. He's decided we need to increase the population of the community – but with good, strong blood – his blood.'

'Christ, he's mad.' I sat up in bed. 'What are you doing?'

Sarah began to pile her clothes into a suitcase.

'Wait ... Sarah, are you on the list?'

'I'm right at the top. He says he's got a hard-on, and it'd be a shame to waste it.'

I stood and stared at her. The blood roared in my ears.

She looked at me, waiting for a reaction. Then she sighed and went to look out of the window, arms folded.

'No, that's not fair, Nick. I tried to provoke you into actually doing something about those two.'

'There is no list?'

'Oh, there's a list all right ... I'm not on it. Do you know why?'

I shrugged.

'Those two have obviously taken a shine to you, Nick Aten. You're allowed to keep me as your own personal plaything. Kitty's on the list, though. And I imagine in another two or three years so will my sisters. As Curt put it this morning, "when girls are old enough to bleed they're old enough to butcher."'

'It's sickening.'

'It is, but until someone does something about those two we're just going to have to grin and bear it.'

'Where are you going, then?'

'I'm moving in with Martin and Kitty. It's not as far away from here as I'd like but it'll have to do. Any time you want a chat you know where I'll be. Bye.'

I dressed and went outside. A cold wind blew and I knew we'd seen the last of the summer. Someone had rigged up the sound system's speakers under tarpaulins and the music still blasted as loud as it had done through those hot summer days and nights.

It was like walking through a deserted funfair. The music still plays. Only there is something mournful and lonely about it now.

Curt and Jonathan – and their bodyguards, now known as the Crew – were lining up cars on the drive. They were planning a couple of hours chasing one another across country. No doubt firing their Uzis at the sky as they went.

Sarah had said the two thought enough about me not to turn me into one of their slaves as they were doing with the rest of the community. I had got on well with them over the last few weeks, we'd had some good laughs together. But there had to be more to it than that.

I had the answer two minutes later.

One of the Crew was a car short. He saw Slatter sitting on the Porsche on the lawn.

The Crew member, looking like a rebel warrior with shades and bandanna, shotgun cockily over one shoulder, swaggered across toward Slatter.

I knew what the bodyguard intended. He'd go across to Slatter and tell him to shift off the Porsche.

Anyone else would have jumped off the car as if it was hot enough to sizzle steak.

Slatter's eyes came down from where they had been gazing over the treetops. He didn't move, he didn't say anything, he just stared with those two laser eyes at the kid.

You could see the kid just droop – his shoulders dropped, the shotgun hung down limp in his hands. He tried to treat it lightly with a nervous laugh, but you could see that Slatter had scared him.

'I'll go get the Audi,' he shouted back at his mates, then walked away from Slatter as quickly as he could.

Over the last few days I'd kept an eye on how people reacted under the new leadership – who were the lickspittles, who kept their mouths shut, who complained too much and who was likely to rebel.

Slatter was a hard case; he wasn't afraid of the terrible twosome like we were. Then, neither would Slatter side with them, nor would he try to oust them, so they knew he wasn't a threat.

At that moment I saw how they viewed him. To Curt, Jonathan and their cronies Slatter was a god. Okay, he was a Dark God, a Savage God, but a god all the same. They could have shot him as easily as they would a sheep. But we lived in superstitious times. They would have been too afraid of his ghost stamping up the stairs for them at the dead of night.

I was the only one who ever stood up to Slatter. Of course, once I nearly got my head busted, but I wasn't afraid to argue with him. So that set me apart from the rest. They respected me.

As the days passed life went from bad to worse. Beatings were run of the mill events.

Curt developed a sadistic new sport called *Carrying the Can*. People guilty of misdemeanours would have a steel pipe, six inches long and as thick as a cucumber, handcuffed to their wrist. From the end of the pipe protruded a fuse.

The game was simple. At the top of the church tower in the village was a glass jar. In the jar a key.

Back at the hotel, the victim stood on the entrance steps while the fuse was lit.

It took ten minutes to reach the gunpowder in the pipe. And it took ten minutes for a fit person to reach the top of the church tower.

You run fast enough. Hey presto. You get to the top of the church tower in time, unlock the cuff and chuck the pipe away from you just in time to see it go up in a puff of smoke.

If you're not fast enough (or for extra laughs they lock the gates to the drive) you're running like billy-oh and – BOOM. You have flash burns on your hands and arms, scorched hair and you're deaf as a post for a couple of days.

Dave pleaded with them to moderate their behaviour. They laughed, then stood on his hands whilst they stubbed cigarettes out on his face.

I saw nothing of Sarah, and when a chance came for me to bring back more fuel for the generators I volunteered fast.

Curt told me they couldn't spare fuel for a car to take me to Ulverston, where a tanker full of fuel waited to be picked up (though they had all they needed for their mindless races), so I'd have to walk which would take me a full day.

Again, I didn't really mind. Eskdale was getting claustrophobic. You hardly dared breathe in case one of the Crew took it as an insult. Then you, too, ended up *Carrying The Can*.

I headed south, seeing no Creosotes as I walked along the country lanes.

I still hoped that Curt and Jonathan would settle down. That they'd see the place would fall apart if they didn't start people working for the benefit of the whole community, not just for the luxury of a lucky few.

Dave Middleton didn't share my optimism. Even as I walked out of Eskdale on that cold October day he must have been planning what he'd say, and what he'd do when I returned.

Chapter Thirty-Five

CARRYING THE CAN

Because of shit weather and deteriorating roads, it took me two days to get the tanker back to Eskdale.

After parking up, I was walking toward the hotel entrance when Simon ran toward me like he was on fire.

He was *Carrying The Can*. His eyes bled terror; he was sobbing as he ran down the drive in the direction of the church.

Nothing's changed, I thought. But it had.

'What's wrong with Simon?' I asked Trousers, who stood watching the youth run. 'It's only a spoonful of gunpowder. He'll do himself more mischief running like that.'

Trousers looked at me, his face blazing with a mixture of terror and sheer heart-pumping excitement. 'They've changed the rules. Curt's stuffed the pipe with gelignite!'

'Jesus Christ . . .' I turned to watch. Dozens more leaned through the hotel windows to watch, too.

Simon belted through the gates at the bottom of the drive, followed the road down through the village to where it crossed the stream, then climbed steeply up to the church.

At this distance he was tiny, but there was something desperate in the way he moved, the silver pipe clutched in his hands.

The time. I looked at my watch. Seven minutes had gone by. He'd time to climb the stairs in the churchtower, pluck the key from the jar, then—

From the distance came a faint ripping crack that echoed from the outbuildings.

I looked across toward the church. A puff of smoke was drifting down-wind. Simon was no longer running.

Someone had shortened the fuse.

Above me I heard a cheer, then laughter. The sound suddenly went faraway. I walked down to the orchard. There I was sick, cursed God and wished I'd never returned to Eskdale.

On the last day of Dave Middleton's life he asked me to go with him to repair the pump that pushed water from the spring to the hotel. During the ten-minute walk he talked about the usual subjects that troubled him.

'Curt and Jonathan are out of control ... They're so unpredictable ... It must be the pills they're taking.'

'I don't see there's much we can do,' I said. 'They've got their own army.'

'There has to be a solution ... I'm too exhausted to carry on. It's down to me that the generators keep turning and that there's fresh water in the tanks, and the toilets work. Look at that.'

His bare arms were stained brown. 'At six this morning I was digging human excrement out of the sewers. When there was no gas to cook their majesties' breakfast they did this ... there, on my eye lid ... There's more on the back of my neck. See? Cigarette burns.'

'You could just walk away from it all.'

'We've got children as young as six weeks old here. You think I'm going to leave them? It's called responsibility, Nick. You can't shrug your shoulders and walk away into the sunset.'

I pulled open the door of the pumphouse. 'Right, what's wrong with it?'

Dave shrugged. 'You're the expert.'

'There's still plenty of fuel.'

'You remember what was said in the orchard the day after Boxer was murdered.'

'Yeah, the revolution. You might as well sit on a pig and hope it sprouts bacon wings to fly you to paradise.'

'Curt and Jonathan can be deposed. With a little forward planning.'

'And with a truckload of guns with people willing and able to use them . . . Hey, there's nothing wrong with the pump. Someone's just switched off the motor.' I fired it into life, then looked up at Dave. He was trembling.

'I wanted to bring you down here so we could talk privately.' Dave held out a plastic carrier bag. 'Take this.'

'Dave. What're you playing at? If Curt finds out you've been messing with the water supply you'll end up *Carrying The Can*. Jesus Christ . . . Where did you get this?'

Lying in the bottom of the carrier bag like it was a tin of baked beans was a handgun.

'It's loaded,' said Dave. 'I found it under the seat of the Mercedes Boxer used to drive.'

Dave looked weird now. Like he'd begun a dangerous sequence of events that he knew would soon be out of his hands. He wiped at the sweat running down his face.

'Dave. I don't want this. Get rid of it.'

'You'll need it.'

'I'll need it! For crying out loud, why?'

'If you're courageous enough to face up to Tug Slatter you're courageous enough to ask Curt and Jonathan to step down as leaders.'

'What are you talking about? Step down? You make it sound as though they're in charge of the local chamber of commerce. Those thugs can't be politely requested to step down.' I pulled out the gun. 'You have to take this, blow out their brains, take control, and not be afraid to use this again and again to keep it. Being a leader is a lump of damn rock tied round your neck.' Dave's eyes burned at me as I talked. 'If you're leader and there's not enough to eat and people go hungry it's your fault. If people get sick and there are no drugs to cure them, then it's your fault. If the Creosotes attack and someone gets killed it's your fault. There are a thousand things to think about, it'd be like keeping a thousand plates spinning on poles – and all the time you are looking over your shoulder to make sure no one's creeping up to stab you in the back.'

Dave said, 'In a situation like this a leader would have perks. Best room in the hotel. Food, drink. Creature comforts. I'll admit times have changed; the new leader could have a dozen wives and no one would mind.'

'I don't want a dozen wives, I want Sarah. I—'

The clever bastard had tricked me. He never even had to tell me I should be leader; I'd said it myself.

'Oh, no way, Middleton. Not me.'

'Nick, you're the natural choice ... No, listen to me. Don't walk away. I've asked Sarah, Kitty, Martin who they think should be leader – I never mentioned any names – but they all gave me your name. You're the only one who can do it.'

'Why me? I failed every exam at school. I'm not bright. I—'

'You *are* bright. No, not in Martin Del-Coffey's way. You're no scholar. But you are intuitive. When you want to, you have this chameleon quality of being like the person you talk to. I can't. People only see me as the toffee-nosed church boy. I admit it. I am.'

'So...' I shook my head. 'I'm a man of the people.'

'Yes.'

'No way. Even if I could get rid of those two tyrants, being boss is too big a job for me.'

'Nick, there's no denying it will be a burden. It's going to be painful at times, but you don't quit. That's called responsibility.'

'I'm not accepting. Here, take this.'

I pushed the gun back into his hand. 'And I'd advise you to hide that very carefully, Dave, or they'll have your hide.'

'You know your trouble, Nick? You are yitten. That's the new phrase they use these days, isn't it? Yitten. It means you're frightened. Scared to death. No, not by those thugs. Basically you're a child, Nick. You just like to play the loveable rebel. You take personal risks, there's no doubting that, the way you stand up to Slatter. What you're afraid of is people relying on you. You are afraid of making a wrong decision and letting them down. You are afraid of that thing called RESPONSIBILITY.'

'Bullshit.'

'So...' Dave pointed the gun at me. His face ran with sweat.

'You are going to do what I say. You are going to oust that gang of sadists up there, then you are going to become our leader.'

'Do you think you could force me to do that at the point of a gun? Dave, you need a long, long rest.'

'Nick. I have done a lot of thinking and a lot of praying. And I believe God has shown me a way.'

'Put the gun back into the bag, Dave.'

'I knew I couldn't point the gun at you and force you to become leader. But what if I point the gun at my own head ... Look.'

'Stop it, Dave ... Take your finger off the trigger.'

'I couldn't shoot you. But I find it easy to put the gun to my head, here, then pull the trigger. Very, very easy. In fact – desirable.'

His eyes had turned strangely shiny. He shook like something was about to erupt from his body.

'Dave ... Put away the gun and rest. You don't want to kill yourself.'

'Why not? I know in a couple of days they'll force me to *Carry The Can*. I've been upsetting our new leaders by questioning their behaviour. I'm too exhausted to run. I'd never make it to the key at the top of the church tower.'

I shook my head. 'Well, you've certainly picked a weird way to blackmail me. "Become leader, Nick, or I'll blow a hole in my skull."'

'That's what I'm saying, Nick.'

'And I'm saying NO WAY. I'll see you later.'

I turned and began to walk away across the pumphouse floor.

'Nick ... If it's the last thing I do on God's Earth, it's this. I'll force you to remember what I'm going to say now: I believe you will make a good leader. You see solutions to problems that I can't solve. You have the guts to follow them through. Remember that obstruction on the bridge over the motorway? You busted right through it. Apply that ability to leading this community and give everyone here, all those children, the only chance they'll have of surviving. They need you, Nick. Without you they're already dead.'

His voice had changed. I felt cold.

'And remember this, Nick Aten, my spirit will watch what you do forever and ever. Our Father, which art in Heaven. Hallowed be Thy name ...'

I thought for a second if I kept walking he wouldn't go through with it. But I had to turn round.

He stood there, reciting the prayer; his eyes fixed on me.

His finger tightened around the trigger.

I don't remember the bang, but I remember the way his brains left his head.

Chapter Thirty-Six

LIFE IS GROTESQUE

Life goes on. Or in some cases it is death that marches on.

When Dave's body was found I was ordered to see Curt in his suite. After being frisked for weapons I was escorted inside.

Curt sat behind a desk, his loose lips sucking a cigar. 'You killed Middleton, didn't you?'

'No.'

'Come on, Nick. You can tell me ... Jesus, it's not as though I'm going to grass you to the cops, is it, now?'

Curt had made up his mind on the matter – and in a way I *was* responsible for Dave's death.

I nodded.

Curt laughed. 'Good for you, pal. I never could stand the shitter anyway. Have a cigar ... Go on, take two.'

I took them.

'You know, Nick, we ought to knock around more – we had some good laughs this summer.'

I made a matey smile. 'Yeah ... Sure.'

'Have you seen anything of Slatter lately?'

'No. With any luck the stupid twat will have fallen down a hole somewhere.'

That was a deliberate gamble on my part. No one dared say anything insulting about Slatter, even behind his back. Curt and his crew believed that Slatter could somehow supernaturally hear every-thing they said.

It paid off. Curt raised his eyebrows, impressed. 'Come on. Let's have a drink. You're wasted just dossing around here. It's time we discussed your ... prospects, yeah, ha, ha ... Your career prospects. You made a spectacular mess of Middleton's brains, you know. How close were you when you pulled the trigger?'

We spent a couple of hours joking, laughing.

At lunchtime topless girls served us with steaks and champagne.

'Where's Jonathan?' I asked as Curt swigged from a bottle.

'Remember that Asian girl ... wassername ... Kitty? He's got her in his room. He's breaking her in for Del-Coffey.'

We laughed hard, then Curt said, 'Look ... You can see the Church tower from here.' He opened the veranda window and stepped out onto the patio.

'Right you are, Sam.' He called down. 'Light the fuse, but remember to stand well back.'

Lunch rested in my stomach like a bowling ball.

'There's some binoculars on the table ... You know, with those you can actually see the expressions on their faces when ... boom!'

TV villains are supposed to laugh off their sadism in a cold way. Curt was hot, sweaty, even scared.

I watched a heavily built girl with ginger hair *Carry The Can*. She ran barefoot, clutching the silver pipe to her chest like it was a puppy. I didn't use the binoculars, and I didn't want to see her face. But I laughed when Curt laughed and jeered when Curt jeered.

The girl ran along the drive, through the gates, and then down the road into the village, her bare feet cracking against the stones. I knew she didn't feel it. All her concentration was focused on reaching the top of the churchtower and the key in the jar.

Normally she wouldn't have made it to the bottom of the drive before stopping to pant the air back into her lungs.

With the pipe fizzing in her hands, she ran like her feet had sprouted wings.

'Bet she doesn't make it,' panted Curt, his lips dripping spit.

'Bet you she does.'

'Right ... The stake is ... your girl Sarah for ... the Chinese girl who brought in the champagne. Yeah, I saw you eyeing her up. Shake?'

Mouth dry, I smiled. 'Shake.' We shook on it. Then we turned to watch the redhead run. My head began to buzz and my smiling face began to feel like a wooden mask.

As we stood side by side on the balcony, I pretended to drink from a bottle of champagne. Champagne's not something I like, but it was the heaviest bottle.

The seconds ticked by – the redhead was running for her life; frantically she raced across the bridge and began hacking up the hill at the other side to the church. I stood there hardly breathing, and weighed up my chances.

If the girl exploded I decided I would bring the bottle down as hard as I could across the back of Curt's head. However, a couple of Curt's Crew watched from the room ... Well, maybe I could take care of them too before they reached their guns.

Up, up, up, she ran. I glanced at the clock. Eight minutes had gone.

I turned back to watch; the tick of the clock felt like a rod slowly tapping the side of my head.

'Any second now...' Curt laughed. 'Then have Sarah Hayes washed and brought to my tent.'

The three were jumping with excitement now like punters at a racetrack.

'There she goes ... There she goes...'

'Any second now.'

The redhead disappeared into the church. She'd be climbing the spiral stairs now. I stood there, expecting to see the puff of smoke.

'There she is.'

A tuft of red appeared to frantically bob and duck on top of the tower as she ripped the key from the jar. I imagined her trying to jab the key into the cuff, hand shaking, expecting any second to be with the lord of hosts, and the singing frigging heavenly choir.

'Shit ... No!'

A speck of silver curved away from the tower to bounce down into the cemetery. Smoke burst out amongst the headstones.

'Correction. Have...' Curt had to breathe deeply three times

before completing the sentence. 'Have the Chinese girl washed and
sent to Nick's tent.'

I used the champagne to wet my dry throat. 'Bit of a laugh, eh?'
The redhead was already walking unsteadily back toward the hotel.

Curt laughed, then he said to one of his Crew, 'Find out who set
that fuse. Then break his fingers.'

'Sarah.' I caught up with her as she walked briskly through the
deserted village.

'What do you want?'

'I get the feeling you don't want to talk to me.'

'I don't particularly.'

'Wait. You don't think I killed Dave, do you?'

'No ... I know you didn't. Dave told Martin what he was
planning the other night. He was irrational and crying. But we
didn't think he'd carry it through.'

I sighed. 'For the last couple of days I thought you were going
round thinking I was a murderer.'

'What have you been doing with yourself, Nick? From what I hear
you and Curt are best buddies.'

'I'm going out with them on a hunting trip this afternoon.'

'That will be fun. Have they asked you to join the Crew yet?'

'No.'

'They will.'

'Forget that now...' I dropped my voice. One of the Crew
was swaggering down the hill toward us. 'Listen. I want to talk
to you, Del-Coffey and Kitty. Your house. Eight o'clock tomorrow
morning.'

Sarah stared at me, expecting me to say more.

'Eight o'clock. It's important.'

The thug walked up, winking when he saw me talking to Sarah.
He said, 'Nick. Have you seen what Curt's done in the churchyard?
Take a look.'

After leaving Sarah, I crossed the bridge and walked up to the
church. Slatter sat on the stone wall smoking a cigarette and
laughing.

'Aten. Get your faggot face across here. Take a look at this.'

'If it makes you laugh, Slatter, it has to be a piss-poor joke.'

It was.

Six people who had carried the can hadn't made it. Curt had ordered that the bodies be sat on chairs or tied to posts so they appeared to be alive. Most had parts of their bodies missing. Mainly hands, faces, stomachs. But now they looked happy.

They could have been relaxing in the garden, a can or a bottle in the hand they had left. They wore funny hats and someone had painted big clown smiles where their faces had been.

'Look at Simon,' Slatter pointed with the cigarette. 'I've drunk so much I've been legless. Never like him, though.' He laughed, his animal eyes glinting between the tattooed blue birds.

I walked away. I felt as if I was being buried in ice.

That evening, as the wind blew cold from the north a seventeen-year-old, Ian, was found guilty of not showing enough respect. Ian never bothered anyone. All he wanted to do was look after the puppies and kittens he collected on his walks around the valley. I think he was a bit simple. If you talked to him he answered in nods, a big smile cracking open his childlike face.

The pipe was chained to him and I stood with Curt on the hotel steps to watch.

I didn't want to see what happened so I let my eyes range up over the hills. In the distance I saw figures moving on a hill top. They were too far away to identify but the way they moved and watched us I knew who they were. The Creosotes were back.

No one else noticed: they were too busy watching Ian *Carry The Can*.

It was only the sound of the explosion that brought my attention back. For a while I could see nothing.

Then I saw a figure loping up the driveway, shoulders rocking from side to side.

'Ian's made it!' shouted a girl.

He had. Sort of.

One of his arms was missing, along with most of the shoulder. His stomach was ripped open. With his remaining hand he held his intestines in a bunch against his chest. A piece trailed behind him like the skin of a long grey snake.

'I'm alive. I'm alive ... Look, I'm alive,' he repeated over and over as he loped up the drive towards us. 'I'm alive, I'm alive.' One eye shone like white glass through the red mess. 'I'm alive. Curt, I'm alive!'

He was ten yards from us when the intestines slipped through his fingers to the ground. They tangled around his feet and he fell face down onto the gravel.

Ian lay and cried and bled there for ten minutes while Curt and Jonathan tossed coins to decide who would put the gun to his head and blow his tears away.

Earlier in the day I had made a decision. Now I knew it was the right one.

Later, I went to bed and counted the hours away until I could go down to Del-Coffey's house and tell them my plan.

Chapter Thirty-Seven

CUT AND RUN

At ten to eight I walked through the gates into Del-Coffey's garden. The lower windows of his house had been bricked up. Del-Coffey said it was because he was afraid of attacks by Creosotes. I guessed, however, it was to make entry more difficult for Curt and his Crew. Del-Coffey'd already crossed them more than once. There might come a day when they wanted him, too, to *Carry The Can*.

'Good morning, Nick.' Del-Coffey looked down at me from an upper window. 'You'll have to use the ladder to climb up here, I'm afraid. I took the precaution of bricking up all the doors as well.'

'You've got yourself a nice little castle,' I said, climbing the ladder. 'Is Sarah up?'

'Yes, she's waiting.' He stood back as I climbed in. 'We're all interested in what you have to tell us, Nick. Sit down.' He indicated a table with four chairs. I noticed his broken fingers were still bandaged.

'Tea?'

I nodded and he poured three cups. Now, he no longer played the superior intellectual. He looked tired and frightened. Sarah walked in. She looked at me, suspicious of my reasons for coming here. She nodded a hello and sat down.

'Where's Kitty?'

'I've just put her to bed,' said Sarah. 'It was her turn to spend the night with Curt.'

'Christ. How is she?'

Sarah's face flushed red with sheer fury. 'How do you think? I've dosed her up with tranquillizers.'

Del-Coffey, hands shaking, rubbed his face; he was on the edge of tears. 'What a mess . . . What a – what a fucking, stupid mess. How did we let ourselves get like this? We're worse than the adults who went mad. We've gone mad too, only in a different way . . . *Carrying The Can*. Bureaucratic rape. Torture. What next?'

'Well, before you start, Nick,' Sarah sounded cold. 'We've been discussing what we should do.'

'And?'

'And we've decided to pack what we can carry and hike out of here.'

'I don't think that's a good idea.'

'So you think we should stick it out here? Ruled by those sadists?'

'Sarah, Curt's asked me to join the Crew.'

Del-Coffey wasn't saying anything – he just stared at me through his red eyes.

Sarah hissed. 'So you're one of the boys now. Congratulations.'

'Sarah, if you will let me explain. Curt asked me and I accepted . . . Hey. Listen, Sarah. Hitting me won't do any good. Listen . . . I said *listen!* I told you I disagreed with the plan of walking away from here. Now let me tell you why. Did you hear the commotion up at the hotel this morning?'

'We heard some cars driving by, that's all.'

'Well, at about four this morning Trousers and a couple of others did just what you and Martin are planning. They tried to walk out of here on the quiet. I think someone warned Curt. By seven the Crew had found them and brought them back. Curt is furious that they tried to run away. Treason he calls it, so you can guess what Trousers will be doing this afternoon.'

'*Carrying the Can.*'

'Exactly. And that's exactly why it's suicide to try and get away on foot.'

'But how are we going to escape!' Martin threw out his arms, his voice breaking. 'No one has access to the vehicles now.'

I held up my finger. 'Unless you're a member of the Crew. So, Sarah, you see why I accepted.'

She squeezed my hand. 'I don't know, Nick. Every time I have you down for a bastard you end up surprising me.'

'I'll take that as a kind of compliment.' I turned to Del-Coffey. 'There's another reason for quitting this place fast. Have you seen any more Creosotes lately?'

'No. To be honest I've been too discouraged to even bother looking.'

'Well, I saw half a dozen of them last night. They were watching the hotel from the hill across the valley again. And I agree with you, Martin, I think they're watching us for a purpose. And from what's been rammed down our throats in the past, that purpose is to kill us.'

'So how do we get out of here?'

'This afternoon at two o'clock all those bastards will be watching Trousers. That's when I'll drive out of here in the bus. I'll go the back way so they don't see me. With luck they'll have the sound system belting out music so loud they won't hear the bus either. You two be waiting with Kitty at the white farmhouse at the end of the valley. I'll pick you up there. Oh, and expect some more passengers. I'll be having a quiet word with a few others who want out.'

Del-Coffey's hands began to shake with excitement. Sarah stared at me surprised and pleased.

'I'm using the bus because it's built like a tank. The Crew are bound to follow us – and it'll be easy to now the roads are covered with dirt; these days tyre tracks show up as clearly as if you've driven through fresh snow – if they do catch up with us I'll use that bus to knock them off the damn road and to kingdom come.'

'Any ideas where we go?' Del-Coffey was thinking hard now – almost back to his old self. 'It needs to be far enough away from this place. And somewhere that we can make self-supporting.'

'Perhaps the coast?' Sarah's eyes were bright. 'We can supplement what food we can scavenge with fresh fish.'

Minutes earlier both Sarah and Del-Coffey had looked as depressed as convicts on death row. Now they looked alive again. Sarah, smiling, kept flicking back her hair and talking quickly, constantly interrupted by Del-Coffey; he seemed to have forgotten his broken fingers and slapped the table every now and again to emphasise a point.

I watched, quiet now, satisfied I'd done the right thing at last.

'We'll build a new community . . .'

'. . . this time we'll be more selective with who we take in. Dave, he was a great guy, but he'd have anybody. He could only see good in people – we ended up with delinquents and jailbirds.'

'We'll have a programme of education – and a three-year plan . . . that's what we need, forward planning . . .'

'Processed fuels are bound to run out. We can build wind turbines to generate electricity.'

'Or watermills . . .'

'It's October now, but by the Spring we can be planting our own crops . . .'

I was content to let them talk. The look of hope on their faces made me believe I could pull it off this afternoon.

I'd made it sound easy. There were problems. I'd have to sneak away the keys, then hope the bus would start. The motor hadn't been run in weeks. And when Curt found out, first he'd piss pure rage; second he'd be tearing after us, guns blazing. I knew full well that if we were caught I'd have to *Carry the Can* for this.

After we spent another hour running through the plan Del-Coffey went to his room to pack.

Sarah looked at me, her eyes twinkling. 'You came through for us, Nick. You're a hero.'

'Don't praise me. I should have thought of this before. I suppose I hoped if we stuck it out Curt's behaviour would improve. The one thing that does bug me is that we're going to have to leave a lot of kids behind who aren't going to get the chance of a decent life.'

'You're not God, Nick. You can't do everything.' She smiled. 'Do you mind if I sit on your knee?'

'I don't mind at all, Miss Hayes.'

It felt good to be close to her again. She sat on my knee and kissed mer softly at first, then suddenly passionately.

'Oh sweet Jesus, Nick Aten. I've missed you.'

As we kissed she pulled the shirt from her jeans, gripped my hand and pushed it up underneath to her bare breasts. They felt firm and tight, her nipples hard. I stroked them feeling my heart beat faster. Christ, I didn't just want her, I hurt I craved for her so much. I massaged her breasts, hard. And I imagined what it would be like when we found a new place. A hotel on the coast perhaps. In a night or two Sarah and I would be sharing the same bed once more. And, believe me, we had some catching up to do.

'Sorry.'

'What for, Nick?'

'I'm being too rough with you.'

'Oh, no you're not. Squeeze harder. I like it ... Harder, Nick ... Ah ... That's it.' She breathed out into my ear and it felt like the warm winds of paradise.

And as I held her there on my knee I realised that one of the reasons I was taking them away from Eskdale wasn't just the régime, or the fact the Creosotes were returning, it was because I was scared Curt would take Sarah from me.

'Sarah, I'm taking the disks, files and – oh, sorry. I didn't, eh ...'

Del-Coffey backed out of the room, flustered. Sarah and I laughed.

'It's all right, Martin,' I called. 'We'll have to break the clinch anyway. I've got to get back to the hotel and make a few preparations.'

I climbed out of the window.

'Take care of yourself, Nick.' Sarah leaned out to watch me go, looking for all the world like Rapunzel with her long flow of blonde hair hanging down the wall.

'Don't worry. I will. Just make sure you lot are in the right place at the right time. There's a bus coming to take you away from all this.'

I kissed her again, and she hugged me tightly in a way that frightened me. As if she had a premonition she would never see me again.

Waving, I walked away back into the village. I kept looking back. Sarah still watched me; each time I looked back distance had shrunk her. At the school I took the shortcut back through the wood.

I walked thinking about Sarah, about what I would have to do today, and about the new community. I was still thinking hard when a figure appeared in the clearing in front of me. For a second the sun broke the cloud and lit the space in the trees like a spotlight. Half dazzled, I squinted against the brilliant light.

The figure stepped forward and recognition winded me.

'Mother . . .'

Mum smiled but it wasn't mother love. It was the smile of a hunter who's made the kill.

The first blow came from behind. I fell forward, my skull ringing with pain. I pulled myself to my knees as I saw mum lift the rock above my head. She smiled again. Then swung the rock down. Then all I remember is seeing blood dripping red onto fallen leaves – and nothing more.

Chapter Thirty-Eight

CRUISING ETERNITY'S WAY

What I heard first were the words: 'It's about time, Sleeping Beauty. I thought you were never going to wake up.'

My eyes were open but I saw pig all. Total darkness. 'Trousers? Is that you?'

'It's me, Nick Aten. How you feeling?'

'Sore . . . Shit, make that agony. Christ . . . What they done to me, Trousers?'

'Same as everyone here. Cracked our skulls, tied us in sacks and chucked us down into this hole.'

I felt round in the dark until I found an arm.

'I know we're in the shit, Nick, but I'm still not going to sit here in the dark and hold hands with you.'

'Where are we? Ouch, my bleeding head . . . How did you get here? You're *Carrying The Can* this afternoon.'

'This afternoon? That was yesterday. They chained me to the can. I ran like hell-fire. Managed to make it to the top of the church tower, unlocked the cuff and tossed the thing ten seconds before it blew. After that I legged it.' Trousers chuckled; there was no humour though. 'I got about a mile when wham! The next thing I know I'm lying tied in a sack. There was a hole in it so I could see I was lying on a river bank. The next thing I know I'm carried onto a boat or barge and dropped down into the cargo hold. You were already here, but I couldn't wake you. They'd given that lump of stone you call a head a sound battering – but I reckon if you can survive being stamped on by Slatter you can take most things.'

I felt around. I was lying on a pile of sacks. The whole place smelt of old, cold piss.

'Shit,' I whispered, 'I wish I could see. Have they left us something to drink?'

'Yeah. Cans of tonic water and lemonade, if you can find them amongst all the empties. And there's some potatoes and apples in a sack across there.'

'Where?'

'Take it easy, Nick. I've left some cans alongside you. And if you give it five minutes you're eyes will adjust.'

'Trousers, have you any idea what they're going to do with us?'

It wasn't Trousers who answered. The voice sounded as if it belonged to a thirteen-year-old boy. 'They're going to kill us, that's what they're going to do with us.'

'No, they're not,' said Trousers. 'If they wanted to do that, they'd have topped us when they caught us. They need us. They're taking us somewhere.'

'Where?'

'Search me ... Shh. Do you feel it? Every so often you feel a turning movement as if we're moving on the current. Sometimes we bump into things, the bank or other boats or something ... Then we're pushed off again. And don't even think of trying to escape. The walls are smooth as glass, there's nothing to climb up. We're like woodlice at the bottom of a glass.'

I opened a can. It was tonic water. Normally I couldn't stand the stuff. This time I drank it like it had come sparkling fresh from the Holy Grail. I touched my head and felt a crust of scabs near my hair line. Mum had certainly held nothing back when she belted me with the rock.

I shook my head dazed. What were they going to do with us? Why did our parents haunt us like the ghost of Christmas frigging past?

'I reckon they're taking us for slaves,' said the thirteen-year-old solemnly. 'That's what they did in wars. We did it in history.'

Another voice came from somewhere behind me. 'Or maybe they're taking us for food.'

'Shut up,' I snapped. 'Trying to frighten ourselves won't help.'

'He's doing a good job,' said Trousers. 'I'm scared. Hell, Nick, you remember what parents did to their kids six months ago?'

'Course I do. But ... but listen. Adults changed, just like that.' I snapped my fingers. 'Maybe the Creosotes are changing again. Look at the evidence. We've been captured alive. They've left us with food and drink. We should sit on our butts and be patient. Maybe the Creosotes are recovering, maybe the madness was temporary.'

'And maybe Santa Claus really does come down your chimney,' grunted Trousers.

I looked in the direction of his voice. Already I could make out the golden gleam of his trousers in the gloom. Around me were shadow shapes of another six people sitting or lying on sacks – all except one who lay in the corner.

'Why doesn't that kid deserve a mattress?' I asked.

Trouser's voice was low. 'Because they hit the poor sod just that bit too hard.'

We waited in silence, feeling the rock of the boat as it drifted down stream. My head ached viciously with every movement. Above us came the scrape of feet passing across the decks.

Well, Nick, I thought. *Mummy and daddy have come to take you home. Or to hell. Somewhere anyway.*

I slept. When I awoke the rocking had stopped but there was still a sense of motion. The more I lay there, just sensing how we moved, the more convinced I became that we had left the river and were moving along a still body of water – a canal, maybe. There was no motor sound so I could only guess the Creosotes were pulling the barge by lines. In my mind's eye I could see them. A team of a dozen apiece walking along each banking tugging the barge along toward its appointment with destiny.

'How long has it been now, Trousers?'

'By my Casio ... It's been precisely ... Ninety hours and sixteen minutes.'

'Christ, they've been pulling this tub nearly four days.'

Now Eskdale was far, far away. I rubbed my face, feeling the scrape of the scabs against my fingers. What had happened to Sarah? She must think I was a carcass now, rotting away under a bush somewhere.

'Hungry?'

'Starving.'

'What's it to be, then?' Trousers picked up the sack. 'Potato or apple?'

'Sling us another apple.'

'Maybe they're going to starve us to death,' came a voice out of the darkness.

'Shut up.' I bit into the apple; it was sour enough to make your eyes water. 'We're alive, aren't we?'

As we were eating we heard a sudden grating sound. Above our heads the hatch lifted. Sunlight blasted into the hold, forcing us to screw shut our eyes.

When at last I could open them I looked up. Heads in silhouette looked down at us.

'Here it comes,' someone whispered. 'Say your prayers.'

'You . . .' It was the voice of an old man. 'Up here.'

One of the Creosotes lowered a rope.

'You. Up here.'

Trousers reached for the rope.

'No . . . No. You!'

The old guy was looking at me. Suddenly the piss-stinking metal box was the place I wanted to stay.

'You. Up here.'

'Good luck, mate,' whispered Trousers.

Feeling like the lamb to the you know what, I climbed up the rope.

It took a good minute to orientate myself when I reached the deck. It was a frosty morning with laser-bright sunlight shafting through the trees. I saw we were on a long barge tied to the canal bank.

All around, watching me, were the Creosotes.

Quickly I scanned the faces; all were thick with dirt.

My dad squatted like a madcap ape on a mound of tarpaulins. He stared at me like I'd just beamed down from the flipside of the cosmos.

'You! You!'

I twisted round. It was mum. She stared so hard at me her head twitched. Her hair was long and wild now.

'What do you want from me?'

She stared harder.

'Mum . . . What do you want? Why can't you leave us alone?'

Her lips parted. 'You. You.'

'Christ . . . Can't you speak English any more? What are you doing to us? Why did you kill John?'

'John!' The name meant something to her. Moving her head like a bird, she tilted it to one side, then looked behind me.

I looked in the same direction. Against the wheelhouse was a row of little figures.

I swallowed. They looked like ventriloquist dummies. Their faces were shrivelled. They wore toddler's clothes but there was something over-large about their heads. I saw one had its face stitched with a series of clumsy cotton crosses in a line like this: XXXXXX. From mouth to ear.

For the first time in days the heat came back to me like a furious rush of steam through my veins. 'You mad bastards! What on Earth have you done?'

The Creosotes watched me, their eyes bright and expectant like kids waiting outside Santa's grotto.

I screamed at them, swearing and shaking my hands. 'What made you do this? Can't you think for yourselves? Can't you talk properly? What's happened to you? Is it God? Is it? When I talk to you does God, or Martians or – or the fucking Holy Ghost listen to me? Does it?'

They stared.

'I mean have you been taken over by aliens? You don't wear the same expressions on your faces any more! You don't know how to drive a car . . . you don't wash yourselves . . . What's going on inside your heads? Can't you talk to me? Can't you tell me what you're doing?'

I turned on my father as he squatted there, lips slightly parted showing the gap in his teeth.

'Dad! Who am I? Look at my face . . . Recognize me?'

He stared at me, like I was the weird one.

'Dad! Wake up! You know me? *Our Nick. He'll either end up a millionaire or in jail*. Remember John? Loved his computer, loved doing homework. Uncle Jack. People treated him like a retard, but he was the only fucking one out of the Atens who had a mind of his own. You know he – he could play that guitar – really play the bastard . . . He was a fucking genius and not one of you lot could see it. You fucking humoured him, like you fucking humoured me . . .'

I wiped at something wet on my face. I thought I was bleeding from the head wound again. I wasn't.

'Well done, you fucking twat,' I howled at him. 'I was ten years old the last time you made me cry. You've done it again. Jesus, sweet bleeding Jesus . . . You know something, Dad. I wished *YOU*'d died of cancer. Not Uncle Jack.'

'Don't talk like that to your father.'

I turned round to look at my mother. Her face had changed. She looked in pain. 'Don't say that to him, Nick . . . 'S not fair. Nick, he did the best for you, he . . . You . . .' For two seconds, maybe three, she wore a look of such confusion. It shattered the alien expression. Her eyes watered, and there was a flicker of warmth there – even recognition.

'Oh, Nick . . . Oh. What have we done? Sweet Lord, what have we done?' The expression was of someone waking in a strange place. Her eyes darted about as if seeing the people for the first time.

'Nick. I am so sorry. Poor John. We . . .' She clenched her fists. Her eyes shut. 'It's so . . . so special.' She smiled, eyes still shut. 'It's so special. It's marvellous. It's a miracle.'

Her eyes opened – the expression of alien calm had returned; her eyes turned cold.

Behind me the whistling started. Dad sat there, crouching on the tarpaulin. As he whistled he shivered. His eyes moved quickly like a frightened animal caught in a trap.

He whistled the carol *We Wish You a Merry Christmas*. When we were young he'd whistle it Xmas morning as a signal to get up and open our presents.

He whistled it then, lips trembling, blowing out white vapour in the ice-cold air. I sensed some sane part of him was still hidden beneath the madman. The weight of his madness was too great for him to talk sanely even for a few seconds as mum had done. He tried to communicate everything in those few whistled notes.

Sanity had flashed like a light across his dark world of madness. For a moment he knew, lucidly, what he had done, murdering John, and the madlands they now lived in.

Then the madness took control again, snapping off the light of sanity. He whistled no more and lifted his face to me and stared and stared and stared . . .

I sat down on a crate feeling empty – a cold, crying emptiness that a whole universe couldn't have filled.

I sat there, watched by the dry eyes of the ventriloquists' dolls that weren't dolls.

Later they pulled a sack over my head and tied me.

Were they going to drop me over the side into the water and leave me to drown?

Right then, I did not give a shit.

I heard them moving about the boat. Then hands lifted me and carried me the length of the barge.

No one spoke. All I could hear was my own breathing – a flat dead sound.

We left the barge and they carried me for perhaps ten minutes. Then they tied me to a tree. I could see nothing but dots of light needling through the sacking.

Then it was quiet.

I waited for a long, long time. Would I be beaten with sticks, or have rocks dropped on my head? Were they hungry and building a fire nearby?

I shivered against the tree until my legs buckled and I sagged against the ropes.

Eventually, I made up my mind. If they killed me, they killed me. But I wanted to see the sunlight.

No one bothered me as I twisted round like a Houdini wannabe, working out of the ropes, then eventually the sack.

There I sat on the forest floor. Not a soul in sight.

I found my way back to the canal. The barge had gone.

For half an hour or so I tried to follow it, but I wasn't sure which direction it had taken.

At last I turned my back on the canal and headed deeper into the forest. I was alone again.

But it wouldn't be for long.

Chapter Thirty-Nine

CROPPERS

I reached the edge of the forest. The ground sloped up ahead of me to the brow of a low hill. The sun shone on the frosted grass. Any other time it would have been great walking weather.

All I felt was cold, hungry and miserable. For all I knew I could be hundreds of miles from Eskdale. Sarah probably thought I was dead. And so would Curt. When he knew I wasn't coming back how long would it be before he went looking for Sarah?

As I trudged up the slope I heard the trucks. Four of them rounded the edge of the forest to growl up the incline toward me.

For some reason they came in pairs, two side by side.

A pair of trucks stopped right next to me. I saw that metal bars had been welded to the front making them look like homemade snowploughs. A head came out of the window. The kid was as surprised to see me as I him.

'Damnation . . . Where do you think you're going?'

'Home,' I shouted above the snarl of motors. 'If I can find it.'

'What's your name?'

'Nick.'

'Nick – if you don't get your arse up here, the only place you'll be going is straight to Baby Jesus.' The kid pushed open the door.

From the look on his face I didn't hang around. In three steps I was in the passenger seat and banging shut the door.

'Nick, old mate, haven't you seen the beggars? The whole place is cheesy with them.'

'Seen who?'

'Kaybees. That's who.'

I shook my head, lost. 'Kaybees?'

The kid exchanged a grin with the eighteen-year-old girl driving the truck. Her dark eyes flashed as she laughed.

'Kaybees. Short for Crazy Bastards. I'm Sheila, by the way. This gangster's Jigsaw.'

'Jigsaw on account of the face.' Grinning, he pointed at his face criss-crossed with scars. 'When my parents decided I'd look better without a head I decided the quickest way out was through my bedroom window. Which I didn't bother opening first. I'm the human jigsaw. Sheila had to tape all the pieces together.'

'From memory. I think it's an improvement.'

'You brother and sister?'

'Neighbours,' she said. 'That first night in April, when the shit started flying, the first I knew about it was the sound of Jigsaw breaking glass with his face . . . Excuse me, Nick.'

She picked up a CB handset. 'We've picked up a traveller. Name's Nick. We'll take him along for the ride.'

'Okay . . . Okay.' The voice vibrated the speaker like a robot on speed. These people were tense. 'Let's do it! We haven't got the fuel to hang around!'

Sheila expertly slipped the gear and we rolled forward up the hill. The truck to our right stayed by our side like it had been welded there.

'So where are the . . . Kaybees, then?'

'Nearly at the top of the hill. We should see them any time . . . Now.' She let out a scream, a blend of excitement and pure, pure terror. 'There they are, God love 'em.'

Shit. Creosotes. There must have been thousands of them. They stood on the grass plain like a forest of saplings in the sunlight.

'Jigsaw. Sheila. I know I'm only a hitchhiker . . . But shouldn't we be driving away from them? *Not toward them.*'

Sheila accelerated the truck across the grass. The other truck stayed by our side.

'You've got us wrong, Nick. We're not running away from

them. We're farmers,' she yelled. 'We're going to crop some weeds!'

Over the CB a voice hollered. 'Go ... Go ... Go!'

We picked up speed, wheels crunching across the frozen turf. The truck at our side started to peel away from us. It stayed parallel, running at the same speed, but the gap widened.

I twisted round to get a better view. The other pair of trucks was doing the same, occasionally the steel plough on their noses would splatter a bush ... Shit. There was a steel cable tied between the two trucks.

I looked back at the gap of blurring grass between our two trucks. It, too, had a silver cable that stretched out between them at maybe waist height.

'Now! Go for it!' Sheila shouted into the CB mike. 'Turn when I turn!'

Jigsaw gripped the rail on the dash. 'Hang on tight. Here we go!'

I looked forward as the Creosotes came up in front. They did not move. They only stared at us with those light-bulb eyes.

We plunged into them.

The trucks were hitting fifty and we were like the scythe of Mr Death himself. I couldn't take my eyes away, as the cable, pulled tight now, cut through men and women as easily as a blade. Windows splashed red.

More Creosotes popped like balloons on the steel plough bolted to the front of the trucks.

Sheila hit the wiper switch to scrape away the spray that turned the glass crimson. Now the ground was more bumpy, or at least the tyres bumped over lumps there.

And all the time someone yelled hysterically into the CB. God knows what – the volume distorted the voice into a mechanical crashing sound.

Then it was over. The trucks were slowing. I looked at Sheila: her dark eyes burned out from her face, sweat dripped off the end of her nose. Muscles stood out in her neck like rods.

She shot me a look. 'Hang on tight, Nick. We're going back. That's right, buddy, we're going to do it all over again.'

I gripped the dash rail and stared forward through the strawberry

jam on the window. My teeth clenched. The engines roared. I saw
the faces of the Creosotes getting nearer and nearer.

This time I closed my eyes. But I could not close my ears.

After we'd driven a couple of miles in formation the trucks stopped.
The Creosotes were a long way behind us now.

One kid from each truck jumped down and unhitched the cables,
then using sweeping brushes, they wiped the red shit off the sides of
the truck. Jigsaw pulled at pieces wedged in the snowplough (or
should that be meatplough?) I heard him shout to a kid working on
the next truck, 'Can you manage that, Smithy? Here, let me give
you a hand.' He threw something at the kid who ducked and
laughed.

I felt sick. I turned to Sheila. 'Why did you do that? The
Creosotes, I mean the Kaybees, are different now ... They're not
violent. What you did was a bloody massacre.'

Sheila's dark eyes widened. 'Where have you been, sunshine?
The North Pole? In the real world we're fighting for our lives.'

I told her where I'd come from and about the few Creosotes we'd
seen in Eskdale. 'Until a few days ago all they'd done was watch our
camp.'

'You said until a few days ago. What happened then, Nick?'

I told her how I'd been kidnapped and carried by barge to this
place. Wherever that was.

Sheila nodded. 'Then they just let you go.'

'Yes, how do you know?'

'Same pattern, sunshine. They came, they watched us for a bit.
Then a few of us were taken when we were out foraging. Some were
taken by their own mothers and fathers. They carried them a
hundred miles or so then they turned them loose. Most got back
safely.'

I shook my head. 'What the hell do they do that for?'

'At first we guessed it was nothing more than a loony game of cat
and mouse. Now we know they were studying our behaviour ...
what we'd do in certain situations ... Hey, Jigsaw, hurry it up.
We can't hang around here forever. I'm hungry.' She turned back
to me: her smile died. 'Then, five weeks ago, I remember it because
it was my nineteenth birthday, the Kaybees came back. I mean

they came back mob-handed. We woke up one morning to find thousands surrounding the camp, pressed right up to the fence.'

'And I take it they weren't there to sing you happy birthday.'

'Correct. They just piled in at us, Nick. Oh, we'd got guns by the crateful. We blasted them . . . They kept on coming. They just don't know fear. They walked over the ones we'd shot, then we shot them, then some more and more.'

'What saved you?'

'Not guns . . . In the end it was our brains. Or rather a kid we call Doc. We'd dug a ditch all around the camp. He got us to dump most of our kerosene stocks into the ditch, then lob in a burning rag. And that was the end of the attack. And the beginning of the world's biggest barbie.'

She laughed but she wasn't smiling. A muscle twitched in her face. 'It was awful. I've been terrified ever since. I can't sleep . . . Every time I close my eyes I see burning men and women.' She took a deep breath, looked at me keenly for a second then smiled. She gripped my hand and slapped it onto her stomach and held it there. 'Feel that. I've lost twenty pounds in five weeks.'

Instead of taking away her hand she held mine there against her warm stomach, while searching my face – for what, I don't know.

I licked my lips, feeling suddenly hot. 'So what's the business with the trucks? Surely you can't kill them all.'

'No. And we're running short of diesel. We're having to cut down on the cull runs. But the cull was the Doc's idea. He noticed after the first attack, when we killed so many of them, they didn't touch us until more Kaybees joined them. He thinks they need a critical number before their instincts tell them to attack. You know, like sparrows flap around for a few days before they've got enough in their flock then, bang, a switch flicks in their heads and suddenly they're off south. So we do our best to keep the number of Kaybees as low as we can. And it seems to be working. We've had no mass attacks since the big one five weeks ago.'

'But surely you can't go on like this?'

'No. And lately we've had a few individual Kaybees attacking us. It usually turns out to be one of the kids' parents. But that might be something to do with their building projects.'

'Building projects? What do you mean? What are they building?'

A horn sounded. 'I'll tell you later. It looks as if you've got a lot of news to catch up on since you hid yourself away in the back of beyond.'

We drove along a dirt track. Jigsaw had jumped back in the cab and was wiping at something with a rag. I saw they were gold rings. He slipped a couple of wedding rings onto his little finger and sat admiring the way they glinted in the cold sunlight.

I sat there trying to work through what had happened that morning. I'd wanted to catch up with the barge, then at the first opportunity release Trousers and the other kids. But they would be miles from here by now; also their situation didn't seem so perilous now I'd heard what the pattern would be. Sheila was confident the captives would be released as part of the Creosotes' experiment.

Another event that morning that I found almost shocking was making contact with another community of sane human beings. In Eskdale we'd come to accept that we were the only ones left on the face of planet Earth. Now it looked as if there were communities of kids dotted all over the place.

Most troubling was hearing about the behaviour change in the Creosotes. They were murderously hostile again. They were flowing back north from wherever they had migrated to. My only hope was that Sarah would be safe. Maybe the Creosotes wouldn't find a place as remote as Eskdale.

Sheila sang out, 'Home sweet home.'

The place seemed to be little more than a collection of farm buildings and farm labourers' cottages. Around the place was a high barbed wire fence making it resemble a prisoner of war camp. Outside the fence ran a ditch. That still had lumps of burnt stuff clinging to the sides.

The leader was a nineteen-year-old called Boss. He'd been a trainee security guard when civilization went belly-up and he appeared to rule the place firmly but reasonably fairly.

I did see, though, beneath his eyes, black half-moons and when he spoke his breath nearly cut me in two. The last five weeks of virtual siege had taken their toll on Boss. He was boozing hard to get through it.

First off they took me into the farmhouse kitchen and fed me with bowls full of rabbit stew and pancake-shaped things that they called bread.

It hit me as I troughed out on the stew that these different communities were each developing their own cultures. At Eskdale the thing was to tattoo your face. Here it was jewellery. Everyone wore gold bangles and rings; so many, in fact, that if someone waved you were blinded by the flash.

Another thing I saw was that they were less reliant on scavenged stores for food. The vegetables in the stew were fresh, they had hutches full of rabbits, chickens roamed all over the place, and everyone looked fit and lean from hard work. If it wasn't for the four thousand-odd Creosotes thirsting for their blood they would've seemed certain to survive.

Sheila stuck close by me, listening to what I'd have to say. Those big dark eyes of hers constantly watched mine.

Doc, the brains of the community, reminded me a lot of Del-Coffey. Same wire-rim glasses and a fuzz of blonde hair. He didn't show off as much as Del-Coffey, though, and I found myself liking him. Christ, I was changing. Ten months ago I'd probably have spat in his eye.

'Tell me about Eskdale,' he said eagerly. 'Did you get a chance to observe the Kaybees much? At first everyone thought they were just plain crazy. But there seem to be patterns to their insanity. They go through distinct stages – like they are evolving.' He rattled on, pumping me for what I knew. I told him some secondhand stuff I'd got from Del-Coffey.

Doc's theory was that the build-up of electromagnetic radiation from TV, radio and radar transmissions had finally scrambled humanity's brains. Like a computer floppy disc being left too close to the monitor eventually leads to it corrupting. 'Obviously, Nick, adult biology differs from that of children and adolescents – you know, hormone levels and stuff like that. So everyone over nineteen – ker-poww.'

'But we're safe now,' I said. 'I mean, Sheila here turned nineteen five weeks ago.'

He nodded. 'Yep, we're safe. All the transmitters in the world are now as dead as my Granny Sally.'

'Not all of them,' said Jigsaw, enthusiastically mopping up gravy with his bread.

'That's true. Not quite all.' Doc grinned. 'You finished, Nick? I've got some things to show you. You're going to be amazed.'

'Well ... Thanks for the food, and saving my bones. But I've got to get back home. I'm going to have to warn my community that the adults are a threat again. We'll need to be ready in case they attack.'

Sheila grabbed my arm as I stood up. 'Nick. You can't just walk out of here. It'd be suicide. They've circled the whole camp. You'd never get past them.'

'I can't just sit here and leave everyone at my place like sitting ducks. I don't even know how long it'll take me to walk back there. A week at least.'

Doc said, 'Take it easy. We'll work out something to get you home. The thing is not to rush it. But I'd recommend you stay here at least tonight ... Come on, I'll show you round our metropolis. We've got forty-five people here. The youngest is three months. Now that was scary – delivering a baby. Lucky it's as natural as going to the lavatory. We've had two more since – and not a single complication.'

Sheila walked round with us, linking arms with me.

It had become an essential part of meeting someone for the first time that you told them what happened to you on that BIG DAY 1. I told them mine. I'd heard Sheila's already. Doc lived on a houseboat with his parents. They chased him round the deck until he jumped into the dinghy and floated away like Moses in his basket.

I said, 'You told me that you'd got some amazing things to show me.'

'Sure ... First we climb this ladder. It's the watch tower. Go on, Nick. It's safe.'

I climbed to the top of the timber tower that looked out over the flat farmland. Doc and Sheila followed me up. In the watch tower a mean-looking machine gun rested on its mount. Next to that a telescope.

'Nick. Take a look through the telescope. I've trained it on what I want you to see.'

I put my eye to the eye-piece. From a field in the distance rose a pyramid. It was dark in colour and what it was made from God only knew.

'I reckon it's a good two hundred feet high.' Doc polished his glasses on a tissue. 'They started building it about two months ago.'

'What is it?'

'It's where the adults go to die.'

'A graveyard?'

'Sort of. A cross between a hospice and a graveyard. You see them go there when they're old and sick, or injured – after they tried to bust in here they crawled there by the hundred. Most are still alive when they get there. They just haul themselves on, then wait to die.'

'Jesus ... They behave as if they have no will of their own. They're like robots or ants.'

'That's it, Nick. They behave collectively. The individual is unimportant. It's the species that matters. It doesn't matter to them if ten thousand die so long as they can crush us.'

'But why the pyramid?'

Sheila shrugged. 'At least it's tidy.'

Doc smiled. 'Thank God it's winter. When it was hot you could catch the stink from here. And it's a good seven miles away. Even further away they're building what look like temples out of the skulls of their children. Lucky you can't see them from here. Come on, Nick, we've more surprises to amaze you.'

In a stable was a room filled with electronic equipment.

'As Jigsaw so rightly said, there are still some transmitters in operation. This is one. We have a hand-cranked generator to charge those car batteries there in the box.'

I whistled. 'It looks impressive. But is there anyone out there to talk to?'

Doc pulled out an exercise book and flicked through the pages. 'We've made contact with fourteen other communities. They're dotted all over the world: New York, San Francisco, Toronto, Iceland, Denmark, Israel, Ireland; there's the full list. We've also picked up Morse, which we can't understand unfortunately, and some distant broadcasts have been bounced off the ionosphere from, I guess, the Far East, but seeing as we've no linguists we don't know what they're saying.'

A question I knew I had to ask, but was afraid to, came out. 'It's all like this, then – everywhere?'

'It is, Nick. It is. Some time on that Saturday night in April. Every adult human being on this planet went mad. Then they killed their children. Most of the young must have died. We're the lucky ones.'

Sheila held my arm tight. 'And sometimes I wonder if we really *are* the lucky ones. It'd be tough enough surviving like this even without the Kaybees wanting to kill us at the first opportunity.'

Doc nodded. 'She's right. Some communities are going under from natural causes.' He pointed at a page full of handwriting. It had two red lines running across it, and the word CLOSED.

'That was a community in France of more than two hundred. A couple of months ago they told us their people were falling sick with fevers and lumps under their armpits.' He shook his head, grim. 'Three weeks ago they told us all of them were sick. A hundred had died. The guy I spoke to sounded half dead. Two weeks ago we had the last transmission. He just kept repeating, Good luck, Leyburn. Good luck, Leyburn. Pray for us, Leyburn, pray for us.' Doc shrugged: his eyes had grown shiny behind his glasses. 'Over the last few weeks two more communities have gone off air. One in Greece and one in Portugal. Both reported they were under heavy attack from adults. I can only imagine they've been overrun.'

'So one by one, all over the world, we're being snuffed out.'

'That's about the size of it. The luckiest beggars we've come across live on St Helena. Have you heard of it?'

I shook my head.

'Napoleon Bonaparte was locked up there. The reason the Brits chose St Helena is because it's a titchy island in the middle of the Atlantic. The community of kids there didn't hang about. They armed themselves and hunted down and killed every single adult on the island.' Doc looked wistful. 'They've got it cushy there. A town, a power station. Huge reserves of fuel. Fertile fields, and thousands of flaming miles of ocean to fish in.' He looked at me hard. 'We should learn their lesson, Nick. We've got to find some way of exterminating the adults – shoot them, burn them, gas them, bury them ... Anything to just get rid of the bastards.'

'Just how do you hope to do that?'

Doc smiled, tired. 'In a crazy, illogical way, Nick, that's what I was hoping *you*'d tell *me*.'

Chapter Forty

BREAKER OF THE DARK

During breakfast I asked Doc something that had been troubling me all night.

'Doc. Yesterday in the radio shack you said you expected me to show you how to exterminate the Kaybees. What made you say that?'

He blushed. 'I should have kept my mouth shut. But it's ... well, to put it bluntly it's weird. We talk amongst ourselves. We talk to the community over in Harmby, and then we're talking on the radio every day to other communities around the world.'

'You're losing me, Doc. What's this got to do with me?'

'Nick, there's a basic message, or flavour if you like, coming out of these dialogues. There's a sense of expectancy. I call it the Messiah syndrome. People from Alaska to Malta are developing this gut feeling that a stranger will come who will give us the answers to the questions we're all asking. And more importantly, this person is going to rid us of the Kaybees and lead us ... if not to the promised land ... at least show us how to survive.' Watching me intently he sipped his coffee. 'Didn't you feel this in Eskdale?'

'No, we had a lot on our minds.' I thought of Curt and his band of sadists making our lives hell.

'I know it seems illogical. That one person could do this. Perhaps in times of trouble we all wish for a messiah to come and save us. I've read enough psychology to sit here and dismiss it as delusional crap, but I admit it, Nick. I feel it here.' Doc pressed his hand to his chest.

'Why did you think it was me?'

'Wishful thinking. We want our messiah to come so much that the first mysterious stranger that arrives we say, by God's flesh, here he is! Sheila was saying last night she thinks there's something special about you. She says she can see something in your eyes that she's seen in those ancient portraits of Christ.'

I chewed my bread and began to sweat. *Christ*. These people were one short of a packet of three. Especially if they thought I was some messiah, a supernatural hero, come to lead them to the promised land.

I nodded at Boss who sat sullenly eating at another table. 'What does he think?'

'I think he'd just like someone to take the responsibility of leadership off his shoulders. Since the attack five weeks ago he's really taken to the bottle.'

I shook my head. This was so crazy I wanted to laugh out loud. 'You know, I'm sorry to disappoint you, Doc. I'm a nobody. I left school with zilch qualifications. Before this happened I was just an odd-job man for a bent dealer. My ambitions stretched no further than the next night out on the beer.'

Doc seemed embarrassed to have mentioned it; for the rest of the meal he looked down at his food as he ate.

By the time I'd zipped up my leather jacket I knew what I'd do.

I didn't say good-bye. I just walked straight out of the camp gates and down the road. Above, the sky looked like a concrete roof: drops of rain began to splat on the ground.

My feelings were mixed. Concern for Sarah. Horror at meeting my parents again. Bewilderment at what Doc had said in the canteen. I was confused; the only cure was to walk until I dropped.

The road signs were still clear. It might take a week but I'd make it home.

For the first half-mile I saw no sign of the Creosotes. Maybe Sheila and Doc had over-estimated the threat.

I walked fast. The roads were skimmed over now with moss, giving them the appearance of being covered by a green peach fluff – but there were no obstacles.

Then I saw the first Creosote. A guy of about forty lay on his side at the edge of the road. He used one elbow to prop up the top half of his body. He didn't move but he watched me walk by.

When I rounded the next bend I stopped and breathed in sharply. Twenty adults stood and watched me. Their eyes had taken on that fierce glare.

This time I was the fool. I'd simply quit the camp with no preparations. Being eager to get back to Eskdale had knocked any sense I had from out of my skull. This might get me killed.

I turned and ran.

I passed the guy at the roadside. Now he sat up to watch me pass. To my left in the field were more Creosotes streaming across the grass.

Shit, you stupid twat, Aten!

I ran harder, panting raggedly. Behind me I heard the bushes rustling like fury as the Creosotes forced their way through into the lane.

At last I saw the camp. I did not stop running until I was safely through the gates.

Sheila was waiting for me. Her eyes were wide with shock. 'What the hell did you do that for? You haven't even got a gun, for pity's sake!'

I pulled in lungfuls of air. 'I need to get back home . . . They don't know the danger they're in . . . You'll have to drive me past them in your truck.'

'I can't do that, Nick. Not without Boss's permission.'

'Well, let's go ask him.' I coughed and spat. 'I need to be moving on before the winter sets in.'

'Surely you can stay a few days, Nick. Please?'

I shook my head and went to find Boss. He leaned against the wall, smoking a cigarette. He looked like death.

I asked him for what I wanted and he looked up through those hungover eyes. 'No. Not yet.'

I started to press him but he suddenly snapped, 'I said no! That is my decision. No. No. No!'

He stamped off into the yard to shout at some kids chopping wood.

Angry, I turned to Sarah. 'Shit ... It wouldn't take someone ten minutes to run me out past the Creosotes. Then I'd walk the rest of the damn way!'

'Nick. He has his reasons – he's—'

'I'll work the price of my fare, then. What needs doing in this place?' I stormed off, determined to do something so worthwhile they'd be forced to reward me with that ten-minute truck ride.

Here they relied on candles and kerosene lamps for light. They were adequate but at night the communal lounges looked not just dim but damn well depressing. It'd get worse as winter brought the long dark nights.

I found the generator they had used to generate electricity when they first arrived there. Then I collared the first kid I saw and asked, 'Hey, just a minute ... Why doesn't anyone start the generator? There's nothing wrong with it.'

'Boss's orders. We're too low on fuel to waste it on electric lighting.'

'Why not go and get some more? There must be a billion gallons out there in towns and cities waiting to be picked up.'

The kid looked worried, obviously wondering why he'd been picked on for my irritable cross-questioning. 'Lots of reasons, I suppose. We've got the Kaybees all around the camp. Also fuel and stuff's getting harder to find. There's other camps in the area. It's all getting used up ... Doc and Jigsaw once drove all the way to Birmingham to get supplies but kids there have put up road-blocks. They shoot at you when you get close. If they—'

'Shit.' I stalked off. Irrationally, I wanted to prove myself to them. That I could pull their lives round and stop them sliding into the dark ages.

I prowled the camp like a wolf looking for something to vent my talents on; something that would dazzle them into giving me what I wanted.

I felt as if a clock had started ticking in my head. Up in Eskdale

Curt and his crew partied while the Creosotes slowly massed. Any day now they might attack.

'How does the radio work if there's no generator?' I snapped at the next kid I saw.

'Uh? A hand generator. We take turns to charge up some—'

I walked on. In one of the barns I found a huge collection of stores. It looked as if they'd tried to salvage everything that wasn't nailed down. There were tyres, car parts, window panes, kitchen sinks, washing-up liquid by the crateful, surgical gloves, licorice-flavour condoms, ice cream cones, barbecues, wall paper ... Everything under the sun whether vital or as useful as a chocolate fireguard.

As I dived through the store mountain an eerie feeling crept in through the back of my head that somehow, unconsciously, I was striving to fulfil Doc's messiah prophecy.

I shook my head trying to dislodge the feeling. But as I worked through the stores the conviction took shape in my head that I was looking for something specific. God knows what – but when I saw it bells and lights would go off in my head.

Sheila came to watch me. 'Be patient, Nick.' The tenderness in her voice made my skin tingle. 'Believe me, the fuel stocks *are* really low. Apart from what's in the trucks, all we've got is the reserve tank behind the barn.'

I made a noise to acknowledge she existed and carried on sorting through the stores.

'No one's had a chance to catalogue this stuff yet,' she said. 'We just brought as much as we could. A lot of it's useless.'

She watched me, probably more than a little bit frightened, as I continued what had become a holy quest.

'I'll see you later, Nick. Grub up at one.'

I grunted and she walked reluctantly away.

Ten minutes later, grinning more like a devil than a messiah, I hissed, 'Eureka.'

The sky was wedged so solid with storm clouds that the candles were lit at lunchtime as they sat down to eat. Boss sat looking gloomy. In his glass was something that sure as jiggery wasn't water.

I stood there and watched them. I felt a mixture of triumph and sheer craziness. They must have seen it in my face, so most sat there, forks in hand, looking at me and wondering if I was going to strip bollock naked and dance a tango.

Casually, I asked, 'Why are you all sitting in the dark?'

Boss paused, the glass at his lips, and watched me steadily.

'The candles are lit,' said Jigsaw. 'This is as bright as it gets, buddy.'

I smiled. 'Let there be light.' I swung my hand down brushing the light switches.

Squeals, gasps, yells – you name it. And the expressions on their faces should have been framed for posterity.

Sheila cried out, 'Nick. How did you do it ... Sweet Jesus, I'd forgotten what they looked like.'

Everyone stared up at the blazing light bulbs, big grins all over their faces. Only Boss looked unhappy.

'We can't spare the diesel, Nick ... Turn off the generator.'

'It's not running, Boss.'

Jigsaw stared open-mouthed at the lights. 'A miracle ... Nick's worked a bloody miracle.'

Doc watched me, his eyes gleaming behind the glasses.

I sat down at the table and began to eat. 'No miracle. What you didn't know is that buried beneath all that crap in the barn you had a brand new, boxed, twelve-month-guaranteed generator that runs off bottled gas. And I know you don't use bottled gas here for cooking and heating. You use wood. And seeing as someone has dumped eight full LP Gas cylinders in that clump of nettles out by the fence I thought I'd use those.' I spooned in the rabbit stew. 'I reckon on the gas stocks you've got, you can run the generator two hours a day, every day, through the winter.'

'Christ, he's right.' Doc was gobsmacked. 'And after the LPG's gone we can ferment animal excrement for methane. We can have electricity all the time, for lighting, for the transmitter and ... Just a minute, Nick, how did you know the generator was there?'

'I didn't. I'm just a nosy sonofabitch.'

I carried on eating. The rest did not – they sat and stared at me.

That night, with a sound system belting out music, the electric lights burning, Boss came across to me and handed me a glass of whisky.

'You're a hero, Nick.'

'I wish people would stop saying that about me . . . Really I do.'

Boss was full of booze and looked jolly. 'Listen, Nick old son. You coming here has been like a . . . an injection of life into the place. Look around this room. What ya see? I'll tell you. You see happy faces. You see hopeful faces. And that's all down to you.'

'You've not done bad yourself, Boss. You're a decent leader; you keep the crazies at bay.'

'Hmm . . . I thought I'd got what it takes to be boss . . . but every day I die a bit. Keeping these people alive is just too big a weight to carry alone . . . Here, more whisky. There. Get it down you. Listen, Nick. Why don't you stay here? Join us. You could be my second-in-command.'

'Sorry, Boss. I've got to get back to Eskdale. There's someone there who means a lot to me. I've been thinking. If you could just drive me to—'

'Nick, Nick. We'll talk about that tomorrow. Come on, this's turning into a party. Hey, will you look at that, they've barbecued some chicken.' He nudged me and winked. 'Sheila's sat by herself . . . She likes you, you know . . . Hey, Jigsaw, you vagabond. Haven't we got any different music to this? 'S crap, man.' He staggered away.

Sheila smiled gratefully when I sat beside her on the sofa. 'Chicken?'

'Please . . . Hell. This whisky's gone to my head. I'm not used to it.'

'Look at them, Nick. I've not seen them as happy as this in weeks. You're a hero.'

'Don't you start.' I laughed. 'The name's Nick Aten, it rhymes with Satan, and I'm nobody doing nothing.'

'Oh . . . Is that what you think?' She handed me a plateful of barbecued chicken and fixed me with those eyes, as dark and as glossy as polished coal.

'Right, Mr Aten,' she smiled and slid across the sofa toward me. 'Tell me your life story.'

The next day Boss, more hungover than ever, fobbed me off every time I asked about a ride past the Creosotes that hung about outside the fences like refugees from Bedlam.

I ended up servicing the trucks. It was a big hint what I wanted in return.

By evening the rain showers turned to snow and I was grateful to have a hot shower and get beside the log fire that shot flames up the chimney like a flame thrower.

Sheila brought a plateful of those bread pancakes and began toasting them on pieces of wire over the fire. She told me to help myself to honey as she explained, 'We used to do a bit of trade with the people over in Harmby before the Kaybees got too cheesie on the ground. They've got huge orchards there and beehives.'

'When we pick ourselves up that's what we're going to have to do,' I said, 'Begin trading with other communities. Just think. We're just a bunch of kids with no experience and no real training and we're going to have to build civilization from scratch. How long do you think it'll be before we have our own space research programme again?'

'Never, I hope.' Sheila snuggled down beside my legs and watched the flames. 'Perhaps we can live simpler lives from now on. You know, like the old Red Indian tribes. If you're comfortable, have enough to eat, and if . . . and if you have someone to love who loves you – that's enough.'

'I'd like to say you're right. But you know like it's in a wolf's nature to howl at the moon, or for sparrows to fly south? There is something in human nature that drives us to explore, colonize, develop. We won't be satisfied until we can take the whole universe apart like a clock and find out how it ticks. And that won't be the end of it. Then we'll want to know how to make one of our own. With all the imperfections ironed out, of course.'

She looked up at me steadily, her dark hair falling across her breasts. 'Why do you talk like that, Nick? Most of the time you're just one of the lads, then you talk like you know things we don't.'

I laughed. 'Take no notice. I'm beginning to sound like Del-Coffey.'

'Who?'

'Oh, just some egg-head I know back home.'

'Is there anyone else back home, Nick? I mean who's special. I know I'm—'

'Listen – everyone shut up and listen!' Jigsaw shouted. 'Doc's on the radio to Dublin. They're under attack. They say it's the biggest yet.'

Chapter Forty-One

BREAKER OF THE LIGHT

In thirty seconds flat everyone who could squeeze in was in the radio shack. Doc sat at the table, staring at the transmitter switches like he could see what was happening at the other end. Over the speakers a voice came clearly over a faint static crackle.

'Hello planet Earth, this is Dublin. Welcome to the big one. Jesus, Mary and Joseph, these guys are thick on the ground tonight. Well . . . We've got the flood lights on and we can see them just sort of . . . sort of shuffling up to the fences.'

For my benefit Doc said, 'The Dublin camp have taken over a prison. There's a thousand kids in the place. They're probably the best armed of the lot.' He drew two squares in the air one within the other. 'On the outer boundary they have high barbed wire fences. Then there's a concrete inner wall that's thirty feet high.'

As Doc quickly talked other voices crackled over the speaker, which I took to be other communities calling in across the world with messages of encouragement.

'Good luck, Dublin,' came a girl's voice with a German accent.

Then a public school English voice, 'Tally ho chaps. Give the blighters hell.'

Then came Dublin: 'Is Sheila there, Doc? I promised her a moonlit walk through old Dublin town one day soon. Am I still on a promise?'

Sheila blushed. 'You are, Jono. You look after yourself, d'ya hear?'

'Blow me a kiss for luck, sweetheart, and I'll chip you a piece of the Blarney stone for ... Jesus, did you hear that?'

It sounded like a burst of static. 'We've just fired our howitzer at the beggars. The mother just vaporised a path straight through them.'

It was like a radio play. We brought in drinks and barbecued chicken and listened to the story. Only it wasn't a story. A thousand people, not one beyond their teenage years, were fighting a war against an enemy that were no longer human.

'. . . machine guns now,' said the soft Irish voice calmly. 'I can see through the window ... The bullets. Like a long line of sparks, flying from the roof above my head ... out into darkness. We don't have to aim. Just fire in the general direction and you're bound to hit the bastards. There are thousands of them ... They started massing this afternoon. They've done that before, then they disperse; this's the first time – shoot, that was the howitzer again. And now we're wheeling the tanks out of the gates. They're going to fire point blank through the barbed wire fences...'

Small arms fire sounded like sharp cracks on the speaker, the big guns came over like fat bursts of static. I looked round the faces in the room. They listened hard to every word. It wasn't blood lust. Every gunshot was an assurance that we too might survive.

The hours passed. More food and drink was carried in. Sometimes we'd cheer as the Irishman described another success. They were confident, they felt safe behind their thirty-foot concrete walls. We felt safe, too. Although when I went out for a leak I did notice that the Creosotes in the fields were shuffling restlessly as if somehow they knew what was happening in Ireland.

'Nick, you missed it. The lads in Ireland have brought out the flamethrowers.' Jigsaw held up a burnt drumstick. 'They're frying tonight!'

'. . . now we're firing parachute flares. They light up the whole place, so I can describe the scene...' The calm voice paused. When it came back everyone in the room sensed it had changed. It sounded almost puzzled. 'We've popped off hundreds of the mad so-and-so's. They're still coming though. They haven't got the sense to quit ... There go the tanks again ... Wait. Wait! The tanks are pulling back to the gates. Our guys are running back! Sweet Mary, they're not stopping to pick up their guns ... Wait ... Shit ... I see what's happened: the Crazies have broken in through the fence to my left. They're just pouring in like flood water ... Come on, come on ... That's it. We've closed the gates in the wall. Now the mad bastards are going to have to sprout wings and fly over.'

The sound of gunfire crackled over the speakers. By now we'd stopped eating. All that mattered was to hear the next words from that soft Irish voice.

By eleven the gunfire sounded as heavy as ever. The Dubliners stood on the prison walls firing straight down at the Creosotes as they pressed mindlessly at the slabs of concrete, like an incoming tide that had reached the sea wall.

Whatever drove them to the walls wouldn't let them go as fuel was poured onto their heads, then the burning rags.

'Oh, boy ... I'm glad you can only hear this. Not smell it. The flames are nearly forty feet high ... The smell is indescribable ... The Crazies are still coming though. There are thousands of them, they walk out of the darkness then just – just wade into the flames.'

I saw them in my mind's eye. And I knew then that this wasn't any pointless mass suicide by the Creosotes. Somehow they'd formed a strategy. And they would stick to it. Inside I felt cold. An arm slipped around mine. Sheila looked up, her face serious, then she looked back at the speaker.

The Irish voice sounded flat and distant now. Like a computer relating an itinerary.

'Still shooting. There go the mortars. The Crazies've made it easy for us. They're a lot closer.'

I listened and inside my head I saw the Creosotes advance. They walked over their own dead. Then they died too. More came. I knew what they'd do: they would build a ramp of human corpses from the ground to the top of the walls.

Doc said: 'The Dublin kids'll make it. They've got stuff to equip an army in there. They've done it before, they'll do it again.' He wasn't smiling; sweat dripped onto his glasses.

'Hello.' The Irish voice was calm. 'I know you are all listening and praying for us. I have to tell you they've reached the top of the

walls.' The voice sounded apologetic as if the Dublin community
had let us all down. 'They're in the building now. There is gunfire
outside in the corridor . . . Well, it looks as if I should chip in and do
my bit. Good night, everybody. Good night, Sheila, God bless. I'm
sorry. We did what we could . . .'

The final crack from the speaker rang on in our ears for a long
time.

We sat silent. Silent.

It was still dark when I felt the covers being pulled back from the
bed. I saw nothing. For a moment I lay there locked tight with fear,
thinking the Creosotes had broken in.

Someone climbed in beside me. There was no mistaking it was a
girl. She was naked and her breasts stroked across my bare arm.

'Nick?'

'Sheila. Are you all right?'

'I'm so frightened I just want to bury myself away.'

'Uh . . . You feel cold.'

'I'm frozen. Nick. Let me sleep with you tonight.'

I admit I lay there with Sheila holding onto me tightly, feeling
every naked inch of her against me and I thought of Sarah. And I
thought of all the sitting ducks at Eskdale and what had happened in
Dublin. And I knew I could not make love to her.

'Do you mind . . .' I sounded awkward. 'If we don't try anything. I
don't think I'd be much use tonight.'

She kissed the side of my face. 'I'm glad you said that, Nick Aten.
You're a gentleman. But will you put your arms round me and hold
me . . . There, that's it. Thanks.'

I made a decision. Tomorrow I'd face up to Boss, demand that
truck ride – and not take no for an answer.

Chapter Forty-Two

GHOST TOWN

'Do it for me. I've earned it.'

Boss looked up at the electric light. His eyes were black holes through which pink glinted. 'You have,' he said. 'And we're eternally grateful, Nick. But I made a decision. Those trucks do not leave the compound.'

'For Godsakes, a mugful of diesel'd get me past the Kaybees. Then drop me off; I'll walk home.'

'No, Nick. That's final.'

He began to walk away but I grabbed him. Those in the canteen watched us, their eyes wide.

'I need to get home, Boss. I've got to try and stop happening to my people what happened to those poor bastards in Dublin.'

'I appreciate that. But it's not our problem. We need that fuel to continue the culls. If we let the numbers mount up beyond a certain point it triggers an attack.' Then he hissed under his breath so the others wouldn't hear. 'And how long do you think those fences would keep them out?'

'You've enough diesel for the winter. There's a hundred-gallon reserve tank out back.'

He breathed out heavily, sending a booze stench into my nostrils. 'Nick . . . Come with me. No, Doc. You stay here. I want a private word with Nick.'

Bad tempered, Boss marched out of the farmhouse round the back of the barn to the reserve tank. He walked up to it and kicked it savagely.

'Did you hear that, Nick? Did you hear that echo?'

'I was told there was a hundred gallons in there.'

'And that's what everyone believes. The truth of it is, old son, I filled it myself in the days when we had diesel coming out of our ears – but I never bothered to check the damn tank first. It leaks. The fucking thing leaked and leaked, week after week, the ground soaking up the diesel so no one noticed.' Tears leaked now from the black eyeholes in his face. 'That's why you get the echo, Nick. The damn thing's empty . . .'

'Shit . . .' Realization oozed through me. No diesel. No Creosote culls. When they reached that critical number they'd come tramping across the fields, crush down the fences and overrun the place.

Boss looked like Dave Middleton in the days before his suicide. He was a walking corpse, going through the motions, and knowing he had failed.

'What am I going to do, Nick? Those kids in there are relying on me. They think I'm going to save their skins. I know I could do it, if it wasn't for those murdering psychopaths out there. We've got a good thing going here. We can grow crops, we've learned to look after livestock . . . But I've killed us. My fault, my bastard fault.' He sat down with his head in his hands. Tears dripped onto the soil.

'Boss.' I crouched beside him. 'How much fuel is there left?'

'The four trucks we use for the culls . . . They've probably got quarter of a tank apiece. And there's five gallons in the drum in the garage.'

'Let's see . . . There's the little Honda car. That's diesel, isn't it? Those things will get you to Timbuctoo and back on a ladleful of fuel.'

Boss looked up. I could see suspicion and hope working in his face. 'Why do you want to know?'

'Listen, I've got a proposition. Give me the car and two gallons of diesel.'

'No way, Nick. Every gallon we have gives us another week of life.'

'No. Listen to what I have to say. What I'm going to do is give you all the diesel you need for the next six months. In return I get the car and a full tank which will be enough to get me home.'

'And how you going to pull that off? Work another miracle? Like when you found the new generator?'

'Come on, we'll grab a coffee and I'll tell you all about it.'

Doc and Jigsaw volunteered to come with me. Sheila wanted to as well but I persuaded her to drive the truck.

I climbed in behind the wheel of the car. It seemed in good nick. The only things that didn't work were the indicators and the fuel gauge. I wasn't going to lose any sleep over that. Jigsaw sat at my side, nursing a sawn-off shotgun on his knee. In the back Doc, armed with a machine pistol, fired questions at me.

'The plan is this,' I told them. 'Sheila will lead us out through the Kaybees in the truck. I don't trust this go-cart of a car to get us through. We've got two gallons in our tank. That's enough to take us where we're going.'

'But not back,' said Doc.

'That's right. It just makes us look harder for fuel.'

'But where will we find it? The whole area's been picked clean now by us and other communities.'

I pointed to a dot on the map. 'Weybeach. I remember it from when I was a kid. It's a little town on the coast where folk retired to – you know the kind of place, one of God's waiting rooms. There will have been very few kids there when the sanity-crash came. So there'll probably be no colonies of kids. In turn, that means there will be no reason for the Kaybees to hang around. They'll have quit Weybeach to go and gang up on survivors in other areas.'

'Let's hope you're right.'

'Pray that I'm right, Doc. It's a long walk back ... Right, here we go.'

I kept the car close to the truck as we drove out through the gates. There were no adults this close to the camp. Sheila put her foot down and I had to do the same to keep up with her. She was good. She flew that truck down the roads, ripping up the green fuzz from the road in a spray.

'I only hope she doesn't brake,' I said, 'otherwise we'll disappear under her back axle.'

'That's right,' grunted Doc from the back seat. 'Cheer us up.'

We took the bend to find a line of Creosotes across the road. Sheila didn't even slow down. The truck parted them like a cleaver through cabbage.

At a crossroads Sheila turned the truck round and brought it alongside us.

'There's no more Kaybees now. Not our lot, anyway.' She looked down at me in an intense way that made me uncomfortable. 'Take care, sunshine.'

A sudden rush of affection for her swept through me. I climbed out of the car and jumped up onto the step beneath the truck's door.

'Thanks, Sheila. You look after yourself. We should only be a couple of days.'

'I'm glad they brought you to us, Nick Aten. You're special, you know that?'

She kissed me on the lips. Jigsaw whistled.

'There . . .' She smiled. 'Remember, there's more where that came from. A lot more . . .' She squeezed my hand where it rested on the door. 'Nick. When you come back I'm going to do all that I can to make you want to stay with us.'

She kissed me again, holding my face with her hands. I stood on the step not knowing what to say. She looked so beautiful as she sat there, hair blowing in the breeze.

'Now, get off my truck, Nick Aten. You've got a journey to make.'

Wiping her eyes, she hit the pedal and the truck went off, swaying down the road back to camp.

The road to Weybeach is long, flat and boring. We drove for sixty miles non-stop. We saw no Creosotes and no camps of survivors. Although we did see in the distance something that looked like a huge doughnut in the middle of a field.

Through the binoculars I could make out that the doughnut ring consisted of dead Creosotes – hundreds of them, lying heaped one on top of the other. In the centre of the ring were a few buildings that had been burnt to shells.

The ring had formed where the Creosotes had pressed up tight against fences before they had died. A sick feeling ran up through my stomach as I handed back the binoculars to Doc.

We drove on. Doc and Jigsaw were quiet. I knew what they were thinking. How long before the Creosotes attacked *their* camp?

Five miles from Weybeach we cruised by ten geriatric Creosotes limping down the road away from the town. Their hair had grown into white manes. These were probably too infirm to have kept up with the earlier mass migrations of adults.

Weybeach was a ghost town. The beach was as I remembered, complete with a pier that ran out over the sands. Dad took John and me out onto it when we were little kids.

'It looks as if God loves us today,' I said. 'He's given us one hell of a peach.'

The town was untouched. Even the supermarket was locked up and looked as if it was only waiting for the manager to come whistling down the street to open up as if nothing had happened.

We found a truck in a nearby coal depot and I began work getting it running. More than six months had gone by since the big DAY 1. The vehicles were still there but tyres and batteries were flat. In most cases the hot summer had evaporated the fuel. Another year or two and cars'd be running to rust.

It was time-consuming but straightforward. Within three days we'd got the truck running, and hitched a huge trailer to the back. We loaded that with enough drums of diesel to see the Leyburn Croppers through the winter. From the supermarket we took food and clothing. I even found space in the car for some bottles of perfume for Sheila.

'When we tell Boss about this,' said Doc, heaving sacks of rice into the trailer, 'he's going to come back mob-handed to pick the town clean.'

On the fourth day we left Weybeach. The truck led the way; I followed in the car. Piled high around me in the passenger seats were cases of canned food and cartons of chocolate.

As I drove I couldn't stop smiling as I imagined the happy faces of the kids as we drove back into the camp. I grinned at myself in the rearview mirror. 'So, Nick old son, this is what it feels like to be Santa Claus.'

Chapter Forty-Three

STAIRWAY TO HEAVEN

I drove back singing to the REM tape on the car stereo. A chocolate box sat open next to me and I stuffed my face. The truck in front, carrying Doc and Jigsaw, lumbered along under its axle-cracking load.

Shiny, Happy People ... Count me in! I sang so loud the steering wheel vibrated against my palms. '*Shy-nee! Happ-pee* ...'

Nearly back at the ranch. Ahead blue smoke billowed from the truck. 'Hey, slow down, guys. We haven't got a ferry to catch ... shit.'

Something was wrong. The truck speeded, whipping by trees, shearing branches.

The road was so narrow I could see nothing but hedge and speeding truck.

Jesus. The brakes had failed on the truck. My hands gripped tight around the car's steering wheel as I followed, tyres slipping on the muck. We were running down hill. A hundred more yards and the road levelled out for the last half-mile to camp.

If Jigsaw kept his cool he could just ride the hill out and slow down using the gears on the flat.

No, was it *shit*. It wasn't the brakes. Jigsaw was hammering the truck's engine, powering the thing faster than it was safe to go, even if you had St Christopher himself in the driving seat.

Jigsaw wasn't running away from something either. He was running toward it. My mouth turned dry.

I powered after the truck hoping I wouldn't skid off into the ditch. Wherever Jigsaw wanted to go, he wanted to be there yesterday.

Down the hill, splash through flood water in the dip, onto the flat, ground opening out into fields – and then I saw what Jigsaw had seen.

'No. No. I don't damn well believe it. You bastards ... You bastards!'

We'd set off five days before, leaving a camp of more than forty people. From a few weeks old to nineteen years old.

We came back to no camp and no people.

The truck skidded to a stop. Doc and Jigsaw jumped out and ran toward the torn fences. I stopped the car and ran after them.

Crows flew up, wild dogs scrambled out of our way. I ran across a carpet of bodies. These were adults pocked with gunshot wounds.

When I reached Jigsaw in the compound he was crying uncontrollably, beating his forehead with the palm of his hand like he wanted to knock out his brains.

Doc stood still, face white, panting, 'How did they do it? How did they do it? Boss could have used the trucks to crop them ... If – if the numbers were reduced below ... They wouldn't attack ... They.' He looked round, winded by what he saw.

Dead Creosotes littered the compound. Here and there were the bodies of people from the community. I ran from outbuilding to barn to house shouting.

'Sheila ... Sheila!'

Sheila lay on the stairs. She'd died trying to stop the madmen reaching the attic room where the baby was. I knelt on the step and held her broken face to mine.

I whispered. 'I want to die now. Jesus, let me die. Let me die.'

After a couple of hours we were in a state where we could actually make a search of the camp.

We found Boss's body beneath some Creosotes by the gate. He must have been one of the first to fall. Spent cartridges and guns littered the place in a shining carpet. The Creosotes themselves hadn't used any weapons, other than a single-minded drive to push their way into the camp. In the end that had been the most devastating weapon of all.

A few of the Creosotes had survived their injuries and lay or sat silently in the carnage. They ignored us. Jigsaw loaded a rifle.

As I continued my search for survivors I heard the slow crack of the rifle echoing round the dead buildings.

Doc found me hunting through the stable. 'They're all dead, Nick. You don't have to check each one. The Kaybees were thorough. They weren't going to spare a single one of us.'

'You're right ... But I'm not leaving here until I've accounted for everyone.'

'I found out why they didn't use the trucks to crop back the psychos,' Doc said. 'The trucks' tanks were empty. Apart from the one truck Sheila used to escort us out there wasn't a drop of diesel left in the camp. Boss had given us the last few gallons for the car.'

Blood thudded through my ears. 'Jesus, I only asked him for two.'

'He gave us eight. He told me not to tell you. He even disconnected the fuel gauge on the car.' Doc shrugged. 'Boss wanted to make sure we, and particularly you, Nick, made it back here in case we couldn't find any supplies.'

'Damn ... Damn him!' I roared every obscenity I could think of. 'Boss has made me responsible for all these deaths. If I'd thought that bit harder maybe we wouldn't have needed the fuel. Boss could have cropped back the lunatics ... These kids would still be alive!'

I looked round at the fields. They were a bleak wasteland now. A cold wind ripped across the grass. Family Creosote had moved on now. Their work here was complete. One by one we, their children, were dying.

I breathed in sharply, struck by an idea that felt as if it had come whistling from out of the cosmos like a bullet. The sensation was the same as when I was looking through the stores before I found the generator.

'Where you going?' shouted Jigsaw.

I ran back to the house, then up the stairs to where Sheila lay. 'I know, sunshine,' I said gently. 'I know what you did.'

I went to the cot where the youngest baby slept. Cold lumps twisting in my stomach, I pulled back the blood-soaked quilt.

Then I turned over the tiny figure on the mattress. It felt stiff . . . I pulled back the bonnet.

'Sheila . . . Whatever they did to you, you won in the end.'

In my hands, in baby clothes, was a plastic doll.

I pushed back the hatch in the ceiling where the water tank sat in the roof void. After climbing up, I lifted the lid of the tank. The water had long gone. Inside it now was a thick layer of blankets. On the blankets was the baby. It opened its eyes and smiled at me.

'How did you know? Nick . . .' Doc followed me as I carried the baby across to the truck. 'How could you possibly know the baby was there? There was no note. Nothing.'

'Sixth sense. When you've survived in hell this long you develop one. Jigsaw, stop wasting bullets . . . That won't turn the clock back.'

'Sixth sense my arse. What made you look for the baby?'

'To be honest I don't really know. I just felt, here inside, that Sheila would do something to protect it. By the time they broke into the compound she must have known no one would escape. And that even though she could slow them down as they came up the stairs to the nursery, she couldn't stop them. And that they'd find the baby.'

Doc nodded. 'So she hid it in the empty water tank and just hoped we'd return and find it before it starved.'

I said, 'Look. You can see where the Creosotes have pulled out all the stores across the yard: they searched this place meticulously. They were going to make sure no one that was under nineteen walked out of here. I reckon our people managed to hold out in the house for a little while. Sheila must have watched the murdering bastards from the window. She saw they were counting our dead. Sure, they've been watching us for weeks to see how we behave, but the bastards have been *counting* us too. They knew we were away from camp. But if they counted even one short they'd have torn the camp apart until they found the baby. Sarah dressed the doll in baby clothes and covered it in blood to make them think the baby was dead . . . Jigsaw, put the gun down and feed the baby. Here's the bottle. You're going to have to give it plenty of fluids. It's dehydrated.'

Doc shook his head. 'Messiah syndrome, Nick. I know it's delusional crap ... but I look at you and, Christ, do I wonder.'

'Let's get back to reality.' I said briskly. 'Doc, help me move the bodies into the house ... No, not the adults. Let the bastards rot. Then you two've got to find somewhere new to live.'

'We've decided.' He nodded at Jigsaw who clumsily held the baby in one arm while holding the bottle for it to drink from. 'We're going on to the community in Harmby. They might let us join them.'

'When they see you with that truckful of supplies they'll welcome you with open arms.'

'You're going back to Eskdale?'

I nodded. 'You two take the truck and the car. There's a motorbike in the garage. I'll be able to get home on one tankful of fuel.'

Doc nodded grimly. Then we moved the bodies back into the house.

'I'll do it,' said Doc pulling out his cigarette lighter.

For half an hour we stood the way mourners stand at gravesides and watched the flames engulf the house. Then I said goodbye to Jigsaw, Doc, and the baby who was gurgling happily now, slung a rifle across my back and climbed onto the bike. It started first time. I waved, then rode away in the direction of home.

In front of me I saw the road stretching out into the distance. In my head I saw Sheila: her bright smile that always made me smile, and the way she looked at me with those eyes that flashed like black diamonds.

And behind me the smoke column from the burning house rose into the sky like a stairway to heaven.

Chapter Forty-Four

HEARTBREAK HIGHWAY

That's the point, I think, when I stopped feeling horror or shock. Perhaps I was in a kind of psychological withdrawal.

I rode the motorbike hour after hour. Sometimes the road was blocked by floods or land slips and I'd have to find another route.

That night I slept in a barn. I found a diary there. It told the story of a sixteen-year-old, Mark Woodley, and how he'd survived the first days of the sanity crash.

My parents are close behind me now. I don't know why they hate me. The world has gone mad. I understand that. But I can't understand why it's happened to mum and dad. The truth just won't sink into my head. All I can do is run and run. I'll find a place where they'll never find me. An island. I'll live there like Robinson Crusoe.

In the corner of the barn lay a skeleton picked shiny white by rats. In a detached way I noticed his quartz battery watch still kept perfect time. The second hand swept round and round, ticking away the seconds for its dead owner.

I dropped the diary by the skeleton.

'Mark . . . You didn't run fast enough, old son.'

The next day I was back on the road by, according to Mark Woodley's watch, 7.09.

I found a motorway and headed north. Although flurries of snow blew across the empty lanes there was no reason why I shouldn't be pulling up in front of the hotel in Eskdale by suppertime.

Then I came to the line that stretched along the central reservation as far as I could see. I drove along them for three miles before actually registering what they were.

I slowed down. Every ten yards a wooden frame in the shape of a letter Y and six feet tall had been set in the turf. To each frame someone had been nailed.

This was crucifixion on a scale the world had never seen before. I rode past the nailed bodies and inside I felt nothing. All I wanted was to get home and see that Sarah was safe. This was just another atrocity. No worse than the latest ... or probably the next.

I had gone another mile when I saw the flash of gold ahead. I slowed down to a crawl. The material of the clothing of one of the corpses was shiny.

I stopped alongside the body.

'Trousers ... I'll get the bastards for you. Believe me, I will.'

The blood on his dead face was dry; his hands nailed to the top of the two prongs on the Y-shaped frame were blue.

Then a finger moved.

'Trousers?'

With an effort so huge it hurt me to watch, he lifted his head to look at me. There was no expression on his face as his eyes fixed on mine.

'Jesus ... I'll get you down, Trousers. You'll be all right.'

He shook his head. Again the movement was painful to watch. I looked down at his feet.

Whichever bastard Creosote had nailed him there had also removed his feet. Leaving him with the choice of hanging by the nails through his hands, or bearing the weight on his two frozen ankle stumps.

He watched me through the crust of blood.

'I'll do it, son. You know I will.'

Slowly he turned his head to one side. I slipped the rifle off my shoulder. At first I was shaking so much I could not aim properly. Then I took a deep breath. The shaking stopped. I squeezed the trigger.

The birds flew up from their feeding grounds at the sound of the shot. I fired again. Then again.

After I made sure his hurting had ended I rode off the motorway at the next exit.

I rode slowly along the silted-up roads, the back tyre sliding at every bend.

I was perhaps seventy miles from home when I saw the mountains rising up ahead of me to merge with the cloud. I pushed on faster hoping to cross them before dark.

But I should have known HOPE was an animal in danger of extinction now. Before I even reached the foothills the bike's motor gave an almighty bang and seized.

It didn't take me long to discover the piston had cracked. I shouldered the rifle and backpack and began to walk.

Ahead the mountains looked bleak. The wind cut through you like a blade. Then the snow flurries became a blizzard.

Chapter Forty-Five

THIS COLD WILL KILL ME

The road took me up the mountainside. I'd never been as cold as this. Christ, it was a supernatural cold that felt as if it blew in through my chest, punching through blood and lungs and heart like ice nails, then tore out through my back.

I crunched on through the snow.

Every so often I'd stop to scrape snow off a road sign so I'd know I was still heading in the direction of home. Would I be glad to see Sarah. Thoughts of snuggling up to her beneath the covers warmed me. It kept me going.

Ahead the road ran up the mountainside but it would be suicide to follow it now. I'd have to find shelter for the night otherwise the cold would kill me. I took a fork to the left which ran steeply downhill toward a lake in the valley bottom. There'd be a house or barn there.

At least going downhill was easier. I even ran for a while to stamp the blood round faster through my body.

I reached the edge of the lake and began to follow the shoreline road. The lake itself was massive, stretching away into the distance like an inland sea.

Here and there yachts wallowed cock-eyedly in the water where they had been abandoned all those months ago.

After a while, the road took me into a forest. At least it was more sheltered from the wind there. The snow fell gently like feathers to the ground.

It grew darker. Another hour of daylight left. I had to find shelter. Already my feet were numb and lights began to twitch in front of my eyes.

'One day you'll do something right, Nick Aten...' I bollocked myself to keep awake. 'You screwed up in Eskdale, you screwed up in Leyburn ... if you'd got half a brain you could have kept Sheila alive ... you could have kept the bloody lot alive ... Doc said they thought you were the bloody messiah sent to save them. Now, that's a joke. You let them die, Aten ... You could have saved them ... You could, you stupid shitter, you could...' I was trying to feel pain, remorse, guilt ... anything. Because at that moment I only felt a numbness icing its way into every part of my body.

'Could have done it. Could've built them a balloon ... could've floated them out. Cabbage brain, Aten ... Cabbage brain...'

How I did it I don't know but I found myself deep in the forest. Somewhere I'd lost the road in the snow.

'So you're taking the easy way out, Aten. You're going to lose yourself, then you're going to curl up in the snow and die ... Ha, bleeding ha! Coward. You've found a way to escape the truth at last.'

And what is the truth, Nick?

'Simple, St Dave Christ Almighty Middleton of Doncaster ... I should have listened to you – done what you said. I should have stayed in Eskdale and run the place myself. There, I've said it, so you can take that Holy Joe smile of your face or I'll—'

I lunged at the face with its sincere smile ... My hands hit a tree. I looked round, panting. 'Hang on, Nick, old son ... You're coming apart at the seams.'

Cutting down to the water's edge, I headed along the shore. I was tripping over my feet now, like a drunk trying to make his way home.

Someone was swimming in the lake. Cold in there, Trousers. Best wait till Spring at least. Cold mountain water ... I shook my head and saw the swimmer was a branch floating by.

I walked on through a world that had lost all its warmth and colour to become black and white. White mountains, black trees, white ground, black water...

Going to die, Aten ... Maybe this is best ... feel nothing no more...

'Hello. Are you lost? Hello? Can you hear me?'

Standing in front of me on the beach were two figures, wrapped like Arctic explorers.

The tall one said to the other, 'Timothy, put the bow down and help me get him to the boat.'

The shorter one, a chubby mongoloid boy of about sixteen, with a concerned look on his pink face, grabbed me by the arm and all but carried me down the beach to sit me in the back of a rowing boat. Then he and the thin one rowed us out into the lake.

I sat there like the ice man of Alaska. My brain had stopped working, so at that point there seemed nothing bizarre about riding in a boat across a five-mile-wide lake in the middle of a blizzard.

Eventually, I could see an object ahead, floating on the water. Just a collection of lumps. Nothing recognizable. The two rowed hard toward it.

We were nearly alongside it before I realised it was a group of huge steel barges, the kind they use to shift coal or rocks. They tied up alongside a low platform, then the mongoloid boy lifted me out.

Suddenly there were young kids milling about, the thin kid was giving orders in a low voice, and I was being pushed up a set of steps into an enclosed passageway.

With a clutch of excited kids pulling me by the arms and coat, they took me through a doorway into a room. I stood there blinking in the brilliant light from neon strips in the ceiling.

'Josie, switch on the fire. Yes ... On full. Good girl. Here you are, friend, sit down.'

I sat down in front of a three-bar electric fire and stared blankly at the glowing elements.

It seemed distant but in the room there was a lot of excited movement as children pulled off my coat, gloves, boots.

'Put his rifle somewhere safe ... Carefully now. That's right ... In the cupboard. You'd better lock it and give me the key ... Now, something warm to eat.'

A girl of around seventeen put down the sewing she'd been working on. 'I'll get it. There's hot soup in the galley.'

I sat there in the armchair, feasting on the heat beating out from the fire, and feeling my feet and hands hurting as they thawed. More than once I wondered if I was dreaming all this, and that I was really lying unconscious in a snowdrift. But as I looked round at the paintings on the walls I reckoned even my brain couldn't come up with those.

Adam, that was the name of the thin one, was open and friendly. After I'd changed my clothes and returned to the lounge, he told me about themselves. 'We're a small community. Thirty-eight in all. At first we lived in a hotel overlooking the lake but we had too much trouble from the afflicted people so I was told to collect the barges from the quarry at the far end of the lake, moor them here as far from the banks as possible and build houses inside of them.'

'You were told?'

'Yes. The Lord spoke to me. He told me how to keep these children safe from harm.'

I just nodded. So he was a religious nut but who cares? They'd got somewhere bright and warm, and for me that was all that mattered.

'I was seventeen when it happened,' he said, putting his long fingers together like he was praying, 'I worked at the monastery in the next valley. You see, I was too young to become a monk but I had already decided to devote my life to God ... It was His will that the brothers and Father Abbot became sick. So I went out and gathered all the children I could find. Eventually I moved them here to the Ark.'

Sitting on the carpet looking up at Adam was virtually the entire population of his community. With the exception of the mongoloid boy, the girl who'd brought me the soup and a pair of Oriental girls, the rest were under the age of eleven.

Adam continued speaking in his soft monk's voice. The children gazed up at him in adoration. 'The Lord instructed me. He showed me where there are generators on the shore that are powered by water from mountain streams, and how to run the cable out here so we have electricity to warm us and cook our meals.'

While we talked I found my eyes being drawn back to the

paintings hanging from the wall. They looked like primitive cave paintings showing stretched-out men and women building houses, farming, sitting with children on their knees listening to musicians playing flutes. On the end wall was a painting running from ceiling to floor showing a tall man in that stretched-out style with his arms raised in praise to the sun rising above a mountain. The mountain looked like the one I nearly died on. The young man looked like Adam.

'Interesting paintings,' I said. 'Who's the artist?'

'That's our Bernadette.' He smiled at the seventeen-year-old girl who sat sewing on the sofa. She pushed back her short dark hair and smiled shyly.

Adam said, 'She paints what she dreams. And I believe the dreams are sent to her by the Lord. These paintings are very special to us. They are signs from Him for all of us to see. They show us images of ourselves in this Ark; and of how we will live in the future.'

I didn't go for this The-Lord-Will-Show-Us-The-Way business but these kids had certainly got themselves a nice place to live. And it was safe. The Creosotes were showing single-minded determination in destroying their young, but I couldn't see how they could get their paws on this place.

Adam talked. I politely listened. After all, I was their guest so it seemed a way of paying for my lodgings to listen to his God-given plans.

Adam was just describing how they were bringing in the sheep to fields nearer to the lake when I was hit by a fit of sneezing.

'I think that long walk took its toll on you, Nick. Bernadette, find something for Nick's cold, will you, please?'

Obediently she put down her sewing and disappeared from the lounge.

'You look exhausted, Nick. And these days we have to be more careful of coughs and sneezes. You'd best spend a couple of days in bed.'

'Thanks, that's kind of you. But I need to be moving on in the morning. I have to get back home. There's a community of people in a lot of danger. Only they don't know it yet.'

'If you must, you must, Nick. At least get a good night's rest.

You'll have a room of your own and tomorrow we'll send you off after a good breakfast with our prayers.'

'Eh ... thank you, Adam.' Awkwardly I smiled at the clean faces looking up at me like I was the Bishop of Bangor. 'Thank you.'

Bernadette came back with a bottle of grey liquid and a spoon. I had hoped the something for my throat would have been a mugful of brandy. This, which she spooned into my mouth, tasted of cough sweets and kerosene.

I was then shown my bedroom, very cozy with sheepskin rugs on the floor and Bernadette's wacko pictures on the wall. I turned to say goodnight to Adam and saw all the children cramming into the corridor to watch me.

'Goodnight.'

'Goodnight, Nick,' they said in chorus.

I shut the door, peeled off my clothes and hauled myself into bed. The comfort and warmth were exquisite. For a while I tried to stay awake and work out how the Ark was composed. Inter-connecting Portacabins inside the barges, I guessed. Certainly a neat trick with the waterpowered generators, though. Hats off to Adam with his bucketsful of divine inspiration.

I yawned. Suddenly I felt so tired I ached, as if Slatter had done a clog dance all over me in his pit boots. The old monster Slatter. What was he doing now? With any luck someone would have shot him, or maybe he'd ended up *Carrying The Can*.

I dreamt that night Sarah made love to me. I lay on my back and looked up to see her there in the gloom, her long blonde hair trailing forward over her face to brush against my chest.

'It's all right, Nick. Everything's all right. Lie still ... Don't try to move ... ah ... That's it ... Oh! That is perfect.'

A confused dream. I only remember fragments. Sarah. Her long hair. Behind her the wacko pictures of long men on the wall. Then the burning rush that comes bursting and sparkling through your body.

Chapter Forty-Six

THIS IS WHERE WE START TO GET ANSWERS

The days that followed were, in the main, a blur. Bernadette thought I had some kind of infection or 'flu. I was weak, feverish. Nights I would soak the sheets with sweat and dream that Sarah made love to me. In the near darkness I would see her silhouette on top of me, her long hair flowing down across her breasts.

During the day I would take short walks around the decks.

Children fished from the platform. They'd sing as they cast out the lines. One morning they were singing carols.

'Only ten days until Christmas,' a boy told me cheerfully. 'Adam says we can have a tree and decorations and things.'

Christmas? I leaned against the railing. Hell, how long was it since my parents took me from Eskdale? Eight weeks? I needed to get back. And now.

All I wanted was to get to the shore, then I could hit the road again. Maybe I'd find a car. With a car I'd be back in a day. If I walked it'd take a week.

Adam walked by. He wore jeans and a lumberjack shirt but he should have worn a monk's habit. 'Don't overdo it, Nick. You're still unwell.'

'I feel fine,' I lied. 'Have you a car? Or a truck?'

'No. In a dream the Lord told me not to use them. Too noisy. We don't do anything that will bring attention to ourselves. We light no fires that would make smoke. By night the windows are shuttered so no one will see the lights across the lake. When we hunt we use bows so there are no gunshots. Come on, friend. Inside where it's warm. I'll ask Bernadette to bring you tea.'

'Yes ... Oh, that's it. Nick. Keep it there, keep it there, I-ah ... Oh, yes. Yes ...'

Sarah came in the dream again. Swaying backwards and forward above me. In the dark all I could see was the shape of her head and her swaying hair.

'Still not feeling any better?' Bernadette spooned more medicine into my mouth.

'I don't feel ill ... Just weak. I can hardly climb the stairs.'

'Do you want me to ask Timothy to help you back to your room?'

'No, thanks. I like it in the lounge ... Are you still painting the pictures?'

Smiling, she nodded. 'Mmm ... When God puts the dreams in my head.'

She left singing. I wondered if she was a bit simple.

I'd spend the day sitting, watching the Ark's inhabitants. They all worked hard, even the youngest children. They were clean, obedient. When Adam spoke they listened with love and respect. Twice a day they held services and sang hymns.

All I could do was sit there, hoping that tomorrow I would be fit enough to continue back to Eskdale.

That night as I got ready for bed I saw something catch the light on one of the sheepskin rugs.

My heart beat harder when I picked it up.

As long as my arm, it was a hair. I put it against my dark jeans. There was no doubting it. It was blonde.

I rubbed my face trying to get my sluggish brain in gear.

The dreams I had. Sarah making love to me. Dreams can be funny, unsettling, erotic – but one thing they do not do is leave physical evidence behind. I wound the hair around a pencil and put it in the drawer.

Then I went to bed, my heart beating fast, thinking hard.

I intended to stay awake but once more tiredness beat me. I lay down and closed my eyes.

The dream girl came again. I tried to lift up my head but it felt as if it had been bolted to the pillow: my arms were too heavy to lift more than a few inches. The figure above me rocked and panted.

Afterwards she dropped forward, breathing deeply, her breath hot on my face. She balanced herself with an arm at each side of my head. With an effort I turned my head to one side. I could see only a dark shadow of an arm. I rolled my head the other way. This time I saw more.

A little light leaked under the door from the passageway. At first I could see a bare forearm and wrist. No jewellery. Featureless skin ... No. I forced myself to see more. There was a birthmark. A red patch on the skin in the shape of a letter C.

I tried to speak but all that came out was grunt. Trying to sit up was worse. It was like trying to move in a dream. Nothing worked.

With a huge effort I snapped into a sitting position and opened my eyes.

It was morning. Daylight seeped through the curtains and Timothy was thumping the door. 'Breakfast, breakfast, breakfast.'

'Okay, okay ... I'm awake. Timothy, I said I'm AWAKE!'

I ate breakfast feeling like something slimy had made its grave beneath my tongue. As I slipped back into focus I began looking round at the hands of people eating.

I drank four mugfuls of tea, hoping it would crank up my brain cells.

When Bernadette left the lounge to take the plates back to the galley, I followed.

'You don't look as peaky as you did, Nick.'

'I feel a lot better. Let me help wash up.'

She began to run hot water onto the plates. 'That's very kind of you. But you need to rest. Anyway, I enjoy washing up. I always sing as I scrub. You know it–'

I grabbed her arm and pulled up the sleeve. A birthmark showed up like a red C.

'Bernadette. It was you.'

She looked up, her dark eyes startled. 'I'm sorry, Mr Aten. I don't know what you mean ... Don't look at me like that. You're scaring me.'

The Chinese twins who were making bread at the far end of the galley turned to watch me.

'Bernadette, you damn well do know what I'm talking about. Where's the blonde wig, Bernadette? You've been coming into – Hey ... Come back here. Bernadette.'

She looked back as she ran. The grin on her face transformed it. 'You'll have to catch me first!'

I followed her down the passage, through a door and into a labyrinth of more passages, then across bridges that linked the barges.

My eyes blurred and I could barely manage a jog never mind a run. Bernadette was fit. She could easily have outrun me but every so often she'd slow down so I could catch up. In the barge where they kept their stores she unlocked a door and ducked inside.

I followed.

I expected a store room. Instead it looked like a professor's study. I blinked in the light. Thick carpets, rugs, a desk, a swivel chair beside a table on which stood a computer, racks of computer disks.

On the walls there weren't any wacko stick men paintings. There were charts, graphs. A map of the world covered with red and black thumbtacks. The red outnumbered the black.

Through an open doorway I saw a bedroom.

'You didn't expect this, did you, Nick?'

Astonished, I looked back at her. Her voice had changed. It had lost the I'm-a-simple-backwoods-girl accent. Now she didn't look away with a shy grin. Her gaze was direct, the smile confident.

'No. I didn't expect this at all, Bernadette. Is this Adam's office?'

'No. It's mine ... Now, do you want to know a secret?'

Chapter Forty-Seven

THIS IS WHAT DROVE ADULTS INSANE

'Sit down, Nick. If you want answers, then I've got answers. And probably far more answers than you can imagine.'

I sat beside her on the study sofa. Bernadette looked at me in the way I'd seen my Uncle Jack look at guitars in music stores, weighing them up, gauging what they are capable of.

'Nick, this might seem a foolish question, but are you interested in learning what happened to the adult population? And what will happen to them – and us – in the future?'

'Yes, of course. But why did—'

'Nick. I'm going to have to make demands of you. First: be very patient. I've a lot to get through. And some of it's going to seem pretty strange. Second ... please accept my apologies. I've under-estimated you. You come across as a bit of a devil-may-care bad boy but there's a brain working away in that skull of yours. Also I hoodwinked you with my just-a-simple-girl performance. Another thing, as you know now, I've been raping you every night.' She grinned. 'It wasn't to slake my perverted lusts. Everything I do, however bizarre it may seem, has a purpose. By the way, you're no longer ill. I have to confess that for the last few days I have been drugging you.'

'What kind of bastard trick is that?' I stood up sharply, blood flaring furiously. 'I can't afford to piss around here out of my skull! I've got to get back home. There's three hundred kids' lives at stake. Obviously you know damn all what's happening out there in the world. There are communities of kids being picked off one by one by the Creosotes ... Jesus Christ, woman, we are becoming extinct and you keep me here, drugged up to the eyeballs so you can shag my brains out!'

She looked at me steadily. 'Hit me, Nick. But I only ask you hit my face, not my stomach.'

'Jesus ... I feel like giving you a slap but I'll not do that. Every single one of us is important now. You know, I've just come from a camp where more than forty people have been slaughtered.' I took a deep breath. 'Just get this into your head, Bernadette, forget about hymn-singing, arty-farty painting on the wall and get yourself into the real world. Good kids are working hard and fighting hard, and dying hard.'

She nodded. I saw no remorse in her face. If anything I felt as if I'd satisfactorily answered questions at an interview.

'Nick ... Listen to me please. I know you're upset—'

'Damn right.'

'Sit down. I know you want to get back to Eskdale. There's someone special to you there called Sarah.'

'How the hell do you know that?'

'You talk in your sleep, Mr Aten.' Bernadette's smile was sympathetic. 'You want to get back there in a hurry but believe me, Nick, you're stuck here for a couple of days anyway. The weather's improving but those mountain roads are still blocked by snow. You'd die trying to get through now.'

'But I must get—'

'Yes, just give it a couple more days. It's beginning to thaw. With luck you'll have a few clear days before the snow sets in for the winter. Fancy a beer?'

'I could murder one ... You said you had answers, Bernadette. 'I'm all ears.'

'Patience, Mr Aten. I'll get the beers, then we'll talk. First, though, I must ask you to promise me something.'

I shrugged. 'Fire away.'

'Whilst you're here on the Ark you must stay here in my

apartment. If you go back and the children find out what's happening here, and what I'm really like, everything will be ruined.' She touched my lips as I started to speak. 'No, I'm not on a weird ego trip. What I'm doing here – it won't guarantee our survival but it will go a long, long way to help. And when I mean our survival, I mean the survival of our species – the human race.'

I nodded. My mind had taken to revolving in its skull. Today the surprises were coming thick and fast.

'One beer coming up. You sit there, Nick. It'll be a few hours before the drug's completely out of your bloodstream.'

As she went to a well-stocked refrigerator I looked round numbly at the maps and charts. Shelves full of books with titles like *Archetypal Psychology* and *Man And His Symbols*. By people with strange names like Jung, Freud, Progoff and Laurens van der Post.

Bernadette returned with the beers as a voice crackled over a speaker. She went to a stack of electronic hardware in the corner of the room and picked up the mike.

'Hello, Abraxas . . . All quiet in Luxor? Good . . . Abraxas, I can't talk now. Something came up. I'll contact you at 1900 hours. Fine . . . Catch you later.' She came back and handed me the beer. 'See, Nick. I *do* know what's happening in the outside world.'

'Do you talk to many people on that thing? The last camp I visited they were in touch with survivors all over the world.'

'I know. I even heard your name mentioned by someone called Sheila.'

The blood thudded in my ears and I had to look away.

'Yes, Nick.' She squeezed my hand. 'I know what happened. They began broadcasting when they were attacked. They only stopped when . . . You can guess.'

'I don't have to – I know.'

'Look.' She pointed at the map of the world covered in red and black thumbtacks. 'I've plotted on there the communities that are broadcasting. Of course there must be thousands more that don't have transmitters. Yours at Eskdale is one. The red tacks are surviving communities. The black tacks are those that have stopped transmitting. Why they've stopped transmitting is unfortunately obvious. The insane adults are doing an efficient job. They target a

community, then something triggers them to attack, which they do
with utter dedication. They don't care how many of their own die.
As long as they achieve the total destruction of the community – and
the death of every single person within it.'

'You talk as if there's some kind of masterplan behind it all. Like
the adults are being controlled.'

'They are, Nick.'

'By who?'

'That's a long story. Before we get down to that, tell me about
Nick Aten.' She grinned. 'Even though we've fucked like crazy I
don't know anything about you. Although...' She nodded at the
transmitter. 'I heard Sheila talk about you with something close to
religious awe.'

'The Messiah syndrome?'

'Ah, you've heard about it. Yes, in times of great danger there *is*
this instinctive craving for the appearance of a messiah, or hero who
will make the world safe again.'

'Well, they got the wrong man with me. I'm nothing but shit.' A
million images burned through my head as I said it. Sarah. David
Middleton begging me to take control, then blowing his brains out.
Being away from the house the night mum and dad killed John. The
Singing Sisters hanging in the barn. Guilt, guilt, guilt! I could have
saved them all if I'd been half as good as people expected me to be.

I sucked on the beer. It felt like a glacier going down my throat.

'You looked as though you needed that,' said Bernadette. 'I'll get
you another.'

When she came back we swapped stories. As always these days
you tell people what happened to you the night the world went
crazy.

Bernadette lived with her mother, who was a surgeon, in the
village at the end of the lake.

On the Sunday, DAY 2, Bernadette had woken at nine. Nothing
seemed unusual. She thought her mother was having a lie-in after a
heavy week at the hospital. At mid-day she went to check on her
mother.

She found her dead in bed from a drugs overdose. Her mother's
diary was on the bedside table. An entry in odd little print only
vaguely resembled her mother's usual scrawl.

It was written on the night of the sanity crash and timed at 2 a.m.

Hating Bernie. Noises in room. Voices shouting. No one there. They shout, kill Bernie, kill her. Save yourself, kill Bernie. Feel confused. Voices demand. Hating Bernie ... no I don't hate Bernie, I love Bernie. Clear signs I am suffering from mental illness. Feeling of great danger. Can only save myself if I kill Bernie. No, Bernie's in danger.

2.45 a.m. For the last twenty minutes I've rolled around my bedroom, biting sheets and my own hands. Feels as though I am fighting a battle with someone in my head. Someone very strong. They are winning. I feel it. My sanity is slipping. I managed to swallow tranquillisers. For now I feel very calm, very clear headed. I know it won't last long. Already I can feel the thing in my head fighting to take control of me.

When it does, the real me, Mary Christopher, will be lost forever. Then whatever is in my head will use my body to kill Bernie. I know what I have to do.

Good-bye, Bernie. I am sorry to have to leave you like this.

You were always very special to me, Bernie.

Love, mum.

Then came some scribbled marks that meant nothing.

Bernadette's eyes were glistening as she carefully returned the diary to the drawer.

'Within a few hours,' she said, 'I saw that it wasn't just my mother who'd lost her mind. It was the whole adult population. Now, Nick, what happened to you?'

We talked. When I told her about being kidnapped by my parents and the weird experiment they seemed to be conducting, seizing kids and dumping them miles away, Bernadette sat up straight.

'Mind if I record this conversation?'

'If you want to. Go ahead.'

'It's not a question of want – it's a question of need. I need to compile as much information about the behaviour of the adults as I possibly can. Every tiny bit more we know about them improves our chances of staying alive.'

I told her everything. She seemed particularly interested in the systematic destruction of the Croppers at Leyburn. How the adults had carefully counted how many were in the community – and kept a count of those they killed.

Two hours later, my throat sore from talking, Bernadette snapped off the tape.

'Right, I've got to get back now. We've got hymns before lunch.'

'But you were going to tell what happened to the adults. Why did they go crazy? Why are they killing their own children?'

'All in good time. Make yourself comfortable. There's microwave meals in the refrigerator, the kitchen's through the yellow door across there. And there's plenty of movies on disc if you want to watch TV. Now ... I know you've lots of questions but you'll get your answers later.'

The answers that were to come – not just about what happened to the adults, but answers to questions men and women have asked for ten thousand years – would, as near as dammitt, blow my mind.

Chapter Forty-Eight

THE MYSTERIES

For three hours I had the run of Bernadette's apartment. For lunch I ate microwave lasagna, swilled a couple of beers and watched a disc of *It's A Wonderful Life* on the TV.

The experience was weird. In its own way as weird as seeing the mass migration of Creosotes, or the flooded towns I'd visited, or the mass crucifixion on the motorway. Here I was sitting in a snug apartment, bottle of beer in my mit, watching Jimmy Stewart doing his thing in small-town USA.

I could have been in someone's city home where everything was fine and the adult population hadn't gone ape-shit and murdered their kids.

After a while I felt reality slipping through my fingers so I opened the window and looked out over the lake to the snow-covered mountains.

No. Here I was on a place these people called the Ark. A whole lot of steel barges floating bang in the middle of forty square miles of cold water. Eskdale was maybe sixty miles away. What did Sarah think had happened to me? Did she care any more? Was she alive or dead?

I breathed in deeply, feeling the cut of iced air. The world sharply focused once more.

'I hope you're not thinking of swimming for it.' Bernadette locked the door behind her. 'The cold would kill you long before you reached the shore.'

I smiled. 'No. Before I do anything I want to hear what really happened back on that weekend in April.'

'Grab a seat, then we'll begin.' Before she sat down she switched on the radio receiver. A low babble of foreign voices mixed with static crackled softly from the speaker.

'This place.' I looked round the room. 'Does Adam know anything about it?'

'Do you mean, is he aware of the conspiracy?'

'Conspiracy?'

'Yes, he's in on it. And so are you. Come on, sit down, Nick. Once I've told you a few things it'll all become as clear as that window why I've done the things I've done.'

'Like the ages of your people here in the community? I mean it seems odd that apart from you, Adam, Timothy and the two Chinese girls, everyone else seems to be under the age of eleven.'

She nodded. 'There is a reason. When I created the community I deliberately chose young children with minds I could mould. Clearly Timothy is a special case. The Chinese twins are from a Christian mission school and are devoutly religious.'

'Like Adam?'

'Yes, he was. He'd planned on becoming a monk.'

'You say he *was* religious.'

'After the collapse of society in April he went off the rails. He'd either spend hours cursing God or going round every church in the district and burning it down. At that time our group lived in one hotel. It got to the point where I had to lock him in his room. He even tried to kill himself.'

'Someone worked a miracle on him. To look at his drive and stamina now you'd think he's on a mission from God.'

'In a way he is.'

'So he's returned to the flock, then?'

'No. Not in that sense. But he has a faith.'

'Are you being deliberately mysterious or am I thick as pig shit?'

Bernadette laughed. 'I'm sorry, I've kept you in the dark long enough. Now . . . Do you believe in God?'

'No.'

I thought then she would try and sell religion to me like some doorstep Jehovah's Witness. Instead she sighed with relief and said, 'Good. If you were religious I'd have to give you the edited version of events to spare your feelings. Religious people might find what I'm going to tell you too controversial, and too disturbing.'

I leaned forward. 'You've got my interest now. Keep talking.'

'Here it is then, Mr Aten. The truth, the whole truth and nothing but the truth. My next question to you is: do you believe that there is a force which is invisible and beyond your control, but a force that has the power to affect, even control your life?'

'No. Not at all.'

'Ever fallen in love?'

'Yes, but...' The bit that should have followed 'but' wouldn't come. I remembered getting the hots for such and such a girl and making up excuses to myself to pass her house twenty times a day in the hope of bumping into her or even catching sight of her. I didn't want to do it. That damned thing called infatuation forced me.

Bernadette smiled, knowing she'd got me on that one. 'A few more examples of this power that can affect our lives. We're young enough to remember what it's like to be adolescent. Along with the spots come loads of strange feelings and desires. Things you wouldn't dream of doing at eleven obsess you when you're fourteen. You spend hours staring at the mirror worrying about the shape of your nose, you listen to sad songs late at night and you feel like you're from another planet, and that people no longer understand you.'

'Yeah, that happens to everyone.'

'Agreed. And then there are things that happen to people individually. You've heard of the empty nest syndrome? This affects women when their children grow up and leave home. They go through a period of feeling useless and ready for the scrap heap. Then there are people who can never shake off a penetrating sense of loneliness even when they're in a crowd. Some feel life is pointless, or that something vital is missing from their lives. They might be wealthy people with families, but they can't shake off this feeling that there's a hole in their lives which, however hard they try, they can't fill – sometimes it drives them to drink or drugs.'

'Okay,' I said, 'some men and women feel as if there *is* a force

that controls their lives. But it's just one of those things that affect
certain individuals. Like some people get depressed for no real
reason.'

'No, Nick. This force I'm talking about affects all people to a
lesser or greater degree. All people. Me, you, the Pope, the
President of the United States. For example, have you ever been
frightened by a dream, amused by a dream or even had a dream that
makes you sexually aroused?'

She smiled when I blushed.

She continued, getting into the rhythm now. 'Why are people
interested by apparently illogical pastimes like football, tennis,
horse racing, music, dance, stamp collecting, watching TV and a
million other things?' She took a breath. 'Right, imagine this.
There's a hall with a hundred people sitting in it. You get up on the
stage, Nick. You're going to make a speech. How do you feel?'

'Nervous.' I grinned. 'Very, very nervous. Trembling legs, butterflies in stomach, dry mouth. Probably start stammering.'

'Me too. Why? Why do all these physical symptoms torment us
when we stand up to make a speech, or sit an exam, or go on our
first date?'

I shrugged. 'Human nature.'

'Yes, human nature. And it is natural that our behaviour is
affected by a force we do not control, cannot see, or even fully
understand.' She opened a beer and poured it, noisily, into a glass.
'If I did this in front of twenty people – the sound of running liquid.
What do you think'd happen?'

'Some of them would want to go to the toilet.'

'So, running liquid instils in all people, if they have a full bladder,
the urge to urinate. Why?'

'You're the one with the answers, Bernadette.'

'Did you know that for tens of thousands of years in prehistoric
times man was nomadic? We roamed in small tribes, never settling
anywhere longer than a few weeks, carrying everything we owned
including our babies. We were on the trail of the mammoth that
migrated with the ice cap. Following us were all kinds of predators,
wolves, bears, big cats.'

'So what's this got to do with wanting to piss when you hear
running water?'

'Stands to reason, doesn't it? Think of the danger you're in if people in your tribe are stopping every five minutes to urinate. It might make the difference between catching that mammoth you're hunting or starving – or maybe the wolves will catch up with you. Far better if the tribe synchronises its toilet habits. And that's what happened. If one person urinates the sound of water hitting the ground makes everyone else want to urinate too. So they all empty their bladders at more or less the same time then they can carry on walking without interruptions for another few hours.'

I nodded. What she told me was sinking in.

She smiled. 'I just wanted to establish that you accept that there *is* a force beyond us that can have some degree of control over our lives. Now, I've been working hard all morning so I'll let you make me a coffee before we crack on with the next revelation.'

As I poured coffee I said, 'Now something tells me you're going to peddle me this Freudian psychological shit.'

'I agree. Sigmund Freud, the man who made the first significant discoveries about the human mind, believed everyone had hang-ups about sex. In a nutshell, he was more screwed-up than his patients. You can safely ignore eighty percent of Freud's work. In fact, most psychologists screwed up. They portrayed human beings as crummy animals made up of a rag-bag of psychological mechanisms. You got the feeling psychologists' studies of the human mind were on the level of a zoologist dissecting buffalo shit.'

'I suppose something like that pissed me off about religious education lessons. Basically all we were taught was that men and women were evil, or weak, or jam full of sin.'

She grinned. 'Good point. I think we're on the same wavelength. Human beings are the most brilliant stars in creation. We're the highest developed. We're capable of working miracles. Sure, there are a few bad apples but that shouldn't rot the whole barrelful.'

'Hang on, Bernadette. You sit here and tell me this. Then you go through there into the Ark and you're singing hymns and telling those kids how wonderful God is. That makes as much sense as an open-ended condom.'

'Bear with me, Nick. As I said, by the time we're finished everything will make sense. Religions do have their uses. Problems arise when they get confused, or twisted by tyrants who realize they can use religion to control the population. Or more commonly religions simply get past their sell-by date: that happened in the nineteenth and twentieth centuries.'

'So we should ditch religion and make the world a better place.'

'That, Nick, would be throwing the baby out with the bathwater ... An example of a religion that benefited all its members was Gnosticism which flourished around fifteen hundred years ago. Most religions say this: Suffer on earth because you get your reward in heaven when you join God. Stuff that, said the Gnostics, we believe we can join God on Earth and have the happiness we're entitled to while we're alive. They believed they achieved this.'

'Cheeky. I bet the Gnostics upset some powerful people, didn't they?'

'They did. The established church of the time were so frightened of the Gnostics they tried to stamp them out. They spread all kinds of foolish propaganda about Gnostics being devil worshippers. They weren't, of course. What the Gnostics had done was develop a religious faith that resulted in its members leading happy and contented lives free from hypocrisy and fear. No, Nick, I'm not trying to peddle you Gnosticism, either. Just that some people were successful in developing meaningful faiths that gave them, here on Earth, while they were alive, peace, satisfaction and prosperity. And just to give you a clue where I'm taking you with all this, here's a saying of the Gnostics: Man is a mortal god. And God is an immortal man.'

I struggled to work all this through the gut of my brain. Bernadette was trying to make this explanation easy for me. But I'm no intellectual. Sure, I spent a lot of time in the school library – chatting up girls or having a sly smoke behind the encyclopaedias. The only book I ever took from a shelf was *The Complete Works Of William Shakespeare*. I belted Tug Slatter round the back of the head with it.

'Man is a mortal God. God is an immortal man ...' I said half to myself. 'Does that mean that we're—'

'Shit,' hissed Bernadette and jumped to her feet. 'Problems.' She ran to the radio transmitter in the corner. She had left it on low, monitoring the worldwide conversations while she talked to me.

'What's wrong?'

'It's the colony outside Berlin,' she said cranking up the volume. 'They're under attack.'

'Adults?'

'Yep. They've been expecting it for some time. They reckon there's more than five thousand of them massing on the banks.' Quickly she explained, 'There's a colony of a hundred kids living on an island in a river. There were some scrappy attacks before from adults using boats, but the colony is well armed and nothing came of it. Now the adults are trying something different. They're ... sorry, Erich's talking again.'

We listened. I don't understand German but it was the emotion carried by the voice that set the hairs on the back of my neck on end. It wasn't just fear – I could almost reach out and touch the sheer astonishment, almost a sense of wonder.

'Shit, shit, shit,' hissed Bernadette. 'This isn't good ... Nick, you told me how the Creosotes were studying us, and that they now planned their attacks? Well, their ability to solve problems is coming on in leaps and bounds. From what Erich is saying it appears the Creosotes are forming a human bridge to the island. It's the middle of winter; the water must be near freezing but hundreds are standing in the water.'

She listened to the transmission, staring with glistening eyes at the map covered with thumbtacks. She must have been imagining what it was like there on the river island.

The tone of Erich's voice frightened me more than I could have admitted to anyone.

As I stared out of the window at the snow-choked mountains, I found myself willing some part of me to fly to Eskdale to see what was happening. All I could see in my mind's eye were the Creosote swamping the hotel like a dirty great ocean. Sarah, fighting like Sheila had done, to the last, to save her sisters and the babies.

Erich's broadcast went on for hours. I slipped into a kind of trance, only conscious of cold, a kind of supernatural cold that bore through me.

At six p.m. Bernadette sighed heavily, stood up, pulled a red thumbtack from the world map – and replaced it with one that was black.

Chapter Forty-Nine

THE REVELATIONS COME THICK AND FAST

8 p.m.

You remember those tigers in their cages at the zoo? Pacing backwards, forwards. Up onto the rock. Down to the water bowl. Pacing again.

I was like that. The death of the German kids had twisted my gut. Now I did want to swim for the shore and run across the mountains back to Eskdale. Sure it would be suicide but I felt I had to act. I had to move physically with a sense of purpose. Even running like a crazy man through the snow would be better than being caged on this clump of barges they called the frigging Ark.

'Nick . . . Sit down. Unwind a little.'

'I can't. I keep thinking what if what happened to the Germans happens to Eskdale. You know they've got two sadistic thugs in charge there that couldn't organize a piss-up in a brewery? If even fifty Creosotes attack they've got no chance. They're babies and little children there. With no one to protect them.'

'And you can save them, Nick?'

'Yes.'

I stopped pacing. The belief I could save them struck me like lightning. Before I was just too plain scared to accept responsibility. Me, boss? No way! Somewhere along this shitty route from Doncaster to the lady of the lake I'd lost the old Nick Aten and grown a new one.

Yes! I could save them. If only I could get back to Eskdale.

'Nick . . .' Bernadette's voice was gentle. 'I believe you can save your community. Only you didn't believe it yourself before. Now you can. Something wonderful has happened in here.' She touched my head. As her dark eyes studied mine, my skin goose-fleshed.

'I've got to get back, Bernadette. I can't wait here any longer.'

'You've got to be patient. Listen to me. Those roads are still impassable. Give it another forty-eight hours.'

I looked at my hands. They were actually vibrating they were shaking that much.

'I'll get you a beer. Meanwhile, you go through into the bedroom and take off your shirt . . . Don't look at me like that. I'm not seducing you. I'll give you a massage to relax those muscles of yours. Let me feel your back. I thought so, like a slab of concrete.' She leaned forward, looking into my eyes. 'Relax, love. If you are going to be any good to your people back home you need to arrive there in one piece.'

I did what she asked. Bernadette's hands were magic, working at the knots of muscle in my neck, shoulders and back. As she worked on me I felt my muscles relax like twisted pieces of rubber unravelling.

Sheer bliss. Pure comfort. The cold in my blood gave way to a warmth that stroked its way through my body.

She said gently, 'That better?'

I grunted a yes. The beer helped too.

After a while we began to talk again. I told her about the rumours I'd heard about the Creosotes talking to God; or that it was a weapon that had caused the breakdown – a mind scrambler.

'Or that it was the cumulative action of radio and TV signals on the mind that caused the madness? Yes, I've heard them all.'

'So what did happen, Bernadette?'

She continued to massage my back as I lay face down on the double bed. 'We've talked a lot about religion and God. Would you like to know where God fits into all of this?'

'You're certainly an enigma, girl. You talk like you don't believe in God. Now you're telling me there *is* a God.'

'More than that,' she said stroking my shoulders. 'I'll show you where he lives. No ... Lie still, Nick.' Her voice was still gentle. 'I'm not mad. Only enlightened. You will be too if you lie there and let me talk as I massage your back.'

'Jesus, Bernadette. You know how to shock. Where God lives? You mean we can just leg it round to his place and say hi?'

'Patience, Nick Aten. Patience.'

'What's this got to do with adults going crazy?'

'I'll tell you, Nick. In one word: EVOLUTION.'

'Evolution? That makes damn all sense. Evolution is supposed to improve animals. Not make them less well equipped to survive. Listen, Bernadette, adults just went psycho, then killed their children.'

'That, Nick, is just one phase of what is an ongoing process.'

'This is all natural, then? Some kind of metamorphosis like caterpillars changing into butterflies?'

'See, I told you, you're smarter than you think. All I can say is while I talk keep an open mind. As I said, some people would find what I'm going to say controversial, even distressing, it would change people's lives forever.'

'All this religious stuff for the kids on the Ark is a charade, then?'

'Not charade in a cynical sense. What we do through there is very useful, teaching them values, a new morality. A faith to give them a sense of safety and security. When a child is old enough they will be told the truth.'

'So you were pulling my leg about telling me where God lives?'

'We're getting ahead of ourselves here. You wanted to know why everyone over the age of nineteen apparently went insane in April?'

'Of course I do.'

'Right, back to the beginning.'

I listened to her gentle voice as she spoke and felt the tender touch of her hands massaging me.

'We don't go back to April, Nick. We go back fifty thousand years. To the time of Neanderthal man. You remember your history lessons, don't you?'

'Only roughly. I wasn't a model student.'

'In a nutshell Neanderthal man was our predecessor in the evolutionary line. We succeeded them. They had receding fore-heads, heavy jaws, ape-like features – but they had big brains, walked liked later men and made tools; they even buried their dead.'

'I get the picture.'

'So, you have a physically strong intelligent man-creature. Capable of defeating any other living creature on Earth. Why, then, did they suddenly die out to be replaced by us?'

'Search me. I suppose they started giving birth to human babies. Eventually Neanderthals were replaced by homo sap.'

'But if you look at the animal kingdom, mature animals destroy or abandon offspring that're born mutant or deformed. Surely the same would have happened to Neanderthals. They would have killed their mutant babies before they had a chance to grow up and threaten them.'

'So what happened?'

'Science shows us that evolution often occurs in dramatic leaps. And when it makes that evolutionary leap nature drives the new stage to destroy the old one.'

Understanding flashed. 'So you're saying fifty thousand years ago the same happened to cavemen. Adults went mad, then destroyed their young.'

'Broadly, yes. What happened wasn't an evolutionary jump that changed the physical body. It was an evolutionary jump of the mind. Scientists got it wrong thinking the young always succeed the old. In this case, the adults succeeded their children.'

'But I still can't see that driving adults insane is an evolutionary improvement.'

'They didn't go insane as such, Nick. What happened was a profound change in the mind. Listen, up to that point Neanderthals had the mind of an animal. True, a highly developed one, but still an animal mind. It wasn't aware of itself as an individual, it wasn't conscious. What happened in one explosive moment across the Neanderthal population was that the conscious mind was born. You can imagine one morning they woke up in their caves and suddenly they knew they were individuals – they could actually think for the first time, they could make decisions, ask questions.'

'Why the madness, then?'

'It wasn't an easy transition. First it was a tremendous shock. Imagine if you woke from a coma where you're only very, very dimly aware of what's happening in the world around you. Then *bang* ... You know.'

'Am I right in thinking this has something to do with what you were saying about this invisible force that we can't see but that can control our lives?'

'You're getting there, Nick. Now, turn over, I'll do your front ... That's it. Now ... In effect what happened was that this new consciousness was a completely new mind. Also it was separate to the old mind that Neanderthals had possessed before. Nick, are you familiar with the scientific concept of the conscious and unconscious mind?'

'No.'

'Well, anyone could check the reference in an encyclopaedia, but I'll come back to that in a moment. Just imagine this, then: one night the conscious mind came into being. Neanderthals would feel as if they'd woken from a coma. Then what happened in their heads was nothing short of a civil war. The new conscious mind battled with the old animal mind for control of the body. We don't know how long they fought one another, but during this transition period the confusion would be so great they would appear stark, staring mad. Control would switch back and forth between the conscious and unconscious mind. Also during this time would come the instinctive drive to destroy their own children. After a while, the new conscious mind defeated the old animal mind.'

'So there were two minds in one head? Fighting one another?'

'Precisely. Imagine them struggling for control. You've seen movies where two people fight for the control of a car. Anyway, eventually the old animal mind was pushed into the back seat where he's stayed as a backseat driver ever since.'

She left me to digest this as she made supper. My head was spinning. And it wasn't just the beer. Questions spat into my mind.

As we finished the pizza Bernadette licked the tomato sauce from her finger and said, 'Right, we're at the point where Neanderthals have suddenly acquired this new mind which has seized control of them and has turned them into conscious human beings who can reason and make decisions. For the first time they can think like you and me.'

'Like I can think to myself, my name is Nick Aten, I'm sitting in a room, drinking a beer. That's the conscious part of me?'

'And that's something no other animal on earth can do. You're getting there, Nick. Right, let's get back fifty thousand years to Neanderthal man. Their young still have the old animal mind. So basically we have two different species. There isn't room in their territories for two competitors. One species must die. Now evolution has another trick up its sleeve. See that computer across there. If you hit the right keys you get my work files up on screen. If you hit other keys you get computer chess. Another key: war games. Buried in the computer's memory banks are dozens of different programs – all complete. They're just waiting for someone who knows the codes to summon them up. Your mind, Nick, and everyone else's mind contains hidden programs like that computer. If you know the right code then you get access to them, and you can use them. You don't believe me?'

'I guess I do; it takes some digesting, though.'

'You'll have heard women say that until their first child was born they thought they'd never know how to raise children. Then as soon as baby's born, ping! Suddenly, they feel like a natural born mother. Now, Nick. Imagine you're eight years old. What would you do if a girl kissed you?'

I grinned. 'Want to hide in a hole. Boys hate girls at that age.'

'But if a seventeen-year-old girl was to kiss you now?'

'Ah, that'd be different.'

'That's because during your early teens your body clock pressed the right button and called up the new software program into your head. Not only did it overturn your old dislike of girls, it made them fascinating. It gave you information on how to get a girl for yourself and what to do, more or less, when you got her.'

'I remember when I was thirteen, one of my friends wrote SEX, SEX, SEX all over his desk. It sounds banal now but we sniggered our heads off for hours.'

'So fifty thousand years ago another software program was activated in the mind. And that was an overwhelming craving to destroy their own young. We're seeing it happening now. A systematic and dedicated crusade by adults to annihilate their children. Because now we form a different species.'

'And they won't stop hitting the genocide button until we're all dead.'

'Or until we destroy them.'

'So . . . It's us or them?'

'Correct. That's why there are no Neanderthals left alive today.'

'Why don't we look like cavemen then, all hairy with heavy jaws?'

'Once the profound mental change had taken place overnight, the physical changes into what we look like today probably happened quite gradually over a few generations.'

'But what about the conscious and unconscious minds? How does that fit in today?'

Bernadette smiled. 'Lie down. Let me massage your back again. You know I'm getting as much pleasure from this as you are . . . Right.' She took a deep breath and plunged in. 'This might come as a surprise. The fact is you have two minds in your head. Again, if you want to go into it in more detail there's a rack of psychology books there, help yourself.' She poured massaging oil onto my back and began to work it beneath my shoulder blades. 'One mind is the thing that makes you *you*. Your personality. Your likes, dislikes. Why you like to wear that leather jacket or why you prefer such-and-such a movie.'

'This is the new conscious mind that overthrew the old animal mind, right?'

'Right. But the old animal mind is still there in your head. He's a back seat driver now. Now, here comes the big, BIG problem. The old animal mind was beaten, and he was locked away in the back of your head. But as the man Jung said, the ancient animal man inside your head, the unconscious mind, is actually more intelligent in some respects than your conscious mind – the Nick Aten part. To make matters worse the unconscious part is a powerful force. He still wants control of you. And over fifty thousand years locked away like a genie in a bottle he's learnt ways to do it. He has access to that buried software I was talking about. And he can trigger it. Sometimes when we don't want him to. When it's inconvenient like when we want to speak to an audience and we get an attack of nerves. Sometimes the manipulation is more subtle – for example a passion for buying new clothes or that new car you can't really afford.'

For some reason I found myself thinking of Uncle Jack Aten, his craving to be a musician, then slowly rotting with cancer.

'If you upset your unconscious then he can really make life tough for you.' Bernadette worked at my neck muscles, fingers slipping smoothly across the oiled skin. 'That hairy old manbeast in your head can inflict mental illness on you. He can make you feel depressed or anxious for no apparent reason at all. Stress you out so much you develop physical illness such as ulcers, heart complaints or even cancer.'

I thought again of poor Uncle Jack and I knew she was right.

'So,' I said, 'the war goes on. But the unconscious is now fighting a guerrilla war, using terrorist tactics.'

'True. But over the last few centuries he's also been saying let's call it a truce. We both want the same thing. We want our physical bodies to be healthy and live long. So the unconscious says: from now on let's work together. We'll be an unbeatable partnership. One mind ancient and wise, the other, fresh, young, inventive, adaptable.'

'But it wasn't as easy as that.'

'Correct. The conscious mind and unconscious mind are still radically different from each other. Imagine if you hook up two powerful computers so they can exchange information and work together. That's what the two minds were straining towards. They have a problem, though. The link between them is far from perfect. Yes, you have your two computers, but you've got the wrong cable connecting the two. Okay, some information gets through, but then you hit the other snag. You discover the two minds don't speak the same language. With me so far?'

'I reckon. Just.'

'Please excuse all these comparisons to computers but it's important to me that I convey what I understand to you. Again, imagine the conscious mind is the captain of a ship. Imagine he's Russian. Now he can steer the ship, but it's the engineer down in the engine room who controls the ship's speed. We'll say he is Scottish. Imagine there's a problem. The engineer is trying to communicate with the captain but can't get through. Every so often the captain shouts down Full Speed Ahead. But it's in a language the engineer doesn't understand. All the time they are shouting warnings and orders at one another but becoming more and more frustrated because they don't understand each other's language.'

'And in the meantime the ship is rushing toward the reef.'

'Exactly. Both the unconscious and conscious want to co-operate with one another. The unconscious only wants to be a good co-pilot, instead of the interfering back-seat driver.'

'But how, if they can't speak the same language?'

'True. Our Russian captain can't understand Scottie, our engineer – but there's nothing to stop him learning the language.'

Chapter Fifty

MAKE LOVE TO ME

I fetched the beers. Bernadette lay back on the bed, looking at the ceiling. She was thinking hard. It was hugely important to her that I understood what she told me. But I couldn't help wondering: WHY ME?

'Cheers.' She sipped her beer, a faraway look in her eyes. 'Imagine, Nick. The benefits if we could get the two minds working together in harmony.'

'It sounds great in theory. But would it make any difference to us in real life – I mean practical day to day benefits?'

Her eyes widened. 'I can't even begin to guess the benefits. They would be enormous. You wouldn't be able to achieve union with the Unconscious mind straight away – only in stages. But someone beginning to achieve this in their lives would begin to reap the benefits pretty quickly. Crudely put they could turn their fifteen thousand a year life-style into a twenty thousand a year one. Men and women who find happiness difficult to achieve would discover happiness. For example, instead of having a series of troublesome affairs, they'd find a satisfying long term relationship; people who feel lonely would now enjoy eternal companionship. I'm not suggesting all problems would vanish but you'd find them less of an obstacle and easier to solve. Are you with me so far?'

I nodded.

'People would be healthier physically and mentally,' she said. 'You would be less likely to suffer from even common ailments like colds or 'flu; and if you did you would recover faster. People might admit to being completely happy thirty percent of the time. How would you like to be completely happy sixty percent of the time? Now, faced with genocide from the adults and having to rebuild civilization all over again, the benefit of going into partnership with the old mind in your head is simple: SURVIVAL.'

She took a sip of beer. 'Old religions promised lots but rarely delivered. Even believers were troubled that they had more than their fair share of misery – and that when they spoke to their god he did not answer. *This one does*.'

'Bernadette. Stop it right there.' The beer nearly slipped through my fingers. 'Earlier you said, not only was there a god, but you'd show me where he lives. I thought you were pulling my leg. But now you're telling me there is a god and—'

'And he's closer than you think.' She gently touched my temple. 'The unconscious part of the mind. The old one in your head. This is what ancient people recognised as god.'

'But they believed ancient gods lived in rivers, up mountains, in the sky?'

'They did. But the human mind has a very clever trick called Projection. This is where people, without consciously doing it, transfer what they don't like about themselves, or their fears, onto other people. Or even onto the world around them. A classic example is the Nazis' hatred of the Jews. If the mind can't handle a problem it simply boots it out of your head. When the sanity crash came for Neanderthals they projected the battle going on in their heads outwards. I know it takes some swallowing but don't take my word for it. Pick up a book about ancient religions and right at the beginning there are myths about war in heaven. Look at the myths of hundreds of different tribes and civilizations and they all tell of a war between the old god who once ruled and the new god. The new god always wins, and the old god is always banished or imprisoned somewhere – never killed. Think of the struggle between the two minds, the new one wins, the other is banished to being backseat driver.'

My face felt hot. 'Christ Almighty, Bernadette, I shouldn't be believing this . . . The trouble is, I am.'

'Those legends are folk memories of what happened all that time ago.' Deep in thought she gazed at the bottle in her hand. 'The myths continue the story. The new god still struggles with the old god. And while the old god never succeeds in regaining power he finds subtle ways of interfering with humankind. I imagine that sounds familiar to you? The myths also say that in the future there will be a reconciliation between the old god and the new god. And that they will rule together.'

'But let me get this straight. This unconscious mind that the ancient people identified as god didn't, as the story goes, create the earth, the stars and – and—'

'All creatures great and small?' She smiled. 'No. But it does have tremendous creative power. When we learn to listen to intuition which flows up from the unconscious what are we capable of? Great music, life-saving inventions, miracle cures, sending people to the moon . . . You name it. If you asked most inventors, scientists, artists and so on how they came by the idea to do what they did most will say they don't really know – it just came in a flash of inspiration. Einstein actually dreamed solutions to some of his problems while he slept.'

'Ah ha. You talked about dreams when I first came here. Adam was always having dreams where God tells him to do this or that.'

'See, you're hitting all the buttons now, Nick. Until Adam began to tune in and listen to the old mind in his head he was a suicidal neurotic. Look at him now. Happy, energetic, brimming with ideas. In fact the idea of this Ark and running power lines from the water turbines on shore actually suggested itself to him in a dream. That's when the unconscious mind is most active, and most successful in communicating with us.'

The blood was singing through my body now, tingling me from head to toe. I found answers to my questions leaping into my head before I could even ask Bernadette. 'You talked about learning the language of the unconscious mind,' I said quickly, 'I'm right in thinking that one of the languages it speaks to us in is dreams?'

'Yes.' Her eyes shone. 'I think deep down you knew this all along. It just needed someone to give you a few clues.'

'Okay, I have dreams but they make no sense.'

'And I imagine Russian wouldn't either. The Russian might be telling you if you continue walking along the road you'll fall down a big hole. But you think it's just some agitated foreigner talking nonsense. It'd take too long to explain in detail now but one day you'll want to look into it more. Just remember that dreams are the language of the old unconscious mind. It's not talking to you in words but in pictures. And once you understand what these pictures or symbols mean, then you can begin your first real conversation.'

'But how do you do that?'

'One way to start is to remember your dreams: if you get a chance, write down a few lines of what you remember. It seems nonsense at first but as the days go by a pattern will begin to emerge. You may even begin to feel a change in yourself. People sometimes find dreams frightening, you know, loved ones dying or futilely groping round in the dark for something you've lost. That's only the unconscious mind getting frustrated and turning up the volume high to get you to listen.'

'My mother once had a book about the interpretation of dreams to learn what's going to happen in the future but—'

'But you're right: that's fortune telling mumbo-jumbo. Forget those books. Listen to the real authority on the subject, the old wise one who knows.' She touched my head. 'The old gentleman in here.'

She must have seen puzzlement in my face.

'Here's an example, then, of a dream which is basically a good dream but which seemed frightening at the time. When Adam went off the rails he dreamt he was wandering round the house he once lived in. Everything was familiar but he found himself being drawn to the top of the stairs. There, there was a door where no door existed in his own house. The door inexplicably frightened him. He didn't want to enter but as this was a dream he had no choice. He opened the door. Beyond was a passageway. Beyond that he knew there was a room with something inside he didn't want to see. He was terrified. He didn't want to go to the room and he'd wake up screaming.'

'So what is the old mind saying to Adam then?'

'First the dream symbolism needs to be interpreted. When you dream about your home you are actually dreaming about yourself, your own personality. This dream is commonplace and simple to interpret. The unconscious mind is saying look, there are parts of you that are hidden, that if you can only find them you can use them. It revealed Adam's solution to his problem as finding a new room in the house.'

'So in dream language the hidden room was really the unconscious mind that lay hidden in Adam's head?'

'Precisely. It was saying look, there's far more to you than you realise.'

'But why the fear?'

'Because it was new. That's all. The new and the unfamiliar tend to make you nervous, even frightened. I remember I was terrified when I had my first driving lesson. Only because it was something new.'

'So you got Adam into the hidden room.'

'Yes. That's when the transformation began into the new Adam you see today. It doesn't always happen overnight. But sometimes you do experience intense feelings of what in olden times people would describe as *seeing the light*.'

'So,' I said, 'in ancient times people weren't as dumb as I thought, worshipping all these weird and wonderful gods.'

'No, they weren't stupid at all. What they were doing was experiencing a gut feeling that there was a powerful but invisible being that could affect their lives and thoughts. They looked very hard for this being, so hard in fact that they began to believe they saw him in the stars or the oceans or forests. The gut feelings were right, it's just they were looking in the wrong places.'

'I don't know if I'm talking a load of crap,' I said, 'but it's just come to me now that for thousands of years there's been this urge, maybe an instinct, to communicate with this supernatural being. A being who we believe, deep down, has an important message for us. One that, if we could only receive it would allow us to live happily ever after.'

'You've hit the nail on the head, Nick. In all cultures believers look for guidance from the gods in the form of signs – astrology, palmistry, reading tea leaves, they're all part of the same thing. It all points to the hereditary belief that someone OUT THERE desperately wants to speak to us. And, deep down, WE desperately want to speak to them. And it's not only ancient people. Scientists feel it too, but they try and rationalise it. They try and communicate with dolphins, or try to teach chimpanzees our language. Billions were spent on radio telescopes and research programmes like SETI, the Search for Extra Terrestrial Intelligence. They hoped they could tune into the transmissions of alien life forms. Scientists, too, believed these beings out there in space would have an important message that would transform humankind. Doesn't that, too, have a religious feel to it?'

'So in effect ordinary people, priests, mystics, even scientists, have been striving and striving to contact a being who they instinctively know exists. Who wants to speak to man, and to help man. But instead of looking outward to heaven and the cosmos they should have been looking in here.' I pointed to my head.

'And you don't need a billion dollar radio telescope, or a gaggle of holy men. You only need to go to sleep at night and to listen to your dreams.' She smiled. 'And remember: don't ignore the old mind. After all, he's the friend inside.'

Midnight. Bernadette sat on the bed looking tired but satisfied. Getting the truth through my thick skull had been hard work.

I wanted to sleep now but there were still some loose ends. 'So I'm right in thinking this. Fifty thousand years ago the new mind took control, pushing the old mind into the back seat. Neanderthal man then changed into us. Ancient people dimly remembered what happened and it became religious myth?'

'Yes. For thousands of years men could talk easily to the old mind. Gradually they forgot how, and they began to believe that the old one they'd talked to long ago was god.' Her eyes, sleepy and huge, looked up at me. 'Yes, Nick. Now you know – like you've always known deep down.'

'And that eight months ago this battle between the two minds erupted again?'

'That's right. Although we didn't know it, humans were already moving into a chain of events that would lead to their eventual extinction. Humankind was beginning to lose its way, its drive for development had turned into a drive for self-destruction. Nothing spectacular like nuclear war. Just a slow rot from the inside. A cancer of the species. We'd lost our faith in ourselves; people believed they had no real reason for even existing ... *What's it all for?* they'd ask one another.'

'And no one could supply them with a plausible answer.'

'And even though instinctively we knew there was a being who could help us, we could not find it. In fact we were becoming more and more divorced from our second wise old mind.'

'So, last April, in a desperate attempt to save the species mother nature kicked our conscious mind out of the driving seat, then she put the old animal mind back in charge again.'

'That's about the size of it. The adults are in the grip of something that seems like madness now, but the next phase will see them settling down to establish themselves as the new superior species on earth. *Homo Superior*. They will be alien to us. You see, the unconscious mind is identical in everyone. The new species will behave collectively like ants. Individuals will be of no importance. Only the hive will matter.'

'Then we're wasting our time. The adults will take over anyway.'

'Perhaps. But I don't want to die, do you? Also mother nature has got it wrong before. The new species may turn out to be an evolutionary dead end – doomed to extinction.'

'But if we survive it will only be because we learn to co-operate with the second mind in our heads? The unconscious?'

'Yes. We must or die. It's as simple as that.' She smiled and rubbed her neck. 'It's already beginning to happen to you. You listen to your intuition. You're ready to follow a hunch even though you don't know where it's taking you. You told me about finding the generator and then, after the massacre, the baby.'

'Just a couple more loose ends ... I understand now why you are creating this religious community. Having a faith will unite the children, give them a sense of security. Then when they're old enough the big secret is revealed, like you revealed it to me?'

'Yes.'

'Why not just stick with the religious stuff? It'd be simpler to let them grow up to be God-fearing folk.'

'Because it won't wash anymore. Even those children know

enough about biology and astronomy to work out by the time they're fourteen that they're being told a white lie. After all, you can easily persuade a young child to believe in the tooth fairy and Santa Claus, but how many teenagers do you know who still believe Santa slides down their chimney every Christmas Eve?' She took a deep breath. 'I'm doing what adults should have done for the last thirty years. They should've bitten the bullet and created a faith that even hardened scientists and ghetto kids can believe in.'

'But what I still don't understand is why you drugged me, and . . . well, climbed into bed with me?'

'Adam's celibate.' She pointed at her stomach. 'And every new religion needs a messiah.'

She stood up. 'It's late. I'm going to bed. But I want you to do me one last favour tonight.' She smiled, her dark eyes locked onto mine. 'I want you to make love to me one more time.'

Chapter Fifty-One

GHOST MUSIC

4 a.m. I stood outside on the apartment's private balcony and looked out over the lake. The night was clear. A full moon poured light, as white as a ghost, onto the water.

It was cold. But I needed that air.

Bernadette lay asleep in bed, her face smiling. I knew she was dreaming. That second mind in her head, the wise old unconscious one, was talking to her. Something good that she was pleased to hear.

A sound came from behind me. It was familiar but I'd not heard it in years. The sound of someone tuning a guitar so quietly it wouldn't even disturb a sleeping baby.

'Uncle Jack.' I turned round to see him sitting on the guard rail between the platform and the water, his electric guitar across his lap – and then I knew I was really asleep beside Bernadette and softly dreaming too.

'Hello, Nick-Nick.' He used the old upper-class joke voice again. 'I say, old boy, am I alive?'

Jack Aten was long dead.

He smiled knowingly and angled his head to one side as he waited for an answer.

I nodded, the beginnings of a smile on my lips. It felt so good to see him. 'You're alive, Jack. You're alive.'

'I've been listening to your conversation with Bernadette. If this second mind, the unconscious bit, is plonked intact into our brains in the womb, then that means my unconscious mind is the same as yours, so in effect, part of me is the same as part of you.'

'And that means, part of you will live forever.'

'Fancy that. There I was dying of cancer, miserable as sin, and all along part of me is flaming immortal.' He grinned. 'You grew up a lot like me. Bit of a rebel, eh, kidda? A taste for the beer and the ladies . . .' He looked serious. 'But you've grown bigger than I ever could, or your dad, for that matter. You know what you've got to do now?'

I nodded. 'Go back to Eskdale. Take charge.'

Jack began to play softly on the guitar, the electric notes humming around us like fireflies.

'Another thing, Nick. Listen carefully to Bernadette, very carefully – you know deep down she's right.'

He hit a guitar string.

A single, brilliant note – and sustained it. The sound was tremendous, vibrating the planks beneath my feet, it seemed to hang suspended there, and although the note never altered in pitch, music ran through it, singing of a deep yearning of something or someone you have loved but lost.

The note faded slowly into the distance.

Jack did not move, his face remained turned up to the sky, glowing in the moonlight.

Then came the echo of the sound as it kicked back from the mountainside. It came howling across the snow, the forest, the valley and the lake like some great spirit that had once been lost in the depths of the universe.

As the sound rushed back on us, Jack hit a string, giving birth to another note of pure sound.

The echo merged with the new note, then it went soaring out across the lake, like a god moving across the face of the water to shake the mountains and the moon and the stars.

Chapter Fifty-Two

OUT OF THE DARK

'Here, catch.'

'What're these?' I shook the box.

'Ammunition.' Bernadette handed me another box. 'They go with this.'

'A pistol. I've already got the rifle.'

'Believe me, Nick, you're going to need all the protection you can get. It's a long walk back to Eskdale. Those are dum-dum bullets. If those Creosotes get in close to you, you want something that will stop them dead with one shot.'

'Thanks. Thanks for the survival gear as well.'

'Don't mention it. Every single one of us is precious now.' Her dark eyes fixed me. 'You more than most. Three hundred lives depend on you, Nick Aten. And if my intuition serves me right, and it always has done, you're going to be more important to our people than you realise.'

'Bullshit, Bernadette.'

'Maybe. Maybe not.'

Adam had called into the apartment to tell me that yesterday he'd been as far as the mountain road. The snow hadn't gone completely but at least it was passable. Now it was six in the morning and the moon was setting behind the mountains. Within the hour I'd paddle a canoe to the shore, then I'd be burning a trail back home. What I'd find there Christ only knew. But I was itching to start.

As Bernadette packed my rucksack she listed what was essential for the survival of humankind.

First: Find a safe haven from the Creosotes.

Second: Ensure you can feed your community.

Three: Adequate shelter.

Four: Believe in that new faith of hers. Stage one: Give young children religious instruction as had been done in the past. Second stage: Re-acquaint teenagers with the wise old one that lives in your head. The one ancient people identified as their god. 'If scientists and doctors can believe in it, so can anyone. Particularly if you can prove to them the practical benefits. As the saying goes: Two heads are better than one. In this case it's: Two minds are better than one. Remember, if you can get to know the god that lives inside your head, you can work the real miracle and save your life.'

Bernadette, smiling, squeezed my hand as I loaded the pistol. 'I'm sorry to bang on about it like this. Even though it sounds highbrow, it is a matter of life and death now.'

'Don't apologise. It's a miracle you got the truth through my thick skull at all.'

'There's another thing I haven't had a chance to mention yet,' she said. 'We'll call it number five on your list. For a while these small communities will, if they can defeat the Creosotes, survive. But the gene pools will be small. Soon there will be inbreeding which will one day wipe out the communities as effectively as the Creosotes. Communities on remote islands are going to suffer from this quite quickly.'

'What do you suggest?'

'There are several solutions. For example, ensure social contact between settlements: this way boys will marry girls from other communities. Another way could be a more deliberate mixing of genes. You know how they used to have wandering minstrels in days gone by, going from village to village playing their songs. What we could have is men who are basically wandering studs who go from village to village impregnating women to keep the gene pool fresh.'

'Sounds like nice work.'

'See, even with the collapse of civilization some people are going to enjoy satisfying careers.'

We laughed. I suppose it was tension as much as anything but we laughed and laughed until tears ran down our faces.

When I could speak properly I wiped my eyes and said, 'One thing, though, all this you've told me, about the second mind in your head, actually being, when it boils down to it, the thing we once called a god, well ... how do you know all this?'

'It wasn't in any book, but the information was lying about for anyone to see, even in any school library. All it needed was to put these bits of information into the right order to make a clear picture.'

'But this is your own theory, right?'

'I can't claim it as my own. Look, this is how the ... revelation, if you like, happened. At school a basic psychology course was on the curriculum. I did it, learning about Freud and Jung, all that stuff about the ego, subconscious, collective unconscious, super releasers, archetypes, etcetera, etcetera, and to me it was just another lesson on the timetable. What really interested me was civil engineering. Then six months before that big DAY 1 something clicked in my head. I rushed back and read my old notes. Then I read every book I could on the human mind; next I had this interest, call it passion, to read about world religions, mythology, even stuff by mystics like Richard Rolle of Hampole; next I studied human evolution. It got to the point where I thought I was going mad.

'Then a few weeks before the sanity crash I lost interest in it, I thought I'd just had a bee in my bonnet and now it was all over. BANG. Civilisation went out the window. For the first week I was too busy surviving. Then again, BANG! I was fetching water from a spring and suddenly it hit me. *Eureka*. The answers came streaming into my head. It was like a computer booting up a new program or ... or throwing the pieces of a jigsaw up into the air and it all coming down complete in one piece.'

'In short. Your second mind, the unconscious one, had been working on the problem in partnership with you, then delivered the answer in a flash of inspiration.'

'You've got it in one, love.'

The word 'love' must have slipped out accidentally, because she blushed and turned away from me.

'Of course I thought I was nuts,' she said. 'It was only when I began to speak to people around the world on the radio that I found another five people who'd reached the same sudden conclusion. It's a bit like the discovery of the evolution theory. Darwin got there first. But others all around the world were reaching the same conclusions independent of one another. It was as if the time was right.'

'So. The information was lying about like the parts of a model. It just needed someone to realize all these funny little parts would fit together to make, say, a car.'

'Exactly. Remember when I spoke to Abraxas in Egypt the other night? He was the first one who told me he'd reached the same conclusions. It was a big relief to him, too. He though he'd gone insane. Now all of us exchange information so we can increase our knowledge about what happened and what will happen.'

'And what will happen?'

'Marvellous things. Abilities that today would seem like miracles. It won't cure all the world's ills but it's a start. Pretty soon we'll be using the mind to heal the body. There's a girl in Argentina who's talking about immortality. Frankly I find that scary – but that's because deep down I believe her.'

'Immortality. Live forever? But how—'

'I've told you the truth about what happened, any more and we'll be going headlong into wild speculation.' She slipped a plastic envelope into the haversack. 'Everything I told you, plus a guide to educating your people is in this document. When you get the chance, study it. You'll see I say that perhaps the only way to defeat the Creosotes is by all the little communities banding together to form a single nation. I hope they'd do it democratically but in the end it might need a single powerful leader to unite them.'

'An Alexander the Great?'

'Exactly. Whoever it is, they're going to have to be ruthless. It doesn't matter how he, or she, unites the communities, whether it be by persuasion, coercion or even invasion.' She looked up at me. 'Nick Aten. Do you think you're up to it?'

'What, me? Alexander the Great? Conqueror of empires?' I

laughed. 'No ... not me, Bernadette.' I slung the haversack onto my shoulder.

'We'll see.' She smiled. 'Come on, you have to go before it gets light ... and before I think of an excuse to make you stay.' She kissed me, then patted her stomach. 'At least you've left me a permanent reminder of your stay.'

I felt myself blushing as I kissed her and wished her luck.

Adam came and helped me load the canoe which was tethered to Bernadette's private landing stage. The lights from the open doorway sparkled on the dark waters.

'As soon as you're on your way, we're going to have to switch off the light,' said Bernadette. 'We can't risk anyone spotting the Ark from the shore.'

I nodded. 'I'm ready, anyway. Good-bye, Adam. Thanks for everything.' I used the paddle to push the canoe away from the Ark. 'Good-bye, Bernadette. I hope we'll get a chance to talk again.'

I saw her eyes glistening with tears as she raised her hand. 'Don't hope,' she said. 'You can count on it. Come back and see us one day ... Good luck, Alexander.'

Steadily I paddled in the direction of the mountains that cut up into the star-spattered sky. When I looked back they had already turned out the light. It was so dark I couldn't even see the outline of the Ark anymore.

Chapter Fifty-Three

INTO THE LIGHT

As Adam had asked I hid the canoe in the undergrowth beyond the shore. Then I pulled on the haversack, shouldered the rifle and began walking, the frozen snow crisp as biscuits beneath my feet.

Walking wasn't easy but by the time it was light I was over the first mountain and the lake behind me was out of sight.

Soon I fell into the rhythm of walking on the snow-covered road, and I found myself thinking of a million things. About DAY 1. The cottage where Sarah, her sisters and I had stayed. My first night with Sarah in the motel after Slatter'd tried to flatten my head, and everything else that had happened in the last few months.

At first it had all been confusing and terrifying. Now, if anything the danger seemed greater. Would the Creosotes wipe us out, would we starve, could we learn enough practical skills to survive? But after hearing what Bernadette had to say, I felt stronger, more clear-headed, more purposeful. I felt like an engine that had been revving uselessly away for years, but at last, someone had finally switched me into gear.

As I walked up the next mountain, my breath blowing out in white clouds, I did begin to wonder if what she told me was true. But did it matter?

Did it matter *what* we believed in, as long as we believed in something?

Then as I crested the top into sunlight I knew the truth.

I grinned and said, 'Hello, in there. It's a beautiful morning. I don't know if you can see through my eyes but there's miles of forest, blue skies, and a spread of snow that looks like a million tons of white sugar.'

Then before I could stop myself, I did the weirdest thing. I took a great breath and let out a mighty roar that went echoing away into the blue-white distance.

The kind of roar that told Mother Earth I was glad to be alive.

The miles ticked by, my legs ached, but I felt good. I was hitting new energy reserves inside of myself.

The first night I found a barn and slept there.

The next day cloud built up in the sky until it made the day not much brighter than night. Still I pushed on, keen to reach Eskdale. That night I camped out by a river.

From then on I followed the river for two days. It grew so wide I could hardly see across to the far bank. When I reached a fork in the road, the map told me to take the right. Once more the road took me up into the mountains. It was then it started to snow.

It was still early in the day so I kept pushing on. The snowfall became a blizzard.

High on the mountain I found a farmhouse occupied by a small community consisting of a teenage husband and wife, who had actually worked the farm with the man's father before the sanity crash, their two babies, and eight teenage schoolboys who'd been on a field trip. After civilization hit the fan they didn't go home but ended up at the Murphys' farm where they'd stayed ever since.

They made me welcome, sitting me in front of the fire and giving me a hot meal.

'You'll stay here, of course,' said Murphy Junior. 'You wouldn't put a dog out there today.'

'Believe me, I'd like to,' I told him. 'But I've got to get home. There are people in danger there. And I don't think they know it.'

'You can't walk in this, man. You'll be dead by nightfall.'

Mrs Murphy said, 'We've got a radio transmitter. One of the lads rigged it up last month. If they've got one, we could get them a message through and tell them what the trouble is.'

I shook my head. 'I only wish we had. Eskdale's pretty isolated and we deluded ourselves we were the only ones left in the world.'

'Well . . .' Murphy poured me a whisky. 'You're going nowhere tonight so we'll make you a bed up.'

'Thanks,' I said. 'I'll be on my way as soon as it's light.'

It never did get light the next day. Cloud and snow blotted everything out.

The day after was the same. Then the next. Murphy told me this was it for the winter. Once the snow set in here, it gripped tighter than a boa constrictor.

Of course, we talked a lot round the kitchen fire. It wasn't easy passing on what Bernadette had told me about why the adults had gone psycho, or the two minds stuff – I fumbled over the words and sometimes I wondered if they thought I was crazy. Some of my metaphors for the human brain were a bit shaky too: 'Imagine you've bought a video recorder . . . That's your brain. With the recorder comes two video tapes. One's blank – that's mind number one, that becomes you. The second tape is pre-recorded with lots of information; you can't add to, or remove anything from tape number two – this is your unconscious mind; mind number two . . .'

Then one blonde-haired kid who'd sat there quiet as a plastic head said, 'Shit . . . You know earlier this year I thought I was going freaking crazy, but I was thinking something along those lines. I'd learned about this Dr Jung guy at school. And how we have not just one mind in our heads, but two.'

For me it was one hell of a relief to know I'd got someone to understand what I was talking about.

We talked for another twenty-four hours with everyone getting very excited about it.

My excitement nose-dived every time I looked out of the window when I saw the snow coming down not in feathers but lumps.

I'd been there a week when I dreamed I saw myself in a big house, writing something down that seemed so important to me that I felt my neck would go permanently crooked from bending over the desk.

In the dream my brother was there. 'What you doing, bro?'

'I'm writing a book. I've got to write it all down in case anything happens to me.' I looked up puzzled. 'But why should what happened to me be important to anyone else?'

'Keep writing the book, bro, keep writing the book.'

The second I woke up I knew what I had to do. It was a clear enough message from the wise old number two mind inside my head. Write everything down. That way it's easier to give people the knowledge that'll save lives.

As I got stuck into bacon and eggs it struck me I'd become a kind of new apostle for the new age. Christ, my old teachers would have had heart attacks if they'd known I was going to write a book.

Murphy understood what I wanted and helped me find this house by the river. Miles from anywhere, it gives me the peace I need to write the thing.

Even though the house is barely seven miles from his farm it took us six hours to walk here through the blizzard.

Naturally I wanted to get back to Eskdale quick. The need burned inside of me like molten metal, but I knew it'd be suicide. The weather was nothing short of Arctic. In a way that helped. I guessed bad weather for me would be bad weather for the Creosotes; it would hold up their march on Eskdale.

So here I am, sitting at this table, looking out over the river. Apart from the river which looks black, everything else is white with snow.

I've got all the food I need, gas lamps for light and coal for the fire.

I ate my meal alone here on Christmas Day. Boy, was that weird. I sat here and thought about everyone I've ever known. At one point I thought I heard Jack's electric guitar upstairs. I searched the house and found nothing.

I poured a tumbler full of whisky ready to blot out the rest of the day in a booze-out, but suddenly I had an incredible feeling of presence. Like there was an old friend in the room with me. So strong came the sensation, I could almost feel it.

The number two mind was there with me. In my head. It strained to make its presence felt. That I wasn't alone. And that I always had a companion who was rooting for me.

I tipped the whisky back into the bottle and began to write.

Now I write all day; the pencil burns across the paper like someone else is moving my hand. I smile. My immortal partner and I are working together.

In late January I began to see the things in the river. They looked like logs floating slowly by. It was only when I got close I saw the holes where the eyes were.

They were dead Creosotes. And they'd been in the water a while. Maybe somewhere miles upstream kids were desperately fighting to stop them over-running their community.

This went on for day after day, week after week.

Late February the thaw began. But it was so slow it was painful.

I'd stand and watch the icicles drip, willing them to turn to water. Once the snow started to thin I could begin the walk back to Eskdale.

The following day I sat scribbling away like a demon when I heard a thunderous knocking. The urgency in the noise sent me running to open the door.

On the doorstep stood Murphy.

His face looked grim.

He said: 'Nick ... Do you know some people called Martin Del-Coffey and Sarah Hayes?'

My heart lurched. 'Yes.'

'We've got them on the radio. They're in big trouble.'

THE THIRD PART

HERE COMES THE CLIMAX

Chapter Fifty-Four

START OF THE THIRD PART

'What's wrong, Murphy? What did Del-Coffey tell you?'

Murphy stamped the snow off his boots before stepping inside. 'To be honest, Nick, not a damn lot. Either they haven't got the hang of the transmitter or it's on the blink. We haven't been able to make much sense of what they've told us.'

As he pulled off his coat, gloves and boots he talked. 'First thing this morning we heard it. They're putting out a general call to everyone. It sounded urgent so Gary called me down to the shack. They were asking over and over: did anyone know the whereabouts of someone called Nick Aten? And that they were up to their eyeballs in deep, deep shit.'

'Did they say what kind of trouble?'

'No. They went off air before we could ask. Anyway, as soon as I heard they needed you I kitted up and got down here. It took me nigh on five hours solid walking.' He sat down with a sigh. 'What we've got to do with you, Nick old mate, is get you back up to the farm so you can talk with your folks.'

'Damn.' I looked out of the window. The sun had hit the mountains across the river. 'We're going nowhere tonight. It'll be dark in half an hour.'

Of course I couldn't sleep. I prowled the ground floor of the house.

Sometimes I'd sit at the table and blaze away with the pencil. I felt old number two taking me over, so all that I became was a hand to hold the pencil while it poured out the words like machine gun bullets across the page. We both knew that time was running out. Events were moving to a climax.

We were kitted up and walking before sunrise. In the haversack I carried Bernadette's document and a bundle of paper covered in my own scrawl. Across my shoulder I'd slung the rifle; the pistol I'd pushed into my belt.

Murphy put his head down and crunched through the snow like an Eskimo. He was born to this kind of thing and I had to push hard to keep up.

The thing that kept me going was the sheer hunger of wanting to speak to Sarah. What was wrong? Why the urgency? Had Curt and his crew harmed them? Maybe the Creosotes were attacking?

The hotel defences were a shambles. I remembered some idiot had driven a truck through the perimeter wall at one point; the gates were bust.

Del-Coffey's place might be the safest, now he'd bricked up the lower floor's windows and doorways. But I remembered what'd happened to the kids in Dublin, with their thirty foot high concrete walls . . . and the Croppers with their fire moat . . . and the German kids on their island. Shit.

It took us seven hours to cover the seven snow-choked miles back to Murphy's farmhouse.

The first thing we did was go straight to the radio shack. One of the kids sat at the mike, tapping the table in frustration.

'Just when we think we're through they go off the air,' said the kid. 'I think their set's on the fritz.'

'Who are you talking to?'

'A guy called Martin Del-Coffey. There's a girl with him as well.'

I shrugged off the haversack and rifle and pulled up a chair beside the kid with the mike. 'The girl. Is she called Sarah?'

'That's her. Sarah Hayes. She said she's . . . Hang on, here we go again.' Static burst from the speaker, then came a voice that sounded like a geriatric robot.

'What's he saying?'

'Your guess's as good as mine, Nick ... Del-Coffey. Del-Coffey. It's no good ... I still can't understand you ... Too much distortion.'

There was a series of mechanical growls then a loud snapping sound. '... better. Is that any better?'

It was Del-Coffey's voice. I was ready to rip the mike out of the kid's hand but he handed it to me. 'Go ahead and talk, Nick. Make it quick, I don't know how long they can keep on the air.'

'Del-Coffey.'

The voice coming over the speaker shot higher in astonishment. 'Nick Aten? Is that you, Nick?'

'It's me, Del-Coffey ... Shit, I never thought I'd be so glad to hear your voice. What's the problem?'

For a full three minutes I got no sense out of him. It wasn't the set, I could hear him holding an excited conversation with someone near him. 'It's Nick ... Yes! The bloody sod's alive!'

At last he came back shooting questions like where on Earth had I disappeared to? Why didn't I come back home?

In about twenty seconds I managed to explain about the kidnap, the long haul back and being stranded, snow-bound, in the back of beyond. Then my patience gave out.

'What's the trouble? Is Sarah there? Is she all right?'

'... but we've got ... think you'd ... get back here as quickly as poss ...'

'Shit,' I hissed. 'It's breaking up again ... Del-Coffey. I can't hear you. I asked, is Sarah all right?'

'... danger ... it's Sarah that I'm ... If you get back be careful of ...'

'Del-Coffey ... Del-Coffey ... What's happened to Sarah?' I was shouting into the mike. 'Has she been hurt? Del-Coffey?'

Everyone in the shack looked at one another, their eyes round.

Static sizzled the speakers then Del-Coffey's voice came clear, 'Can you hear me? Nick? This wiring is held together with paper clips. They keep slipping off.'

'I hear you, Del-Coffey. Sarah. What's happened to her?'

The pause seemed to last for an hour. I sat there staring at the speaker, sweat beginning to ooze from my skin. Then came a female voice. Quiet, almost a whisper, like it was coming from a planet a billion light years away.

'Nick ... Are you all right?'

'Sarah! Thank God it's you ... Listen. You're okay?'

'Oh yes ... I'm fine.'

'I heard you've got some trouble.'

'We have. Big trouble. But first I've got some news for you.'

'News? What kind of news?'

The pause seemed to spin away the seconds, my hand ached I held the mike so tightly.

Then she spoke: 'Nick ... I've had a baby.'

The walls of the shack seemed to rush in on me. I rocked back. The first stupid thing that came into my head was: 'A baby. Whose is it?'

'Whose is it? It's yours, you idiot ... Nick Aten, you are a dad.'

That was when the world really did jump out of focus. Murphy's wife had to nudge me three times before I rejoined the rest of the human race.

'Mine?'

'Yes. Whose do you think? You were the only one.'

For the next few minutes we had the kind of breathless, astonished conversation you could imagine. Separated for months, then to suddenly find out I'm a dad? 'Yes, the baby's fine. He's three weeks old.'

Suddenly I realized I'd difficulty in speaking: people were hugging me and slapping me on the back.

I snapped out of it when I remembered that Eskdale was in trouble. Right up until then I'd assumed it was the Creosotes. I asked them if they'd been attacked.

Sarah sounded puzzled. 'No. It's nothing to do with Creosotes. It's Curt. He's completely insane. About six weeks ago he ordered that no food should be given to anyone but his Crew and their harem. Del-Coffey, Kitty and I have managed to feed the rest, that's over two hundred people, one hot meal a day. But it's only boiled turnip and potato. It's a starvation diet, Nick. Soon we're going to start losing people.'

'Can't they send out scavenging parties – there must still be canned foods waiting to be picked up?'

'When I say Curt is insane, I mean he's really out of it. He's paranoid. He won't permit anyone to leave Eskdale. By chance Martin found this transmitter in a house down the valley. Like he says it's a heap of junk; he's worked wonders getting the thing to work at all. The other problem is, if Curt finds out about this radio Martin'll end up *Carrying The Can* for it.'

'Jesus. They're still doing that?'

'*Carrying The Can?* Oh, yes, they are. They've killed thirty-eight people with that little game so far.'

We talked hard for another twenty minutes then Sarah's voice started to fade.

'Sarah, listen,' I said. 'Have you had any trouble with Creosotes?'

'No. Not at all. No, the weird thing is, there must be two thousand camped in the next valley. No trouble, though. They keep themselves to themselves.'

Holy shit almighty. My mouth turned dry.

'How many, Sarah? Two thousand?'

'Yes. What's the—'

'Listen. Do the numbers stay the same? Or are more joining them?'

'. . . few only.' Sarah's voice barely made it above the static now. 'Seen more joining them. They come in twos and threes.'

Shit, shit, shit! 'Sarah,' I shouted into the mike. 'Listen very carefully to me. This is important. You are in danger. They have begun massing. When there are enough of them they will attack you. I've seen it happen. They will stop at nothing until they have killed you all. Curt won't be able to defend the hotel from them. You must get away from there . . . Find a way to run for it. You've got to— let go of this fucking mike. Let go or I'll fucking kill you . . .'

Murphy said gently, 'Nick . . . Nick. You're wasting your breath. They're no longer transmitting.'

'It keeps happening,' said Gary. 'They cut out for a few hours before they can get back to us.'

I could say nothing. I marched out into the snow-covered yard. There I stared out across the mountains, my heart punching away at my chest. I wanted to scream down the sky.

After a while I rubbed snow into my face, then I went back inside.

'I'm sorry about that,' I said. 'I find out my girlfriend is still alive.

I find out I'm a father. Then I find out that they'll probably be dead in the next few hours.' I took a deep breath. 'And I didn't even get a chance to warn them.'

They watched me silently. Mrs Murphy leaned across and hugged me. 'I'm sorry, Nick. If I was in your place, I'd want to grow wings and fly home.'

For a second I looked at her then I planted an earth-shaking kiss on her forehead.

'Thank you, Mrs Murphy. That's exactly what I'm going to do.'

'What're you talking about? You haven't got wings?'

'I know ... but I've got two damn good legs. I'm going now. Don't try and stop me.'

Murphy smiled. 'We won't, lad.'

'If Del-Coffey manages to get that set of his working again, warn him that any time now they're going to be attacked by the adults ... That they've got to get away from the area. And tell him I'll be back in Eskdale in three days.'

Seventy miles in arctic conditions? In three days? Impossible.

But right then I made up my mind. From now on I would force the impossible to become possible. We all have to – or we are dead. It's as simple as that.

Ten minutes later, haversack on my back, rifle on my shoulder I was on my way, waving to the Murphy clan as I went.

When I reached the main road East that'd take me to Eskdale, I said aloud: 'Okay, you in there, number two mind, the wise old man or whatever we call you, listen to me. You know we've got to get back. We're talking about the survival of the human race here ... If you're as powerful as Bernadette says, I'm going to give you a challenge: get us both back to Sarah. Fast. And in one piece.'

I hit the road, following it as it hugged the shore of the great river.

At long, long last, we were going home.

Chapter Fifty-Five

ON THROUGH MADLAND

Head down, I went for it, ploughing through mile after mile of snow drifts. To my left, the river thick with drowned Creosotes. To my right, frozen mountains.

Sometimes the drifts on the road were so deep I'd have to detour across a field.

There were no settlements. No surviving ones, anyway. I did pass a burnt-out church. A broken-down barbed wire fence surrounded it. People like us had lived there once but they'd either fled or were dead.

I didn't stop but powered on. I felt like a loco with a roaring fire in its belly and a head full of steam. Nothing could stop me now.

The map told me that in three miles I'd reach a suspension bridge that would take me across the river. Then it was downhill to the flatlands: the next hills I'd see would be Eskdale.

Two miles on and I saw why there were so many bodies drifting down river.

For a full five minutes I had to stare at what spanned the river from bank to bank. I saw it, but what I did see took some time sinking in.

Running across the river in a C-shaped curve, fifteen feet wide, a hundred yards long, was a causeway. It was built out of human beings. There must have been a thousand or more of them. At first I thought that corpses had been tied together but as I edged nearer I realized that the causeway was made out of *living* adults, standing chest deep in the water, their limbs woven together to form a solid bridge of flesh and bone.

As I watched, one of the adults let go, probably killed by the cold water. The body drifted away downstream.

So this was what I'd seen floating by the house. Discarded parts of the causeway.

From the trees on my side of the river, a Creosote walked out across the living causeway. Without any kind of hesitation, he took the place of his dead colleague in the freezing water.

The process continued. Dying adults would crumble away from the causeway; immediately they'd be replaced by a fresh one.

See a line of ants across your back yard? Scrub out a hundred with your foot. The line of ants reforms with more ants from the nest. And they carry on just as before. They ignore their own dead. No pain, no remorse, no grief. The new species of Man behaved like those ants.

As I watched, I saw a steady stream of adults begin crossing the causeway to the other side of the river.

The causeway did have some mad purpose. They needed to cross the river – so this is how they did it.

I carried on, carefully now. Creosotes were coming out of the forest to my right, crossing the road then heading down to the causeway.

The bastards were migrating north. I knew why. To snuff out every community of their children they could find.

Eskdale. How long before they targeted the three hundred kids there?

I got through the Creosotes' lines without them seeing me and pushed on quickly to the bridge.

When I saw it I realised why the Creosotes had built the living causeway.

The suspension bridge now lay in a tangle of steel cables down the valley side. It didn't take a genius to guess what had happened. There'd have been a bunch of kids living somewhere on the other side of the river. In an attempt to stop the Creosotes swarming over the bridge and wiping them out they'd managed to dynamite it. But the Creosotes, driven by that remorseless, indefatigable instinct to kill their own young had found another way.

This left me in deep shit. I pulled out the map. I had to cross the damn river to get back to Eskdale. There was another bridge twenty miles upstream but there were no guarantees that that hadn't been blown too. Probably the next one as well. It might take me a week to find a way across.

The other alternative, Nick? Swim for it. In summer maybe, but this water's so cold it kills as sure as a knife.

With luck there might be a boat somewhere along the banks. Then again, there might not. This place was pretty remote. It could take a week to find a stupid boat. In a week everyone in Eskdale might be food for the birds. Including Sarah and my son.

The idea I had then took my breath away.

'You suicidal cretin,' I said to myself. But there was no other way.

If the people bridge was good enough for the Creosotes, it was good enough for me.

The light was beginning to fade by the time I reached the causeway. In half an hour it'd be dark. If I was going to do it, I'd have to do it now.

As I cut down through the wood to the causeway, wondering how the hell I could pass for a Creosote I walked into two in a clearing. They were standing, staring into space, in that switched-off way they had.

If I kept going then maybe they'd not bother me.

No such luck. The tallest one with long grey hair went for me like a wrestler on acid. Swinging his arms, mad, blazing eyes locked onto mine.

I wasn't ready for the ferocity of the attack, the rifle was still strapped across my back, the pistol in my belt.

When he hit me, I fell back.

Deliberately, I continued to roll back, finishing the roll with an upward stamp.

The sole of my boot smashed upward into the guy's chin as he came after me. His hand snapped up, then he went down.

As I struggled to my feet the other Creosote grabbed me. He was short and dumpy, but was he strong.

He got in front of me and held me in a bear hug so tight I thought my spine would snap. As he crushed me in his ape arms he pushed me back. I couldn't breathe, I couldn't see where he was pushing me. For all I knew he was pushing me into the arms of a whole mob of Creosotes.

I felt the ground slope up sharply behind me. He kept pushing, his face turned up to stare at mine. His breath stank like shit.

My heels hit something as he pushed and I fell back. He didn't loosen his grip and he came down on top of me knocking out what breath still stuck in my lungs.

I was going to die. There in the muck, crushed by this psycho. I stopped trying to punch his face and stab out his eyes with my thumb. Nothing hurt him.

I felt the ground around me, hands going like frantic crabs, searching through snow and sticks and Creosote shit.

My left hand closed over a cold lump the size of a football. It was hard.

With the world starting to turn dark and faraway as I suffocated, I gripped the rock with both hands behind his head.

Then I brought the mother down.

Hard.

I felt his head kick forward to thump into my chest.

Suddenly the pressure around my spine was gone. I pushed him off and stood up, ready with the boulder to hit him again.

No need. I'd done a good job. The back of his skull curved inward in a mess of blood and brain.

This was the first man I'd killed.

For a second I stared at him, trying to hold down the feeling that was coming up inside of me. I couldn't hold it for long. Up it rushed.

The feeling was good, very good indeed. The old man inside was congratulating me.

I ran down to the river bank. It was do or die now.

Now I was closer to the living causeway I could see it was low in the water and every so often it would move – a kind of undulation as the people shifted slightly to get a better grip on the next, causing the causeway to dip down into the water.

If I got my boots wet I'd never get them dry again. One thing I did need now was to keep my feet in good condition. Quickly I took off my boots and tied them onto the haversack by the laces. Then, rifle at the ready, I walked barefoot down to the river bank through the snow.

This time I kept my wits about me looking for any sign of Mr Creosote coming through the forest.

I worked along the banking until I was perhaps thirty yards from the causeway. Creosotes were still walking across, but there weren't so many now. I counted only four on the causeway itself. All walked in the same direction from this bank to the next, then they climbed a hill at the other side and disappeared over the ridge. No doubt homing in on another bunch of kids.

I inched nearer to the causeway, trying not to be freaked by the weird sight of all those men and woman hanging onto one another to form the meat road across the water.

When the causeway was clear and there were no more Creosotes heading down toward it, I ran across the frozen mud to where the causeway began at the water's edge.

For a second I hung back. The idea of walking across all those people was repulsive. You wouldn't stuff worms into your mouth – I didn't want to do this.

I looked back to see a dozen more Creosotes walking down through the wood toward me.

This's it.

Like I was walking on light-bulbs I gingerly stepped on the first human link in the causeway. The man shifted under my bare foot and turned his face to look up at me; it was a swollen mask punctured by two red holes where the eyes had been.

I walked on to the causeway, bodies shifting slightly. I didn't stop now, walking as quickly as I dared across the slippery backs and heads of hundreds of men and women.

To my left a woman died with a groan, released her grip on the people next to her and floated away in the current. The causeway dipped and suddenly I was ankle deep in freezing water.

The people braced themselves beneath my feet and lifted up out of the water again. A wave of coughing spread through the living causeway, make it shudder from end to end, but still they gripped each other tightly, so tightly I couldn't tell where one man ended and another began.

In the middle of the roadway a few of the people were already long dead, held there only by the those around them. I trod on one belly that was so rotten my bare foot went through with a crunch. Like stepping onto a rotten melon, fluid squirted up my leg.

Shit to this.

I ran across the yards of skin, and the heads packed as tightly as street cobble stones, my boots swinging crazily from the haversack, my feet thumping down on chests and backs and stomachs and faces, knocking the breath from their bodies. As I ran I was followed by winded

uh-uh-uh-uh-uh

sounds, and the meat road writhed and groaned and panted beneath my feet.

uh-uh-uh-uh-uh-uh-uh-uh

My pounding feet would smash down on a nose or a finger or a forearm, snapping them like dry sticks.

By the time I was three quarters of the way across, the meat road was gripped by convulsions, bucking out of the water like a sea serpent. Hands clutched at my ankles but I didn't stop.

And I didn't stop when I hit the beach at the other side. I ran on through the forest until I'd left the river and the thing in the river far behind.

For the next forty-eight hours I was a walking machine. Nothing stopped me – night, snow, gales, hunger, exhaustion. They should have been obstacles but I drove through them like a tank drives through solid walls.

I ate as I walked – sometimes I think I even slept as I walked.

After I left the mountains the snow turned to slush and it rained for mile after mile.

When at last I knew I had to stop and rest, soaked and exhausted, I found a car on its side against a stone wall. I took my rifle and put a bullet through the tank. As the fuel streamed like piss from the hole I lobbed a match into it.

For the next two hours I roasted myself in front of the inferno. It was so hot it melted a circle of snow fifty feet in diameter. My face burned and my clothes steamed until they were dry.

Then I walked on through the night, through deserted towns alive with dogs and cats gone wild. Across empty countryside. I saw no communities of kids – only signs there had been once. Mr Creosote is a thorough bastard.

As I walked I imagined what I'd find in Eskdale. The pictures that came into my head pushed me on faster.

On the second night of my journey, at five to midnight, I came across a road sign that seemed to shine in the moonlight.

ESKDALE COUNTRY PARK

I'd done it. I was home.

Before I could go on I had to reach out and touch the sign to prove to myself it was real.

It had taken four months to come less than a hundred miles. A year ago a leisurely drive would have taken a couple of hours.

The hotel and Del-Coffey's house were three miles away.

What now?

As I walked on, slowly now, I realised I hadn't got the remotest idea what I was going to do when I arrived.

Broadly the plan was to kick out Curt and his Crew and take charge. Then get rid of the Creosotes. How I'd actually do it ... God only knew.

Chapter Fifty-Six

IF ONE GREEN BOTTLE SHOULD ACCIDENTALLY FALL...

I walked up the road with the moonlight shining on what was left of the snow.

After a quarter of a mile I heard the whistling begin.

I carried on walking, thinking maybe it was some kid far off in the distance whistling in the dark. But these days what kid would be out in the countryside at midnight?

Ten Green Bottles Hanging On A Wall, If One Green Bottle Should Accidentally Fall...

I'd just walked through an Arctic wilderness but I'd never felt as cold as I did then. I knew who was whistling.

And I knew I'd been seen. And that the whistling was some kind of mind-twisted greeting, or warning. Or threat.

'Yes, I hear you, dad,' I said to myself. 'Your son's come back.'

With the whistling floating across the moonlit fields and woods I carried on up the hill.

I was just two miles from Del-Coffey's house when I saw the fire as I crested the hill. It lit a group of farm buildings about a hundred yards to my right.

Follow your instincts, Bernadette had said, listen to the quiet voice inside. I wanted to hurry down the hill into the village and see Sarah – and the baby; my son; for Chrissake's I didn't even know his name yet. But instinct told me to check on the keeper of the fire first.

This is what I saw as I approached. Sitting around the bonfire in the farmyard were seven teenagers. Six of them looked wild bastards, dressed in army gear.

The seventh I knew instantly.

Tug Slatter. He sat on a log in front of the fire.

As I crossed the yard toward the fire the six kids stood up, surprised to see someone come strolling into their bonfire party in the middle of the night.

Tug Slatter just glanced up, then took a long pull on his cigarette. Far from being surprised he looked as if he'd been expecting me all along.

I crouched on the opposite side of the fire and held out my hands to warm them.

The firelight sent flickers and shadows prancing across Slatter's ugly tattooed face. He looked back at me and said nothing.

We sat like that for a minute. Slatter's army-style buddies looked at one another, then at Slatter for a lead.

I stared at Slatter's bad-beast eyes. And I knew something had changed. Something was missing.

I searched my mind for it.

That's it . . . I nodded. When I looked at Slatter I knew I was no longer afraid of him.

Before, fear of him, though I wouldn't admit it even to myself, forced me on the defensive. I'd insult him, make a cutting remark or even physically attack him.

Now, for me anyway, Slatter was a monster no more.

Bernadette had told me about all that software lying around in the back of your mind. Most of the time you don't use it, you're not even aware that it exists at all. But if you hit the right keys it comes to life and transforms you.

You can become an Einstein, a mother, a father, a warrior, a leader, a messiah – anything that the situation demands. All you need is that access code.

Somewhere on my journey back here I'd found it. Changes had taken place in my head. I was a different Nick Aten now.

I looked round at the faces watching me to see what I'd do next. 'I could murder one of those beers.' I took one without waiting to be asked. The cronies looked at Slatter again, waiting for his lead.

Slatter spat into the fire. 'You old bastard . . . I thought you were dead.'

I sensed Slatter's change in attitude to me. The words were pure old Slatter, but the tone had altered. This was probably the nearest thing to a friendly greeting he'd come to in his life.

'Well . . .' I drank the beer in one. 'You can see I'm alive. And I'm back for a reason.'

'What's that?'

'Because you need my help.'

'Piss off.'

'You need my help, Slatter. And I need yours.'

'What makes you think I'll help you? I wouldn't piss on you if you were on fire.'

I opened another beer, then I told him what had happened to me. That they were in danger – the Creosotes were massing. As soon as there were enough of them, something would click in their heads, then they'd go hell for leather to kill every single one of us in Eskdale.

At first they found it hard to believe and laughed, saying that sometimes for a laugh they'd walk through the middle of the Creosotes who'd just stand or sit about and not touch them.

I asked why Slatter and his cronies were sitting up here in the yard of a wrecked farmhouse. What was wrong with the creature comforts of the hotel?

Slatter's eyes narrowed and he gave me some crap about Curt paying them in booze and cigarettes to camp out here and keep watch.

'If no one's afraid of the Creosotes, who are you keeping watch on?'

'God knows,' said one of the cronies, and with the exception of Slatter they all laughed.

Reading between the lines I guessed Curt had got nervous of having Slatter around and bribed him to live out here.

'Slatter. I need your help to get rid of the Creosotes.'

'How you going to do that? There's more than three thousand of the bastards.'

'I was hoping you'd tell me.'

Slatter laughed.

An eighteen-year-old called Burke had been a mercenary in Africa before the sanity-crash. He said he knew weapons and explosives inside out. 'We've got a garage full of Semtex. We could blast the bastards.'

'You could if you could get them all to nicely wait in a big enough building,' said one of the other cronies. 'Those fuckers are spread out for two miles along the valley floor. You could blast hundreds of them but you'd not get them all.'

'It's as simple as this,' I told them, 'if we don't wipe them out, then they'll wipe us out ... What if we use the explosive to blast as many as we can, then use guns on the rest?'

Slatter spat. 'What, seven of us chasing thousands of the mad bastards through the forest? Sure we'd blow away hundreds, but even if they fought back with their bare hands they'd soon tear us a set of new arseholes ... Think again, Aten.'

'Maybe I'll leave it to Martin Del-Coffey. He'll come up with an idea.'

'That faggot? He'd wipe their arses and try to teach them algebra.'

'Come on, Slatter, I bet you can come up with an idea.'

'Of course I could.' The ugly ape face split into a grin. 'But I'll not tell you.'

'There's three hundred lives at stake. If you can—'

'Aten. Hey, Aten, shut up, I'm talking now. D' ya want to know something interesting?'

'And what's that, Slatter?'

'That ponce father and tart mother of yours are back as well.'

I stared at him, the blood drumming though my neck.

He pulled on the cigarette, staring at me. 'They're hanging out with the rest of the bastards.'

'Tell me something new. I already know.'

For the first time he can't have seen the thing in my face he used to feed on: shock, surprise, fear, whatever it was – wasn't there. He shrugged, broke eye contact and looked away.

I smiled. It felt as if I'd won my first small victory.

'The other thing I want you to help me with,' I said, 'is to get rid of Curt.'

'So, Aten, who'll be the new leader?'

'I will.'

'Oh yeah ... Me help you become new boss man. No way, Aten. No friggin' way.'

I left it at that. Anyway I was knackered from walking for forty-eight hours solid. I took my haversack to the barn, pulled out the sleeping bag and climbed.

Deliberately I kept awake, watching the stars through the open door – and listening to Slatter and his cronies talk around the fire.

Burke entertained them with a few dirty limericks, then they started talking about the Creosotes in the next valley.

'Aten's thick,' I heard Slatter say. 'All you have to do to get rid of those psycho bastards is stick Semtex against the wall of the dam, light the fuse, and bang ... The water would wash the bastards all the way to kingdom come.'

I'd heard what I wanted to hear. Now, I could close my eyes and sleep.

Chapter Fifty-Seven

START OF THE LONGEST DAY

I slept right through until eight a.m. When I'd eaten breakfast Slatter came up to me and grunted. 'Follow me. I've got something to show you.'

I followed him along the spine of the hill. The grass was crisp with frost, the sun blazed in the sky and you could see for miles.

After a mile he stopped. 'Down there.'

Along the bottom of the valley that ran parallel to Eskdale valley Creosotes sat or lay along the banks of the stream as far as I could see. At the top of the valley the dam wall ran from one side to the other in a curtain of black concrete a hundred feet high.

Slatter said, 'Burke reckoned there were three thousand of them. There's more now. Look . . . There's another bunch coming over the hill there.'

'So, Tug, what now?'

'I reckon you're right, Aten. They're getting ready to crush them pansies in the hotel.'

'Listen, Slatter. I'm going to tell you something now. It's going to sound like I'm slagging you off. I'm not, this is the truth. You're a parasite, Slatter. You hate ordinary people. But you can't live without them. You've got no one out here to terrorise respect out of; there's no one to watch you parading about and think, '*Christ, there goes Tug Slatter – he's a hard bastard.'* Stuck out here living in that ruin you're like a man who's slowly being starved to death.'

Slatter said nothing for a while, then he looked at me. 'I reckon you're right about that as well ... You said you wanted Curt and his cretins kicking out of the hotel ... When are we going to do it?'

'Now.'

As we walked back to the farm I told him, 'I heard what you told the others last night, about blowing the dam and drowning the Creosotes ... It's a pretty good idea. Burke says he knows about explosives. Can he do it?'

'Yeah, he can do it.'

'Tell him to get started then. We can't risk another day, we've got to blow the wall of the dam tonight.'

'You tell him. You're going to be the new boss.'

Back at the yard Slatter sat on the wall and smoked cigarettes while I talked to his cronies for an hour. They were the usual sad bunch of retards, headcases, and thugs that Slatter hung out with. But they had guts and when I told them the plan they jumped around like kids who'd been told that Santa Claus was coming.

'It'll take a block of Semtex about the size of a house to do it.' Burke's voice quivered. To him this was better than sex. 'We'll get the JCB, dig out a pit at the base of the wall. Stack in the explosive, then mound earth back over it. That'll do the trick.'

'You've got enough Semtex?'

'We've got plenty.'

'Good. If you get it done by nightfall we'll blow the dam tonight at midnight. In the dark the Creosotes won't know what's hit them.' I picked up the rifle. 'There's going to be some Creosotes who aren't taken out by the tidal wave that'll come thundering down that valley when we blow the dam. We'll have to be tooled up with all the guns and ammo we can carry to finish them off.'

'We're going to kill all of them?'

'By this time tomorrow those bastards are going to be extinct.'

Then this bunch of psychos cheered and whistled and slapped me on the back. Slatter watched without moving a muscle of his tattooed face.

Then his cronies hurried away to prepare for the biggest bang Eskdale had ever heard.

The time was eleven o'clock.

'Come on,' I said to Slatter. 'I want to see Sarah Hayes first ...
Did you know I've got a baby son?'

'I heard ... But I didn't believe. Pansy like you wouldn't know
where to put it.'

We both laughed as we set off down the hill toward Eskdale. Me
and Slatter laughing together? Almost liking one another? Christ,
surely this was a day of miracles. I only hoped the miracles kept on
coming my way. This was going to be the longest day of my life.

But first I wanted to see Sarah and the baby ... Our baby.

Then Slatter and me were going together to call on Curt ... and
make Curt an offer he could not refuse.

Chapter Fifty-Eight

JUST LIKE OLD TIMES

Noon.

'Nick ... Hey! Nick Aten. We heard you were back. Curt wants to see you.'

Two hundred yards down the road I could see Del-Coffey's house in the village. Sarah would be waiting for me there.

'Okay,' I said. 'I'll be about an hour, I'm just going to see Sarah. You know, I've got a baby son now.'

'Don't mess Curt about, Nick. He said now. He means NOW.'

Shit. I squinted up against the sunlight at two teenage members of the Crew who sat on the ten foot high wall that enclosed the hotel grounds. They carried shot guns. They weren't aiming them but I noticed both were pointed in my general direction.

The kid I was talking to pulled open the gate. 'Come on, I'll take you up there. You'll have to leave your bag and guns in the gatehouse. I'll have to search you as well ... No, not you, Tug.' The kid looked nervous. 'Curt wants you to get back to Hill Top Farm. He'll send a case of beer up for you.'

Slatter shrugged. I went inside and the gate banged shut behind me.

Looking back I saw Slatter undo his jeans belt. Nervously the gate man asked, 'What you doing, Tug?'

'I want a frigging dump, that's what.'

'There? In the road?'

'Good a place as any ... You can stand there and watch if you want.'

The gate man shook his head quickly and told me to follow him.

Shit and double shit ... It'd all gone wrong. Yes, I wanted to see Sarah and my son so much I hurt inside. But also I wanted to map out some strategy with Del-Coffey to kick out Curt and the Crew.

Now I was on my own, unarmed, and that idiot Slatter was taking a crap in the road. Shit, I knew I couldn't rely on the moron.

I breathed deeply.

'You okay?' asked gate man.

'Tired. I've just walked eighty miles.'

'You're some tough shit now, aren't you? You didn't have those muscles when you left here. What you been doing? Body-building?'

'Muscles? I never noticed.'

What good was muscle? I was alone now. How was I going to do anything to Curt apart from try and talk some sense into his thick skull?

Alone?

Didn't you listen to a word I said? Bernadette could have been speaking into my ear. *You're not alone, no one's ever alone. All you have to do is tune into that second mind inside your dense brain, Aten. He's waiting in there to help you. He's intelligent, he's powerful, he's creative. Now ... Switch off ... Think about something else and let him help you. Let him start piping that intuition into the front of your brain.*

I tried ... I looked up at the hotel building. It was a wreck now. Windows smashed, tiles missing, ivy growing wild across the walls. The grounds were littered with bottles, cans, rusting cars, the old Shogun that had saved my skin lay on its side burnt out. A dead cat rotted at the side of the driveway.

A line of children walked toward the hotel carrying cases of beer on their heads. Their eyes, looking too large for their heads, wore a dead shine. The children were beginning to starve to death.

Someone had tried to repair the break in the wall where the truck had crashed through with bits of timber, barbed wire and house doors. Never mind the big bad wolf, even one of the little piggies could huff and puff and blow that piece of crap down.

That's it, Nick. Think about anything but what you need to do . . .

I only hope you're right, Bernadette. If you're wrong I could be as cold as that dead cat by tonight.

We walked round the back of the hotel to the swimming pool, still covered in ice, and the hotel terrace. A bonfire was burning.

Curt, Jonathan and the Crew, about twenty of them, sat round a huge table.

They were pissed. Laughing, talking, shouting.

Curt sat at the head of the table like the Queen of bleeding Sheba.

The racket cut to silence as they saw me walk up.

Curt looked like shit, a burnt-out kind of look, his eyes seemed to peer out to his left and right both at the same time.

'Hey, hey. My old buddy, Aten. Sit down. Grab a drink!'

I thought he was going to start firing questions but he continued a conversation with Jonathan who sat on his left hand side. It was something scintillating because they leaned toward one another, heads nearly touching, chuckling themselves breathless.

A sixteen-year-old girl came up to me as I sat down.

Even though the temperature couldn't have lifted its belly above zero centigrade she wore a cut down T-shirt, mini-skirt and sandals. Her hands and feet were blue. A smile was nailed to her red mouth but her eyes bled sheer bloody agony.

'Refreshment, sir?'

My hatred for Curt turned from simmering to boiling.

The girl looked down at the tray she carried: there were bottles, cans, cigars and bowls of multi-coloured pills. 'The blue spirit is very warming,' she said, 'but it's neat alcohol so you might want to mix it with a beer if you're not used to it.'

From the smell rolling out of the jug of blue spirit I guessed it was the same stuff that I'd used before now to clean engine parts. These guys were out of their fucking mind.

'Sir?'

'A beer . . . Just a beer. Thanks.'

Jonathan, pulling on a huge cigar, turned to look at me. 'Nick. Everyone reckoned you'd kicked us into touch. We were all saying you thought you were too good for us.'

'That's right.' Curt looked at me with his splayed eyes. 'We were pretty cut up about it. We had people out looking for you.'

'I was kidnapped,' I explained, 'by my parents. Along with Trousers.'

'So we found out ... Where's Trousers now?'

'He's dead...' I was going to give them the whole story about the mass crucifixion; my intuition sang a different song. 'I killed him.'

'You killed him?' Curt and his Crew exchanged surprised looks.

'You're all right,' said Curt gratefully. 'I always said you should have joined the Crew. Look at the benefits.' He waved his hand, taking in the table full of food, booze and drugs, and the servant girls shivering in tart make-up and mini-skirts.

'Curt,' I said, 'the reason I got back here as quickly as I did is to warn you. You won't know this but the—'

'Warn me? Warn me what?'

'You don't realize the danger we're in. Now that—'

'Danger? Warning? We're in no danger, are we, Jonno? No, Nick. We're as safe as frigging houses...'

'But, there's—'

'Shush, Nick. Tell me later. It's party time. And we've laid on some entertainments for you. We've got some buckets of water. These girls want to take part in a wet T-shirt competition, don't you, girls?'

'Yes, Curt.' The girls shivered and desperately, desperately smiled. Their lives depended on it.

'Do you want to see the wet T-shirt competition, Nick?'

'No. I want—'

'Today, Nick Aten's the boss ... Oi, Billy, bring out the two bitches. It's time we did it to them.'

I sat there and made myself feel like concrete. These pathetic sadists wanted to watch my face as I watched whatever they'd planned. Already I'd seen them touching the servant girls' bare legs with cigarettes, then howling with laughter as they jumped. The girls never screamed. Their pained smiles did not budge.

A seventeen-year-old girl was brought out along with a labrador. It whimpered and leaned against the legs of the girl.

One of the Crew kicked the dog then pulled it from the girl who began to cry.

I grew cold inside, as they strapped one of the steel pipes packed with explosive onto the dog's back.

Jonathan grinned. 'Watch this, Nick . . . *Carrying the can* with a difference . . . Clever, eh? The dog belongs to the girl. They love one another, together all the time. You know, she even made it a Christmas card.'

Inevitability set in like a truck going over the edge of a cliff. All you could do was sit and watch the tragedy happen.

With his cigar, Jonathan lit the fuse on the pipe strapped to the dog's back.

'Go on, girl – run!' shouted Curt.

The girl ran. Then they released the dog. It ran after her.

It was a grotesque twist of what you see in the local park. A girl and her dog running together. The girl runs fast. The dog runs faster. They dodge backwards and forwards around the trees. The dog wags its tail; its pink tongue flaps out of its mouth. Excited barks.

Jonathan said, 'Do you think she'll outrun the dog?'

Curt grinned. 'She'll have to run faster than that.'

In the end what happened surprised them both. A hundred yards away on the lawn . . . the girl stopped running.

She called the dog, got down on her knees and held it tight in her arms.

The shock wave from the explosion cracked one of the windows.

The Crew roared with delight. Happy days for them.

Old man in my head, help me make this their last happy day.

More booze, laughter . . .

I was stone cold sober. I said, 'Curt. Just let me explain. The adults are massing in the next valley. Any day – any minute now – they might attack. If they do we are dead meat.'

'You're talking a bag of shite.' Jonathan blew out clouds of cigar smoke. 'Them Creosotes have been there weeks. They've not moved out the valley . . . They wouldn't hurt a fly.'

'Don't you believe it.' I started to tell them what I'd seen since leaving Eskdale, the ruthless extinction of people like us.

Curt's eyes widened than narrowed. I'd hit a raw nerve. Deep down he was afraid.

'Liar.'

'I'm not lying, Curt. Why should I lie? If we don't do something now, this fucking minute, we're going to die. If it comes to it, we'll have to think of moving people out, particularly the young children and babies.'

'No ... No! No! No!' Curt's face blotched red. 'No one leaves. We stay here. All right? All right!'

I carried on, listing the communities wiped out by Family Creosote. Curt wasn't listening.

'Well, get a load of this, Crew. It looks as if our buddy, Nick scaremonger Aten has broken the law ... Billy, get another one. Nick's going to do the business.'

I knew full well what he meant. After all this time, it was my turn to *Carry The Can*.

Chapter Fifty-Nine

CARRYING THE CAN AGAIN

Billy pointed a shotgun in my face as they snapped the cuff around my wrist. Attached to that, a foot long piece of chain. Attached to that the Can.

Picture it. A sealed piece of metal pipe as thick as a cucumber and as long as your forearm from wrist to elbow. The fuse ran down another tube inside the pipe with just the tip of the fuse poking out through a small hole. No way could you rip out the fuse once it had been lit.

I held the thing in both hands. It was as heavy as death.

All you could do was run like Satan wanted a piece of your arse. Down the driveway, through the gates, down the road into the village and up to the church.

Then you climbed to the top of the church tower, tipped the key out of the glass jar, unlocked the cuff and chucked the bomb as far as you could.

Some made it, some didn't – sometimes for a laugh Billy would short fuse the bomb. Then you didn't get as far as the end of the drive.

I sat there. I did not move. I showed no expression. This was it, I shouldn't have expected any more from the bastards.

I'd have to make the run, and unlock the pipe bomb from my wrist. If I didn't, Sarah, my baby son, everyone would be dead within the week.

'See, Nick Aten . . .' Jonathan pulled deeply on the cigar, making the end glow white. 'You brought this on yourself. If you'd toed the line you could have joined the Crew. Got yourself some nice ladies to keep you warm at night.'

Curt smiled. 'If you make it to the church on time – you're welcome to join . . . Just make sure you run hard enough.'

Jonathan pulled hard on the cigar again. 'Ready, steady . . .' He touched the tip of the cigar against the stub of fuse that poked from the hole. '. . . Go.'

The fuse hissed, sparks flying, then the flame disappeared into the pipe. All I could see now was a trail of blue smoke oozing from the drilled hole.

I licked my dry lips. 'What if I stay here . . . with you? And we all watch what happens next.'

The Crew looked at each other in alarm and started to back away.

Jonathan stuck the cigar back in his mouth and pulled a pistol from his jacket pocket. 'What if I blow your head off . . . Then we'll watch what happens from the hotel . . . Now, Nick Aten, I reckon you've got a hundred seconds left.'

I ran.

The Can clutched in both hands, chain jingling, I belted in the direction of the driveway with the Crew jeering. When I reached the bushes and they could no longer see me, I cut back up across to the back of the outbuildings.

If I knew Jonathan he was jealous of Curt being matey with me. He wouldn't risk me surviving this run; he'd make sure that the Can had been short fused.

The outbuildings came up in a confused blur. Then I stood there, panting, looking round at the sheds, stables and garage not knowing what I was looking for – only hoping I'd recognize it when I saw it.

I ran behind the boiler house.

Come on, Aten! This thing's going to blow you to buggery in ten seconds flat!

I ran faster.

Bingo!

Behind the boiler house a heavy timber trap door was set in

the earth. It was the coal shute that led down into the cellar.

I grabbed the iron ring in the trap door and heaved until my shoulder muscles cracked. The trap door came up, rotten with age. *Pray the thing holds, Aten.*

Quickly, I dropped the pipe bomb down to the full length of the chain into the shute, then I slammed back the trap door with the chain pulled tight between the iron frame of the hatchway and the trap door itself.

Chained there, I squatted down onto the trap door. The bomb smoked away ten inches beneath my feet, separated only by three inches of one hundred year old timber planking.

And waited.

. . . And waited.

Picturing the sparking fuse creeping closer and closer to the charge.

I never heard the bang.

One second I squatted there, eyes fixed on the chain as it disappeared under the trap door, the next second I lay against the boiler house wall, trying, but somehow failing to breathe.

I coughed, pulled myself to my feet, then dropped back against the wall. My legs were shaking, my head was ringing, my feet and knees were throbbing like hell.

I touched my forehead. When I took my fingers away they were jam red with blood.

The trap door had been ripped off by the force of the explosion and lay ten feet from the cellar entrance. I'd been standing on that.

Then I noticed my arm. The hairs had been scorched from my skin; from the handcuff swung five inches of blackened chain.

Come on, Aten. This is it!

As soon as I could, I limped back in the direction of the hotel, skirting round the far side, so I came back on the Crew's backs.

They were all stood there, shielding their eyes against the sun's glare. Through the ringing in my ears, I heard them asking one another what had happened to me. They'd heard the bang for sure.

Jonathan was chuckling and pulling excited drags on his fat dick cigar.

I walked up to the table, picked up a bottle of the blue spirit and twisted off the top.

As one, they spun round to look at me in amazement.

'You look as if you've seen a ghost,' I said.

Jonathan looked at the snapped chain swinging from my wrist as I lifted the bottle.

'You never made it to the church ... What did you do, cut the chain?'

I smiled.

He clenched the cigar between his teeth. 'Bastard cheat ... You'll *Carry The Can* again ... properly this time.'

I walked to within a few paces of him and looked into his face behind the swirling cigar smoke. I felt a gun muzzle jabbed into my back.

'All right,' I said. 'But first I deserve a drink.'

I took a deep mouthful of the blue spirit.

Then spat it into Jonathan's face.

The spirit hit the cigar.

With a pop it ignited, enclosing the bastard's head in a brilliant orange flame. He went jerking back howling, rolling about on the terrace, his hair burning and melting into a cap of bubbling tar.

Curt and the Crew just stared, mouths open, like Judgment Day was upon them.

It could only have taken a second but it seemed to take forever.

I swung back hard with the spirit bottle, smashing it across the nose of the guy holding the gun to my back.

He keeled over stiff as a stick.

Billy stood behind him. He was fumbling with the safety catch of an Uzi.

Before he could pull back the bolt, I managed to slam five beefy punches into his face, splitting his nose, lips and eyes.

Then I dragged him forward, wrenched the gun from his hands and shoved him down to the ground.

It was chaos. The Crew were shouting, scared, panicking, some hiding under the table, some running. Only Curt sat watching it all in a doped-up way, completely amputated from reality.

Two of the Crew across the table had pulled out revolvers, but as

they lifted them, I squeezed the trigger of the machine gun, empty-
ing the whole magazine at them, just hosing them down with hot
metal. Minced by the bullets they dropped down dead.

As I groped round amongst the screaming men for another gun I
looked up.

Jonathan had lifted himself up on one elbow. His two round,
lidless eyes stared like white discs out of his burnt face.

I froze, he had the pistol in his hand and he was aiming it at my
chest.

Then came the noise.

So low at first you feel it rather than hear it. A low, low pounding.

Jonathan heard it too. Even though his face was a burnt mess I
saw the look of sheer, bloody awful terror as he saw who came
towards him.

Jonathan looked at the gun as if it had turned to chocolate in his
hand. He knew what was going to happen now.

Slatter loped across the terrace, his pit boots pounding the
slabs.

Jonathan turned as he lay there, propped up on one elbow. The
last thing he saw was Slatter's boot swinging forward to crunch his
chin, kicking him, non-stop express, into the evergreen gardens of
eternity.

Now the Crew were gibbering with terror as Slatter walked
toward them. They kept glancing from his pit boots to Jonathan
lying dead, then to Slatter's tattooed face.

I'm glad I wasn't on the receiving end. The look in Slatter's eye
must have been terrible.

'Put it down,' he said to one of the Crew who carried a shotgun.
The guy dropped it like it was diseased.

'Now . . .' Slatter stood and watched them as they cringed back
from him. 'Everyone get into the pool.'

The Crew didn't wait to be told twice. They ran to the pool and
jumped in, the weight of their bodies breaking the ice.

'Now. Wait there till I come back.'

They all nodded frantically, shoulder deep in freezing water.

Slatter walked back to where I stood holding a revolver to Curt's
head. The sad bastard hadn't moved. The look on his face was a
regular stew of bewilderment, surprise and fear.

I offered Slatter a shotgun. He shook his head.

'Guns are for faggots, rubber necks – and cowards ... Isn't that true, Curt?'

Curt trembled, his flabby lips drooling spit.

Slatter reached forward and picked another pipe bomb off the table. He snapped the cuff onto Curt's wrist.

'You've shit your hole, Curt.'

Six months ago I'd have tried to stop Slatter.

Not now. Not after I'd seen Curt and his Crew rape and torture and murder and starve this little fragment of sane humanity that'd hung grimly on while the rest of the world was dying.

I stood back so the rest of the Crew in the pool could see.

As Slatter lit the fuse fear drove Curt's eyes back into focus. 'You can't,' he screamed. 'You can't do this!'

Slatter's beast eyes just stared into Curt's.

'Help me! Help me!' he yelled at the Crew shivering in the pool. They stared back, too scared to move.

With a howl of frustration and fear Curt ran down the drive in the direction of the village, hugging the bomb to his stomach.

I watched him go. I felt no pity. 'Do you think he'll make it?'

'He might. He's fast ... But ...' Slatter reached into his pocket and pulled out a small silver key. 'I got there first.'

We waited in silence. I pictured Curt's wild run, then climbing the stairs up the church tower, his heart feeling as if it would rip up through his throat, then Curt out on the tower roof, scrabbling about for the jar, picking it up, seeing that the key had gone, crying out in terror, maybe wishing he could turn back the clock and undo the evil he'd done and then –

The distant explosion broke the spell.

'What do you want me to do with them in the pool, Nick?'

'Tell them they've got a choice. Those that are ready to become good citizens of Eskdale can put on dry clothes. Those that don't, take them down into the orchard and stamp on their heads. We'll bury them with Curt and Jonathan.'

Chapter Sixty

HERE IT COMES

At first it was chaos – like trying to fit the pieces of a huge jigsaw puzzle together without any picture on the box to help you.

Then as I got a grip of the situation it started to come together.

I stood in the foyer of the hotel. At two o'clock I was asking people if they would do such-and-such a thing. By two-thirty I was giving orders. And I realized people were more than happy to obey. They looked like slaves that had been kept underground – now they were out in the light and free. And what they wanted was security and order.

Shivering in the pool, the Crew cried out that they wanted to become loyal, hard-working citizens. Suddenly all of them were saying they were as much victims of Curt as the rest and that they'd been intimidated into joining the Crew. An hour ago they were strutting gang members, hard men, now they sobbed in the freezing water like scared schoolkids.

Slatter told them to get out, get changed, then obey every single order I gave – to the letter. Pathetically grateful, they scrambled out and ran back to the hotel.

Word went ahead that Slatter was roaming loose in the grounds like one of the old gods – one of the vengeful kind.

What was left of the Crew dropped their guns before he even reached them and raced to congratulate me as their new leader, and how they'd waited for this to happen and how much they hated Curt, blah, blah, blah . . .

Mid-afternoon Del-Coffey came loping up the driveway, shoe laces still trailing. He couldn't believe I was there. For five minutes he talked no sense, grinning, laughing, and shaking my hand over and over.

'Nick, you're all right, you're all right! What happened to you? Your head's bleeding. I heard Curt and Jonathan are dead. It's unbelievable, everyone's over the moon – it – it's like we were dead – now we've come back to life again . . . Hell, it's great to see you . . .'

Between this I managed to shoot out orders. 'Ben . . . go down to the gatehouse please. You'll find a rifle, a handgun and a green haversack down there. Bring them up here to me. And be careful with the bag.'

Del-Coffey looked round amazed at the happy faces of kids from four to nineteen charging about on errands or just running to find others to share the news and slap one another on the back.

In the corner two of the servant girls were using brass candlesticks to beat one of the Crew members around the head.

Del-Coffey was astonished. 'What are those two doing?'

'It's called revenge. There's going to be more of that in the next few days. And whoever wants to pay those sadists back gets my blessing . . . Hey. You, you were one of the Crew, weren't you?'

The guy stopped dead in his tracks, his hair still wet from the pool. 'Yes, sir.' He trembled.

'Get the rest of the Crew together,' I told him, 'Then you can cook these kids you've shit on for the last six months a meal – no, make it a feast. And you, or your old buddies, don't eat a crumb until these kids can't eat another thing. Got that?'

'Yes, sir.'

As he started to walk away I couldn't stop myself grinning mischievously as I said, 'And remember, wherever you are, whatever you do, Slatter is always watching you.'

The ex-thug ran like he was scalded.

Del-Coffey shook his head in wonder. 'What happened to the old Nick Aten? You look as if you were born to be king.'

'You know about computer software . . . Well, I bought some new software for up here.' I tapped my head.

Del-Coffey looked puzzled.

'Don't worry, it's a long story.' I pulled Bernadette's book from the haversack. 'Do you believe in God, Del-Coffey?'

The puzzled look deepened. 'No.'

'Good. You can be our first bishop . . . Now, listen. Did you get my message from Murphy?'

'No. Our transmitter's bust. I couldn't fix it.'

'Shit . . . You don't know about the Creosotes, then? And what's been happening to communities like this all over the world?'

'No. The Creosotes are harmless now; we can see—'

'Sarah. Where's Sarah now, and the baby?'

'The baby's being looked after by Sarah's sisters at my house in the village. Sarah's helping out at the hospital.'

'What hospital?'

Del-Coffey explained Curt didn't want sick people in the hotel or even the village. A pub up the road had been roped in to serve as a hospital. 'She's there with Kitty right now.'

I said, 'Listen. It's not safe now. The Creosotes are . . . Hey, what the hell's this?'

At that moment I was mobbed by dozens of kids, shaking my hand and patting my arms and back; all of them talking at once in excited voices.

Del-Coffey was forced back by the crowds. Grinning, he shouted over the racket, 'What's it like to be popular?'

Me? I couldn't stop smiling. 'Weird . . . Damn weird.'

Half an hour later we were sitting drinking coffee and eating cake.

We were talking about what we had to do. Sarah's absence was nagging away at the back of my mind but there was a mountain of work to get through. Del-Coffey filled me in on what supplies the Community had to live on, that the fuel was long gone, no electricity. No vehicles worked. In short the place was a mess.

We were talking when I heard a horse clattering outside on the driveway.

A ten-year-old raced across the foyer. 'Nick . . . Nick. It's one of Slatter's men. He's got something important to tell you.'

Outside the kid on horseback told me they'd set the charge against the wall of the dam. 'There's a ten-minute delay fuse. Do you want Burke to blow it now?'

'No.' I looked at the sun dipping down toward the hills. 'Tell him to detonate it tonight at midnight when the Creosotes are asleep.'

As the kid prepared to ride off, Del-Coffey told him to wait and ran into the hotel. He came out minutes later with a pair of walkie-talkies. He handed one to the kid on horseback.

'Now, at least we've got instant communication,' panted Del-Coffey.

After the kid had ridden away we returned to the hotel.

Life was beginning to settle down. I got some kids to make inventories of stores while I decided who could be trusted with guns to help guard the place.

By late afternoon I stopped, suddenly uneasy.

'Christ, I forgot all about Sarah. Where is she?'

Del-Coffey looked up from his clipboard. 'I sent word an hour ago ... Don't worry, Nick. She'll want like mad to come, she's talked about you night and day ever since your parents took you. It's just that they're so damn busy with the children suffering from malnutrition.'

I looked across to where ex-Crew members were handing out plates of steaming food to young kids. 'I've a good mind to nail up some of the old Crew as an example ... The bastards should have to pay for this.'

'Let them pay. Now you're in charge, Nick, they'll be happy to work until they drop.'

'It's Kitty! It's Kitty!' someone shouted. 'She's running ... Nick!'

Kitty nearly fell into Del-Coffey's arms as she came gasping up the drive, blood streaming from her mouth.

'Nick ... I'm sorry, Nick...' Kitty panted. 'We were walking back to the village ... A man and a woman jumped out at us. They've taken Sarah away. I tried to fight them...'

That cold feeling came sliding back.

'Creosotes?'

'Yes.'

'What did they look like? Exactly.'

'Woman ... I don't know. Dark hair. Forty. The man had grey and black hair mixed. And just here.' She pointed to her mouth.

'He had a gap in his top front teeth,' I said.

'Yes ... how did you know?'

Understanding thudded inside of me. Suddenly I felt so weak and tiny – as if I was a little child again. 'Oh, mother. Why do you always have to interfere?'

Del-Coffey looked startled. 'Your parents?'

'Yes. I know it's them. They've been following me all along. They were probably watching me when I was at the Cropper's settlement ... They probably watched me from the bank of the lake when I was on the Ark. Then they followed me all the way home ... And now they've got Sarah ... Jesus Christ Almighty ... When is all this going to end?'

Del-Coffey asked Kitty, 'How long ago was this?'

'Half an hour.'

'Half an hour? Kitty, why didn't you come straight here? They might have—'

I interrupted. 'Give her a chance to speak. Kitty, what happened after they took her?'

'I ... I followed them. They took her over the hill into the next valley. I watched them take her to that little white church on the hill.'

'Go on.'

'I waited a few minutes, but nothing else happened. They just took her into the church.'

I got my rifle and pushed the pistol into my belt.

'I'll get some people to go with you,' said Del-Coffey.

'Don't bother ... The speed I'll be shifting none of them will be able to keep up.'

'For chrissakes be careful.'

I nodded at Bernadette's book in his hand. 'Read that – learn it from cover to cover. It might seem strange ... But you've got to have faith in it ... Whether it's true or not doesn't matter. We've got to believe in something or we might as well feed those children cyanide. At least they'd die quickly.'

Del-Coffey looked bewildered.

'If I don't come back ... There's something in the bag I've

written, too. It'll all become clear when you read it ... It might just save those poor devils' lives.'

I'd started off down the driveway when I heard Del-Coffey, shouting and running after me. He held the walkie-talkie to his ear. 'Nick ... Nick! It's Burke up at the dam ... He says the Creosotes have started moving.'

'This is it, then.' Mouth dry, I looked at Del-Coffey.

I felt I was living out a series of prophecies that were, one by one, becoming fact. Once I would have ranted and sworn. Now I felt calm. I knew what I had to do.

'They've begun to move in our direction, Nick. Burke reckons there's more than four thousand of them.'

I looked at the faces of the hundreds of kids as they came out of the hotel to watch me go. They didn't shout now. Their expressions were serious, more than that there was a look of deep, painfully deep trust in their eyes.

'Nick. What shall I tell Burke?'

In my head I could see Sarah's face as well as I saw those in front of me.

'Nick ... The dam is in the same valley as the white church.' Del-Coffey went grey. 'If they blow up the dam wall a tidal wave a hundred feet high is going to tear down that valley. Nothing will survive that.'

'I know.' For a moment the world became unreal – then suddenly I had the strongest conviction in my life what I must do.

I looked at Del-Coffey. 'Tell Burke to blow the dam. *NOW*.'

Del-Coffey, trembling, nodded and began talking into the walkie-talkie.

I turned my back on the hotel and the hundreds of watching eyes. And I ran.

Chapter Sixty-One

SOME KIND OF REUNION

The trees lining the driveway blurred into a dark tunnel as I ran, the rifle strapped across my back.

Through the hotel gates, down into the village, by Del-Coffey's house, across the bridge, then up the other side of the valley.

As the road began its zig-zag climb up the hill I cut straight up across the turf, willing myself to keep running up the steep hillside, my eyes burning in the direction of the hill-top and the darkening blue sky.

My throat rattled, my body burned and pains pierced my legs, but something inside of me wouldn't let me slow down.

A hundred yards from the hill-top I heard the sound. A thumping great crack that sounded as if the sky had been torn in two. To my left, in the distance, white smoke billowed into the sky.

The dam had gone. I ran harder, wanting to see what would happen next. The last hundred yards were the steepest. At times, I had to climb on all fours. As my hands touched the ground I felt a powerful vibration running through it.

Then I was at the top of the hill, looking down into the next valley. It had already been and gone.

The tidal wave must have torn the two miles down the valley like a hundred foot high concrete wall, moving with the speed of an express. Its force grinding boulders to gravel.

Nothing living even had a chance to drown in the flood: the crushing wave would have shattered every bone in their bodies.

I turned right and ran along the top of the long spine of the hill, looking down into the valley bottom.

Already the flood waters were dropping as I watched, leaving behind on the valley walls a continuous slick of mud, uprooted trees and thousands upon thousands of dead men and women.

No. Not men and women. They weren't human any more. They had become an alien species, dedicated to destroying us. I felt no pity. All I wanted now was Sarah.

The church in which she was being held was perhaps another mile down the valley, where it began to broaden out.

The sun rested on the hill top when I saw the church, making its white walls and spire glow pink.

The church and the top of the hill it stood on were clear of the flood. But still surrounding it was a black lake, streaked here and there with clumps of pink froth.

Now it was downhill all the way.

I went down that hillside in huge leaping strides. Slip now and I'd break my neck.

From bushes in front of me a figure lurched out, arms grasping forward.

Not all the Creosotes had been caught in the flood.

I didn't stop running as I slipped the rifle from my shoulder and shot him in the chest. I jumped over the body as he fell.

Five or six more stragglers came at me. These were ferocious bastards – they wanted my blood.

I shot one after another, willing each bullet to count.

Several more were working along the valley behind me but I ignored them.

Only the ones that stood between me and the church I blasted.

When the bullets ran out I broke the rifle across the head of the last one that stood in my way.

Now I was running across the valley floor, through six inches of liquid silt. Bodies were twisted mud shapes; they were everywhere. In the end I had to run across them they were so tightly packed together.

From trees that had survived the tidal wave more bodies hung from branches like dead fruit where they'd been left as the flood waters dropped.

A hundred yards from the church the liquid mud deepened until I was wading waist deep through this freezing shit, pushing floating corpses away with my hands.

The slope began to run up, I moved quicker as the water shallowed to my knees, ankles, then I was free of it and running up the hill to the white church.

At the doors I stood panting. What I'd find in there God only knew – but I wanted to be in control when I went in.

Gingerly, I pushed open the door.

Inside, the church was filled with dappled greens, pinks, reds, golds and deep, deep shadow.

Silence pressed hard against my ears, the only sound my heart that seemed to fill the void with a deep bass thump.

I pulled the pistol from my belt. It was still dry. I eased back the hammer and holding the gun high walked slowly down the aisle.

The millions of colours moving across the inside of the church came from the setting sun shining through the stained glass windows. They were full of Biblical scenes – ten foot high saints, lambs, angels and a green hill far away.

I couldn't manage a shout, only a whisper. 'Sarah?'

Jesus Christ . . . No.

I'd seen so many things. But this was so bad I had to turn away.

Ahead of me, leaning against the altar rail, a dozen tiny figures. They were like the ones I'd seen on the barge, just before I'd been released.

Cut down and mummified bodies of teenagers. They watched me with their biscuit-dry eyes. One of them had a split face, roughly repaired by a row of stitches: XXXXXX.

Candles burned on the altar. More burned in candlesticks around the walls. The place was deserted.

Quiet as a cat I hunted through the shadows. Where were mum and dad? Where was Sarah?

There was a purpose to all this. My parents had seen my return to the valley. I'd heard my father whistling.

They couldn't walk into the hotel and get me. So they'd taken Sarah. Knowing I'd follow them here.

Here was the trap.

And here, Nick Aten, their first-born son, was the prey.

'Mum ... Dad ... Here I am ...' My voice echoed in the cavern of the church. I looked up into the shadows. 'Aren't you going to say hello to your loving son?'

'Nick ... Nick ...'

I twisted round, finger tightening on the trigger.

'*Nick.*'

It wasn't the voice I expected.

'Sarah. Where are you?'

'Straight in front of you. The door ... They've locked me in here.'

In the shadows I saw the door. Behind a steel grille the size of a TV screen was a gleam of blonde hair.

'Sarah ... You're all right?'

'Yes ... They're using me as bait, Nick ... It's you they want.'

'Well, they've gone now. You're safe.'

I forced my hand through the grille, felt her grab my hand and kiss it; and then hold it to her face. It was wet with tears.

We stayed like that for minutes on end, just feeling the touch of one another. After all these months it was so overpowering I couldn't speak.

Sarah whispered, 'What was that noise? I heard a clap of thunder, then the whole building began to shake. I though it was going to come down on top of me.'

'Don't worry. That was the sound of our lives being saved.'

She began to tell me about Curt's atrocities and the starvation but I told her that was over too.

'Let's get you home,' I told her. 'Is there another way out of here?'

'No ... It's the crypt. There's only coffins down there.'

'I'll have to find something to break the door down.'

'Don't you leave me, Nick Aten ... Not now. Don't you dare.'

'I won't. There's a cross on the wall made out of iron. Stand back and I'll break the door down with that.'

Sarah must have seen them first. I saw her eyes go unnaturally wide beyond the door grille.

Next came a cold sensation at the top of my back.

The cold became flaming agony and I twisted away and fell against the wall.

Standing there side by side were my parents – wild and dirty-looking now, with long hair and blazing eyes. My mother held a knife in her hand. Her fingers gleamed red with fresh blood.

I moved my left shoulder. The pain from the knife wound stabbed through my back.

Panting, I raised the pistol and looked at my father's face through the sight.

My hand began to tremble.

They stood and stared at me, heads shaking slightly from the tension twisting up the muscles inside of them.

I forced myself to keep aiming at the face. Only now I didn't see the wildman hair and mad eyes.

I saw my father's face. His lips parted and I saw the gap in his teeth.

'Nick ... Nick.' I heard Sarah behind me. The voice seemed faraway. 'Nick. Shoot them ... They're not your parents any more ... Fire the gun.'

I pulled the trigger. The explosion echoed around the church.

Ten feet above my father's head the bullet knocked a lump out of the wall.

'Mum ... Dad.' My throat hurt as I tore out the words. 'I don't know if there's some part of you deep down can hear me ... But listen. I'm a father now. I've a new family. And you've no right to do this. It's time for you to go away now. You've got to leave us alone.'

I fired above their heads again. They did not flinch.

'Nick ... Don't let them do this to you,' called Sarah. 'They're not your parents. If you don't kill them they'll kill you ...'

My mother began to walk slowly forward, the knife held straight out in her hand. I was so hypnotised by her eyes that I forgot everything else until the blow knocked me sideways.

My father held the cross I'd intended to use to break the crypt door down with.

He swung it again.

I jerked back and the heavy ironwork bit into the wall.

'Stop it ... Dad, stop it!'

He kept moving forward. I lifted the gun.

He swung again and the cross splintered a wooden pew.

With my free hand I began picking up prayer books laid out on the pews and threw them at him.

He kept on coming.

'Dad, don't ... don't ...' I felt six years old again. My dad was coming to punish me and there was nothing I could do about it ... He could run faster than me, he was stronger than me ... Here he comes to smack me and carry me crying to bed.

Slash with the cross; sometimes to beat thin air, sometimes hitting the wall, sometimes hitting my arms.

'Dad ... No ... Leave me alone.'

The wall at the end of the church met my back and I could walk backwards no longer.

All I could see were my father's eyes. Staring into mine. And they were getting closer and closer.

The sound of the gunshot came from nowhere. The echo crashed from wall to wall. My head jerked from left to right to see where it had come from.

Then I looked at my own hand. Smoke oozed from the gun-barrel. My finger still pulled the trigger so tightly it had turned bone white.

Slowly I looked down along the aisle.

My father lay flat on his back, arms stretched out at either side. Above his head was the cross. A spreading pool of blood fanned out around his head.

My mother came at me snarling. The force of her leap knocked me flat; the pistol skidded away across the floor.

She crouched on my chest, both hands in my mouth trying to tear my jaws apart.

I crunched my teeth together on her fingers.

But she didn't let go. She only used the grip to pull my head up then crack it back down onto the stone slabs.

She did it again, and a droning sound started running through my brain.

Consciousness was slipping away from me.

Give you birth ... Do you know the sacrifices we had to make for you ... You failed us ... You betrayed us ... dirty, dirty son ... We gave you everything . . . You failed us . . . Now we're taking it all back . . . Everything . . .

Mum's voice. But it was only in my head as my mind began to slip. Somewhere a girl was screaming my name . . .

'Nick! Fight her, Nick! Fight her!'

The strength came thundering back from somewhere deep inside. I kicked up, pushing her off.

I pulled myself to my feet and backed off, choking.

From her ragged clothes she pulled out the knife and came forward, eyes burning, her lips parted.

Then she ran at me.

I sidestepped her, grabbed her by the huge bunch of tangled hair. And using the momentum I spun her smack into a stone pillar.

The first time her head hit the pillar it was accidental.

The next time was not. Nor the next.

When she was gone I lowered her to the floor.

I found the key to the crypt by my mother's body.

Sarah came out and we hung onto one another like children.

As we walked toward the doors we heard it.

A low, breathless whistling. Arms around one another we walked down the aisle to where my father lay.

He looked up at the ceiling, whistling: blood had spread out like a red blanket on which he lay.

When he saw movement he stopped whistling, and turned his head to look at me.

Sarah says that's when he died.

I say the same. But deep down I know that for a few seconds he was my old dad again. Sane, tranquil, and knowing that I'd still love him and mum until the day I stopped breathing too.

Chapter Sixty-Two

MIDNIGHT, THE LONGEST DAY

Del-Coffey's house. Candles burning.

My injuries weren't serious – even so, I wore so many bandages I looked like something from *Return Of The Mummy*. Sarah sat beside me on the sofa, as the girl brought in the baby.

'Look at him,' said the girl, staring at the baby in awe, 'just look at him – the way he sees things. He's been here before.'

After the girl had put the baby in Sarah's arms Del-Coffey ushered her out of the room.

'I'll leave you to it.' He smiled. 'You got a lot of talking and . . . and stuff to catch up on . . . Give us a shout when you're ready for bed; the girl will look after the baby tonight.'

'Here you are,' said Sarah. 'Your son and heir . . . He's four weeks old today. Come on, hold him.'

'I can't. I'll drop him.'

'No, you won't. Hold out your arms . . . That's it, support his head with your other hand . . . There, you look like a natural born father now.'

In the last ten months I'd never trembled as much as this. He lay there content in my arms, his clear eyes looking from one candle to the next. In that face and those eyes I saw my whole family – John, Uncle Jack, mum and dad, grandparents, and, of course, someone far older, who we'd forgotten was there all along.

Sarah kissed both of us.

I whispered, 'What's his name?'

'I hope you don't mind. I called him David. After all, even though Dave Middleton never knew it, he probably saved our lives ... He deserves some kind of memorial.'

I shook my head smiling. 'I don't mind at all ... Well, young Dave Aten, I'm your dad – not a pretty sight, eh? Never mind, we'll have plenty of time to get used to one another.'

Chapter Sixty-Three

THIS IS IT – THE END BIT

The stream at the bottom of the garden sounded musical and relaxing. David played on a blanket in the shade of a tree. Sarah sat checking sheets of computer printouts.

The hot August sun gently baked the twelve young men and women as they sat around the table, cold drinks in their hands. The mood was quietly cheerful and there was gentle laughter as well as talk.

'Think of it like this,' I was saying for the hundredth time since I returned to Eskdale. 'Imagine a newborn baby is like a new video recorder.'

Sarah giggled. 'Can't you come up with a more picturesque example?'

I stuck out my tongue and ploughed on. 'Think back to the days when you could actually buy a video recorder. You know, when we had money and shopping malls and traffic jams. Anyway, the video recorder is the newborn baby's brain. It comes with a blank tape on which you record your own personal memories, likes and dislikes on. That is YOU. Also, though you don't know it, it comes with a pre-recorded tape that's packed with thousands of programs, movies, documentaries – this is the unconscious mind. The trick is to be able to access these pre-recorded programs: if you can do that you can transform your life, be healthier, become anyone you want to be – servant, warrior, scientist, teacher, leader . . .'

'Tinker, tailor, soldier . . .' chipped in Sarah.

More gentle laughter.

This dozen were our first school teachers. I looked at them each in turn. 'Remember, for the sake of the children – we have this conspiracy – we all pretend there is a God . . . like we pretend there is Santa Claus and the tooth fairy. When they're old enough, then they learn the truth. That's when they move into the adult phase of their life. Jewish kids had Bar Mitzvah, we will—'

'Nick. Sorry to interrupt.'

Del-Coffey loped awkwardly across the lawn, laces eternally trailing.

Breathless, he sat down and poured himself a lemonade. The bloke is worth his weight in gold.

It is due to his intellect that we, two thousand of us now, live safely in a territory twenty miles across that's free from Creosotes. Armed patrols pick them off as they cross the borders.

It was Del-Coffey who rigged up the wind turbines that give us electricity; and his meticulous organization of scavenging expeditions means we have food stores to keep us going until we learn how to properly farm the land.

You can read Del-Coffey's account of what happened from DAY 1 to the present day – it's scholarly, extremely detailed, big words, maps, photographs, the whole sausage. You'll find it in the four big leather-bound books in the library, along with the video archive.

Now, as we get to the end of this, a little bit about me. Yeah, I did become leader – that's when life really did get tough. *Responsibility* is the hardest word in the English language.

After the day we blew the dam we mopped up the last of the Creosotes. Slatter did that virtually singlehanded. He moved amongt them like an avenging angel. An ugly one with a tattooed face and pit boots – but an angel none the less.

A week after that he left without telling anyone where or why he was going. We've not seen him since. One day we'll name a town or something after him.

But if he ever came back . . . Sometimes I wonder. I might reach for the rifle I keep by my desk.

* * *

Del-Coffey's face was pink from the walk in the hot sun. 'I've spent the morning on the radio ... Jigsaw and Doc are all right, but their camp took a battering from the Creosotes last night ... Don't worry, they reckon they can hold out. The bad news is two communities have gone down in Florida and France. New tactics. Half a million Creosotes at a time just roll over the camps like a tide ... Oh ... and I'm getting this weird message from some lady called Bernadette who says she lives on the Ark.'

I sat up, suddenly tense.

'She's not broadcasting to any particular community. It's going out worldwide. She says...' Del-Coffey read from his clipboard. 'This message is for Alexander the Great. The time has come to build your empire ... Remember December.' Del-Coffey took a swallow of lemonade. 'Then the message gets weirder. This Bernadette says, tell Alexander the Great he has a girl child and she has been named Alexandra. Mother and baby are both fine.'

I said nothing. I picked up my son and walked down to watch the stream bubbling around the rocks. Then, softly, softly, I began to whistle him a tune I learnt a long time ago.

> Ten green bottles hanging on a wall,
> If one green bottle should accidentally fall,
> Then there'll be nine green bottles hanging on a wall.
> Nine green bottles hanging on a wall,
> If one green bottle should accidentally fall ...

There's not much more to write. For now, anyway.

If you're ever in the area don't be afraid to call in. Just ask anyone the way to Nick Aten's house. It's the yellow one in the middle of the village.

There's only one more thing to do before I do the customary author bit and write The End at the bottom of the page. And that is to say: *Remember what's inside your head. You, too, can do wonderful things and have a wonderful life. And whatever happens, you are never alone. DO NOT FORGET THE FRIEND INSIDE.*

THE END.

End Note – Year Three

APPENDED BY M. C. DEL-COFFEY

Whether you believe Bernadette's explanation of what happened on DAY 1, and her theory of the unconscious mind being the personality ancient people identified as God, is entirely up to you.

I confess, I did not swallow the theory hook, line and sinker. No one should accept such radical hypotheses without question. Therefore, I ask that you should undertake at least a little corroborative reading of your own.

First, I recommend you see the following entries in an encyclopaedia:

DREAMS
COLLECTIVE UNCONSCIOUS
SUPER RELEASER
MYTHOLOGY

Then if you wish to probe deeper I would suggest an elementary introduction to Psychology followed by a book about Dr C. G. Jung.

That last day in August, when Nick Aten heard the message from Bernadette beseeching Alexander to wake up and to build an empire, he changed. He became quieter, seemingly preoccupied with a huge problem. At the time I was mystified. However, when I read what you now hold in your hands all became clear.

Up until he handed me the manuscript he'd kept it under lock and key in his study. I'm sure Sarah is not even aware of its existence. For obvious reasons, as you will appreciate.

Last November we learned that Cheswold, a small town, twenty miles from Eskdale, was besieged by Family Creosote. Before we had done nothing. We have limited resources. Our own survival was always paramount.

However, Nick changed all that. He led a force of thirty armed men and women to Cheswold and eradicated the attacking Creosotes. Cheswold is now a protectorate of Eskdale. We have installed schools and a new administrative centre there.

Ten days ago Nick spoke to Bernadette on the radio. As far as I am aware this is their first direct communication since he left the Ark in the December of YEAR 1. I don't know what passed between them; however, Nick became yet more introspective and began taking long walks to be alone with his thoughts.

Three days ago Tug Slatter returned from nowhere. He and Nick talked for hours.

Perhaps as a result of this conversation, and the one with Bernadette, Nick raised a force of three hundred men and women and announced plans to make his way south liberating every community that is under siege from the affected adults. En route they would take Harmby (Doc and Jigsaw's community) into our protection.

Nick Aten's aim is to travel into the very heart of the territories of the insane adults, find their HQ (if one exists), and destroy it. The ultimate aim being to annihilate all of the affected adults and ensure our country is a safe place to raise our families and begin rebuilding civilization.

I will keep this book locked in my safe. One day, when Nick Aten returns, I hope to place *BLOOD CRAZY* where it belongs, in pride of place in our library.

And, the fates willing, there will be a second volume of his to go alongside this one. That will tell the story of how, after fifty thousand years, we were reunited with the Old Self that resides within our hearts. And that together we fought for the World.

And together we won.